DREAMS OF THE INFINITE YOU

Cedrix E. Clarke

Cressy Publishing

For Suzanne
who is always First Reader

CONTENTS

INTRODUCTION

◆ ◆ ◆

T he best tool in a writer's back pocket is the question
what if? I could have the vocabulary the size of a dic-
tionary, but without that question getting under my
skin, you wouldn't have the stories in this collection. The question is like the flint that starts the fire. Admittedly, sometimes
it sputters and goes out, but more often than not, the question
starts a flame that burns down the forest. Maybe, all the for-
ests. You see, the question is greedy. It's unrelenting. It wants
the writer to play God with the lives of men and women in the
pages, and I willingly go about this business, telling myself no
one really gets hurt. No one dies.

They don't. Do they?

That's a rhetorical question, of course. No one is hurt. No
one dies. Although, it doesn't mean you won't feel their pain
or their grief in these pages. I want you to see the Universe
through each character's eyes. I want you to feel what they feel.
When their hearts race, I want your heart to race. I want you
to cry for them. If you have a heavy heart, it's because I wanted
you to.

You will find many conundrums in this collection. There
are at least two maybe three murderers you may cheer on (to a
degree). Death comes in several different forms, not all of them
bad. Several gods show their faces, and they are not what you
expect. In these pages, holidays are not necessarily for family
gatherings (you may have known that). War shapes us into
what we are (and this is not a conundrum, just a statement

of fact). You will find that curiosity doesn't always kill, but it will change you. Take note, old monsters live with us, and new monsters are created by us. After reading, you may find being senseless wouldn't be so bad. The world isn't always what you think it is.

Life isn't about silver linings. It's about passage. From one state of being to another. Out of the light, into the dark. Out of the dark, into the light. Through hell and back. Over the river and through the woods. What's the payment for passage? Your life? Your soul? Friends? Family? Does it matter? This is fair warning: There always will be darkness within the light, and light within the darkness, and I only ask that you be aware of both in these pages.

Cedrix E. Clarke
Richmond, KY
April, 2021

All hope abandon ye who enter here.

Dante, *The Devine Comedy*

Every cell
Of your body
Holds a universe
& you exist
In the universe
Of every cell
& what you dream
Are the dreams
of the infinite you

Cedrix E. Clarke
Twitter, 2014

SOMEONE ELSE'S LIFE

◆ ◆ ◆

The line on Craigslist caught Edward's attention: Do you wish you could live someone else's life? He didn't even have to think about it. His answer was immediate and surprising. Yes, he thought, I want to live someone else's life. But that's not what made him click the link. The line was in the Lost & Found section of the website, and he couldn't figure out what living someone else's life had to do with something lost or something found. He had to know. And it was a distraction, something to take him away from Molly, his lilac point Siamese that had jumped the wooden privacy fence two weeks before, probably in pursuit of a bird or another cat. Edward was distraught over losing her. He'd walked the neighborhood for the first few days, calling out here kitty kitty, then widened the search to the adjacent campus. He and his girlfriend, Marlene, put flyers on every flat surface in a nine-block square, and knocked on every door in that square, but no one had seen her. Edward went to the animal shelter in hopes a good soul had brought her there. But she was lost. His last-ditch effort was to put a notice in the newspaper and, as a half-thought, Craigslist. He didn't know if anyone still looked at Craigslist, but what could it hurt?

Once he'd placed the ad, he began scanning the lost and found section of Craigslist daily, but it was mostly dogs that had been found. A boxer. A collie. A beagle pup with no collar that answered to the name Ralphie. Edward wondered *how* the person knew to call the beagle *Ralphie* if it didn't have a collar. Did he start yelling out random names until the dog began wagging its tail? How many names did he yell before the beagle responded to Ralphie? It was funny, but Edward couldn't bring himself to smile. Not while Molly was missing. So, he moved on. Right below the ad for Ralphie, Edward saw the line "*Do you wish you could live someone else's life?*" His curiosity impelled him to click on the link. The web page came up, and the ad was striking for its simplicity, no fancy graphics, no pictures of beautiful people, only words.

```
Do you wish you could live
someone else's life? Walk
in their shoes, step for
step, every moment of the
day? Feel their joy, their
passion, their love? Do you
feel lost? Do you want to
be found? Do you want to
escape your everyday life?
The Mendelson Foundation
can help. Call 1 800 555
HELP now and be a part of
this amazing journey. This
is not too good to be true.
```

Edward didn't know what kind of happiness potion the Mendelson Foundation peddled, but he didn't believe the ad for a second. He figured it was a bait and switch fraud where the scammer promised the world, but gave only illusion, so long as the credit card held out.

Still, Edward wanted to live someone else's life, and this caused him to lean and peer over the edge of his life, but not too close. He didn't want to fall. The tipping point had not yet come.

And it didn't come when Marlene, his on-again off-again

girlfriend, dumped him for a teaching job at a small university out west. She'd known for a couple of months but hadn't had the guts to tell him. She said she'd planned to tell him a few weeks before, but then Molly went missing. In a few days, she'd be gone, so she had to tell him. When he asked why she was leaving, she blamed it on the seventy-year-old English Department chairman who wouldn't let professors discuss or teach writing published after 1950. The chairman was an annoyance, Edward knew that, but he couldn't understand why Marlene had to go so far. There were closer teaching jobs at better colleges. He decided the job in Arizona was her way of running from their relationship. In her mind, the only way she could escape Edward was to put distance between them.

The night before she left, Marlene looked like she'd rather be anywhere than with him. Perhaps, it was guilt. Was there someone else in Arizona? Or did she just want to get away from him?

The moving van had left earlier, and the cleaning had been done. They sat on the floor of her empty apartment, not really talking. "You should really get another cat," she said.

He was feeling passive aggressive, so he blurted, "And another girlfriend, too, I guess." Then he added, "I want to find Molly." Another long silence followed, and the room grew dark. He didn't want it to end on bad terms, but he had to say what was in his heart. "Why didn't you tell me?"

"I wanted our remaining time to be good," she said. And it had been. Edward had started thinking it might be permanent *on-again*. The way Marlene had helped him search for Molly had brought them closer.

"Well, you could have asked me to go with you."

He imagined her sideways frown, but couldn't see it in the dark. "Don't start, Edward. Don't. You'd never have come anyway."

"Yeah, I know," he admitted. He'd been with his engineering firm for seven years and thought he'd make partner in the next year. "I'm entrenched and can't pry myself lose."

They made love at his house that night, and it felt good. Maybe it was his way of trying to save the relationship, but she left the next morning. It was over. Forever off-again. Never on-again.

When he arrived at work the same day, he was called into the Keeley brother's shared office and told the depth and the density of rock for the Library project at the Rosedale Branch had been miscalculated. The estimated price tag of rock removal was half the project cost. Edward had spent more than a year working on the project, late nights, early mornings, weekends. He'd lived and breathed the job. It wasn't just a new library, but also a tornado shelter for an area of town that had few basements. The limestone in this flat area of town made constructing basements cost prohibitive. A tornado two years before had made a shelter a political issue.

"I started this engineering firm thirty-five years ago," Don Keeley said, "and there's never been such a costly mistake. The Library's demanding your head, and I'm giving it to them."

Edward looked from Don to his brother, Greg, and then back to Don, but neither yielded their stern expression. "You're firing me? Is this a joke?" When neither brother answered, Edward squinted at Greg. "You remember, right? I told you those borings and soundings were wrong. I requested a different geologist, but you said *no*."

"There's no record of such a request by you," Greg said.

"I sent you an e-mail."

"There's no e-mail."

"But—"

"Listen to what Greg is saying," Don said. "*There's no e-mail.*"

Then it dawned on Edward. All evidence of the e-mail had been removed from the server, and he hadn't made backups. He considered bluffing that he had blind copied the e-mail to an off-server address, but he didn't have the heart. Did he really want to work for the two brothers anyway? "You're fucking unbelievable," he said.

"*Edward,*" Don said. "Don't burn bridges."

"You are, why can't I?" He stood, walked to the door, opened and gently shut it, then he cleaned out his desk. He felt sick to his stomach. He wanted to sabotage the Keeley Brothers, but he couldn't. He wasn't that type of person.

He left the office, got in his car, and drove toward home like a man burning up, but he wasn't really. He was closer to the edge and was accepting that all he'd had in his life a month ago had changed. He had nothing left. But he didn't feel invisible. Not yet. But so close.

He was stopped at a light on Rose Street at the intersection with East High, only four blocks from home, when he saw Molly. She walked away from him, up the hill toward campus, like she owned the sidewalk. He almost left his car in traffic to chase her down. But he thought it would be best if he could get ahead of her, maybe park on Maxwell and double back on foot.

He kept one eye on her and the other on the red light. He prayed for it to turn green. As the cat got further away, he began doubting it was her. He'd just lost his job, not even twenty minutes before, and he didn't care, so long as he found Molly. *That* would make the world right again.

The light turned green. He waited for the asshole in front of him to let his foot off the break and accelerate. He followed the same asshole at a crawl up Rose Street, and he feared he would lose sight of the cat—*was it really Molly?*—but he kept his eye on her. When he pulled up next to her, Edward saw the distinctive black splotch on the tip of her tail, a marking he'd seen on no other lilac point. She ran on the sidewalk with the stride of a lioness daring anything to get in her way. Edward considered stopping, to hell with blocking traffic, to hell with everyone else in the world, but he had to get ahead of her.

He drove past Molly to the intersection with Maxwell. He turned left and parked in a *no parking* zone. He jumped out of his car without locking the doors and ran. He crossed Rose

Street and went back toward High, where he expected to find Molly moving toward him.

He reached High, turned back, and walked up the hill to Maxwell. He went down each of the side streets, twice. Molly was nowhere to be found.

This was the tipping point.

He kept walking up and down the same four or five streets, but she wasn't there. He now wondered if she had ever been there. Had he imagined the cat walking up the hill on Rose Street?

When it was too dark to see, he went back to his car, now adorned with a parking ticket. He drove home and drank. First beer, then bourbon. With each drink, the night became fuzzier.

He woke to the smell of vomit on his breath. He ran to the bathroom, gargled with mouthwash, and brushed his teeth, but the smell was still there. Maybe it was on his clothes. His head pounded, right behind his left eye. He swallowed 600 milligrams of ibuprofen and turned on the shower. As the hot water poured over him, he tried to remember the night before. All that came to mind was giving the pizza delivery guy a twenty-dollar tip and saying something about looking for Molly and showing him a picture. He remembered telling the guy his girlfriend had left him, and if he found her, he could bring her back, too. Had he shown him a picture of Marlene? He didn't remember eating the pizza, or anything else about the night. Whatever he ate and drank, he'd thrown up, which he didn't remember at all, thank the gods. Just the smell.

The alcohol may have temporarily lessened the ache of his heart while he drank, but it only made this day worse. He regretted drinking to the point of oblivion. He'd been falling into the well for weeks and drinking only cushioned his landing. He was at the bottom now, laying on his back looking up. He saw the top, but there was no way to climb out. Edward hated this feeling. Even though sunlight poured into the bathroom window, he could only see blackness from the bottom of the well.

His life as he knew it was over, and he realized he'd have to be reborn. The question was how? He considered asking Marlene if he could come out to Arizona to make a go of it with her there. But was that being reborn? Wouldn't it be the same old song and dance? And even though Marlene had been cordial during the breakup, she wanted a fresh start. Far away from him. *She* needed to be reborn, too.

His savings would float him for six months, even with his mortgage payment, and if necessary, he could borrow from his retirement or his parents, but money wasn't the issue. What bothered him was the thought of sitting at home, twiddling his thumbs, nothing to do except dwell on all the real-life issues, but mostly, missing Molly.

Still, the words kept coming to mind. *I need a new life.* At first, it was a bad joke, and then it became a mantra. As he stepped out of the shower and wrapped a towel around himself, he remembered the ad on Craigslist. "Do you wish you could live someone else's life?" More than ever his answer to this question was *yes*, if only for a little while. He still didn't believe it, but he needed to grab onto something that would give him a glimmer of hope, something that would pull him out of the well. He was lost and needed to be found, he told himself. What did he have to lose anyway?

After he'd put on shorts and a t-shirt, he turned on his laptop. As the computer loaded up, Edward figured since it had been two weeks, the ad would have been taken down. Yet, when he clicked on *lost & found*, there it was, boldly calling out to him. Perhaps the ad was a siren set to bash his head against the rocks, but it was worth the risk. Yes, he thought, I want to live someone else's life. He punched the number into his cell phone. It rang twice, before there was a click.

"Mendelson Foundation," a woman said. "How can I help you?"

Edward stumbled at first with an extended *uhhh*. What was he supposed to say now? He hadn't planned a response. "There's an ad on Craigslist," he finally said. "The one about living someone else's life. I was curious about what the Mendelson Foundation is selling."

"The Mendelson Foundation is not selling anything," the woman said.

"Well, how do I get to live someone else's life?"

As if reading from a script, the woman said, "For that question to be answered, you have to come to our office and sign confidentiality agreements, and other legal documents, to protect you and the Mendelson Foundation. You will have to complete a questionnaire to determine whether you're a candidate."

"Is this for real?"

"As real as it gets."

This rang true to Edward, and maybe that was only because he wanted it to be true. He didn't hesitate. "Where are you located?" he asked. He listened and wrote down the address. "Do I need an appointment?"

"You should make one," the woman said. "When's good for you?"

"How about right now?"

The Mendelson Foundation was a complex of warehouses surrounded by an eight-foot fence with three strands of barbed wire at the top. Edward thought it was heavy security, but the gate was wide open.

He'd been told to drive to Lane H and turn right. The office would be on the left. What Edward discovered when he passed through the gates were indistinguishable warehouses. He figured there were ten lanes with six warehouses in each lane. Sixty warehouses all owned by The Mendelson Foundation. Each had four large bay doors, and a regular door on each visible side. If he hadn't been told which lane, it would have taken Edward thirty minutes driving up and down the lanes to find the right building.

When he passed Lane C, a chill went up his spine, and he came to a complete stop. He had an uneasy feeling about the quiet of the place. There were no vehicles. No people. In the middle of the work week, this place should have been crawling with activity, but it was deserted. He considered turning around, but he had nothing to lose. Turning around meant going back to the bottom of the well.

He found Lane H, turned right. Three cars were in front of one of the warehouses. There was a sign on the door for the Mendelson Foundation. He parked and got out, feeling more at ease. That there were cars meant there were people to drive them.

He started to knock, but it was a business. He turned the knob, opened the door, and went in. He expected to enter a warehouse, but he found himself in an office within the warehouse. It was like his doctor's office with a receptionist's desk, waiting room, carpet, fluorescent lights, couches, and magazines.

"Hello. It's Edward, right?" the young woman behind the desk asked.

He nodded.

"I'm Dawn. We spoke on the phone. Here's the questionnaire I told you about. Take your time filling it out. When you're done, bring it to me, and I'll let Dr. Mendelson know you're ready." As he took the clipboard, he stole a glance at Dawn. She could have been on the front of any of the magazines on the table. Why was she slumming here?

He sat on the couch, and checked that he had none of the listed diseases, and filled in his vital statistics, height, weight, education, marital status, children, siblings, parents, on and on. When he finished, he took the clipboard to Dawn and sat back down. She reviewed the questionnaire and clicked on the computer. An email, Edward figured. He flipped through *People* magazine, looking at pictures of people he didn't care about. Twenty minutes later, Dawn stood. "Dr. Mendelson is ready for you now."

He followed Dawn through a door into the warehouse, only mildly interested in the sway of her body as she walked. He was distracted by the flurry of activity he saw. It was a large square room, about a fourth of the size of a football field with a dome ceiling. Everything was white, the floors, walls, ceiling, doors, the desks, and even the computers on the desks. It was antiseptic. All the workers wore white lab coats, and they moved here, there, and everywhere. Edward realized this wasn't a medical facility, but a laboratory.

"What are these people doing?" he asked.

Dawn looked back. "Monitoring people's lives."

Edward didn't know what this meant, but he shut it out of his mind down before he invested more time to figure it out. He noticed there were hallways off the side of what he thought of as the white dome room, and Dawn led him to one these corridors.

"What is this place?" Edward asked.

"When someone asks, I'm supposed to say it's Oz."

"So, you're Glenda the good witch, right?"

Dawn smiled but said nothing.

"And Dr. Mendelson is the wizard? Didn't he turn out to be a humbug?"

"I assure you Dr. Mendelson is everything he says he is," Dawn said.

They reached the end of the corridor and turned right into another corridor, and then another and another. Edward felt like a mouse searching for a block of cheese. Finally, Dawn stopped at a door with a sign that read *Joseph Mendelson, M.D., PhD., J.D, M.E.* "Here it is," Dawn said.

She raised her hand to knock, but Edward stopped her with a question. "What's with the alphabet soup behind his name?"

"Dr. Mendelson has a lifetime of education."

"Isn't *J.D.* a law degree?"

"It is," she said.

He was about to ask why Dr. Mendelson needed a law degree when Dawn's knuckles rapped on the door. Edward heard a muffled *come in*. Dawn opened the door and motioned Edward to enter. He did.

The room was not white, but dark with mahogany wood-work all around, elaborate moldings on the ceiling and book-shelves on the walls. The room was lit with incandescent lights from copper fixtures. The only white in the room were the duel computer monitors.

Dawn followed Edward into the room and handed the clipboard to a dark-haired man sitting behind the desk. Dr. Mendelson, Edward presumed, but the man couldn't have been thirty years old. Edward had thought he was meeting with a wizened wizard, but it turned out Dr. Mendelson looked more like the wizard's apprentice.

Dr. Mendelson scanned the questionnaire, and then handed it back to Dawn. "Oh, okay. This is good," he said. "Thank you Dawn."

Edward had a fleeting thought that Dr. Mendelson's voice sounded old. It didn't match his appearance of youth, but then he was distracted by the movement of Dawn's figure as she left the office.

"Sit down, Edward," Dr. Mendelson said. Edward turned back to the doctor and did as he said. Dr. Mendelson looked at him closely. "Please tell me, what is it about your life that makes you want to live someone else's?"

Edward considered the question and wasn't willing to share much. "A run of bad luck is all."

Dr. Mendelson nodded. "Of course, you have. Do you have debt? Is that it? Did someone die? Did you hurt someone?"

Edward shook his head. "No, no, nothing like that. I mean, I owe on my house, but not much, and no one died. If you want to know the truth, I'm sick of my life lately."

Dr. Mendelson grunted, nodded his head. "Tell me about that?"

"Why is it important?"

Now, Dr. Mendelson sighed. "You see, this is the part where I decide whether you are a candidate for the services of the Mendelson Foundation, and you have to answer questions. If you're resistant, I can lead you out and you can go on your merry way."

Edward shrugged. "I have nothing to hide," he said. To prove it, he told everything. Dr. Mendelson didn't interrupt, but Edward could see the compassion in his eyes, or was there something else? Maybe it was excitement.

When Edward was finished, Dr. Mendelson leaned forward. "So, you feel you have nothing left to lose, right?" Edward nodded. "And you have no responsibilities to anyone, not even to Molly, correct?" Again, Edward nodded, although hesitantly. Dr. Mendelson smiled. "You're free, is what I'm asking you. No ties to anything or anyone?"

Edward realized his jaw had clenched, and he forced himself to relax. "No ties at all."

"Good. Then we can help you if you want. Some people don't."

"Why not?"

"Because they don't really want what we have to offer."

"Okay, tell me what this place is."

Dr. Mendelson smiled. "Well first, some legalities." He opened a desk drawer and pulled out a folder. "You can take your time reading through these documents, but primarily they say that once you sign, you can refuse our services. However, if you do, you agree to not speak about what you've been told about us. If you choose our services, the documents state you will receive our services at no charge. There is a power of attorney in which you appoint the Mendelson Foundation as your attorney-in-fact for financial and medical issues during your time with us. And—"

Edward didn't care about the legalities, so long as he wasn't selling his soul. "Stop. I don't care. If I have to sign before you'll tell me what you do, just tell me where to sign. I don't have the patience to read all of these documents."

Dr. Mendelson passed Edward a pen, and Edward signed document after document. When he finished, he passed them back to Dr. Mendelson, but he kept the pen. He was going to get something out of this.

"So, is that it?"

Dr. Mendelson nodded.

"Well, what is it you do? What is the Mendelson Foundation?"

Now, there was a visible sign of agitation in Dr. Mendelson's face. "You're ready to dive in now, aren't you? No matter what I tell you?"

Edward leaned back in his chair. "No, no, but I'm hungover, and I'm not in the best of moods. Just get to your sales pitch." When he heard his own voice, it sounded hollow, as if he were speaking from the bottom of the well.

"You don't believe."

"I—" Edward started, but stopped. He took a deep breath. "I want to believe, it's why I'm here, but the more you talk, it sounds too good to be true. I'm a doubter. I want to see behind the curtain."

Dr. Mendelson nodded. "I'm not a salesman. I'm a scientist, and I want to offer you the chance to be someone else. That person will control themselves, and you won't be making decisions for them. You'll be in their mind, co-existing, kind of like watching a movie. When they take a bite of chocolate, you'll taste it, and when they get mad, you will as well. You won't just be a passenger, but more of a shadow."

Edward scoffed. "I don't believe it."

Dr. Mendelson held up his arms. "Of course, you don't. It's insanity. But you've been looking me in the eyes. Tell me whether I believe it?"

Edward nodded. "You do."

"So, do you think I'm crazy?"

"No, I don't."

"Then what's the problem?"

Edward held up his right hand, then his left hand. "It's a math problem I see. It doesn't add up."

Dr. Mendelson squinted. This wasn't the answer he expected.

"You have all of this," Edward said and stretched his arms

out. "You own this entire warehouse complex. Sixty or more buildings. You have employees that have salaries. You pay an electric bill, taxes, insurance. I'd guess I'm barely scratching the surface on what all this costs. You need money to run this place, but you offer your services for free. There has to be a catch somewhere."

Dr. Mendelson neither confirmed nor denied these statements.

"Well, if I'm not paying for living someone else's life, who is? The money doesn't add up."

"You're a very practical and intelligent person, Edward. This is not a question that gets asked often, but it does get asked. I'll answer you as I have in the past. This is how it works. You don't have to pay because the hosts—that's what we call them—the hosts pay for you to be inside their heads."

Edward leaned toward Dr. Mendelson. "Why would they do that?"

"What we offer the hosts is life. More life. Longer life. For the time *you* are part of *them*, they don't age. Being a part of the Mendelson Foundation extends their lives. They give up their privacy to one or several individuals, and in exchange they get part of your energy, which regenerates their cells. They pay us money, a lot of it, for this service. Now, we can't guarantee they'll live forever. Even we can't stop car accidents or lightning strikes. We're not God. We can't stop murders either. We can hold off most diseases but not all of them."

Edward stared at Dr. Mendelson, disbelieving, and maybe a little horrified. He had so many questions, it was difficult to settle on one. "How much of my energy am I giving the host?"

Dr. Mendelson shrugged. "Infinitesimal."

"By doing this, am I giving up part of my life?"

"A day for a day," Dr. Mendelson said. "And by that, I mean, if you would live to be eighty-three, then you will still live to be eighty-three, but the week or the month you are part of the Mendelson Foundation, you extend your host's life by that much time. You lose nothing. They gain the time you're there."

"So, for every day I'm inside the host, they get an extra day of life? Their batteries are recharged."

Dr. Mendelson shrugged. "That's kind of what happens. Close enough for this conversation."

"While I'm inside the host, what happens with my body?"

"Your vitals are monitored. You're nourished with a feeding tube and hydrated intravenously. All your business affairs are taken care of. Bills paid. Taxes filed. It's kind of like you're taking a long trip, and you hire a service to take care of details for you. We answer letters. We have your phone directed here and take messages. We explain you're on a vacation or sabbatical. For you, maybe we can tell them you've been hired by a new employer to design a bridge overseas."

Edward shrugged. "Whatever. I still don't believe it."

"Edward, how old do you think I am?"

"Twenty-eight? Thirty maybe."

Dr. Mendelson nodded. "I do look like I'm younger than you, don't I? Well, I'm seventy-eight, and you'd never know it. I can show you my birth certificate, if you want, but I suspect you still wouldn't believe, right?"

Dr. Mendelson was right, of course. Since he wasn't paying anything, he wasn't losing, except time, and right now, he had a lot of time to give. He had nothing better to do. "Is there a minimum amount of time?"

"We suggest increments of thirty days," Dr. Mendelson said. "After you come out of the chamber, and spend a week tidying things up, eating some good food, enjoy the stipend the Foundation gives, you can go back in, if you want. Many do. Some do not."

Questions that Edward should have asked earlier came to him. "Hey, if you're seventy-eight, but look twenty-eight, does that mean you've been doing this for fifty years? And do you have a—well, if you're the host, then is the traveler inside you called a parasite? Do you have a parasite right now as we're talking? Did the parasite hear everything I've told you?"

"We call them travelers," Dr. Mendelson said, and he

smiled. "The name originated 40 years ago, when our organization was focused more on new age beliefs, and yes, I've had travelers off and on for 40 years. I currently have one. Travelers are counseled that the information they learn while inside a host is confidential, never to be discussed."

"How can the Foundation keep them from talking about it?"

"Well, one of the documents you signed," Dr. Mendelson said, "gives the Mendelson Foundation access to you, so while you're outside a host, someone from the Foundation is an occasional traveler inside you. You gain some life then, as a benefit from us. We always know if a traveler discloses information about the Foundation or a host. Trust me. You won't be inclined to talk. It hasn't happened in forty years and won't this time."

Edward didn't believe him. He didn't believe any of it. And yet, he was in the well, and he saw what was being offered as a way to happiness, something to lift him up from the bottom. Even though he knew he should decline, just walk away, he wanted the opportunity to be happy. He made a rash decision. "Okay, I'm in," he said. "Whose mind will I be touring?"

"You have choices," Dr. Mendelson said. "First, I need to know, do you want a male or female host?"

Edward arched his eyebrows. "My host can be a different gender?"

"Of course," Dr. Mendelson said.

"As interesting as a female host would be," Edward said, "I understand the plumbing for a guy, so I'd better stick with a male host. Maybe a female another time."

"Okay. Let's review your options."

What Edward noticed about his host choices was they all appeared in their late twenties and had interesting lives. One was a minor actor he knew. There was a pilot. A stripper ("Didn't you ever want to know what it would be like to be the one being looked at than the one looking?"). Several minor league sports figures. Musicians. A surfer. And then the professionals. Lawyers. Surgeons. Policemen. Firefighters. Soldiers. Congressmen. Edward noticed there were conspicuously no accountants, teachers, engineers, or writers. When Edward pointed out that it was like choosing a career, Dr. Mendelson said, "There are other categories in our database, but career is what most travelers choose from."

Edward nodded. "But why is it all you've got are exciting professions?"

Dr. Mendelson smiled. "It's about marketing. Who wants to be a traveler in a host who has a dull job? Would you want to live the life of a clerk in a grocery store? The hosts have to try to be interesting, so they spend time in careers that draw attention."

Edward thought this through. "So, each host gets a longer life," he said, "but some of the hosts have greater risk, like the policemen and soldiers. What if they get shot? Their longer lives wouldn't mean much."

Dr. Mendelson nodded. "Sometimes the hosts feel desperate if they go a while without a traveler, and they will take on a different career path to get more interest. And we've had three hosts that have died as a result. Others have had injuries."

"What happens to the traveler when the host dies?"

"The traveler dies, too."

Edward bit his lip and shut his eyes, something he did to keep his attention focused. He took several breaths. When he opened his eyes, Dr. Mendelson was patiently waiting. "You said there were other categories besides career to choose from," Edward said.

"That's right, but most people choose by career."

"Maybe I want to know the other categories."

Dr. Mendelson shrugged. "Some of our hosts have—well, there's no other way of saying it—their sexual activity is primordial. Sometimes the host has only one lover, but their lover has the beauty of a god or goddess, and other times the host has several partners. If that's your thing, I can show you—"

Edward waved his hand in front of him. "No, no," he said.

Now, Dr. Mendelson smiled, as if he knew something Edward didn't. "There's another category that's similar but different than careers. It's skills, and sometimes this is a career, but usually different. When you're within a host with certain skills, you learn from it. For example, being a traveler in a host with a different language, you retain some of his or her language skills. The longer you're a traveler within the host, the more of the language you'll retain. But there are limitations to this, of course. It's mental, so being within a professional athlete will only give you knowledge about the game, maybe minor reflex acuity, but it won't give you the physical ability. You could teach the sport, maybe, but not play it. If you're hosted by a surgeon, you won't get the fine skills, but you will get much of the knowledge, not that it will do you much good, unless you're in medical school. Does that explain it?"

Edward was intrigued by this. "What other skills are there?"

"Do you want to learn to read music?" Dr. Mendelson said. "It won't help you be a great pianist, but a good one, once your fingers learn to touch the keys, and even some of that is retained. Another skill is cooking. If your host is a chef, then you learn how to cook. You won't have the knife skills, but it'll give you a good palate, and you'll know what ingredients go with one another, and maybe the wines that go well with a meal, that kind of thing."

Edward made another split-second decision. "I want my host to be a chef."

"So, you want to learn to cook?"

Edward shrugged. "Well, that too, but if I'm stuck inside a chef's head, I know I'll eat well. Food will make me happy, I think."

Dr. Mendelson cocked his head to the side. "You'll eat like a king," he said. He punched some keys on his computer, turned one of the monitors toward Edward. He described three male chefs, all working in larger cities. One of the chefs lived in Sarasota, and Edward had always wanted to live near the ocean.

Grady Watson was a James Beard Award nominee who specialized in Southern cuisine with a Latin flair. Edward read the bio, and all of it was interesting, but there was a picture of Grady with his wife, and when he saw it, he knew.

"Him," Edward said.

"Why Mr. Watson?" Dr. Mendelson asked. "He's not the *best* chef of the three, and he's short and slightly overweight, unlike you. I'm just curious about your interest in him over the other two."

"I want to be where it's warm," he said. It seemed the picture was taken without the Watsons knowing it. They were looking into one another's eyes, and there was such love and happiness in their faces. Edward figured some of that happiness would fall to him and take him away from his own misery. He hoped that's the way it worked. He also knew one picture did not necessarily make a happy marriage, but he didn't believe these two people could fake those looks. "I want to be near a beach."

"That sounds like as good of a reason as any other I've ever heard"

"When will this be ready to go?" Edward asked.

"Now, if you want."

"Now?" Edward asked. "What about my house, my things, my electric bill and cable bill?"

Dr. Mendelson waived those things away with a swipe of a hand. "All that will be fine, but I have one question: Do you have any pets other than the poor kitty that ran away?"

Edward shook his head.

"Okay then," Dr. Mendelson said. "That makes this easy. We'll have your mail and phone forwarded here, pay your bills, and do whatever is necessary. We will visit your house a couple times a week, to make sure all is okay. We've done this thousands of times. I can assure you that part will be fine. It's just business for us. It's what we do."

Edward wasn't expecting it to be immediate, and he was flummoxed, unsure if this is what he wanted. He wondered about loose ends he'd left to come unraveled, and whether he should call his parents to let them know. But let them know what? That he was touring someone's mind? No, of course not. That would only make them think he was crazy. He decided he'd send them an e-mail that he was traveling overseas, and he'd be out of contact.

"Yeah, okay, what do I do?"

"Just go to sleep," Dr. Mendelson said. "We'll hook you to wires, sensors, an IV tube for feeding, a catheter for urination, and on and on."

Edward started to ask how they take care of defecation but decided he just didn't want to know. "Before I do this, I want to send an e-mail to my parents to tell them I'll be away for a few months"

Dr. Mendelson nodded. "And anybody else that may worry about you." Edward shrugged and shook his head, feeling somewhat pathetic. The doctor smiled knowingly. "Okay, I'll take you to the library's computer where you can send them an e-mail."

Thirty minutes later, Edward was put in a small room with a double bed and given two little red pills. He was told it would help him sleep, and when he woke, he'd be a traveler in Grady Watson's mind. He was given a hospital gown, and told it was necessary for access to his body. The door shut, and Edward changed into the gown. He lay in the bed, unable to sleep. The red pills weren't working, and he didn't think any of this was going to happen. All the world crashed in on him, and he wondered if this would help him climb out of the well. There wasn't even a sliver of light at the top of the well anymore. He decided if this worked, he would want to stay inside the chef's mind as long as he could. Why did he need to live his life when he could be a part of someone else's? His life only brought him misery, and he would just…

Edward woke and saw a knife slashing a carrot, a julienne cut he knew from watching the Food Network with Marlene.

The speed of the cut was remarkable, like watching a Jedi Knight slicing vegetables. Edward could feel the touch of the carrot, still slightly cool from being refrigerated. He could feel the rapid movement of the knife, slicing through the carrot like butter. He heard the *click click click* of the knife striking the cutting board, and he heard music, fuzzy guitar chords. He recognized the song, but he couldn't place it at first. Then he heard the chorus. It was *The Spirit in the Sky* by Norman Greenbaum, and Edward realized he was humming along. No. That wasn't right. Grady Watson was humming along, and Edward wasn't *hearing* the song through Grady's ears. It was in Grady's mind only, and with the song, Edward heard and saw a steady stream of thoughts and images. The sensation was like watching a movie but knowing all the character's thoughts. Edward thought he could get lost in this man's mind.

As Grady cooked the pisto manchego, he was focused on the task at hand, and had few extraneous thoughts. There were other cooks in the kitchen, also busy at their tasks, and not talking by Grady's order. It's how he worked, in silence, creating his artistry of tastes without the constant hum of voices around him. Still, certain thoughts or images floated in, and Edward didn't know what it all meant, just flashes of a memory or random thoughts. It was all Edward could do to not go a bit crazy.

So, he stayed in the backseat, watching, being patient, hoping it would all make sense with time. Edward sensed this was prep work for the upcoming dinner hour, and at one-point Grady acknowledged this with a look at the wall clock and yelling, "Thirty minutes. Finish your work, and be ready for orders. It's a full night. Reservations 'til ten."

It all looked like chaos to Edward, the way Grady went from dish to dish, tasting, smelling, stirring, tossing in spices, criticizing the line cooks, but more often than not, praising a particular dish and telling the cook to keep up the good work. When Grady looked at an employee, Edward got a subtle feel for what Grady thought of them. Sometimes it was feeling of trust that a particular job was getting done, and at other times, there was a lack of clarity, maybe because it was a new employee Grady didn't know much about or an older employee who had issues. Edward got a sense of distaste for the maître d' named Harold, something that had nothing to do with the restaurant. It involved a woman, or maybe women, but Grady's thoughts moved on before Edward could get a firm grasp.

The five hours Grady and his line cooks filled orders was invigorating and exhausting. Edward learned little about Grady during this time. The focus was only on getting the food out to tables. Edward doubted he would learn much about cooking during the tour of his host's mind. It was all jumbled, half thoughts, mostly reactions and unexplained emotions. Everything Grady did in the kitchen was instinctual, no real thought to it.

Edward was intrigued. Putting it all together was like having a thousand-piece puzzle. He was content to enjoy the ride, especially the eating part. At one point, Grady began making what he thought of as shrimp risotto with lemon sauce, plated it, carried it off to a corner, and ate standing up. With the first taste, Edward realized Grady's genius. It was the only dish Edward thought he could make himself, so simple, and yet it had the complexities of flavor that made Edward think of a symphony, with instruments playing different parts, but all fitting together.

When there were no more customers, Grady left the cleanup for his employees, changed into shorts and a t-shirt, and escaped out the backdoor. He unlocked his SUV, a big Chevrolet, started the engine, and lifted his iPhone to call Maggie, his wife. He moved the SUV out of the parking lot as he talked to her. He said it had been a good shift, no catastrophes, all was well, but he wanted to take a drive to wind down. When he hung up, he turned on the radio, and sang along to *Ob-la-di Ob-la-da*, and let the thoughts of the shift go through his mind. He reminded himself to tell Simon, the line cook, to not be so fucking heavy handed with salt. Twice orders came back and had to be remade, and this was unacceptable. There were other thoughts, little of it making sense, but when Harold the maître d' came to mind, the thought was clear: *Insolent little bald prick.* The conflict had to do with Harold bedding every waitress in the restaurant against Grady's policy, and now the waitresses were fighting. Grady wanted to put him out on the street, but Harold ran the dining room so well Grady feared losing him.

As these thoughts roared through Grady's mind, he drove the streets of Sarasota, and passed over a bridge, the water below just an inky presence, but the smell of salt distinct. When the SUV stopped, it was in public parking. Grady got out and walked to the beach, tossing his shoes beneath a picnic table. He began running, his thick feet pounding in the sand. Not an easy lope, but a full out run in the sand, maybe a half mile. He stopped, breathing hard, and sat down on the beach, the flats of his feet together and his back straight. He cleared his mind, shut his eyes, so now Edward was in darkness.

Finally, one thought. *Welcome.*

Edward wondered what it meant. *Who* or *what* was welcome.

The next thought. *Dr. Mendelson's email said you'd be traveling with me tonight. I hope I have entertained you thus far.*

With horror, Edward realized Grady was speaking to him.

I can sense you. But you're directing your thoughts away from me.

Edward tried to be still, quiet, but finally he thought, *You can hear me?*

Grady breathed deeply. *Now that it's calm, I can. After a few days, when the connection between us has strengthened, I'll be able to hear you all the time, except when you don't want me to hear you.*

Now, Edward had a concern. *Dr. Mendelson said nothing about this.*

Grady sighed. *He doesn't know. Not all my travelers are self-aware enough to respond. Many of them have the insight of a fish, so I ignore them. Let them watch, but not get to my essence. Dr.*

Mendelson is a genius, but he only gets half of the equation, the half that keeps him young.

What's the other half? Edward asked.

The experience of not being alone. Becoming one with you. Your thoughts being mine, and my thoughts being yours. The goal is for us to think as one, separate but together, synchronicity

Edward didn't respond. He didn't believe.

You are hesitant, unsure of me, not trusting what I say, and I understand this. I am your first host, right? And it's all still new to you. You're not sure whether this is happening the way it should be. I assure you, it is. Grady paused to see if Edward would respond, and when he didn't, he asked, *I sense your unhappiness. Is this a form of suicide for you?*

Not suicide, Edward thought. *Escape.*

There was a long pause, and Edward caught uncertainty, then a sense of Grady choosing his words carefully. *You are welcome to use my life as an escape, to be just a passenger to all I do. I'm fine with that. I don't believe you are escaping your misery though, merely delaying it. And that's okay, maybe you need a respite from your life, whatever it is that has put you in...the word I'm sensing from your mind is* the well. *What's the well? Is that what you call it? It is, isn't it?*

Edward reluctantly confirmed it was. *I'm at the bottom of the well trying to climb out.*

Oh, this is good. We already share thoughts. Earlier I sensed you tasting my supper, as well. You liked it. Edward could feel Grady's lips stretch into a smile. *So, being a passenger is fine. If you like my food, you'll enjoy my life, because that's all it's about. But what Dr. Mendelson doesn't understand is this experience can be more. Before I joined the Mendelson Foundation, I was alone, empty, and no matter what I did, I couldn't fill that void. I had money, women, drugs, booze, everything money could buy. Nothing helped. When people were near, I felt more alone than ever. When I had my first traveler, I realized I couldn't escape the feeling of someone looking over my shoulder, so I accepted it. I didn't communicate with the first few travelers. I didn't know I could, but having the traveler filled my emptiness, as if something had been missing. Maybe it's just me that feels this. Maybe I'm the only host who has discovered the ability to communicate with a traveler, since most of my travelers return.*

Grady opened his eyes, and both he and Edward looked out into the Gulf of Mexico. They could see the lights of a few boats floating on the ocean. Grady lifted his head up to the stars in the moonless sky.

It's all so infinite, Grady thought.

And we're so small.

And alone.

Yes, Edward thought.

You've lost people?

My girlfriend left me for a job, and I lost my cat. I was fired from my job after ten years. All in a few weeks' time. All I had was gone, and that's what put me into the well.

Which loss is worse, the cat or the girlfriend?

Oh, Molly, my cat, Edward answered.

She made you feel less alone?

Yes. She completed me.

Grady stood and started walking back up the beach toward his car. *Oh, pets will do that, won't they? They fill the void, too. Kids will do that. Wives will do that. But nothing will do it so completely as what you and I now have.*

Edward felt the sand below Grady's feet, and smelled the salt in the air. He thought about the ad on Craigslist. He'd been lost without Molly, and now he did feel as though he'd been found.

In the next thirty days, there were moments that felt unreal to him. That first night Grady went home and made love to his wife, Maggie, the three of them sharing the passion. Edward tried to pull away, into the back of Grady's mind, but Grady told him, *No, you have to be a part of this.* So, he was, and it was wonderful, blissful. Edward thought he had an orgasm, too, if that was possible. It didn't matter Maggie was somewhat ordinary. Grady's love for her was intense and filled every moment he was with her.

The food Grady made was unlike anything Edward had ever seen or tasted. Grady took him on a tour of spices and sauces, fish, meat and vegetables, liquors, coffee, and tea, and the combination of all. Grady told Edward the key to being a great chef was knowing how to eat and having a palate to know what was missing.

Only then did Grady begin teaching Edward the basics of cooking, naming the different knives, pans, utensils, and showing the various forms of heat and how each produces a different result. Edward was a sponge, soaking it all in as though he was in culinary school. He kept asking himself if he could ever go back to engineering after this.

Grady's beach house was on Siesta Key, not far from where he'd parked his car that first night. Every day before work, Grady took a late morning walk, when the heat was beginning to rise, and this is when each of them laid themselves open to the other, an intimacy Edward had never had. When Edward told Grady this, Grady suggested maybe he needed to have relationships more like what he had with his cat, Molly, than what he had with Marlene. Edward couldn't deny it. He loved Marlene, but he couldn't live without Molly. Edward would never have come to this conclusion without Grady's insight. Marlene had been someone to hang out with and screw, but she was replaceable. As for Molly, Grady suggested what Edward was suffering from was grief.

It was a grievous loss.

One morning Grady asked Edward if he liked being an engineer, and Edward responded, *I'm good at it.*

That's not what I asked. Do you have passion for it?

Edward considered the question, and finally thought, *It's a job. It pays the bills. I mean, I do like the sense of accomplishment I get when a building or road or sewer line I've designed is constructed.*

But do you wake up excited about it?

Edward didn't have to think about his answer. *Never.*

Grady let it go, but the thought was planted in Edward's mind, and he fought against it, mostly because *his* happiness was never a priority. He hadn't been taught a job should bring joy, or that you should wake up excited about going to work. The only equation he'd ever known was working hard meant he had money to pay the bills. That there was potentially more to the equation had opened his mind.

One Sunday morning while Maggie drowsed on Grady's shoulder after a lovemaking session, Grady thought, *What am I sensing from you? Is this an awkward moment? Are you embarrassed?*

Edward was taken aback and didn't respond. He wanted to hide from Grady so he was unreachable.

Come on. Talk to me, Grady thought. *I want to understand.*

Edward sighed. *I'm embarrassed. I mean it's not the physical act between you. It's that I'm sharing this intimacy with you. What the two of you have is unbelievable. It's sensual. You become one. And while I've had lovers, I've never had a lover like this. So complete. At first, I felt some slight discomfort, but now, each time the two of you touch one another, I feel like a trespasser. I just don't think it's something I should be sharing.*

No, this is exactly what you should be sharing, Grady thought. *It's what you're here for, to experience life as I do, and this, making love to Maggie, is an essential part of my life. When she and I are together there's nothing else in the world that exists. That's the way it's got to be. All your worries forgotten, whatever they are. That your rent's not paid has to be out of your mind. That you're screwing your best friend's wife doesn't matter. Or that your best friend is screwing your wife doesn't matter either. That the world's about to end has got to be gone. In that moment, you have to be fearless. You have to let go of all that could harm you. Only when you can do that, can reach this level of intimacy.*

Edward wasn't sure he could keep the rest of the world at bay, but didn't dispute what Grady was saying, except it wasn't exactly true. *But you let me in,* he thought. *Doesn't that destroy the intimacy?*

No, not for me. You're part of it.

Maybe for you, but not for Maggie. I mean, isn't it like making love to one woman and having someone else in your thoughts. She doesn't know, does she? Wouldn't it upset her?

It's more like I'm talking to myself, Grady thought, *and I get your emotions along with mine. It's like having a dual sense that doubles the intimacy. Maggie doesn't need to know.*

Edward took a long time to respond as he thought about what Grady had said. He had only one more question. *Do you enjoy making love to Maggie as much when you don't have a traveler inside your head?*

Edward could sense the flow of Grady's thoughts as he considered the question, but couldn't get ahold of them. It was like trying to stop running water from going down a drain. Finally, Grady thought, *It's complicated, but yes. Having you in my mind makes it better. Three different people, two bodies, all becoming one. It's beautiful.*

But Maggie doesn't know I exist.

Whether she knows, doesn't matter, Grady thought. *Does it make me tri-sexual? Is there a term for it? I may be the only host of the Mendelson Foundation who knows how good it can be.*

Edward was almost ready to move on, but he asked, *Do you worry that a long time will pass without a traveler?*

I used to worry about it, but so far most of my travelers return. Some of them I've met in real life. I mean, outside my mind. We speak on the phone. When I'm feeling especially in need of having someone with me, I call and ask them to come to me. This doesn't happen often, but there have been times. The dark times.

Why are you so lonely? Edward asked.

I've always been like this. It's part of me.

The evening before Edward was scheduled to return to his own body, he asked, *How did you become part of the Mendelson Foundation?*

Grady was walking on the beach after his shift, whistling *Love Me Do*. He stopped whistling and focused on the question. *You said you answered an ad in the Lost & Found, right? What did the ad say?* Edward told him, and Grady smiled. *The ad I answered was: Would you like to live forever? And I thought it was tripe, but I had turned forty and was financially secure from several different sources, namely my family. I didn't like the thought of getting older. I can't say I was in much of a different spot than you, the love of my life had left me, a wonderful woman, and I was directionless in my life. I was unhealthy, even fatter than I am now, and so I called the number. It was a rigorous process to be chosen as a host, and even when I was chosen, I didn't believe having a traveler would make me young. But then, when three years passed, I could see the lines around my eyes had disappeared, and then after five years, I had settled into what I see in the mirror today, and nothing's changed since.*

How does it work? Edward asked. He couldn't decipher the jumbled thoughts that passed through Grady's mind, so he waited for him to answer.

I don't know, Grady finally thought. *I mean I know your body is acting like a battery for me. There are yearly shots, but I don't know what's in them. It's got something to do with making me a receiver for your energy. How it's done really isn't important, except I had to make sure you and the other travelers were not being hurt. I couldn't do this if there was no benefit to you.*

There was a pause, and Edward pulled away

That's not all you were wanting to know, Grady thought. *There are other questions. I know.*

Edward had other questions, but hadn't planned on asking them. *The questions aren't necessary,* he thought.

Give it up, man.

Edward felt cornered. *Doesn't your wife notice?*

Edward couldn't see Grady's expression, but felt his face muscles tighten. *What the fuck are you asking?*

She grows old, you don't.

Yeah, Grady thought, *but it's not noticeable, yet. It'll cause problems eventually, I guess. But for now, it's just not important. I enjoy the moment. Carpe diem.*

What if you had kids?

To live forever, the ability to procreate is removed.

Edward thought about it. *You mean you—*

Snip, snip.

Edward sensed Grady's humor and would have laughed if he could.

People have kids so they can see their own youth in them, Grady said. *I look in the mirror and I can see my youth.*

Grady was almost back to the house, and Edward had only one more question. *You can't stay* here *forever—*

You mean in Sarasota? Grady asked. *No, eventually, I'll have to move on to some place different, before someone notices my failure to age, and probably take a different name. The computer age has put us at risk, because there are pictures of us all, and the IRS and the government will eventually take notice. They'll wonder why I'm still working well into retirement. And I guess, I'll get divorced when I move. I'll give my wife everything she needs, and keep enough for me to start a new life.*

But you love her, Edward said.

I do.

Then why not give up the Mendelson Foundation? Grow old with her.

Edward sensed upheaval. *That's simply not possible,* Grady thought.

The reason I chose you was because of the picture, the two of you looking at one another, such love. Was that not real.

Of course, it was, Grady thought. *That was a moment in time, a happy time, but nothing lasts forever. You are responsible for your own happiness. When I met Maggie, she made me so happy. She still does, but I can sense it fading. Can't you feel it?*

Edward hadn't felt anything. He wondered if Grady was rationalizing it.

Your last night, right? Will you be back?

I don't know, Edward thought, *maybe.*

39

With that, Grady put Edward to the back of his mind, and Edward was simply a passenger the rest of the night. He was left wondering whether travelers truly cured Grady's loneliness. Maybe Grady was deeper in the well than him and having travelers was his only grasp on reality.

Edward wanted to talk about it, but when Grady returned home, he made love to Maggie and went to sleep.

Edward woke in his own body in a hospital gown. He was stiff, but not weak as he had expected, and he was thirsty. There were three bottles of water on the nightstand. He drank two of them in rapid succession. He stood, and immediately sat down. It was as if his legs had forgotten how to move. The signals from his brain to his legs were slow. Edward raised each leg several times, stretching the muscles. When his legs seemed to finally begin working, he stood again and walked around the bed, holding on. After two treks, Edward felt almost normal. Being in the gown bothered him, but he did not find clothes in the closet or dresser, so he went to the door and turned the knob. It was locked. He would give them a half hour, then pound on the door until someone came. In the interim Edward exercised and stretched, all the while feeling conspicuous and silly in the gown.

Twenty minutes later, Dr. Mendelson opened the door, carrying a bag with Edward's clothes, and asked how he felt. Edward only nodded. Dr. Mendelson excused himself while Edward changed. When Edward opened the door, he and Dr. Mendelson weaved their way toward the front of the warehouse. Finally, Dr. Mendelson asked, "So, how was it?"

Edward could tell it was a question he asked often, but never without great curiosity. It took a few seconds for Edward to figure out how to speak again, and when he had cleared his throat several times, he said, "Great, I think, but I'm still processing it, trying to understand everything."

"You're not sure if you're coming back?"

"I don't know. You were right though. I would never say

40

anything about the Mendelson Foundation." In the lobby, before Edward left, he turned to Dr. Mendelson. "Tell me if I'm wrong. There are thousands of travelers being housed in the warehouses. That's why you need so many buildings."

Dr. Mendelson smiled, but said nothing.

On the drive home, Edward stopped for a burger and milkshake, which he finished before turning onto Maxwell from Broadway. He was out of the well, and he felt like he'd found himself. He was going to wait a few days before deciding whether he would return to the Mendelson Foundation. He thought he would, at least one more time, but he wasn't sure if Grady would be his host. He'd become disenchanted with Grady. Maybe he'd just be a passenger next time. Maybe he'd go with a more exciting host, something for the ride.

His house was as he left it, except maybe a little neater. He felt like having a beer. He didn't care that Dr. Mendelson had told him to hydrate. With his Dos Equis, he walked out on the patio and sat in a chair. It was cooler now, late September, and he realized he'd lost the last month of summer. He never felt like he'd gained so much in a month's time. He was excited about going to the grocery, preparing for and cooking a grand meal. He had much to learn, but felt competent.

Edward was about to get up when Molly appeared at the top of the fence and hopped into the patio. Edward screamed with excitement and joy. He started crying. He picked Molly up. She was fat as ever. He figured she had been fed by a good soul and finally decided to return home. He wanted to tell her she was a bad cat, but couldn't bring himself to do it.

He did feel complete now.

HOW MANY LIVES

◆ ◆ ◆

I t was the silence of flight Jenny noticed. When the tires of the Camry left the shoulder of the road to go over the cliff, the only change of sound should have been the absence of the tread of the tires, but there was nothing. She had a moment that confused her, but realized time had slowed, or maybe stopped, and the sound waves from the engine, air conditioner, and stereo were suspended while she was lost in the moment. The sounds were still there waiting for the moment to begin anew, and it was the oddest part of dying. Jenny knew she couldn't survive the crash into the rocks below. She found irony in the fact she'd been singing along with AC-DC's Highway to Hell. Of all days to die, this is not the one she would have picked. Not the day the divorce was final. Not when she had so much life left to live. She wondered if she could survive, but all she could see through the windshield was white—

—from the glare of the lights in her eyes. She screamed at the top of her lungs as she felt Julia emerging, and it hurt terribly. She squeezed Jack's hand, as if holding onto the pain, for a snapshot of a memory, and he urged her to push, push, push—

—but the ring wouldn't slide on her finger. She didn't panic, but saw Simon was about to lose it in front of all their friends and family, so she reached to his hand and held it and he looked up at her. She smiled. He resisted smiling back until she whispered, "Don't worry." That's when his face lit up, and she looked into his turquoise blue eyes—

—and saw the anger there. Her father held the used con-
dom between his thumb and forefinger and shouted, *"Jesus
fucking Christ. You're only fifteen. If your mother was alive..."*
She wanted to scream she loved Brad, wanted to spend the rest
of her life with him, but she couldn't overcome the self-hatred
for disappointing her father. When he turned—

—he handed her the half-smoked joint and exhaled the
sweet smoke. "Are we going to screw or what?" he asked. She
wished she could remember his name, and it was on the tip of
her tongue. Lonnie? Gale? She wanted to tell him that as soon
as he got out the coke, she'd fuck him, but instead she reached
—

—for the file, opened it, and glanced at her notes. She
looked up at her client and said, "Even if we plead it down,
you're going to spend two years in jail. It's a second offense,
man. I'm sorry." She saw he watched her—

—open the file, glance at her notes like she cared about
him, and when she looked up, he saw the fake sympathy. She
told him the best she could do was two years. It was just a job to
her. Fuck her, he thought. He made a fist, and—

—she rubbed her eyes, trying to get the tears back in.
She didn't want to cry. Her mother wouldn't want her to cry.
They'd prepared for death since Dr. Cooper told them the cancer had spread. She felt the world shift beneath her feet, and
she had to sit down. Jesus. Both parents in a year. A tissue appeared in her hands, and she wiped—

—off as much of her blood as he could from his murdering
hands—

—onto a paper towel and wondered why the hell she hadn't
been paying attention to the fucking game. Brandon was on
second base, and she should have been watching him and not
talking to Alice. But Alice was telling her about the size of her
boyfriend's cock, and that image still wouldn't go away. She
reached into her purse, which was still sticky with the blood
that had gushed out of her nose, and grabbed the baseball
where it had landed and held it up. A fucking foul ball. She'd

give it to Brandon to make him happy despite the loss. Her grip on the ball loosened and it fell—

—down with the urgent pull of gravity as the moment re-formed, and all the sound waves began again with all clarity in the world. A sudden and loud *HAAARUUUMMPPHHH* tolled. Bon Scott sang "*... I'm on the hiiiiiighway to Hellllll...*" Jenny released a scream that lasted long enough for the Camry to slam into the rocks. As she lay dying, Jenny felt cheated. *None* of those memories had been hers. Why didn't she get to see her life flash before her eyes just like the cliché? Why did she have to see moments in the lives of strangers? But they hadn't been strangers, Jenny realized. She knew only what the dying know. She'd been all these people. They'd all had been her, like fingerprints on her soul. She'd be born as another and another until she'd lived all her lives, not in any particular order, for time had no real meaning. Her last breath carried one final thought: How many lives could one soul live?

THE RAIN WOULDN'T
TAKE AWAY THE PAIN

◆ ◆ ◆

"Will your parents even like me?" Mary asked. I could see her out of the corner of my right eye. She sat cross-legged, facing me, seatbelt unbuckled. Her small delicate hand laid across my right leg, unmoving, and yet, I could sense her unfocused energy.

I heard the question but didn't respond immediately. I was listening to the squeal coming from the driver's side front tire, which was impossible to ignore, sounding like a banshee on a death march. The further I turned into the left curve, the higher the pitch became. I thought it could be the brake pad, brake drum, or even the ball joint. The Accord had been making the squeal in left turns for a week, but I couldn't pin down the cause. My father had a mechanical mind, and I hoped he'd be able to diagnose it.

There were dark clouds approaching from the west, not a storm, but a heavy rain. I kept moving to spite the squeal so we could be off the roads before the rain reached us.

When the curve straightened out and the squeal faded, I turned to Mary and gave what I hoped she would consider a smirk. Of course, my parents would like her. It was a silly question, but she'd been asking it all week. At first, it was endearing, even the nervousness, but now I was concerned she might have unresolved self-esteem issues.

"You really shouldn't worry about my parents," I said. "It's my sister who'll be in your face the whole time we're there."

Little sisters should not scare girlfriends, but Mary latched onto it like a security blanket. "In my face? Is your sister a terror or what?"

I should have kept my sister out of it, but I couldn't help myself from testing these waters to see if I could figure out what was wrong.

I'd convinced Mary to spend Thanksgiving with my family when she said she didn't have the cash to go home to New Jersey. A plane ticket for a four-day stay was too costly, and the eleven-hour drive would have exhausted her for the week before finals. She told her parents she had to study, which was true, but not the whole truth. She hadn't told them about me.

We were only twenty minutes from Cressy, and I needed to set her mind at ease. "Agatha is just like any sixteen-year-old girl," I said. "You just have to remember she thinks she's the most important person in the room and that she can control you. She'll ask personal questions, and you either deflect them or answer them. My mom will run interference for you though."

Mary groaned as if I'd just announced my family worshipped the nub of Satan on Tuesday nights, and she followed it with, "Oh now, your mom is my savior? Jesus Christ."

Another left curve was coming up, although softer, and I slowed to see if speed affected the squeal. As I entered the curve, I heard it. I pumped the brakes, and I thought the squeal faded, but just a bit. When the road straightened, I accelerated, and the squeal waned to nothing.

"Did you hear that?" I asked.

"Hear what?"

"That squeal."

From the corner of my eye, I could see her shaking her head.

"You didn't hear it?"

She squinted, unable to make sense of what I was talking

about. "You must have dog ears because there was no sound a human could hear. Or maybe you imagined it."

I didn't think this was true. "Well, maybe. I am pretty sure I heard it though. I guess you have to be in the driver's seat." The next curve was toward the right, so I sped up as we approached it. I glanced at Mary and saw the patient look on her face. She wasn't going to let it go. "My mom's no one's savior, but she'll keep Agatha in line, and make her be polite, which is difficult to do. Agatha likes to be mean."

"Oh great," Mary whispered.

"Give it up," I said. "My mom will love you because you're smart, and that's all that matters."

My mother was a high school math teacher, and she liked anybody who could keep up with her at math. Mary was a fourth-year engineering student, and she was my first girl-friend I thought knew more than my mother about geometry and algebra. I had been Mary's freshman English teacher three years earlier, and she turned in papers on a different level, structurally, technically, and philosophically. The first assignment was simply to write a three page *how to* essay, and she turned in an eight-page paper on turning sand into glass. It was so good even I could have followed the instructions. Her Wuthering Heights analysis was on par with my professors, but was original. I showed it to my best friend, Joseph Rabin, and he said there was no way a freshman wrote the paper. Joseph's emphasis was 19th Century English Lit, so he would know, but he admitted her take on it was unique. When I showed him her other papers, Joseph told me what I had already decided: She's a freaking genius. I gave her an A for the class, and I only saw her on campus occasionally for the next three years, nodded and waved.

Two months ago, she showed up at the department chairman's annual grill at the beginning of the fall semester. Her friend, Renee, was apparently dating another of my colleagues, and she forced Mary to tag along. Mary told me she was glad to see a friendly face, and I told her I was glad to see a face

47

of anyone who wasn't in the department. For hours, we were like a couple ballroom dancing, without music, weaving in and around other groups of people, but it was as if they did not exist. I took her home, and we became inseparable. Even when we were physically apart, the phone calls and texts filled the void of missing one another. She was such a bright light, electric, eclectic, knowledgeable about everything, and almost always wired, but not in the way that she made people nervous. She entertained without being entertaining, effortlessly passing her energy to everyone near her, as though the world was her stage and she was going to perform.

Her only questionable trait was what the hell she saw in me, a third-year doctoral student who could not seem to finish a thesis on T.S. Eliot's *The Wasteland*. Sometimes I thought I was caught in *The Waste Land*. April may be the cruelest month, but my doctoral advisor told me if I didn't finish my thesis by May, it would be necessary for me to move on to make room for students who could finish. I'd been told I could continue teaching Early American Lit in the spring if I had made significant progress on the thesis. Mary stuck by me during the last two months, through all my bitching and moaning, and not once told me to buckle down. She simply listened and offered to help with the research. She told me once that I made her comfortable, probably because my problems were worse than hers, and maybe that's why she was still with me.

When I suggested she spend Thanksgiving weekend at my parents, she had been hesitant. She claimed it was because she didn't want to barge in on my family's holiday, but now I wondered if she simply worried about making a bad impression on my parents.

"Your sister will hate me?" Mary asked.

I laughed. "Well, yeah. Agatha hates everybody. She'll be jealous you're taking my attention, not to mention my parents' attention. Everything has to be about her. She's in high school. Just ignore her."

As we entered the next left curve, the squeal was different. It was deeper and more resonating, and a vibration came through the steering wheel. Then it stopped as suddenly as it started. There was only a faint echo. I wondered what had happened. I thought maybe something had hung up in the wheel well and finally let loose in the curve. It was gone, hopefully for good. I came out of the curve into a straight stretch and could see more than a mile.

"So, why didn't you tell your parents you were spending Thanksgiving with my family?" I asked. This had been bothering me, probably in the same way meeting my parents bothered Mary. I worried it was because she saw us as something temporary, and that could also explain why she seemed to dread the thought of meeting my parents.

She mulled the question over. "Well, I really like you, and if I tell them, it will totally ruin it." I turned to her to ask what she meant, but her eyes were cast down to her lap, so I looked back to the road and let her finish gathering her thoughts. She finally said, "You blow out the candles on your birthday, and you get a wish, right?"

"Yeah."

"If you tell anyone the wish, what happens?"

"The wish doesn't come true," I said.

"*Exactly.*"

I was confused. "So, I'm your wish?"

Mary laughed, and said, "Uh-huh." In a Forrest Gump voice, she said, "You're the whole box of chocolates, Jenny." We had caught the movie on cable the night before, and I was shocked she had never seen it. She had been doing the voice ever since. In her own voice, she added, "You know, I liked you since you were my teacher."

"Yeah, right," I said.

"No, no," she said. "It's true."

I turned back to her, squinting. "You were hot for teacher?"

She slapped my shoulder, but laughed. "No, no, it's nothing like that. I just knew on the first day of class there was something about you bigger than life. You're just so goddamned

49

nice. One day after class early in the semester, we left the class-room building together, you opened the door for me, and after that, I always followed you out, just to see if it was me, and it wasn't. You opened the door for everyone. You went out of your way to open the door for people. If someone was thirty feet away, you would wait for them, then you would open the door, just so you could let them in. Of course, you couldn't notice me when I was your student—not like that anyway—and I understood, but it didn't make me want you any less. You were a nice guy."

"And a good teacher, right?"

"Oh Jesus. You make it sound like I was stalking you. I wanted to get to know you. I couldn't though. I couldn't cross the great divide between student and teacher."

A thought occurred to me. "Is that why your papers were so good?"

I glanced at her and saw she was biting her lip. "Well, I wrote those papers because I wanted a good grade, but I may have done more for you because I liked the way you taught. Plus, I had a crush on you."

"Why didn't you tell me this before? I mean, since the party."

"I thought it made me sound juvenile. I knew you were five and a half years older than me. I needed to be as mature as I could be, if I was going to make this work now."

She always took the intellectual way out of emotional deci-sions, treating our relationship so much like a chess game she had to keep two or three moves ahead of me, not that this was difficult to do. I tend to react to a situation as it arises, without any forethought. I make split second decisions, and I'm just damned lucky I'm right so much of the time. This didn't make me unpredictable to Mary. She seemed to know exactly what I was going to do before I did it, and I wasn't sure how this made me feel about her. I knew I couldn't compete with her, but maybe that wasn't such a bad thing.

I was distracted for a second by another downhill curve to

the left a half mile away. The road had been built into a wooded hillside with a twenty-foot limestone cliff on the right and a deep gulley on the left where the road had been cut into the hill. There were old trees, sycamores, poplars, pin oaks, and large evergreens, on both sides of the road. The canopy going into the curve made it dark, like a tunnel, but I thought I could see well enough without my headlights on. The rain was closer now, but the sun was still bright. I had driven this road enough times I could maneuver it blindfolded.

I forced my attention from the road back to Mary. We had circled the issue, and I decided to go ahead and attack it head on. "Why are you so scared of my parents? And now of my sister?"

It was as though a bomb had gone off between us. She leaned away, folded her arms across her chest, and frowned at me, not angry, but defensive. "Oh, Jesus, I just want it to be right," she said. There was a hint of annoyance, but she said it flippantly as though it was obvious or should have been.

It didn't really answer my question, and I considered just leaving it alone, keeping my hands off it, but that simply wasn't in my nature. "Why do you think you're going to screw it up?" This question wasn't fair because I knew Mary would never consider she was going to screw anything up, but it was a reasonable conclusion. I wanted to rile her a little bit, knock her off balance, and maybe help her get over her fear.

Mary shook her head emphatically. "No, that's not it." She began to explain it mathematically. "There are just too many variables, and I cannot predict how your parents and sister are going to react to me. They may hate me."

I groaned. "So, you're restless because you can't predict how strangers are going to respond to you?"

She nodded.

"You have to trust me. It'll be fine. Can you do that? Stop worrying. It's not like you."

Mary laughed. "It's unbecoming of me."

"Well, no, just unlike you."

I wanted to add that it was irritating as hell, but we entered the curve, and in the darkness of the shelter of trees, I saw the largest deer of my life standing in the middle of the road two hundred feet away.

"Look at that," I said. It was a buck, at least an eighteen pointer, its antlers looking like two oaks had sprouted out of its head. It was painfully beautiful. I expected the deer to jump out of the way as soon as it heard the car, but it lifted its head, looked at me, and held its ground. The deer seemed to be daring me to not slow down, as if we were playing a game of chicken.

"Watch out!" Mary screamed.

I slammed on my brakes. The brake pedal sank to the floorboard with an indefinable hollowness. I cursed the goddamned deer as if it were the deer's fault my brakes were broken. I thought of my dad and how he could only dream of killing a deer this size. Now, I had no choice but to strike and probably kill it. A wave of regret passed over me. If I avoided the deer, the likelihood of injury to either me or Mary increased, whether it was striking the limestone cliff on the right or dropping off into the wooded gulley on the left. My only thought was to keep us from harm, at whatever cost. So, I kept straight, but edged as far to the right as possible.

At the last minute, the deer sidestepped out of the way. I missed it by half a breath. My relief was short-lived. The brakes still didn't catch. We were traveling at an unsafe speed. I pumped the pedal for all I could, but there was no resistance at all. We entered a slight curve on the continuing decline. I couldn't control the car. I felt us spin counterclockwise, and I turned the wheel in the opposite direction to gain control. Just when I thought I had it, the passenger side wheels dropped off the road. I jerked the wheel hard to the left and pulled out of the drainage ditch. Now, we spun clockwise, out of control. I realized, probably too late, we should brace ourselves for the inevitable impact.

"*GRAB HOLD!*" I shouted.

I wished I had let Mary go home to her family for Thanksgiving. Had it been self-serving to invite her to my parents for the holiday? Had I caused her injury by insisting she join my family? The questions thoughtlessly passed through my mind as I pumped the brakes hoping pressure would build up in my last and final attempt at gaining control of the car. We had spun one hundred and eighty degrees and were facing the way we had come. I saw that goddamned deer standing in the road mocking us, the irony noted. Then, like a blur, the deer jumped off the road into the woods down the hillside. I wanted to curse it again, but I let the feeling pass. At that moment, the Honda lurched off the road, still spinning clockwise. We were air born, turning. The gravitational pull pinned me in the seat. I screamed. Mary screamed. There was a bone chilling silence. All I could do was wait for the sound of impact. We hit the first tree. I thought it sounded like the crack of a baseball bat, a home run for sure. That's all I remember about the crash. Not even a dream.

I woke with the rain. There was a pain in my chest and arms I could never have imagined. I was able to move my head, but not without that terrible pain, and I could see bright pink dots splattered against the spider-webbed windshield. Red stripes smeared the dash and side windows. The driver's side window was shattered, and rain drizzled in against my shoulder. The car was twenty-five feet below the road on a slope not quite vertical. The accord was level, but only because my door was wedged against a huge sycamore.

I turned to my right. The pain nearly caused me to blackout. I stared at Mary's motionless deformed body in the passenger seat. The airbag lay impotently in her lap. Her legs were at odd angles to one another. It looked as if her body was corkscrewed, with her left leg twisted in a different way than her trunk. Her head was at a greater than ninety-degree angle to her shoulders, obviously broken. She was broken.

I whispered, "Mary?"

Her hair was tinted scarlet. A stream of blood trickled along her right temple onto the seat and pooled into a small red ocean. She was dying. Her life's blood drained from her.

I moved my arms to reach for her, and that small shift caused such pain blackness wrapped itself around me like a cloak. It did not take me, not this time. As the pain in my broken arms subsided, I breathed deep and the blackness moved away. I took measure of my other injuries. What grabbed my focus was the sledgehammer thud in my lower back. It wasn't the piercing pain of my arms, but more like each end of my spine was being twisted in opposite directions, like the wringing out of a washcloth.

My back hurt, but I felt not a twinge of pain in my legs. When I pushed my feet against the floor to lift myself up in the seat, nothing happened. The airbag blocked my legs, so I couldn't see movement. I rolled my toes in my tennis shoes and thought my toes moved, but I had nothing to base that on, except the ghost of a feeling. I decided to lift my leg with my hip, just an inch, so the airbag would shift, but as hard as I tried, the airbag remained still. Was it paralysis? Temporary or permanent? Were my legs broken or at odd angles like Mary's? Considering my other injuries, I thought paralysis may be a blessing, but I worried it was a curse. I was scared. I wanted to scream. I remained calm.

"Mary?" I called again. I tasted blood in my mouth and with my tongue felt the holes of missing teeth. I put aside my uneasiness and focused on broken Mary. Maybe it wasn't as bad as it looked. "*HEY MARY?!?*" I yelled. "*MARY, WAKE UP!*" It was garbled, but still intelligible.

I wanted to get to her and do something to help, but all I could do was be helpless, and I felt hopeless. I closed my eyes and heard the rain pounding against the metal of the car. The rain wouldn't wash the blood away. The rain wouldn't take the pain away. There was nothing I could do.

I remembered my cell phone and thought it would be easy to call for help if we weren't in a dead zone. Without thinking,

I reached out to my pocket and the sudden movement caused such a wave of pain the black cloak did wrap me up in its fold and take me this time.

I dreamed of walking the trails at Red River Gorge in the Daniel Boone National Forest and leaning over the edge of a cliff and then a little further until I lost my balance. I dreamed of landing. The pain. Oh god, the pain.

When I woke again, it was still raining. My neck hurt. My head ached. My lips were chapped. My arms and back felt like torture but I felt nothing below my beltline. I stared at Mary's dying or dead body, and I wailed. She was dead, I knew it, and part of me wished I was dead. I tried to move toward her again, more carefully this time, but the pain in my upper body was too great to move more than a few inches. I just wanted to hold her and tell her I was sorry. I blamed myself for the accident. I could have had the brakes checked. I could have driven slower. We could have taken Mary's VW Bug, which was only a few years old. I would have felt like the last sardine in the can when getting out of the Bug, but Mary would still be alive worrying about meeting my family.

Mary was dead because we took the Honda. I wailed again, in pain, but mostly grief. I was lost in it. I felt like I was drowning in the grief. I wasn't even trying to reach to the surface.

A voice cut through my noise. "Stop that crying! Stop that noise! You hear?"

My initial thought was we were saved. Someone had seen the car go off the road and called an ambulance. Hope swelled but was crushed when my eyes cleared. I saw an old man with a curly gray beard. He wore a fur-lined red suit and was leaning into the broken passenger door. But he wasn't really leaning in. He was partly in the car, partly out. His image split by the passenger door. I blinked several times to clear my eyes, but the image of this pudgy man didn't change. I thought I must be dreaming. I saw Mary beside him. Like a balloon tied on a ribbon, she was floating. She stared at me expectantly. I glanced at the seat next to me, where her lifeless body lay.

"Come on. It's time," the old man growled. He said it matter-of-factly, almost bored, although his voice boomed. I was speechless. I glanced at Mary's hopeful eyes and looked back to the old man. He extended his gloved hand. "Come on. Take my hand. Now. No time to waste."

I breathed in until I felt a sharp stinging pain in my chest. A broken rib, maybe. I gasped. The old man drifted toward me and reached out his hand. I wanted to shrink away, but couldn't. The thought of his hand against mine unnerved me. He touched my chest instead, although touch is not really what he did. His fingers sank beneath my skin, and seemed to drain the pain out of me, like a sponge. The pressure in my lungs eased. Again, he whispered in that booming voice, "Come on. Come with me." His free hand reached to mine but stopped just short of it. Why wouldn't he grab hold and pull me forward if he wanted me to go with him?

Still, I was lured to him. I painlessly lifted my broken arm to him. Before our fingers touched, I pulled back and dropped my arm into my lap. I was confused by his bright eyes. "Who? Who are you?" I asked. Maybe my question should have been which one are you because there were two names that came to mind, and I wasn't sure which one he was.

He sighed, obviously annoyed, and answered my question with a question of his own. "Who do you think I am?"

I didn't want to say it. It seemed absurd and it was absurd. I felt the witch's fool. This had to be a hallucination brought on by the pain from my injuries, but I said it anyway: "Santa Claus."

And my God, did he look like Old Saint Nick! Just like out of a greeting card. The rosy cheeks. Curly gray hair. Thick beard. Red suit.

He scowled, and I knew I was wrong. He was the other one. "*I am Thanatos*," he said, his voice big in my head. He was an old power.

If I hadn't been so scared, I might have laughed: Santa Claus is Death, and Death is Santa Claus. He seemed aggravated that it wasn't obvious to me. But his scowl was the only scythe he carried. He could not bring me harm this day. Of that, I was sure.

I thought about the Blue Öyster Cult song, and it seemed ridiculous to me when you replace the reaper with Santa Claus. All humor passed when I thought about the line that Romeo and Juliet were together in eternity. Was that line written for Mary and me? Death had taken Mary, and now he was here to take me. I wanted to go with him if it would get me out of pain.

I caught my breath and looked at the motionless body of Mary in the passenger seat. Then I glanced at her bright glowing form next to this crazy old man.

Grief burned like fire in my chest.

"Don't cry," the ghost of Mary whispered. I didn't know I'd been crying. She reached to me and touched my face with her long thin pale fingers. Just as Thanatos drained my pain, Mary took away my grief. If I went with Mary, there was no use for grief.

"My family would have loved you," I told her.

Mary stroked my cheek with her hand, but said nothing. She kissed my forehead and rested her head against mine. I closed my eyes and breathed in her loving healing touch. I was happy.

For a long time, she held me, mingling with my body.

Then the old man interrupted us. "Come on, now. Come with me. You can be with Mary forever if you want." It was as if he'd read my mind.

I had almost forgotten him, forgotten she was dead, and I was almost dead. I realized I didn't want to be dead. I would not simply yield to the pain. I shivered. "I don't want to die," I said.

"Tell him Mary," the old man said "Tell him how wonderful this new life is. Tell him."

As if it were a recitation, she stated, "No worries; no cares; no bad thoughts; nothing. Nothing but love. Pure love. No jealousies; no angers; no sadness; no tears; nothing. Nothing but love. Freedom."

The old man smiled. "Show him Mary."

Mary caressed my neck.

At first, her touch was warm and then it burned. I was on fire. The passion consumed me. I moaned. It was wonderful, the best feeling I had ever had, but something about it didn't feel right. It was empty. I thought about what Mary had said, and the word *nothing* banged around my head like a pinball machine. Every time it hit, something else came to mind. Nothing is easy, nothing good is free. Nothing from nothing leaves nothing. Freedom's just another word for nothing left to lose. Nothing. Death wasn't offering me something. He was offering me nothing, and this is what Mary wanted me to know. She was the mathematician and had told me Death's lie in a simple formula. There was not really love in Death's world. If there is nothing on one side of the equation, there was nothing on the other side, too. Or even worse, for every bit of love, there was pain and hate to balance it.

Before she released me, Mary whispered a final, "Nothing."

If Death heard her, he gave no sign. "That was mere seconds. Now, imagine all eternity," the old man in the red suit said, but he was no salesman. He wanted to take away pain, but pain was life.

I shook my head. "I don't want to die; not yet."

"Come with me," he beckoned. It was the plea of a hungry animal.

"I can't. No, I can't."

"Come with me," he repeated. "Ask him, Mary."

I turned to her. She was silent. She wouldn't look toward me.

"He's supposed to be Santa Claus," I said. "The red suit."

The old man frowned. "No," he said. "I'm Death. Santa Claus is myth. I'm not a giving spirit, I'm a taking spirit. I take life. I take souls."

"He delivers death," Mary said, but she was wrong. This god delivered nothing. He took life and gave nothing in return.

The old man nodded. "She's right, so come with me. You'll be in a lifetime of pain if you don't."

"No," I said. "I can't; I don't want to die."

I shut my eyes.

The old man whispered in my ear, "You'll be in pain. I can be your salvation." I wanted to laugh at this statement until I felt the old man's warm touch, his breath on my ear and his fingers on my shoulder.

The numbness faded.

All the pain returned.

I groaned and opened my eyes, but I couldn't focus.

He touched me again and my suffering stopped. "You'll be weak and crippled. Don't suffer like this."

"No. Pain is life," I said and tried to push him away.

My hands pushed empty air. He wasn't flesh. Inside his cold empty lifeless spirit, my hands found the hideousness that raged within. I jerked my hands back. "What do you get for taking life?"

The old man was silent. His eyes peered deeply into mine, and for a second, I thought he wasn't going to answer, but he scoffed. "That doesn't matter to you. I am Death, the antithesis of life. I am freedom from your pain. You want peace, and I can offer that to you. I can take you from this world of suffering. This hell. Come with me!" The last statement was a demand. He outstretched his hand to me.

I could hear a siren and thought I saw flashing red lights approach from a distance. An ambulance.

"Come," the old man commanded. "I'll get you eventually."

The ambulance. The old man. Which was my salvation?

"Follow me."

I shook my head. I could hear people struggling through the wooded brush above on the hill.

He was fading, and with him, he took Mary. "Bye my love," I said. She blew me a kiss.

"Hey, you okay in there?" a voice asked through the window.

"I'm alive," I said.

When I turned back toward the old man in the red suit, he had gone and ferried Mary's soul with him. Only Mary's dead body remained.

I passed out while the men resurrected me from the car.

It was weeks before I was conscious enough for snippets of it to come back to me. When I mentioned Santa Claus, the nurses thought it was because Christmas was approaching, and Death could only mean the death of my girlfriend, Mary. No significance was placed on any of my medicated ramblings. I had to wait until I was out of the hospital before I told anyone about what had happened. But when I was released, I kept silent, not a word to anyone about any of it, not even to the grief counselor. I didn't want my friends and family or my doctors to think I was delusional. Who would have believed me? You don't. You think I am crazy. You think I hallucinated or dreamed all of it, and that's okay. Even if you believed me, would it significantly change your life?

Years have gone by, and I still cannot get it out of my head. My limp is a constant reminder, and when I wake in the middle of night from dreaming about it, I can't get back to sleep. I lay in bed next to my wife, eyes wide open, unable to move until first light. My daughter is only two years old, and so Christmas is not the annual ritual I know it will become, but I still have to see the fake Santa Clauses in the mall and department stores. I dread the month-long reminder, and I think, if they only knew. If they only knew. I want to tell everyone.

I cherish every moment of life with every ounce of my soul. But most of all, I fear death. I fear the reaper.

He is coming.

SYMPATHY

◆ ◆ ◆

He called himself Satan; sounds presumptuous, doesn't it? Sounds like a straitjacket and a padded room were needed. That's what I thought, anyway.

"Hey man, mind if I sit here?" were his first words, spoken in the deep, rumbling voice of the Jamaican reggae singers— Bob Marley or Peter Tosh, someone like that. *Man* was pronounced *monn*, and *here* was pronounced *hereuhh*, and every syllable was deliberate in its enunciation. I was staring into my beer like it was a crystal ball, maybe looking for answers, maybe some questions. The voice startled me and when I raised my head, I peered into the blackest face I'd ever seen. The whites of his eyes were like moons in a midnight, starless sky, and his smile was like the white tail of a comet painting a grin across his face. I was sure he was in a reggae band. He dressed the part; he wore sandals and holey white jeans and a raggedy green t-shirt. His thick dreadlocks coiled around his shoulders and down his back like black snakes. I wasn't afraid of him; and yet, I didn't quite feel safe. I wasn't sure how to respond to his question, so I stared at him. He asked again if he could sit across from me.

The pub was nearly empty. There were two older men at the bar watching a football game, and a couple in a booth across the way. Otherwise, the place was dead. He could have sat anywhere, but he chose to sit with me.

I nodded, and he slid into the chair. "Hey man. What's

going on?" he said. I was silent. "My name is Satan," he added.

I didn't know how to respond to this. What's appropriate when someone tells you he's the devil incarnate? All I could think to say was, "And I'm Jesus Christ." As soon as I said it, I bit my tongue and drew blood. There must be an unwritten rule you don't tell someone you're Jesus when he claims to be Satan. Besides potentially adding unnecessary tension to the conversation, it could also mean serious trouble if it turns out he is Satan, or even if he thinks he is. But when a chance presents itself for me to make a clever joke, albeit a joke in bad taste, it comes out before I can control it. The little editor in my mind has been on hiatus most of my life, and at times it makes me the wittiest person in the room. Other times, it makes me the most obnoxious, which I don't really mind.

But luckily, this man–*Satan!?!*–laughed, and his perfect teeth gleamed in the dark room. "Oh man! Oh man! That's funny! That's really funny," he bellowed. *That's* sounded as *thattt'z*, and *funny* was *fon-nee*.

When his laughter subsided, he pulled a pack of cigarettes out of his shirt pocket. "Do you want a smoke?" I shook my head. "Don't smoke?" I shook my head again. I started to tell him he couldn't smoke since the ban passed, but I decided *screw it, let the waitress tell him.* A funny thought struck me awkwardly: As Satan he probably has some privileges regular people don't have, like smoking wherever the hell he wants. I pressed my lips together to restrain my laughter. He didn't notice. He was busy tapping the pack of cigarettes against his palm. Finally, he opened the pack, lifted a cigarette out, and lit it with a wooden match he'd pulled from nowhere. He closed his eyes and sucked on the cigarette. The end lit up against his dark face like a lighthouse beacon on a stormy night. He released the smoke in several rings that rushed toward me, exploding and deforming against my face. I considered making a comment about secondhand smoke, but I didn't want to start a conversation about disease and death with *this* man.

Satan opened his eyes and looked at the beer bottles lining

the edge of the table. He pointed to them. "So, tell me about it."

"About what?"

He looked at me as though I were stupid.

I held out my hands. "What do you want me to say?"

"Well, what do you want to say?"

I ran my left hand through my hair. "I don't know. What do you care? I mean, what's it to you?" And I meant this. Who the hell was this guy coming into the bar asking to sit with me and then asking me to tell him about my problems? It made me angry. I wanted to leave, and I almost stood up. But the fact was, I needed someone to be there across from me. Not to listen to my problems. God knows, I knew what my problems were, and I didn't need a pseudo-psychiatrist to tell me I was a self-absorbed, emotionally immature self-aggrandizer. That was what my wife was for. That's what she said earlier in the week, as if cheating on me wasn't enough. With my best friend. In my bed. It should be obvious to anyone the alcohol was to deaden the pain of everything. It was supposed make me oblivious, but it wasn't really working. Maybe having someone there, not to talk about my goddamned wife, but about everything else, might help. Just to have that other voice, even if it came from a crazy Jamaican *monn*. That's all. I didn't want to talk. Only listen. "My God," I whispered, "why does every bleeding heart need to hear what's going on in my mind? Jesus Christ. Why does everyone think they can help me? I mean, because they can't. No one can help me!"

"Have you got a wife?" Satan asked.

I shrugged, and finally nodded.

"Why aren't you with her?"

I shook my head. I wasn't going to talk about it.

"Come on. I can help. Give it up, man." He sounded convinced in his abilities, but I wasn't so sure.

"What makes you think you can help?" I asked.

Satan shrugged his bony shoulders. His dark eyes were wide and round, and his smile was inviting. "It's what I do," he answered.

"What do you mean?"

"You know what I mean," he said, but I didn't, and when I said I didn't, he said, "Come on, trust me. What have you got to lose?"

I squinted at him and gave half of a smirk. To his question, I offered, "My soul?"

For a half second, Satan's face was blank as he processed my response, and then his face broke. He roared. He banged the table, stomped his feet, and he howled. "Oh, man, that's funny!" he said. "Oh, man." For several minutes, he laughed, at times coming to a complete stop, and then breaking up again. He took a napkin and wiped his forehead. "Oh my. Oh dear." The entire time, I sat there, interested in his laughter, but making every attempt to show no emotion, as if I didn't get the joke.

What finally brought his laughter to a stop was a pretty waitress who asked, "What's so funny?"

It wasn't the waitress who had been bringing me drinks all night. This girl was petite and bright faced, like a flower in bloom. The name on her pin was Astral. Her blue eyes were the color of a summer sky, and her hair a shade of honey. She was happy, her smile told me that much.

"He's a comedian," Satan said, pointing to me.

She turned to me. "So, tell me a joke?"

I was speechless, so Satan saved me by saying, "Miss Astral, he's a little bit shy. Could you bring me a hurricane, and bring my friend another beer. Something to loosen his tongue."

She smiled. "Good plan. That all?"

"For now. It's still early in the night."

"Okay. Be back in a second," she said to Satan, and to me she said, "Think of something funny."

She left and Satan flicked his finger in the direction of the empty bottles. "So, you don't want to talk about that. That's fine, but let's talk about something else. I'm looking for the answer to an age-old question, if you know. Which is the bigger evil: Politics or religion?"

I shrugged my shoulders. "I don't know," I whispered, hoping he'd leave me alone with the questions.

"Come on, man. It's really important." It seemed to be a life or death question to him.

"Okay, okay," I said. "Ask a politician, he'll tell you religion. Ask minister or priest, he'll tell you politics."

Satan waved that aside with the hand holding the cigarette, dismissing my unworthy answer. He peered at me menacingly with those dark eyes. "I'm not asking them. I'm asking you, man."

"Then I don't know," I said. "You can't say the institutions are evil–"

"Can't I?" Satan said. His voice was a big bass drum. He set the cigarette in the ashtray and lifted his arms. He splayed his fingers. The air shimmered momentarily between his hands before he slammed them onto the table.

It sent a cold chill up my spine, but I ignored it. "It's an unfair question. Both do some good."

Satan grunted. "Now listen to this: Anything that has power is corruptible, anything corruptible is evil."

I shook my head. "Yeah, men are corruptible. We all know that. But you're saying because man is corruptible, he is evil. That's a generalization, a very broad-brush stroke."

Satan nodded. Emphasizing each word, he rumbled, "*Yes... Man... can... be... very... evil.*" His voice was a storm and his breath fire, but this didn't scare me.

I mocked his emphasis on the words: "But... most... men... aren't."

He laughed. "Most men are apathetic fools. Most men are lambs being led to slaughter." He paused for a second, and then, with a quick rush of words, added, "They let themselves be brainwashed by the soulless, in both politics and religion." There was frustration straining his voice and perhaps his old heart, too. "Can't you see that? Can't anyone see it? Is blindness running rampant about the world? Or is it just me? I say, man is powerless. Man corrupts easily. Too goddamned easily."

"That doesn't mean everything corruptible is evil," I countered. "Only the weak corrode to evil."

Satan slammed his palm on the table again. "Men are weak. I know."

And goddamnit, he did know. His eyes spoke of thousands of years he'd tempted the world with fruitfulness. His eyes told of the suffering he'd seen, the pain he had given. His eyes showed his pathetic sadness, his own suffering and pain. Was this sympathy for the devil? Was he wanting my compassion, my understanding? I couldn't admit it. He wasn't the devil. He couldn't be. A cold chill frosted my skin. I'd fallen into his eyes and couldn't get out. I couldn't turn away. I kept falling.

It seemed hours later I woke from the trance.

He was smoking another cigarette, or maybe it was the same one. I didn't know. The drinks had come and Astral had left without me telling her a joke, or maybe I did and just couldn't remember. Again, I just didn't know.

"How are you feeling, man?" Satan asked.

"Sleepy," I answered.

He nodded and slid the finished cigarette into an empty beer bottle.

I looked into his eyes, unafraid. "Why do they call you Satan?"

"It's just one of my many names." He raised his drink. "To the fools, the priests, the monks, the imams, the congressmen, parliamentarians, presidents, prime ministers, kings, and queens. May they find good souls to rule the earth better than I, better than their gods." He nodded. "That's right, my friend. This is my final drink, my last toast, and I'll be on my way to other places. Away from this *godforsaken world*."

Later, I would wonder whether all the gods had forsaken our world, but for the moment I was dumfounded. I grunted and asked, "Listen. Are you...are you the devil?"

He shook his head. "It's just a name."

I frowned. "I don't understand."

"You're not meant to." He looked away, a starry-eyed gaze,

then reached for the pack of cigarettes, lit one. "No one is. The fools pray to gods that left millions of years ago, the fools hold faith in these gods. The creators." He smiled and shook his head. "I tried through the prophets to teach, but fools misinterpret words. What's that— 'God helps those who help themselves?'"

"Yeah," I said.

"Yeah, man, well that's what I wanted to tell them, what I wanted them to understand, but they turn around and say, 'God will provide for those who have faith,' and they think of faith in God, not themselves. No one can understand. You'd think a world with a thousand and one religions would realize religion is not the answer. If only one religion is the true religion, are the other thousand doomed? What stupidity."

I rubbed my eyes. "Are you the prince of darkness, of evil?"

"I'm Satan. I'm not evil, I'm not a prince. Fairy tales, it's all a fairy tale."

I must have moved away, maybe I even stood up, because he said, "No, don't leave. Stay. I want someone to understand."

"Why? What do you care if no one understands?"

"I don't know." He shook his head. "Guilt, maybe. I'm leaving you defenseless against a species of being hell bent on destroying itself. A species incapable of the simplest of lives. Without me to referee, it's inevitable. Without someone to guide and instruct, this race will destroy itself. It's a sorry place to be, man. It's gotten out of hand." He bowed his head, looking into his drink. "I'm tired. It's time for me to leave this world. I just wanted one more drink, one more smoke, before I left."

I closed my eyes. "Why . . . why are you telling me?"

"So, someone will know."

"But why me?" I closed my eyes tight. The darkness felt safe.

He grunted, maybe it was laughter. "So, you can tell the rest of the world, I guess."

"I don't understand."

"No," Satan said. "I didn't think you would." There was

silence.

I finally opened my eyes. He wasn't there. He had disappeared. He'd left his cigarettes and the smoke. He'd taken his drink and conversation with him. I looked around the bar. I was alone except for the waitress, Astral, who was cleaning glasses behind the bar. The jukebox played a quick-paced, modern tune about the world's decay–*it's the end of the world as we know it*–and I figured Satan had planned it that way. I tapped my fingers to the song's beat and watched Astral clean. She noticed me staring and smiled.

She moved out from behind the bar and walked to my booth. She sat down across from me. "So, tell me something funny."

I smiled and gave it my best shot. "The devil smokes unfiltered cigarettes."

It felt as though I had been chosen as a prophet, and *that* was funny. I was really scared for the world. I looked at the beer bottles lining the table. It took a few seconds to remember why I had been drinking. I considered it and realized it no longer mattered.

GOOD NEIGHBORS

◆ ◆ ◆

S tan stood in the street looking at Zelda Prince's house at
the end of the cul-de-sac. His chest hurt, as if a clawed
hand had hold of his heart and waited for the right moment to crush the life out of it. The anticipation was a bitter
pill really, and he had to swallow it to do what he had promised. He had to man up. Do what a good neighbor would.

But he didn't want to. Lord, no.

A trickle of sweat ran down his spine in the August heat,
and he couldn't bring himself to take another step. He thought
of a thousand excuses to delay, but he had the key. *I can stick
my head in, yell for her, and if she doesn't answer, come right back
home*, he thought. But he wouldn't.

No, that's not right. He couldn't. He couldn't live in his own
skin if he didn't search all the house for her. Turn it upside
down. Top to bottom. Either find her or a clue about where she
had gone.

His conscience would consume him if he merely looked
in and called out her name. He wanted the relief of searching
every room and *not* finding her. He craved the release of dis-
quiet that had grown in him. He needed it.

He believed he'd find Zelda's mummified body in the recliner chair with a well-aged scotch on the coffee table. Or
maybe he'd find her in the garage asphyxiated from the ex-
haust of her vintage Pontiac.

He hoped not. He didn't want to be known as the one who

could have saved her from a fate of dying alone.

Stan hadn't seen Zelda since back in the middle of winter when he no longer noticed her dark eyes peering from the side of the living room curtain. He didn't knock on her door to see if all was well. He didn't call her. It didn't cross his mind he needed to, not until it started warming up in April. By then, he was too embarrassed to request a welfare check from the local police. He feared being asked, *why didn't you call sooner, sir? You could have saved her, you know? What were you thinking?* So, he'd gone about his life, blinders on, but discomforted. He thought it would work itself out. He had watched the yard guy mow Zelda's lawn three times in April. On the first Saturday of May, the yard guy pulled his truck to the curb and marched to her door. He knocked with the flat of his hand three times. Stan stood from spreading mulch around his mailbox and uttered a small prayer for Zelda to open the door. She didn't, and the yard guy left without mowing.

On an early June evening, one of the Murphy boys saw lights in Zelda's upstairs window while he was in the front yard catching lightning bugs. It was Mark, the nine-year-old, and his Mason jar lit up like the moon as he ran into the house screaming for his mom and dad, that something was happening at Crazy Zelda's house. *There were lights!* Even the kids had picked up on the small talk of the adults. They knew Zelda had gone. But when Fred and his wife, Ethel, ran into their front yard, the house at the end of the cul-de-sac was dark, and Fred told his son he'd just imagined it. Mark said he didn't, and then showed them the Mason jar of lightning bugs, which they made a fuss over as if Mark had discovered the light bulb itself, telling him he could use the jar to read by tonight. They didn't tell him the lightning bugs would be dead by morning. They went back inside, and Zelda was forgotten.

Stan had witnessed all of this from his porch, except he hadn't been looking when Mark saw the lights. By the time Mark yelled and Stan turned, there were no lights on in Zelda's house.

The city mowed Zelda's lawn before the long July 4th weekend. As each day passed, Stan's apprehension grew. Every night, when he pulled into his driveway in the evening, he looked at the red brick house, sweating guilt like bullets. Why hadn't he done something sooner?

Stan breathed in, breathed out, gathering himself, but he was not of a mindset to move forward, yet.

He figured she'd drank herself to death. He smiled when he decided she hadn't been mummified after all, but instead was pickled by the scotch she drank like lemonade. Oscar Prince tolerated his wife's drinking, Stan knew, but Oscar didn't drink, except the occasional Budweiser. Stan and Oscar hadn't exactly been friends, but had been friendly. Oscar would borrow gasoline to finish mowing the lawn, and always returned Stan's gas can filled up. In return, when there was an electrical or plumbing issue in the house, Stan asked Oscar to look at it.

Before he retired, Oscar was the maintenance supervisor at the high school where Stan taught chemistry. He kept the school's thirty-year old boiler room running with efficiency improvements only Oscar understood. The year he retired, the furnace retired as well. Oscar was seventy-two and looked like he should have retired a decade before. Stan came with the district superintendent to ask for Oscar's help on the furnace, and Oscar listened to the superintendent's plea, but he said his hands hurt and he didn't feel like getting them dirty. *You understand, don't you?* Oscar had asked. He wasn't looking at the superintendent when he asked it. Stan nodded. He wasn't going to intervene on behalf of the school and make Oscar feel obligated. Stan remembered Zelda stood behind her husband with a glass of what was probably scotch. As the door shut, Zelda said, *You should have taken it on, foolish old man. You could have charged an arm and a—*the door shut, and Stan didn't hear the rest, but he knew.

He'd been thinking of Oscar weeks ago, and he wondered

how long it had been since Oscar's son, Jack, visited his step-mom. Had he been there since Oscar's funeral? Maybe he was too busy, being a Philadelphia lawyer.

One evening, on a whim, Stan googled *Jack Prince attorney* and found his commercials on YouTube. He watched them and laughed so hard his wife, Betty, asked what was so hilarious. Stan replayed the commercial where Jack stood on the steps of a courthouse and a voiceover said *No problems are too big for Jack Prince.* A computer-generated tyrannosaurus rex approached the steps, and Jack calmly looked on. When it appeared the t-rex was going to make him an early lunch, Jack held up his arms and a laser shot out of his hands. The t-rex shrank to velociraptor size, turned, and ran away. *Helping accident victims for twenty-two years. Call the man, Jack the Prince. If you've been hurt, he can help.* Betty sighed and commented the dinosaur was still large enough to do a *Jurassic Park* on him. Stan figured the commercial played on Philadelphia television stations so much every injured person thought of Jack when they were hurt. A good marketing ploy, even though it was ridiculous.

Stan had written the singsong number down, and that night called but he got an answering service promising a call right back. When no one called, he dialed the number again, and was given Jack's office number. He called the new number and was told Mr. Prince wasn't expected in until October, when he returned from Vermont. The receptionist promised to give Jack the message. Five days passed and Jack hadn't called. Stan dialed the number, and this time told the assistant he *thought Jack's stepmother was dead and he had to talk to Jack about it.* He didn't want to be blunt, but needed to get Jack's attention. It worked. Jack called back within a half-hour and listened to Stan's concerns. Jack didn't jump on the next plane as Stan hoped. It's what family would do. It's what Stan would have done. But Jack did promise to overnight a key and authorized Stan to go into the house. Stan was bewildered at this. Jack wanted *Stan* to go into the house to see if his stepmother had died, and Stan didn't know what to say. In the end, he promised to check on her. He doubted the key would be sent.

But it arrived by FedEx just a half-hour earlier.

When he called for Fred, Ethel said he was at Marsha's middle school basketball practice. He considered asking her to go with him inside the home, but he didn't want Ethel's incessant chatter. It was difficult enough to get off the phone with her.

He could have waited for Fred, but it would be dark, and he didn't want to be inside the house when the sun went down. So, he had walked to the middle of the street and was immediately entangled in his reconsiderations.

Maybe she'd gone to Florida for the winter and met a man. Stan imagined not finding her in the house and then walking out the front door to see Zelda and a man, a *younger* man, pulling into the driveway. How could he explain being in the house? He'd say Jack had been worried about her and asked Stan to check on her, making sure she was okay. He even sent a key. Still, Stan kind of hoped she would drive up, despite him being made a fool. He could accept that, but if her corpse was in the house, dead for months, he wasn't sure he would ever get over it. The guilt would haunt him in the lonely hours of the night and lie close when he woke in the morning, all to remind him he'd failed to take care of a neighbor

By now, his feeling of guilt overpowered his dread, and his feet shuffled forward. Heaviness filled his heart. When he reached Zelda's mailbox, Stan opened it and pulled out the mail stuffed inside. It was mostly junk mail, but he saw a few letters had *late notice* written on the outside. He stopped looking at the mail, deciding it was none of his business, and tucked it under his left arm. He walked up the driveway and paused at the garage door. Zelda's Pontiac had been entombed in the garage for six months now, unmoving, the battery probably dead. Or had she driven away in the middle of the night?

He moved onto the sidewalk, every step heavier than the

last, but finally he made it to the porch. His head thudded. *Don't do this*, it seemed to be telling him. Stan ignored it and climbed the three steps. He stood on the porch, key in hand, ready to unlock the door. He turned and faced the cul-de-sac to see if anyone was watching him. He was satisfied everyone was in their air-conditioned houses, making supper or getting laid or whatever people did at seven-thirty in the evening in August. He wondered if maybe he should have left a note for Betty, and he considered going home to write a quick one. Just a short *Hey, I'm going down to Zelda's to see if she breathed in Pontiac fumes or maybe slipped and fell in her tub and broke a hip. Be back in a few. Love, Stan.* But if he left the steps now, he'd never return. It was time to get this foolishness over with. Be done with it. *Take care of thy neighbor.*

Stan opened the screen door and reached the key toward the knob. His cell phone rang. It scared him, and he almost dropped the mail. He felt salvation when he pulled his hand away, like his life had been spared. He reached into his pocket and looked at the phone. It was Fred. Stan tapped the answer button and said *hello.* Ethel had told Fred that Stan had called, and Fred wanted to know what he needed. "Ah, nothing really," Stan mumbled. "It's just I got a key from Zelda's stepson this afternoon, and well, I wanted to know if you'd like to see what it's all about." But *no*, the basketball practice would last another hour. If Stan could wait, Fred would be glad to go on this little adventure. And then he said, *it's what neighbors are for, ain't that right?* Stan shrugged, as if Fred could see him, and then he replied he wanted to go in before dark. He'd call Fred later and let him know what he found, if anything.

When he ended the call, he noticed his hands were shaking, and he didn't know *why*. What made him so scared? A dead body couldn't hurt him. What else did he expect to find in the house?

Stan calmed himself, enough that he could reach his hand out and put the key to the keyhole of the deadbolt, but it wouldn't go in. Had Zelda changed the lock after Oscar's death?

Why would she? He flipped the key over, and this time it slid in as if oiled. He turned the key. The cylinder rolled over. He did the same to the doorknob. It clicked. He pulled the key out and put it in his pocket before reaching for the knob. It was cold to his touch, almost frozen. He jerked his hand back, holding in a scream. He wondered if he'd imagined it. Maybe *something* was warning him away from the house. Some questions aren't meant to be answered, he knew, and sometimes you have to leave well enough alone. Stan rolled his eyes for having even the slightest trace of fear. *Death* was a transformation, from life to nothingness, and anything dead couldn't harm him. There was nothing to be scared of. Nothing at all.

Now, convinced, he reached for the knob again. It was a normal temperature. It had been his imagination. He turned it, and the door creaked open, breaking the silence in the home. Stan stepped inside.

He didn't smell rot, only stale air. It was hot, above eighty in the house. For a second, Stan thought Zelda's air conditioner had failed, but of course, it had never been turned on. When she'd last been seen, the temperature had been below freezing. It had been a cold winter.

He figured most stages of decomposition would have happened earlier in this heat, and gases would have mostly dissipated. Still, there should be a scent of death underlying the staleness of the air. There was nothing. Stan decided Zelda wasn't dead. Not here, anyway.

He laid the mail on the foyer table, and yelled, "*Zelda! Zelda are you here?*" Hearing the echo of his voice alarmed him. He shivered and said *fuck* under his breath. It was his word to say when annoyed, and he had annoyed himself. He thought maybe he'd overreacted. Zelda had gone to Florida with a friend, one of the snowbirds, and had just decided to not come home for the summer. It was simple enough. He'd lived two doors down from Zelda for two and a half decades now, and he couldn't say he knew anything about her. Outside of her being married to Oscar, he only knew she drank too much scotch. She could have friends who went to Florida if she wanted them.

Since Oscar's death, Zelda stayed mostly indoors in the cold months, but in the spring and summer, she walked about her yard every evening, scotch in hand, leaning down to pull weeds from the flower gardens and around the shrubs. In the fall, she stood on her porch and watched the lawn guy rake her leaves. She *liked* a pristine yard, not a blade of grass out of place. Stan knew that. And he knew she was territorial. He'd seen her storm out of the house when Marsha Murphy, only eleven at the time, had kicked a soccer ball into her front yard. Zelda moved with a grace most people her age lacked, reaching the ball before Marsha. She tossed the ball up a few times and said something to Marsha before hurling the ball over Marsha's head. Stan couldn't hear what was said, but he saw the expression of horror on Marsha's face when she turned, tears streaming down her cheeks.

Still in the foyer, Stan thought he could leave and call Jack Prince and tell him his stepmother wasn't home, but what if he was wrong? What if three months passed, and the house was fully searched, and she was found? How could he explain why he hadn't found her? No, he couldn't leave. He had to walk the house and make absolutely sure she wasn't here.

Oscar had twice invited Stan in for a beer. Both times Stan had entered and left the kitchen through the garage. So, he'd been in the house, but only that one room, and now he stood in the foyer thinking about the path to take in this unfamiliar house. To his left was a formal living room, and to his right a dining room that probably connected to the kitchen. He wanted to flip a coin and let it be random, but he chose the living room. The evening sun beamed into the room from the west, and it looked inviting.

His steps echoed on the hardwood floors as he moved through the foyer into the living room. There was a thin layer of undisturbed dust on the coffee table, but otherwise the room looked tidy. The gold pillows were placed against the green cloth of the couch and two chairs, as if Zelda expected company any moment now. There was a candy bowl filled with M&M's on an end table in front of a tiffany lamp. Stan guessed the chocolate inside the candy coating had probably melted in the stifling heat, but when he bent to pick one up, the candy coating crumbled between his thumb and forefinger. There was no chocolate inside. Was it a joke? He couldn't decide whether the bigger question was why the chocolate had been removed or how it had been removed. He checked three more, and all three fell apart in his fingers. It had to do with the heat in the house, he thought. Still, he was unnerved.

He moved away from the candy toward a doorway at the rear of the room and through it into the den. There was nothing here that would indicate Zelda hadn't vacated the premises. He was surprised at how neat Zelda kept the house at her age. The furniture was positioned around a fireplace and a small, older television, not a flat screen.

Stan saw a bookshelf in the corner and moved to it. He saw hardbacks of Robert Heinlein, Isaac Asimov, and J.R.R. Tolkien. It must have been Oscar who was the sci-fi and fantasy fan, and not Zelda. Had Stan known, he would have had one more thing to talk about with Oscar. There were hundreds of romance novels, with a section dedicated to Danielle Steel. These were Zelda's, of course. Had to be, or was he stereotyping? He just couldn't see Oscar reading romance. There was a scattering of early Stephen King and John Irving novels, which could have been either Oscar's or Zelda's. Stan saw 'Salem's Lot and felt an urge to pick it up, but he resisted. He'd read it thirty-five years ago, in college, and it had terrified him.

He had to pull himself away from the bookshelf. A bookshelf tells much about its owner, and this shelf interested Stan because it was so much like his own. His wife read romance, and he read everything else. Stan always had a book with him and consumed them like potato chips.

He moved out of the den into a mudroom. Shoes were lined up on a shelf and coats were on hooks on the wall adjacent to the back door. There was a bathroom, on one side of the mudroom. Stan turned on the light long enough to assure him there was nothing out of place.

He passed out of the mudroom into the kitchen, and trickles of sweat poured down his forehead and neck. The house was steaming hot, near ninety degrees and humid. Almost unbearable. *Before I leave, I'll switch the thermostat to air conditioning*, Stan thought

Again, except for the dust, the kitchen looked like Zelda was expecting guests. Stan heard the hum of the refrigerator, and he considered opening it, but felt odd looking inside. If Zelda hadn't been here for six months, the food would be gross and inedible, but the milk would have a *sale by date*. He could use that to determine when Zelda had left the house. But not yet. He'd look before he left if he didn't find her. Stan glanced in the sink, and found no dirty dishes, only a few dead flying bugs. Had Zelda died in the house, dead flies would be on every flat surface. Flies feast on death. The process of eggs to maggots to flies would continue until the dead body had been fully consumed, and the life cycle of the fly would end all over the house. There'd still be flies buzzing around.

Stan opened the garage door and turned on the light. Zelda's Pontiac was in its space, and nothing was amiss. Had a cab come to pick her up to take her to the airport? Or did a friend take her wherever she'd gone?

Stan went into the dining room and all was as it should be. Zelda was ready for a dinner party, not that Zelda ever had dinner parties. He looked out the large picture window and could see the cul-de-sac. He saw his wife's silver Honda Accord in the driveway now.

Stan noticed the sun was setting, a bright orange to purple sky. Had he been in the house that long? He had spent a few minutes looking at the bookshelf, or maybe it had been longer. He wanted to be out before dark, so he had to hurry.

He went back to the foyer, up the steps to the second floor. Once he was in the upstairs hallway, he knew he would find nothing. There were three bedrooms, and each had made beds and were clean except for dust. Stan heard a noise coming from the master bath and found the toilet running. He jiggled the handle, and it stopped. Her water bill must have been atrocious. He figured the utilities were being auto drafted from her account.

Zelda wasn't here.

As he walked back down the stairs, he remembered the basement. Oscar had once said he and Zelda used the basement for the storage of a lifetime of junk and lamented putting any of it downstairs, but he said Zelda couldn't let it go. He joked that when he and Zelda passed, Jack could have it all and deal with it. He never said it, but Stan believed Oscar didn't like his son much. Stan thought it may have been due to the way his marriage to Jack's mother ended and the way his marriage to Zelda began. Stan never asked. It was private and none of his business.

At the bottom of the stairs, in the foyer, Stan remembered the funeral, Zelda in the front row by herself crying as the minister spouted about *Oscar giving himself to the Lord Almighty only moments before taking his final breath*. The doors opened and Jack walked in and seated himself next to Zelda. He'd given her a tissue but hadn't cried himself. Not one tear. He'd been late to his father's funeral and showed no emotion.

Stan found what he thought was the basement door in the kitchen, and he stood before it, but he couldn't open it. He tried to move his hand to the doorknob, but his arm refused to work. He turned and moved away. Just go home, he thought. She's not down there. She's gone. Just as he couldn't bring himself to open the basement door, he couldn't go home either.

Stan saw the refrigerator hulking against the wall, almost as if it wanted to be overlooked. It was the only part of the house that would be cool. He realized he had to know what was inside. Were there leftovers? Curdled milk? Rotting pork chops? His curiosity got beneath his skin. He moved to the refrigerator, and in a swift motion, he reached to the handle and pulled the door open. He stared dismayed at the contents, surprised in a way he never would have dreamed. It was inexplicable. The jug of milk was on the top shelf, but there was no milk. The half-gallon of orange juice was empty as well. He saw a grape jelly jar, but there was no jelly. There were empty Diet Coke cans arranged in neat rows. He reached in and lifted the egg carton, and knew from the heft of it, there were no eggs inside. The packaging for the four sticks of butter were neatly folded and placed in the box. The ketchup bottle was clean inside, as if it had been washed out with soap and water. Stan saw the plastic wrapping, but no chicken breasts. There was method in the placement of the empty containers, all of it systematically returned to the refrigerator, but Stan, for the life of him, couldn't figure out why. What reason could Zelda have to put trash into the cool of the fridge, or was it even Zelda who had done it? Had someone broken in to play a cruel and perhaps unusual joke?

Stan shut the refrigerator door and wondered if he'd find similar order in the pantry, but he didn't have the resolve to look. He glanced at the basement door and moved toward it. He just wanted to have this over with before his body refused to work. He reached for the knob, turned it, and flung the door open. As soon as it swung wide, the hair on his arms stood on end. Stan wondered what he'd find when he turned on the light. Had she fallen down the steps and broken an ankle or knee? Would he see her cold, lifeless eyes staring up at him? He felt around for the light switch. He found it and hesitated. No one would know he didn't go down the stairs, but he would blame himself. This he knew. It just wouldn't be right. He'd come this far. He had to finish it. Get it over with. Right now. He sighed and flicked on the light. She wasn't at the bottom. *Thank God!* Relieved, he took a deep breath.

He didn't let himself stop there. He decided it was like getting into a cold pool. It was better to dive in and get over the chill of the water than easing in with the cold water creeping up his chest. On the fourth step of the dim basement, he paused. So much for diving in. He could feel the cool of the basement, it made goose bumps rise on his arms and nape of his neck. Was it the cool of the basement or his rising terror? He reminded himself to keep moving so his fear would acclimate quicker. He continued his descent, counting all twelve steps. At the bottom, he saw the basement was lit up except for one corner that had been blocked off by two walls and a closed door. He faintly remembered Oscar carrying two by fours into the house, but never asked what he was constructing. Could it have been this corner room?

The sweat that stained his t-shirt felt like ice against his back and chest in the cool of the basement. He wrapped his arms around himself.

From Oscar's tales, Stan thought Zelda had been a hoarder, with all their junk scattered about in the basement. What he saw was nothing like that. The furniture was together in a corner, old couches and chairs, mattresses and box springs, and tables, like a store showroom. One wall was lined with boxes, each meticulously marked with its contents.

Stan didn't read what was in the boxes. He was curious, but he wanted to get this done and over with, so he moved toward the corner room.

Zelda wasn't in the basement as far as he could tell, unless she was in the corner room. Did he have to check inside? The room appeared to be big, maybe twenty by twenty-five feet. If the basement was for storage, *why* had the room been built? Maybe this is where the secrets were kept. The dark secrets. Stan shuddered. How much could one person know about his neighbors or how much should they know? That he was in Zelda's home uninvited made Stan uncomfortable, like he was prying. He didn't need to know what was in her fridge, on her bookshelf, or in her basement, and yet, he was here to help. But was that true? Helping would have been knocking on the door a few weeks after not seeing her. That's what a good neighbor would have done. Why hadn't he done that?

He didn't want to admit it, but he didn't like Zelda. She was mean, and a little off. There was something else about her, a look in her eye, like she knew more than you, even though she was usually drunk on scotch. She never waved as she drove by in her Pontiac. When Oscar had gotten sick, she hadn't taken care of him. Stan had visited him in the hospital just before he died, and Oscar just wanted to know where Zelda was. Stan told him *home*, but he hadn't offered to drive her to visit Oscar. He knew she wouldn't have gone. It was almost cruel, but did all of this justify letting six months pass before checking on her?

Stan hesitated to let the guilt pass. While he stood there, he wondered if the room could be a sex room, with whips, chains, handcuffs, and other devices Stan didn't want to think about. This was ridiculous. But the thought was enough to wring out the guilt and get him moving again. He figured it was probably a wine cellar, or a liquor room, something to do with Zelda's alcoholism. Had she been in this room consuming scotch for the last six months, except for quick trips up the stairs for feasts on ketchup, butter, and milk, and the chocolate of the M&M's? The fact he was considering this as a serious possibility made Stan want to laugh in hysterics, but he stifled it. Now was not the time to lose it.

Stan was overwhelmed with a sense Zelda was in the room as he continued toward it. The panic rose in his throat. He wanted to run, get out of the house, go home, and forget. Let it fucking go and never return. He should burn the house down to the fucking ground. As crazy as it sounded, Stan thought that's exactly what a good neighbor would do.

And yet, he would do none of those things. He had to check. He was the good neighbor after all, and he owed Oscar at least one favor. He wouldn't let Oscar down, let his wife be alone down here anymore.

He reached the door, discovering a deadbolt. Stan hoped it would be locked. When his fingers drew close, the knob turned. He pulled away. The latch cleared the strike plate. His stomach hurt, like he'd swallowed marbles. He wanted to move away from the door before it opened. But it was as if his shoes were nailed to the floor. He hadn't the strength to move.

The door eased open. It was black inside. The dead didn't need light, Stan thought. He wondered what the dead did need.

A skeletal hand reached toward him, the skin hanging loose on the bone. It grasped his forearm. He did nothing to stop it. He was sickened by the touch of her flesh. He wanted to scream, but nothing would come out. Stan figured Zelda had spent six months wasting away. Yet, she still lived. And she was strong. He wanted to draw away, but he held fast, like a post driven into the ground. "Zelda?" he asked.

The hand gently pulled Stan into the darkness. He didn't resist it. How could he? His first step took him to the threshold. The second into the room. The door shut. He was in darkness. Stan turned and saw no light seeping around the edges or bottom of the door. The blackness was vast, impenetrable. He'd walked into a different reality.

"I knew you'd come. Such a good man," she said. Stan recognized it as Zelda's voice. It came out as a croak, as if she used the last vestiges of breath remaining in her lungs. Lungs that hadn't worked in months.

Stan stuttered as he sought the words for what he most wanted to know, and finally, his words formed a sentence. "What are you?" He regretted asking as soon the words passed his lips.

"I am the eater, and you are the food."

He didn't know whether it was the words or the realization he wasn't getting out of this alive, but his stupor was broken He didn't want to be the food, as she had said it. He ripped his arm from Zelda's hand and turned toward what he thought was the door. It wasn't there. He found only drywall. He moved to his left, slamming his fist against the wall. When he reached the corner, he realized he'd gone the wrong way. He turned and moved back the way he'd come, still pounding on the wall. He heard Zelda's dry laugh. He moved toward her. His freedom was that way, too. He figured he'd bully his way through her. He was twice her weight before she'd—what? Died? Wasted away? She couldn't weigh anything. She was only skin and bones. He moved fast, not quite a run, but with his shoulder lowered, ready to knock Zelda to the floor. The laughter was louder now, and he passed by it. She was behind him. He thought he'd made it.

He felt the door frame and moved his hand down toward where the knob should be. Before he could grab it, her fingers landed on his shoulder and dug in. "Love, don't go," she croaked. "Zelda needs you."

Stan made one attempt to pull away from her grasp. As soon as he moved, she yanked him away from the door with the strength of a thousand men. She held him upright and moaned in his ear. A greedy moan. Hungry. There was no movement for a second, and then she struck his back like a sledgehammer. He screamed from the pain and terror. No matter how hard he pulled to get away, she held him still with her hand. He finally submitted to her.

He felt her other hand wind around his side to his belly, and then lower to his crotch, where it paused long enough to make Stan absurdly think she was checking out his package. It was just their first date. He shivered. Then her hand continued, between his legs and around. She took hold of his ass and lifted Stan up. In one swift motion, she slammed him to the ground. He landed on his back. The air rushed out of his lungs. He gasped for a breath, but he didn't try to get up. What use would it be?

Stan wanted to know only one thing. He tried to ask, but all that came in a wheeze was, *"How?"*

Zelda pressed a bony foot against Stan's chest as he tried to take air into his lungs. "I've always been this, sweet," she finally said. That's what he wanted to know.

She fell on top of him, her mouth impossibly large against his head. He felt nothing as she consumed him. What was her became him, and what was him was hers to control. Zelda's body was gone, nothing remained, not a fingernail or even a strand of hair. Nothing. There was only Stan, but a much different Stan.

She had called herself *the eater*. That wasn't exactly right. She had consumed Stan and took everything of his. He was still Zelda, and all the thousands before. She had existed since time began. She wasn't evil. She just wasn't human.

A half-hour later Stan emerged from Oscar and Zelda Prince's house into the dark of night. He turned and locked the door behind him. He whistled as he walked toward home. He was in a great mood. He hadn't felt this good in months.

Before he reached his house, the headlights of Fred's Camry caught him as it turned onto the cul-de-sac. Stan moved to the side, and Fred pulled next to him and stopped. The passenger window rolled down.

"Howdy neighbor," Fred said. "I guess Zelda wasn't there?"

Stan leaned down and peered into the car. He nodded to Marsha in the backseat before turning to Fred. "Her car's in the garage, but there's no sign of Zelda. I found a snake in the basement. The bastard scared the shit out of me. I put it outside."

Fred laughed. "Oh Jesus. I hope you weren't bitten."

Stan smiled at his neighbor. "It wasn't poisonous."

Not much anyway, he thought.

Stan went into the house, where Betty was making meatloaf and mashed potatoes. She wanted to chat. He stepped into the dining room, opened the liquor cabinet, and poured himself a scotch. He went to the refrigerator, bent down to the freezer, and grabbed two pieces of ice. How long had it been since he'd had a good drink? The liquor soothed him as Betty talked. Ruth McMillan had been at the grocery and told her the good news. She was *pregnant*, blah, blah, blah. Who the fuck cared? Stan thought. He couldn't listen to this incessant, monotonous rant about people he didn't care about. Stan wondered if he'd have to poison Betty like he'd done Oscar before, when he'd been Zelda. Once he retired, Oscar was home too much, and wouldn't get a hobby. Still, he was a saint compared to this woman and her goddamned blathering. He poured himself another scotch.

IN DEATH'S EYES
WEARINESS WEEPS

◆ ◆ ◆

Part I: *Death is Weary*

He claims he's tired; weary, to be exact.

Slumped in an armchair, Death puffs on a cigarette and blows smoke rings into a dusky lamp. His long, bony fingers tap the padded arms of the chair, and he looks around the room, his eyes hidden behind wire-rimmed, mirrored sunglasses. His face expressionless. "I'm so sick of this, and I want to stop, but I can't," he says. His voice is sandpapery, almost a whisper in its harshness, but his words carry with such clarity I do not have to strain to hear. "Don't pass judgment on me. You think I'm a killer, right? You're a little scared of me? There's no reason to be. I'm not what the world thinks."

He is pale, sickly, impossibly thin, but despite the rumors to the contrary, he has flesh. His black hood has been pulled back, his whole head visible for the first time in years. I can see his dark mane of hair and the creases on his flesh. I cannot see his eyes behind the sunglasses. I don't want to see them. He's right, I am terrified. Who's not scared of Death?

"You're wondering why I chose you, right?"

I think I know, but I nod. I can't bring myself to speak. He seems to understand this and is willing to ask and answer his own questions until I swallow my fear. I am prepared, with pages and pages of notes. I know his life from the moment of his birth to when he walked through the door of the hotel here in Las Vegas. Who hadn't heard it all? We have watched his life pass during the last seven years, measuring our own lives by his. We've come to be affixed to what became his twenty-four-hour news channel and watched him become a reluctant reality star. Our lives changed because of him. Mine changed more than most because I was assigned to follow in Death's wake to write an ongoing investigative report for *The Times*. My stories are mostly background noise to the twenty-four hours news cycle on cable.

"You wrote an article six months ago," Death says. "You made a list of ten potential victims, and one of them told me he knew I was coming because of it. He had it on his desk and showed it to me."

The article had been my editor's bad idea, and I resisted, but finally agreed, spending weeks researching and writing. When the article was published, I was condemned and censured by cable news and the bloggers as being sensationalistic and particularly morbid. It had almost died down when a person on the list became a victim, and the hysteria recommenced. When a second person on the list died by Death's knife, the news world made it seem as if Death used my list to determine his kills. My editor let other writers for *The Times* lambaste me when it was his idea. I almost quit, but my wife reminded me it would only be worse someplace else.

The irony was the talking heads who severely criticized me on cable spent weeks adding and subtracting to my list. I started getting offers to appear on cable shows. My editor urged me to go on, anything to sell the paper. My wife said she would file for divorce if I did.

"Your article could have been embellished," Death says, "but it was just the facts. I read it as I walked. I knew you got it. There are other writers who would have listed certain people to sell their newspapers. They would have included a few politicians and judges. Maybe an actor or two. Your list used criteria you developed from having studied my history. It was smart."

I want to say thank you, but I cannot bring myself to thank him for liking something that caused me tremendous grief.

Death's lips curl into sneer. "Most of what is written about me is so full of shit I want to scream to the world. I know much of it is people that knew me a little bit, before I transitioned, telling their stories and cashing in. Writers like you spend your time discrediting these stories, but once it's out there, the damage is done. It's not that you're my biggest fan. You're not a fan at all. That is obvious from the article, but you don't like my victims, either." He pauses, grunts. "It's a crazy, fucked up world that I have fans, isn't it? I mean, it's sickening."

The world fears and hides from Death, and yet he has a cult who follows him, embracing the death he brings. It was through them the request to meet was proffered. I assume Death's fans arranged this hotel suite and are the ones who concealed me coming into the hotel. Not even my wife or editor know of this meeting. The world only knows Death is in the hotel, but not what he is here for or who he is here for. I watched him enter the hotel on the Death Network twenty-five minutes ago from ten different camera angles with the commentary turned down. Those same cameras are probably waiting in the street below right now, while the talking heads are wondering what the hell Death is doing in this room. Inquiries are being made at the hotel front desk, but they'll get only false names.

"Are you going to sell the video tape to the media?" He nods to the video camera on a tripod to my left.

It's a blunt question, and one I have an answer. It's something I have spent the last week thinking about. "No."

"You could make millions. No reason for you not to cash in."

I shrug. "I don't need the money."

Death smiles. He actually smiles. He probably knows I'm lying. The money would be useful. "So, you'll give it to the media when your book comes out to boost sales?"

"There will be a book," I admit, "but the video won't be released while I'm living. Maybe I'll leave it to a charity."

Death sighed. "What? You don't want to make money off Death?"

"I make money off you all the time," I reply. "Every paycheck I get has some of the blood you shed on it."

"Fine. Leave it to a charity, but maybe the money will be hard to turn down later. Or the government will discover the video and take it from you. If you give it up, it's okay. You're safe from me." He means he won't take my life. I can't believe him. I intend to take necessary precautions to protect the tape once it's authenticated.

"That question, why me, was my second question," I say.

Death smiles again, and it is rather charming, not what you see daily on the television. "Okay, I'll bite. What was your first question?"

Now, I smile. "Why give the interview?"

He grunts, surprised I asked the question. "You haven't figured it out, yet?"

I lean forward. "You want to tell your story."

"Well, yeah, a myth has formed, and I don't particularly like it. I want you to dispel it. I'll give you the information you need. Are you up for that?"

I lean toward Death and lower my voice, "I'm not here to tell the story you want me to tell."

Death snorts. "What do you know about what I want you to tell?"

"I know—" I hesitate. "I'm not going to sugarcoat it."

Death thrusts both of his arms out and screams: "I HAVE SPENT THE LAST SEVEN YEARS KILLING PEOPLE. WHY THE FUCK DO YOU THINK I WANT YOU TO SUGARCOAT IT? HOW THE FUCK CAN YOU MAKE THAT SOUND LIKE IT'S A GOOD THING?" The doors to the room shake. I feel his voice press against my skin like a big bass drum. Witnesses have described the power he can evoke with his voice, but hearing about it is nothing like experiencing it. I don't piss myself, but it's a close call.

When I am able to focus again, I recognize I must either leave now and move on with my life, or do what I am here to do. I can't leave. I'll never get this opportunity again, and Death has become my life. I can't let go. "Please don't do that again," I ask, quickly adding, "I only meant, I am not going to say death by you is justified—isn't that the word your fans use?—justified, because your victims are—what is it they say?—they're deserving?"

"Wait, wait," Death says. "I've never said their deaths are justified."

"But your contingent claim it. It isn't that your victims are dying which bothers me. It's that they are dying without due process, no trial."

"And that makes me a bad person?"

"It doesn't make you a good person."

Death smiles again. "Okay. If my victims had a trial and were convicted, would death be a just punishment?"

I shrug. "Whether or not I believe in capital punishment is not the issue. It's that you are acting as the judge, jury, and executioner."

"Well, when we finish, you may see me as a victim, too." He laughs bitterly at the truth of this statement. "You say I'm the judge, jury, and executioner," he continues. "That's part of the mythology. I can't fault you for thinking it. You are looking from the outside in, and I want you to be on the inside. I am not evil, and I'm not the end of the world. I'm not a bad omen. Yeah, maybe I'm just a cancer, but I'm the good kind of cancer. I am taking care of the bad kind of cancer. You know it, even if you can't admit it. You write about it."

I look at my distorted reflection in Death's sunglasses, and I see my own sadness there. Death kills, and I spend my time figuring out why because there is always a reason, sometimes obvious, sometimes not. "Okay," I say, "so tell me why you do it. Make me feel sorry for you."

Death shakes his head. "Shit, you're a tough guy."

"Maybe I am," I respond. "I'm scared, so maybe I'm not that tough."

Death takes a moment, looking in my direction. I don't know if he is staring off into space or trying to see into my soul. I can't see his eyes. He stands and walks to the closet safe. He punches in a number, opens the safe, and closes it. When he turns, I see the familiar red wax top of a Maker's Mark bottle, and he's carrying two glasses. He sits, pours an inch in each glass, and shoves one of them toward me. "This is my only sustenance," he says. He lifts the glass back and pours the amber liquid into his mouth. He grimaces at the burn. He nods to my glass. I follow suit, and it does burn, but it's a good burn. A real good burn.

"You live on this?" I ask.

"I don't need anything else," he says. "Well, I started smoking these." He holds up the cigarette. "I wanted to see if I could get lung cancer, but it hasn't worked, yet. I smoke five packs a day. I am not sure I have lungs anymore, or if I have them, I'm not sure I need them. I could get an MRI, I guess, but I don't have health insurance." He waits for me to laugh at his joke. When I don't, he shrugs, as if to say *everybody's a critic*. "The thing is, I don't know what makes me what I am. I don't know what happened to me. I was normal, and then there was a period I was kind of not normal. Finally, I became the monster I am. I don't eat. I don't shit. I don't piss. I don't sweat. I guess this stuff—" He points to the bourbon. "—is pickling me because it doesn't come out."

Now, I do laugh. He smiles, but it is a gloomy smile. Maybe he is lamenting his loss of normality, although it has been years.

"I have no sex drive," he continues. "No desire at all. Just to kill. Sometimes the desire is so all-consuming it takes up everything. Maybe my killing is as close to sex as I am ever going to get. There is a release when I take a life, and it feels good. There are times it's really good. I'm sure you can't understand it. No one can." He stubs out his cigarette and lights another, before leaning back on the couch. He is so forlorn I know he is doubting his reasons for doing the interview. I am afraid he's going to shut down, and I rack my brain for the question to open the floodgate.

"Help me understand," I say.

"Oh, man," he says in his quiet, raspy voice. "How can I do that? You have to walk in my shoes for a day. You have to feel what I feel."

I nod and try to express as much empathy as I can, although I imagine it falls short. "Walk me through a day. I can't walk in your shoes, but I can hear it from you. Tell me what it's like."

He pours us another glass of bourbon, downing his immediately. He pours himself another. I wonder if he feels intoxication from the bourbon.

"Okay, yeah," he says. "I'll tell you about a day early on, maybe six months had passed after the—what do you refer to it in your writing? The change? I like that. It's like I went through menopause. Six months after, or maybe eighteen months. Time has become meaningless to me. I know I've been doing this for seven years because that's what I've been told. Otherwise, a minute seems like a year, and a year seems like a minute. I only know on that day it was cold. I was in New York City, and there was eight inches of snow. The snow always slows me down, but it doesn't really bother me. I just trudge on."

Death leans back, takes a long drag on his cigarette, too long. The tip of the cigarette glows like the sun, and he blows out the smoke. A blue haze lingers between us. He puts the cigarette into the ashtray, pulls another out of the pack, and lights it with a wooden match.

"I trudge." He stops to laugh. It's a harsh, almost uncomfortable noise. "Trudge. That's just a funny word, but it's what

I do. I trudge. I plod. Nothing stops me. Not sleet, not rain, not snow, not wind, not six fucking Kentucky state troopers putting their useless bullets in me. I just keep on keepin' on. And the question is, why do I keep going?" He looks at me as if he expects an answer, but I stare at him. He finally continues. "The grim truth about it is that I am drawn, like the hound when it gets the smell of a rabbit. That hound can't stop. He has to keep going until he either finds the rabbit, or the trail stops. Of course, it's not really a trail, or a scent I follow. I just know where my prey is. I can't tell you how I know. I can only say it's not really a sense like smell. It's not physical. It's just a knowing."

He runs his hand through his hair. "That night in New York City, it was about midnight, and there were people all over. By then they knew to step away from me, like a parting of the red sea, but they didn't really have a fear of me. I was just a spectacle; nothing to fear for most of them. I didn't look at their faces. I didn't want to see what I guessed would be excitement. There were cameras, but not like it is now. These days, I get more press than the President. In most cities, they know hours before I get there, and I have a full police escort. Cameramen are there, ready to walk with me wherever I go." He stops, rolls his eyes. "That was sexist, wasn't it? There are camerawomen, too.

"Back then, there were only a few cameras, probably CNN, and I think MSNBC may have been following me that early. I remember the pale neon lights shimmering in the cold, windy night, like sirens singing to the sailors, offering warmth and companionship for a little hard cash or maybe a soul. People seemed to flow toward these beacons of light to escape the night, the chill, maybe to escape me, to which there is no escape, of course."

Death takes another drag on his cigarette and looks at me. "You want to know what it's like to be in my shoes? I wanted to go where the people were going. A shop, a bar, a fast-food joint, anything, but I couldn't do it. I was being pulled. It's like I'm a fish that's hooked and being reeled in. I could go left or right. I could turn around and walk the other way. But I would end up there, no matter what. The kill draws me in. All roads lead to the next kill. Do you understand that?"

I want to let him rant and rave, but I can't resist a question. "Have you tried to resist it?"

His head jerks back, and he gives me a look of pain as though I had just hit him in the face. "You don't understand. I can't resist. It's like me asking if you've tried to stop breathing since you've been in Vegas. You can't, of course. It's a reflex. Once I get the trail, there's more than just knowing the roads. I get a sense of who my kill is. That's the pull."

He leans back on the couch, puts his hands behind his head and takes a long breath, almost a sigh, but it seems more like exhaustion. "That night in the New York snowstorm," he continues, "I saw black. Black bubbling from the bottom of the ocean, and I didn't know what the fuck it meant. I had a sense of greed. It had been there all day. Now, it was like nothing I had ever felt. I went mad. I don't know whether I blacked out, or just went into a fog, but I kept walking. Faster. I had a need. I walked out of the city, maybe I crossed a bridge. I don't know. I eventually found myself in a suburb on this empty night."

Death had forgotten his cigarette, and the ashes drop onto the chair. He brushes them off and reaches for his pack of cigarettes and lights another, taking another of those long drags. He leans toward me. "When I stopped, I was in front of this white stone structure with six columns in the front, fortifying the three floors of opulence. I had a feeling of unearned wealth. Or maybe it was wrongly earned wealth. There was this awfulness coming from the house, and it made me want to do what I'd come to do. I stepped up onto the porch and banged the door with my fists. *BAM! BAM! BAM!* There was a hollowness in the sound, as though the house was empty of all life. He was there, waiting for me. I could feel his sins, just like you can feel a headache. It hurt inside my soul, and I wanted to kill him to stop the aching. I knew he'd scream when he saw me. They always do, and usually they beg for mercy, but I offer no quarter."

Death frowns. "Do you see?"

I nod. "I'm beginning to."

"Yeah, of course, you do. Anyway, all the neighborhood was awake, on their front porches, or peering through curtains. Either they heard me banging on the door, or somebody had seen it on television and called to tell them I was in their neighborhood. They must have wondered who I was coming for, but they probably knew. I mean, they knew his crimes. Surely, the world knew his crimes. They had to, didn't they?"

I don't answer, and an uncomfortable hush lingers. Finally, I break the silence. "I do not know. I'm sorry."

He shrugs. "I ignored the neighbors, and I continued attacking the wood. *BAM! BAM! BAM!* Finally, the door opened on a chain, and a crisp, blue eye peered through the crack at me, looking me up and down. She knew me, and it was obvious she expected me. Sometimes when I come to the door, they won't let me in, and I have to wreak a little havoc. This time, the door closed, the chain was taken off, and the door opened wide. A white, brittle hand motioned me in. The front room was dark, but I saw the lady moving across the room. She stopped and turned. This poor woman leaned against the wall with her head bowed and sobbed, but it wasn't for him. 'Take him. I don't care,' she told me. I pitied her because she'd had to live with her husband's crimes for so many years, all the world knowing." Death paused. "With his crimes, how could he still be living?"

Death sips at the bourbon and sets the glass down. He smiles at me. "Now comes the good part. This is what you want to know about, isn't it, writer?"

This is not a slight toward me. Even if it was, it is true. I do not deny it. I acknowledge the truth with a nod of the head.

"Yeah, I thought so," he says. "I moved past the old woman into a hallway and up the stairs. With each step, visions of his crimes slowly took hold of my mind. When I reached his room and looked into his cold, gray eyes, the repulsiveness of it all swept over me. I saw the black ocean, black as coal and thick as mud. Charcoal beaches, with globs of thick black oil wrapped in sand and murky, dead waves. Dead birds littered the shores. Rotting fish floated in the lifeless ocean. All the suffering. I can't tell you who the man was, or what he had to do with the oil being in the ocean. I didn't need to know the details. He had a part in it and for that he had to die." Death pauses and glances at me. I suspect he wants to make sure I am listening. Satisfied, he continues. "It always happens like this. The anger builds, until it must come out. I scream. All my rage is there. All my sorrow. I slammed clenched fists against the wall and shook the house. I slammed my fists again and again and again. Finally, I stopped."

Death's hands are clenched, and he holds them out, squeezing as though he has the man's soul in them. "It still gets to me." He puts his hands down. "I fell to my knees before the man. My head was level with his, and for the first time, I looked at him, and saw a gross, fat, old man without hair, without fear. His crimes must have been ages ago. He was ancient. Sitting in a padded armchair, he glared at me, mad as hell. He said, 'How fucking dare you! How fucking dare you come into my house—' Before he could finish, I slammed the palm of my hand into his forehead with enough force to lift his body up and backward. The chair started to flip over, but before it could crest its balance, I caught and straightened it. I sat the fat old man deeply in the cushions and called him a goddamned fool. The old man whispered, 'I'm going die anyway, aren't I? Aren't you Death?' His words dripped with contempt. He leaned forward and spit in my eye. Without thinking, I grabbed the back of his head with my left hand pulled him forward. With my right hand, I pried his mouth open, grabbed his tongue, and snapped it from his mouth. He wouldn't speak again. He screamed and shook his head, beating his face with his hands. The blood filled his mouth and dribbled down his chin. He tried to spit the blood out, but couldn't."

Death shakes his head and sighs. "Listen. I'm not a violent

person. At least, I wasn't. I always hated violence. Now look at me. There I was holding that old man's tongue in front of his eyes, smiling at him, before I threw it across the room. From inside my cloak, I pulled out my long blade. I said, 'You must die for your sins against Mother Earth. In the name of the Mother, I take your life.' I don't know why I say it, but I always do. It's part of the ritual. Never taking my eyes from his, I slid the blade into his stomach and lifted. The blade cut through the rib cage, and when it reached his old heart, there was a small, red explosion, splattering blood everywhere. His eyes faded and flickered out. He sagged in the chair and died. He deserved to die. Sometimes I love murder. Not the violence of it, not the death of it, but the truth of it."

There are so many questions in my mind I don't know where to start, but finally ask, "Do you know who Harold Stull was?"

"Was that his name?"

"I think so."

"What's got you so excited?"

It's true. I am excited. "It was the tongue," I say. "You ripped his tongue out, and no one knew why. There were theories, but none of them made sense. Rage. That makes sense. He shouldn't have spit in your face."

"Why do they think I ripped his tongue out?"

I shrug. "Most people try to relate it to what Harold Stull had done to deserve a death by you, and that's the problem. Until now, no one knew for sure what he had done. He was the type of man who had multiple reasons, but mostly he ran large companies, made huge profits for himself and his friends before driving the companies into the ground."

"That didn't have anything to do with what I did."

I'm still excited, and I hate to take the time to explain, but I want Death to understand why it's important. I sip at the bourbon. "Well, I think it did. He bought a company called Horizon Star that made concrete. One of the largest oil spills ever was off the coast of Venezuela. It is believed defective concrete made by Horizon Star was the cause, although there is no evidence to support this. The Venezuelan government fixed it, quietly. They cleaned it up. They never pointed fingers. Harold Stull sent the company into bankruptcy and made a fortune. Greed is an understatement for what he suffered from. You should have heard about this. It was in the news before you..." My voice trails off. "You know, before you transformed," I finish.

"Became a monster, you mean," Death says. "Well, there was five years I did not pay much attention to the news. I was nearly a recluse. I found a place where there wasn't much badness."

"You mean Cressy?"

Death nods. "But I am getting ahead of myself. You have to know about me before Cressy."

Part II: *The Policeman and the Junkie*

My fear of Death is passing. He is still human, or at least has the sensibilities of being human. He recognizes he has lost his physical needs, and he misses the hunger of food, the need for love, which exposes his lingering humanity. It's absurd to believe he sustains himself by the lives he takes, as some have argued.

He waits for my attention to focus back on him, and when it does, he looks away, almost shyly. "You've probably spoken to all the kids I went to school with."

"If I haven't, someone else has, and I've read or seen the interview."

"They see it different now than it really was then. You understand that, don't you?"

"I suppose," I answer.

"Tell me, what do they say about me?"

I am hesitant to provide him with details, but it's not a question I can avoid. I suspect he already knows. "They say you were a quiet, smart kid who never caused any trouble and made good grades." He arches his eyebrows. I shrug and continue. "You were also a noisy, dumb kid who always was in trouble."

Death laughs. "So, you writers are left with determining who has credibility and who is lying through their teeth, right? I don't envy your job. I, at least, get to see the truth, and I know it is the truth."

The need for a drink overwhelms me, and I reach for the bottle to fill the glass with an inch of bourbon. I tip the glass back, and the liquid burns as it falls down my throat. I cough as I set the glass back down. The glass clunks against the table and sloshes out the dregs of bourbon. I wipe the bourbon up with the tip of a handkerchief before cleaning the bottom of the glass. This fastidiousness allows me time to put my next words together. "I'll admit knowing the truth is a good trick. It would change my life in ways I can't imagine, but..." My voice trails off because I can't bear to state the obvious.

"But the truth can be a burden," Death finishes.

I nod. "I would never want to walk in your shoes."

"You only know part of it."

"Well, tell me how it began."

Death lights another cigarette. "It's hard, you know. My family has to see me like this. They have to wonder what they did to make me what I have become. I hate that for them. It wasn't anything they did, or anybody did, except..." He pauses for dramatic effect. "Spiderman got bit by a spider. And I saw a cop beat up a junkie."

He puffs on the cigarette, smoke billowing like a freight train. He shows obvious agitation at having to talk about his childhood. "I was the quiet kid, and I made good grades, but you know that already. You've spoken with enough of my teachers to know that through high school, I was the perfect student." I nod in confirmation, and he continues. "I had a good childhood. Normal. I had normal middle-class parents, who could not have done better. I had friends, although my best friend was usually the book I was reading at the time. The rest of the world thought I was fucking weird for reading so much. My parents did, but I never got in trouble, so they let me be." Death blinks and looks at me with concern. "Are my parents okay? Are they taking this hard?"

His parents disappeared shortly after Death transformed, and there were rumors the government had whisked them off and given them new identities and a new place to live. Recently, a story was published online by a reputable journalist whose sources claimed Death's parents had been dropped into the deepest part of Lake Michigan. This was not something I was going to tell Death. "They haven't been heard from in years," I say.

His passiveness is a hint that he knows of the rumors, and I suspect he knows more than I do. Is it possible that his fans reached his parents first and have tucked them away some place safe?

"My father was a plumber," he says. "He could do anything with pipe, and his work was always clean. When he went into someone's house, he put those surgical booties over his shoes. In the summertime, even before I was a teenager, I went with him, almost every day. When he didn't need my help, I sat on a toilet or at a kitchen table reading. I learned to be pretty good with my hands helping him. By the time I was fifteen, I could put in a kitchen sink, faucet, and drain. Plumbers do more than work with pipe. They have to be carpenters, and electricians, and I learned it all from him, although electricity always scared me. I got shocked by a live wire once." He remembers the incident and laughs. "It knocked me across the room. It scared my father half to death, and he shook me until I woke up. He took me to the hospital, but I was fine. Well, I guess I was fine. There wasn't smoke coming out of my ears."

Death lights another cigarette and blows the smoke away from me. "My mom always felt lucky she had me," he says. "She thought she couldn't have kids, so I was always considered a blessing. My parents treated me like royalty. They bought me all the gifts in the world. Whatever I asked for. I could have taken advantage of it, but mostly I wanted books. Just books. Those were the days. The days before…"

Death let this last statement linger, and I had to ask, "Before what?"

I suspect there is great sadness in Death's eyes now, but I only see my reflection in the mirrored sunglasses. "Before I saw the cop and the junkie," he says. "I don't know if that is what turned me, but it was the first time I noticed the world had changed for me. The world went from a place wide open to a place I had to escape from."

I lean toward death and say, "Tell me about the policeman." No one knew this story, and I wanted it all for myself.

Death looks amused. "Oh, now you're the junkie, who needs a fix, right? You want it like nothing else in life. If I were cruel, I'd ask what you'd do for the story. I can see you saying, 'Anything. Anything at all.' I got it right. I do, don't I?" I start to object, but Death waves me off. "It's okay. Really. I understand. We all have our needs."

It's true, but it doesn't make me feel any less bitter about it. "And murder is yours," I say.

He shrugs. "It's more of a compulsion."

"To-may-to. To-mah-to," I say.

"Yeah, right. Whatever," Death says. The humor is still in his face, but he lets it pass. He holds up his hand. "The policeman and the junkie," he says, as if to remind himself of the story he needs to tell. "I cut class that day. It was the first warm day of spring that year, above fifty degrees, and in Cleveland, if you're a senior in high school and you don't cut school that day, you're a loser and deserve to be in school. I cut school to feed my one addiction. I had a hundred bucks my grandmother had given me for my birthday, and I wanted to spend it on books. I could buy enough books to get me through to graduation, when I would work for my father. I planned to blow every dollar I earned, mostly on movies, books, and fast food. It was going to be the summer of my life. Anyway, I cut class and rode the bus to Squire Mall."

He pours another glass of bourbon and sips at it. For now, he has put away his cigarettes, and that may have been because there was enough secondhand smoke in the room to satisfy him. "The bookstore was Edsel & Edelman Booksellers, and everybody called it Ed and Ed's, one of the last great independent bookstores in America, or so they advertised. I spent the entire morning there, and I had a stack of about ten paperbacks bundled under my arms. I had Margaret Atwood's *A Handmaid's Tale*, John Irving's *The World According to Garp*, Kurt Vonnegut's *Bluebeard*, and I even had Dicken's *A Tale of Two Cities*. An assortment of great writers."

Death considers this, and he gives a half-hearted laugh. "It's because I had all those books that I met the girl named Rose. 'That which we call a rose by any other name would smell as sweet.'" He runs his hands through his hair and sighs. "When I remember that day, I can only think *what if*, and it makes me the saddest. I wonder if Rose knows what I have become. Does she know the boy she met that spring day is now a monster? What does she think about it?" Death shakes his head. "It was my last real chance at love, and it was no chance at all. She was a year older than me, a freshman at the University of Cleveland, and stunning. She only started talking to me because she saw all the books tucked under my arm. She told me she thought I looked like I was going someplace where they didn't have books. There was truth in that statement, although it was still five months away. I told her I didn't get to the bookstore often enough and had to stock up. She knew I was a high school kid cutting class, and she said she had done it her senior year. We talked about the books tucked under my arm, half of which she had read, and she wanted to know how I had made my choices. This was a girl I had been hoping to meet my entire life. She liked books as much as I did. All kinds of books. Her favorite was Heinlein's *Stranger in a Strange Land* which she said was the best book ever to define what it truly meant to be human: The ability to laugh." He takes a drink, and says,

"I guess I retain some part of my humanity, according to that standard. What do you think?"

I don't answer, and he continues. "We went to lunch in the mall food court at a sandwich shop, spending much of lunch talking about insufferable writers. Especially the ones who get a lot of press, like James Joyce, Thomas Pynchon, and William Gibson, all of whom did not seem to care whether their readers understood what they were writing. I remember Rose told me I had to read Ralph Ellison's *Invisible Man*, explaining it wasn't just a book about race as most people seemed to think. She said it was about an individual's inability to affect the world around him, and that's what makes most of us invisible. Every good novel has different levels of understanding, she told me. Some are more complicated than others. She said the different levels should never get in the way of the story. I promised I would buy Ellison's *Invisible Man*, and I did, but not for a while."

Death leans close to me. "And so, she gave me her phone number, and I tucked it in one of the books. She said goodbye and made me promise to call her. I never did."

I smell the liquor on Death's breath, but I didn't pull away from him. "Why didn't you call Rose?"

He places his forehead in the palm of his hand, shakes his head. "I lost her phone number. You'll understand in a second. Even if I hadn't lost her number, I don't think I would have called her. I changed that afternoon." He heaved a sigh. "It's the policeman."

I'm on the edge of my seat, and I want to tell him to get on with it, but I keep it to myself. He will get there in his own time.

Death pours us another drink, and he picks up his glass and holds it high. He waits for me to pick up mine, and when I finally do, he says, "To the junkie." Death downs the bourbon, pours another, and drinks that one, too. There isn't much bourbon left, but I am sure he has another bottle in the safe. "When Rose left, it was early. I couldn't go home until school let out, so I left the mall for a guitar shop about three quarters of a mile away. I had an acoustic, but I was dying for an electric. I wanted to be just like Keith Richards, you know, not the flashiest guitarist around, but one that could write the songs. To have never had a lesson, I wasn't bad, but it was persistence, and not talent."

Death sets his glass down and steeples his fingers together. "If I hadn't taken the shortcut, would you be here talking to the monster I am? Well, I don't know. I can only think so, because if I thought it was only that ill-fated walk, it would drive me crazy. The shortcut was along a railroad track parallel to Squire Mall Road, cutting beneath the interstate. It was safer than crossing the traffic at the interchange. I had taken the shortcut fifty times before, even though my mother didn't like it. I always asked if she would rather me cross heavy traffic. I loved my mother, but she worried. The shortcut would give me fifteen extra minutes on that sunburst Gibson I loved so much. The owner of the music shop was cool to let me jam, and he knew when I bought an electric, it would be from him."

Death lights another cigarette and blows the smoke in my face, and I consider asking him to stop smoking, but the bourbon has made me much more tolerant than usual. "At the interstate, the property along the railroad track is grown up with weeds, scrub trees, cedars. Probably, a disagreement about who should clean it, the railroad, the state, or the city. As long as a train wasn't coming, there was no need for me to get into that mess. Beneath the interstate, it was clear, and the other side wasn't as weedy. From there it was only a couple hundred feet to the shopping center which backed up to the interstate. I didn't think it could be dangerous to walk the tracks. I listened for trains, and there were none, but I still fast-stepped it, my plastic bag of books dangling from my left hand. I remember thinking about Rose."

Death leans back in the chair, his hands clasped behind his head, and I think he has shut his eyes behind the sunglasses, but can't know for sure. He takes a drink of bourbon, and then another, as if he needs courage from the bottle to continue the story. "When I reached the clearing underneath the interstate, everything I knew about the world changed. It didn't make sense what I was seeing. The interstate lifts about fifty feet above the tracks. Underneath the interstate, is where I found the policeman and the junkie, but I didn't know what I was seeing at first. There was a man with his back to me. He was a hundred feet away and up an incline, just beneath the bottom of the interstate. His upper body would drop down, and then slowly rise. And then he'd do it again. It didn't make sense what he was he doing. He had something in his hand. It took what seemed like forever for me to figure out he held a pipe. He was smashing it down, and whatever he struck with it would twitch."

Death raises his arms above his head, hands clasped together, and then moves them down in a swift motion. He repeats the motion. "It was like he had an axe, splitting a cord of wood. I hadn't stopped moving. I was probably still beneath the south bound lane of the interstate. I don't know what made me realize it was a man on the ground. He was beating a man to death."

Now, Death continues, but I shut my eyes, visualizing it, but not wanting to.

"That's when I knew the man with the pipe was a policeman, and the man he was beating was a heroin addict. I knew it. I just knew. It had something to do with money not being paid. I can't tell you how I knew. The policeman didn't look like a cop. He was in jeans with a black leather jacket. He faced away from me and didn't see me. I saw more than I wanted. I knew this wasn't the first person he had killed. I knew if he saw me, I would be the next. I couldn't move, and the beating continued. I saw him raise the pipe and strike the junkie seven, eight, maybe nine times. I did nothing. I realize now there was nothing I could do, but I felt bad for months and months after. I stood there, a statue, horrified. I did nothing. During those thirty seconds, I saw the black smoke that wasn't smoke. It was the evil wafting off the policeman, and it hovered around him like a cloak. Tendrils of the smoke seemed to reach out to ensnare me. That's when I dropped the bag of books, one of which had Rose's number, and I ran like hell. I heard the policeman scream for me to stop. I didn't. I didn't turn around either, although I knew he wasn't chasing me. I didn't feel his evil moving toward me. When I got to the shopping center, I still felt danger. He would come searching. He was a policeman, so if he found me, he could take me, and no one would think anything of it. I would be beaten to death with a pipe or something worse."

Death stops, and I open my eyes. I could feel the bourbon making my eyelids heavy, but I see Death's eyes for the first time. He had taken his sunglasses off, and there is weariness there. All the pain of the world is in his eyes.

Most shocking is the tears.

"I had luck that day," he says. "There was a friend of my mom's coming out of Kroger. She asked why I wasn't in school. I told her the truth: I skipped school, and I needed a ride home. I told her she could tell my mom if she wanted. She did. I was grounded for two weeks, and that was okay by me. Anything to get out of the big trouble, even if it meant small trouble. I wouldn't have gone out in public anyway. I was afraid the policeman searched for me. I imagined him going to all the high schools in the area and getting lists of students absent that day. He never showed."

Death blinks back the tears, but it doesn't keep them from coming. He wipes them away with the back of his hand. "This is the worst of it. When the two weeks of being grounded was up, I went to the library and found the newspaper report of the murdered junkie. He had been found by a state worker mowing around the bridge about five days after the murder. The report said there were no leads. Of course, there weren't. It was low priority for the police. The victim was a junkie, and it was barely a blurb in the paper. I kept reading each day's paper, hoping there would be a break in the case. There never was. Four weeks after the junkie had been beaten, there was a headline on the front page that changed everything: 'Detective

Suspended Pending Investigation of University of Cleveland Coed Beating.' There was Rose on the page, looking at me, with her beautiful, sweet face. Next to her in a separate picture was the policeman, his evil spoiling the front page of the paper. I read the article, relieved Rose's injuries were not life threatening. Her worst damage was a broken arm, but she had bruises on her shoulders, stomach, and face. The article was vague about why the policeman had beaten Rose, except charges were pending and expected."

Death reaches for the bourbon bottle, lifts it to his mouth, and finishes off the last inch. His eyes are peering into me and waiting. I realize what he wants. After a respectful minute of silence, I ask the obvious question: "He found her number in your books, right?"

"That's my guess. It was never stated in the newspaper, but how else could he have found her? He must have beaten her to get my name, and she wouldn't give it. She was strong."

He seems to be done telling this story, or maybe tired of it, but there are a few details missing. "Why didn't he kill her?" I ask.

Death doesn't seem interested in this question, but he has an answer. "The account in the newspaper said a student saw the policeman force her into the car and called the cops. The Cleveland police located and arrested him before he could kill her. Miraculous. Usually, no one questions a policeman's actions, but the student said he felt something, whatever that means."

I still have some bourbon in the glass, and I finish it, shutting my eyes as the bourbons burns a path down my throat. "What happened to the policeman?"

"Before he could make bail," Death says, "he was choked to death by another inmate. Good fucking riddance."

"Why didn't Rose tell the police what the policeman wanted?"

I can see excitement in Death's face. "I expected to be found. Wouldn't Rose have told the investigators the policeman was asking about a kid she'd met at a bookstore?"

To answer this question, I know I will have to find Rose. I want to ask more questions, but Death seems ready to move on. So, I let it go. I can flesh it out later with good research. I think I know where he wants to take his story. "You never once tried to contact Rose after that?" Death shakes his head. I ask, "Why not?"

He lets some time pass, and finally shrugs. "Tell me, would you want to talk to the boy who nearly cost you your life? Would you want to have anything to do with him? Fuck no. I won't say I put her out of my mind or that I wasn't tempted to call her. I was. I found her number. It wasn't hard to find. I just couldn't do it. There were other issues, too. There were changes in me." Death lights a cigarette, takes a long drag, and blows the smoke toward a lamp. The light in the room fades until the smokes rises toward the ceiling. "It was like I was going through puberty a second time, I guess. Physically, I was the same, no pimples, no growth spurts, nothing like that, but I would have welcomed those things. What happened instead was I started seeing auras, the good, the bad, the ugly. I knew things I didn't want to know. I knew when someone was sick, and how sick they were. I could see cancer a mile away. I knew what everyone was feeling whether I wanted to or not. Happy, sad, horny, mean, angry, all of it, and it was kind of cool, for a while. Then my new sight became limited to just the ugliness —you know, hate, lust, envy, jealousy, and fear. Every one of us has a little bit of ugliness in us, don't we? Sometimes just a bit. None of us are perfect, and many of us are far less than perfect. By the end of the school year, this new sense was limited to only the evil in a person's aura, and evil only comes in one color. Black. I could no longer see the good in people, only the evil. I knew who to avoid at school, and at the mall, and while this was also a neat trick, it made me want to stay in my room. Evil couldn't be avoided. There are some of us who live truly blessed lives, and in those people, I saw nothing. Most of us have something we aren't proud of, and I saw it, no matter how small. Some of them had only blackness. Pitch black. The absence of light. I was scared of my chemistry lab partner. He was a sadist. I had to pretend to be best friends with him. I was breaking on the inside. By the end of the school year, I wouldn't go out in public unless I had to. Working for my father that summer was the hardest thing I ever did. So, yeah, I never called Rose. I had other things on my mind."

Death rises from the couch and walks to the window to look out at the Vegas landscape. "Down there, there's all types of evil, all levels of badness, all types of sin. This is an awful world we live in." Death slams his hand against the windowsill and the wood breaks beneath. He turns and screams: "THEY'RE MURDERING THE WORLD, KILLING ONE AN-OTHER, AND THEY DON'T SEE IT! THEY'RE FUCKING BLIND! THE WORLD IS BLIND. I DON'T UNDERSTAND HOW THEY CANNOT SEE IT!" His voice has physical shape, and it fills the room almost to the point of suffocation. I hold my breath and count to ten. Finally, I can breathe again. He backs away from the window and stands still for a long time. Abruptly, he walks to the safe, removes another bottle of Maker's Mark, picks at the red wax, removes the lid, and pours us a drink. I need a drink.

Part III: *Cressy*

Until Death puts his sunglasses back on, I don't realize how oppressive his stare is. The room brightens, and my thoughts are not all doom and gloom. His eyes will haunt me forever. I want to curse him for that, and yet, he is already cursed, isn't he? Instead, I bow my head, and say a prayer for his soul, whatever good that will do.

"I tried college," he says as he sits down, "which I'm sure you know, and I failed. By the time I reached Ohio State, the evil had begun to take a physical shape, reminiscent of the smoke surrounding the policeman. The evil pursued me. I was a magnet to it. I couldn't go to class for seeing the smoke. I wouldn't leave the dorm room. My roommate, Randy—I don't remember his last name—bless his heart—he didn't understand. I told him I suffered from depression, that was all, and it was true. All day I would sit in front of the television and cry my heart out. I watched cable news, and the world I saw was terrible; my heart ached over it. The world was mad. Do you understand me? It was lunacy. Madness. It still is." Death pauses while he lights a cigarette. "Randy wanted to help. One day he got the University to send a shrink to check on me—Randy must have gone through hell to get this to happen. The shrink sat on Randy's bed, and I tuned him out the best I could, but I couldn't ignore that he was cloaked in smoke. It wafted from him and reached out to me. It tried to wrap itself around my ankles. That's when I learned I could push back, wall it away from me with my mind. The smoke went scurrying back to its master, the shrink. He finally left, I am sure to report I was non-responsive and needed help. I had to leave before he returned with reinforcements. So, only six weeks in, I left college."

Death takes a drink of the bourbon, and I follow suit. "How long did it take you to get to Cressy?" I ask.

"Not long," he says. "A few days. I spent time in Lexington, but there were too many people there, too much blackness I didn't feel safe. It was no better than Columbus or Cleveland. I got into my car and drove old country roads until I was lost in the Kentucky hills and there didn't seem to be anyone around for miles. I felt safe. It was a coincidence I came upon Will Bardson. I was driving on Bardson's Road in Providence County, and he stood at the end of the driveway of his orchard, getting the mail. He waved me down, like he needed my help, and I guess he did, just not at that moment. I stopped, rolled the window down. He leaned into the passenger side and asked if I was lost. No matter how he meant it, I was lost. I told Will that I meant to be lost. I said I wanted to be nowhere, and he agreed this was indeed nowhere. He told me his wife was making BLT's and an apple cobbler for lunch. He said I was welcome. It had been a year since I felt no threat, so I agreed. I saw no blackness from Will or his wife, Jewell. They were good, lonely people who couldn't have children, and they took me in and treated me as their own. I am so thankful for that five-year reprieve, and their gift of a normal life."

I could interrupt Death and tell him I got to know Will Bardson in the last seven years. I have taken a yearly sabbatical to Cressy not to cover Death's story, but to pick apples and make cider. I send Christmas cards, and the Bardsons send me birthday gifts. More than anyone else, the Bardsons have helped me understand what Death was before he changed. I have done my best to help them understand what Death is now. I convinced them he's not the monster the rest of the world thinks. I don't really need to hear about his time with the Bardsons, but I am curious about his point of view, so I let him continue.

"I became a Kentucky apple farmer," Death says. "It was the happiest time of my life. I worked twelve hours a day most days, sometimes more, and I loved it. I lived in a cabin at the rear of the property. I was a simple laborer, but a little more. I was the only person they kept on the farm year-round. For reasons I can't explain, they trusted me. I became one of their family, eating Sunday meals with them, and an occasional lunch. I worked like a person possessed. It was a simple life, a world without problems. I had no television, no radio, no computers, and I didn't read the newspaper. I didn't have the internet. I wrote my family letters. They visited and saw I was okay. I offered no explanations about what I was doing with my life. I only went to Cressy for groceries and library books. There was evil in Cressy, but I kept my distance. My life at the orchard was a sanctuary, a blessing, and Will and Jewel Bardson were wonderful people. Will knew there was something different about me, and he knew I didn't like going to town or dealing with the public. He let me choose the seasonal workers. He said I had a knack for picking the best of them, and it was true, of course. Sloth is a minor evil, but I could see its shadow in people. The picking season was a busy time, and I worked from sunup to sundown. If it was a cider making night, I worked until after midnight. The rest of the year, my time was spent keeping ahead of the seasons. I pruned in the winter and spring when it wasn't too cold. I mowed and sprayed for insects and disease during the late spring and summer. The seasons passed at a blink of an eye." It is clear these memories are pleasant for him, and he could talk about the orchard for hours. I could listen, but Death understands it's of no use. "All that had to end, of course," he says.

"Why?"

"Damned if I know why. It just did. Does the butterfly ask why she changed from the caterpillar? No, of course not."

"But if you knew why—"

"Then I would know why," Death says. "Nothing else. It wouldn't change anything, only make me angry. I would continue walking my walk, and I would always be unstoppable, I guess." He lights another cigarette and blows smoke toward me in a smoke ring that bursts around my head. "The why doesn't matter. The how doesn't matter, either. Let's just assume I changed because a power greater than me simply decided the world needed a force against evil. This is not about turning cheeks. If it is God who did this—and I don't know it is —but if it is, then he or she is a vengeful God, and not willing to suffer evil. Maybe a force like me will be some break in the decline of the world. I think there probably needs to be a hundred like me to have much effect. I'm being cynical, but that shouldn't surprise you." Death laughs, a deep, less than human sound, and it may be the scariest thing I have ever heard. "So, a power greater than me caused me to be this way. By hiding at the Bardson Orchard, I delayed the inevitable. Eventually I was going to come across some evil so reprehensible, the metamorphosis had to happen. I was the match waiting to be struck. I was the torch ready to burn. It was going to happen."

He has brought us to this point, and I consider another gentle prod, but I slouch comfortably in my chair and wait.

After about a minute, he clears his throat. "That day in August, just a couple of weeks before we started picking, I worked on the cider mill, getting it ready for the first pressing, which was still more than a month away. You can't make good cider without golden delicious apples, and the earliest they would ripen would be the middle of September, but by then, I would be too busy picking to give the mill proper maintenance. So, while Will Bardson worked on the sorting machine, I greased the fittings and bearings, cleaning every inch of the mill, and that includes the pasteurization equipment, the jug fillers, and everything else. That's when I discovered a PVC pipe from the pasteurization equipment to the aluminum barrels had a crack. Will and I agreed all the PVC needed to be replaced, not just the one. I took measurements, made a list, and told Will I would be back in an hour. He offered to go, but I told him I was craving fried catfish from Faye's Diner. I had been to Cressy hundreds of times in the past five years. Why would this trip be any different?"

Death pours us yet another glass of bourbon, and I leave mine sitting. I wait for him to continue as he sips at his. "You've been to Cressy, so you know it's small; there isn't much there. The courthouse is the center of town, and almost everything else is in the courthouse square, the post office, the library, three or four law offices, two banks, two fine restaurants and one greasy spoon... oh, and the furniture store. The only grocery store is one block down Richmond Avenue. The square is large enough so there's always a parking space, but on this day, I had to park a block away at Hanson's Grocery. I walked to the square and then to Faye's for my catfish dinner. The place was empty except for the waitress, who sat at the cash register looking bored. Faye's is the kind of place where there are always a few townies drinking coffee. The waitress sat me in a corner booth next to the window. When I commented about the restaurant being empty, she said everyone was at the courthouse for a fiscal court meeting. I said those meetings usually wouldn't draw flies, and she laughed. But she said the rumor was a factory was coming. A big factory, and that meant jobs."

Death leans toward me, smiles. "Of course, you knew that already though, didn't you? But did you know our state senator had an interest in a company buying land near the proposed factory site? Also, this same state senator was on the budget committee which had approved the widening and straightening of the road to I-75 in Richmond? You didn't know that, did you? Isn't that the way these things usually work?" I shrugged my shoulders, and Death grunts. "Well now, here's what you should be asking: How did I know these things? No one else knew or even suspected. As I sat there waiting for my catfish, I saw it. I saw the green of money, a lot of it, exchanging hands. I knew more than I wanted to know. There was a new company coming to Cressy, a chemical plant of some kind, and it was going to be big, lots of jobs, a great opportunity for Cressy, and everyone was happy about it."

"Everyone but you," I say.

Death nods. He leans toward me conspiratorially and in the lowest voice he can muster, he whispers, "That's right. I saw death." When he says *death*, a chill runs up my spine and the hair on my arms stands straight up. In a regular voice, he says, "I saw people dying. I saw disease. It wasn't the company's product; it was the byproduct, and the deaths were decades away." Snuffing out the current stub, he lights another cigarette, and it dangles from corner of his mouth as he speaks. "I sat there in the restaurant and I saw certain and absolute death. My catfish came, but I had lost my appetite. I was the death row inmate who couldn't eat his last meal. That's what it was for me. After this day, nothing would be the same. I may not be dead, but I am Death, and that's got to be worse than being dead."

Death runs his hands through his thick hair, and he looks sick to his stomach at this memory. "When I saw the smoke seeping out of the door of the courthouse, I thought the building was on fire. It was the color of black rolling up from a burning pile of tires, but it hovered close to the ground like fog. I knew it came from one...one man. What I knew about him—he was the person responsible, and he was aware of the death he wrought. Even worse, he had no guilt. It wasn't that he wanted death—he really didn't—but it was a business decision: Is the legal liability less than the potential profit? If so, then cover it up, hide it, diffuse it, whatever you have to do to beat the onslaught of litigation lawyers, and meanwhile, you collect your profits. The deaths were a minor irritation, and simply didn't bother him as long as the money kept rolling in. It would, too. He knew it."

I consider this and start to respond but decide against it.

I must have made a face because Death says, "You have a question?"

"No," I say, and then I shake my head. "I mean, yeah. But I don't want to interrupt." Death stares at me, lips pressed together, and it's clear to me he's not going to continue until I say what's on my mind. "If that's the criteria you use, why haven't the manufacturers of tobacco and asbestos seen the blade of your knife?"

"Yeah, why haven't they?" Death asks. "It's not like I decide who dies; I only get to know why. This man's soul was black, and maybe it involved more than his greed. I don't know. I just know for the first time I felt this incredible pull, like a vacuum sucking me into this mess. I resisted it, holding onto the restaurant table until I couldn't do it anymore. I stood, knocking the chair over in the process. I walked away without picking it up. The waitress asked me what was wrong as I went through the door, and I didn't acknowledge she had even asked a question. I walked to the hardware store for my first weapon, a long bowie knife. I broke the display glass with my fist. I reached in and took it. As I left, the proprietor, Elias Hackney, yelled he was calling the Sheriff, and I agreed he should. It didn't stop me from moving toward the courthouse. I recognized what I was doing was crazy, and yet, I couldn't stop myself. I was being pulled. The man's black heart had to be splintered into a million pieces. Had to. Simply had to. And I was going to do it, no matter how crazy it was." Death takes a long drag on the cigarette, turns, and blows the smoke away from me. He looks back to me. "You're going to need to dry clean your suit, you know. All the smoke. Sorry about that."

"I don't care," I say.

"Yeah, well, this is a nasty habit I wish would kill me." He holds the cigarette up, as if to make sure I knew what he was talking about. Neither of us laugh at his joke. "As I approached the courthouse, the smoke parted for me, and I followed its trail, although I didn't have to. I felt the pull, like the man was sending a signal. I walked to the circuit courtroom on the second floor, not where the fiscal court usually held its meetings. When I opened the door, it was obvious the location had been changed to accommodate the number of people. Every seat was taken, and people stood in the center aisle. I could see the man at the front of the room, standing between the county judge-executive and the Cressy mayor, who was blustering about what a pleasure it is to have Mr. Gillingham here in Cressy. He said Gillingham was bringing three hundred jobs to town, which was important to the community. On and on the mayor went about this man. I could have listened and assessed the situation, but the compulsion to murder him was overpowering. It could not wait. I shoved my way through the crowd, excusing myself as I moved forward. I slowly made my way to the front, and I felt eyes turning toward me. The mayor's speech faltered when he noticed he was losing the attention of the crowd. He stopped speaking as I took a step outside the spectators and through the short swinging doors separating the audience from the spectacle of the courtroom. Neither the mayor nor Judge Cain tried to stop me as I moved forward. When I stood before Gillingham, two feet away, he looked normal, not like a sociopath, but I had second sight. As I looked into his eyes, my mind reeled, unbalanced. I could see the entirety of his evil, and it made me lightheaded. I turned and looked about the room. All eyes were on me to see what I would do. I wanted to run, but the pull was too strong, and my whole being was filled with rage I had never felt. I was the fuse leading up to the dynamite. I couldn't stop."

Death looks at me, tightening his lip into a frown. "You're on the edge of your seat, aren't you?"

"How can I not be?" I ask.

Death nods because he understands, although it seems to make him sad, or maybe it's simply the telling of his story making him sad. "A man in the crowd saw my knife, and he yelled it: *He's got a knife!* The reaction wasn't like someone yelled *fire* in a crowded theater. No one moved. It was drama they were watching, I guess, or maybe train wreck. They couldn't turn away, just like you haven't been able to turn away all these years. I mean, you've got that itch. You got to know how it all turns out. They wanted to know what I was going to do. I had no choice but to be consumed by the pull, although they didn't know that. I leaned toward Gillingham, and I whispered *you know the death you have wrought and you must die for it. Mother Earth claims you.* I still don't know why I make a reference to the Mother. I've never been a religious person. It seemed silly at the time, and it still does, but I always say it or something like it. As I looked into the blackness of Gillingham's eyes, I saw evil."

Death shrugs. "I guess you've seen the videos of me taking the bowie knife and piercing his heart. I've seen them, and it still bothers me. I look like a madman, but the videos do not show the blackness. When he dies, the videos don't show the blackness fading into nothing either. If they showed that, the world wouldn't have thought I was crazy. The world would have understood why he had to die, and why I did it. I had to. All of you would have wished you had been the one to do it. I pulled the knife out of him, wiped it on his pant leg, turned, and left the courthouse."

I lean toward Death. "That's not what happened."

Without hesitation, he says, "Oh, but it is."

"You're missing a big part of what happened," I insist.

He takes a drag on the cigarette and blows the smoke into

my face, as if in contempt. "There are ten videos of what happened. I know you've seen them. It's that part of all of this I like the least. Do I have to tell it when you know what happened?"

I breathe deeply as I consider it.

"Please," he says.

I shake my head. "I could let it go and move on, but I don't think your truth is in those videos. I don't think the witnesses can tell me the truth of what happened to you."

"The videos don't lie, witnesses didn't lie," Death says.

"The videos show you knocking innocent people down."

"I did that."

"You shoved people out of the away to get out of the courthouse."

Death shrugs. "So, you say."

"In their minds, they were stopping a murderer and you needed to be brought to justice."

Death takes the longest drag on the cigarette yet, and he blows it out. "What do you want me to say?"

I lean toward him. "They were innocent people who didn't know what you were. Three of them died for it. I want you to admit that."

Death holds his hands up. "Wait. Wait. I didn't kill those people. You know that. Two of them were trampled to death by the others, and one was shot by the Sheriff when he was aiming for me. I didn't kill them, but I get blamed."

I wave off what he said. "Yeah, you were misunderstood, but how were they supposed to know why you did what you did? Can you fault them for attacking you? If I had been there, I would have tried to stop you."

Death pours another drink, but leaves it sitting on the table. "You've read the Frankenstein story, right? That's what this was about. You're correct. I was the misunderstood monster, but it's not like I had the ability to stop and tell that crowd it was better for them if the jobs didn't come to Cressy. I was being pulled away to my next killing. I had to leave. So, I turned, still holding the damned bloody knife—you can never get all the blood off a knife, you know? I started walking. At first, it was a parting of the sea, but when I was in the middle of them, I felt the first hand on my shoulder. It slipped off as I took a step, but then the people in front of me closed in. My way was blocked. I had to leave the circuit court room, and I didn't want to hurt any of these people, so I stuck the knife in my belt. When I did that, hands grabbed at me from behind, and I swatted them off. I moved another step toward the door and the throng of people moved back, but not far. The next part is clear on one of the videos. I shoved no one out of my way as I moved forward. I systematically lifted them and set them aside. I had no ill will toward these folks. I knew many of them. It's when they came from behind me and from the sides that people began getting hurt. I simply couldn't be taken down. I had such strength, incredible strength, like a superhero, and I kept moving, slowly. The people who grabbed me were either dragged forward or were trampled by the people behind them trying to get to me. I didn't know until later that two of them had died in the courtroom. It wasn't like I could stop and check on them, and it wasn't like they died by my hand. I'm told in the confusion, one was trampled and the other hit her head on the ground after being pushed down by one of the towns-people. Still, I get blamed, don't I?"

Death takes a drink and then another. "So, I made it to the door, opened, and closed it behind me. I shut them off, but there were still a few of them who had made it out of the courtroom. They were in front of me running down the stairs, screaming their heads off. The Sheriff was at the bottom of the stairs, his gun drawn. He stared me down as I approached. I could hear the throng of people from the courtroom stomping down the steps behind me. They began yelling for the Sheriff to get me. The Sheriff waited until I was on the last step be-fore he discharged his weapon. The first bullet missed and may have hit the ceiling. The second bullet struck my right knee. The third entered my chest next to my heart. The fourth missed me. The fifth struck my left shoulder as I turned. The last bullet struck my heart. I've heard it said I didn't die then because I had no heart, and this may be true. Later, as I walked the highway, the bullets kind of leaked out of me. It's the Sheriff's fourth bullet that caused the commotion. I didn't hear the scream, but sensed it. I turned and caught the fourth bullet's benefactor, a young woman who was just a few years older than me. She looked like a pretty librarian. I laid her at the foot of the steps. Dead. I turned to the Sheriff and called him a fool. He threw his gun at me and ran. I bet he was never reelected. I finally made it out of the courthouse, and a few people followed at a safe distance, until they got bored, I guess."

Death pauses, and I take the break to ask a question. "What did you think was going on?"

He laughs. A bitter sound. "You mean with my body? I had no clue, and I still don't know. I have my suspicions about part of it, but I still don't know the answer to the biggest question: Why the fuck me? There was never anything special about me. Prior to the metamorphosis, I was normal—just a kid in high school who liked to read books and listen to rock music. There is no reason to explain why I was chosen. I was, and I knew I had to walk. I had more killing to do." Death inhales deeply. "I was already sick of this. I had blood on my hands."

"And the state police caught up with you?"

Death shrugs. "Well, they were waiting for me. I was maybe two miles outside of Cressy. I only had a faint feeling about my next victim. He had killed and tortured women, not in St. Louis, where he lived, but in other states where he traveled. I knew the police had never connected these crimes. It was all vague still, coming to me in bits and pieces. I was on my way to him, one foot in front of another, carrying that damned knife in my hand. I crested a hill on Richmond Road and saw at the top of the next hill, the state police had two cars sideways blocking the highway, lights blazing. I saw six troopers standing there, waiting for me, acting like it was a day at the races. After all, I was only one man, walking. They had their guns. What could I do to them? The reports by the Sheriff had been either been ignored, or maybe he had returned to his office and locked his door while someone else had called it in. I was a third of the way down the hill before they spotted me. Two of the troopers walked down their side of the hill. I guess, we were supposed to meet at the bottom, talk it over. They would handcuff me, put me in their car, and cart me off to jail. That was their plan. I could tell from their stride they didn't take it seriously. I knew I could not stop walking. When we were about thirty feet apart, they told me to drop the knife and stop right there. Of course, I didn't. When I was fifteen feet away, both of them pulled out their batons, yelled at me to stop. I kept coming, keeping my eyes straight ahead. I didn't know what would happen when they tried to force me down. I just knew to keep moving."

Death now takes a drink of the bourbon and wipes his mouth with his sleeve. "I don't like this part either." He takes a second sip, swallows, and shakes his head. "When I reached them, the trooper on my right, swung the baton at my right wrist, hoping to make me drop the knife. When it hit, there was a crack, like a homerun being hit. It was like I had armor on. The baton was in two pieces. I didn't feel a thing. The second trooper swung at my head with his baton. My left hand reached up, snatched it out of his hand, and I threw it aside. The first trooper grabbed for my right hand. I think he meant to pull it behind my back, but my arm didn't move. I took a step. The trooper was dragged along, and he fell forward. I think he may have torn his pants and skinned his knees before he let go. The second trooper pulled his sidearm and told me to stop or he would shoot. I believed him, but I had no control over it. After I had taken two steps, he shot my left calf twice. I felt the force, but not enough to hinder my stride. My body absorbed the bullets like a sandbag. Two more shots in my right calf, and I kept moving. I had moved twenty feet and remember the trooper telling me the next shots would be to kill. I wanted to turn and tell him to please kill me. Instead, I put one foot in front of the other. The trooper shot me in the back then in the head until he had no more bullets. He ran to me, screaming, 'What are you? Just what the fuck are you?' I turned to him, and whispered, 'I wish I knew.' He walked next to me, pistol at his side. He was the first person to ask why I was doing what I was doing. I told him the truth: That I couldn't help it." Throughout this final recitation, Death had stared into his glass of bourbon, like it was a crystal ball. He looks up and says, "You know I couldn't help it, right?"

I shrug. I don't want to condone Death's actions.

"All six of the troopers put their guns away," Death continues, "and they walked with me. They were respectful, almost honorific. They talked about how the world had just changed and speculated about what it meant."

I lean toward Death. "What did they think was happening?"

Death laughs. "The world had come to an end."

"They were wrong, of course."

"Yeah, I guess, but I can say it ended for me that day. From this point on, life had no meaning, just endless moving about, and killing. I only saw the worst in people."

Part IV: *Being Death*

Death finishes the bourbon in his glass, sets it down. "I guess we need to talk about what the government did, don't we? You know the military had a hard-on for me for months as if I were a threat to national security."

The politics of Death doesn't interest me much, and I have no real desire to hear Death's take on reactions or overreactions of the national government, but I have less desire to stop him.

He lights another cigarette, but simply holds it to the side. "The military showed up later that same day and treated me like an enemy. For months, resources were spent trying to destroy me. I scared them, and I don't need to tell you why. The military used explosives. Then larger explosives. At times, the ground beneath me shook and then was gone. I would climb out of the pit, shrapnel sticking out of me. They tried everything but a nuke, I guess. They would have used that if I spent more time walking in less populated areas. I really don't know how I survived all the attacks. Maybe my physical body is in another dimension. Maybe I'm between life and death. None of that would explain how my body absorbs and then ejects bullets and shrapnel, would it? Yeah, that I can't explain. Finally, after months of their war against me, the government gave up. There wasn't a warm and fuzzy feeling, but at least they weren't trying blow me to smithereens. Maybe they realized it wasn't such a bad thing to have me killing evil, terrible, and no good people. There was a brief campaign of saving my victims by evacuating areas as I approached them, but I changed directions to where my victim went. The government gave up because it caused too much disturbance to save only one bad person."

I want to tell Death the government gave up the hunt because it was making the fear worse. "Are you sure the government gave up killing you because you were killing bad people?"

Death grins and shrugs. "What else could it be? I know they were convinced I was invincible or maybe immortal. Maybe they decided I was harmless to most people, not that they would ever admit it, though. What they did was turn me over to the world, didn't they? But they never came out and said, *hey, this death guy isn't so bad? He kills bad guys, and that's good for us.* No, what they did was to warn towns as I approached. Just a simple statement like I was a hurricane coming, telling people to stay indoors, or leave town. But people didn't. The news got out about me, and you were either for me or against me, and both sides showed up. Those against me attacked me, with no effect. I have been burned with gasoline. A dozen priests have thrown holy water on me, and others have exorcized me. I have been stabbed with knives, scissors, swords, and poisoned hypodermic needles. I'm still here, and those attacks still come. The government's warnings became unnecessary, because the news media let the world know where I was, every minute of every day. No film star, president, or newscaster has been filmed as much as me, and it would take you a millennium to put it all together."

I reach for the bottle of bourbon, which Death willingly hands over, and I pour a glass. I sip at it. Death is fidgety and I know my time with him is ending—he is being called to his next kill—but I have so much to ask him. "You have an entourage when you come to town now." It is a statement, not a question.

"An entourage?" he asks. "Is that what you call it?"

"What do you call it?"

Death laughs. "A bunch of crazy fucks, or sometimes my fans." He lights a cigarette and takes another impossibly long drag. The end of the cigarette glows like a sunset, and then he blows smoke rings across the room. "All of the networks cover me, and I know many of the correspondents just by seeing them on the road. On occasion, I will talk to them, about the weather, or even sports I've heard about, but I never answer their questions. I am told the Death Network is twenty-four hours news about me and only me. Is that right?"

I nod. "Yeah. Between killings, the network reports your whereabouts, and have talking heads speculate about your last victim. I have been asked, but refuse to go on. It's really senseless."

"Isn't that odd?" Death asks. "Do people really watch it?"

"Like a religion," I answer.

Death snaps his finger. "That's what I've become to some, isn't it? The world has found a new religion, based on their fears of me. They must tell their children, 'Behave or Death will take you away.' I'm their worst nightmare; and I'm real. Of course, not everyone hates or fears me. When I enter a city, my hordes, my fans—or entourage, as you said—are waiting for me and they walk with me. I am offered cigarettes, and bourbon. Many of them worship me, sing hymns, and give me blessings, and a few ask for my blessings. I have nothing to give but death, of course, but I appreciate the cigarettes and bourbon."

"There are some that plot against you," I say.

Death flicks the ashes of his cigarette onto the floor. "Yeah, I hear in Atlanta, they've constructed a wall around the city." He grunts a raspy laugh. "It won't keep me out. Nothing can stop me. Not even myself. God knows, I've tried, but I always end up with the blade in my hands."

"Other cities, too," I say. "Sarasota, Charleston, and Denver are building walls. There are developments all around the country that have built massive fortresses, with the houses being sold at triple the value."

Death shakes his head. "How much money are they spending on these walls?"

"Hundreds of millions, maybe billions."

He shakes his head. "It's such a waste. Don't they realize I'm a product of society? All they have to do is be good, and I won't come for them? It's so simple. Money can't keep me away."

"What about the people who live in their cars, traveling where you're not. Isn't that better than a wall?"

Death bites his lip, sighs again. "I was told by a reporter there's a wealthy man who keeps himself and his family on the other side of the Mississippi from me, by flying around in a private jet. That must cost him hundreds of thousands of dollars each year. If they're one of my potential victims, I will reach them, or whatever created me will have a different way of taking care of them. Earthquakes or hurricanes, or planes that crash, or maybe just a toy on the stairs. Whatever it is, I'm sure it will be a painful and tortuous end for them. Justice." Death says this with a smile, as if he knows several secrets. He frowns and leans toward me. "Like I said, sometimes I just love murder. Not the violence or death of it, but the truth of it. Just before the final moment, when a person's energy fades, I can see the whole story in their sad, unflinching eyes, because he or she no longer needs to keep the lies hidden. There's shame and desire for forgiveness, but I offer only death."

Death takes a deep breath, holds it, and blows it out. Maybe he doesn't need to breath, but he expresses his exasperation with such precision. "A lot of damn good it does them," he says. "If I'm there, it's too late. They're going to Hell, and I am sending them there."

"So, there is a Hell?"

"Other than the one I'm living?" Death asks. "Yeah, well, I don't know. I like to think there's a punishment I can't give, because all I offer is death, and that's easy, isn't it? It's an escape. What I'm doing is protecting the rest of the world from them."

"Is your life that hard?" I wonder out loud. Then, without much thought, I say, "It's not as if you have the struggles of normal people. You're invincible, untouchable. You don't have to worry about the car payment, or a sick child, or whether your teenager is going to get into a good college. All of this seems to be for show." I stop and consider my next words carefully. I've said too much already, but I might as well finish it. "It's not as if providing your type of death is hard, since you are invincible, you know. But then again, I don't have to walk a mile in your shoes."

"Or ten thousand miles," Death says. He's not mad at my judgments, but he is defensive. "You think it's easy killing people and not being able to control the impulse? You think it's easy being hated? There are some cities where they line the streets to shout curses at me and throw rocks. It all bounces off me. It doesn't hurt, but oh, how I tire of the preachers telling me I am evil, thumping their bibles at me, telling me to open my heart and accept their one and only savior. They cringe when I look their way, as though they think I am judging them to see if they need my services. Don't they understand I am already one of the damned?"

"Do you truly feel you are damned?"

"Aren't I?"

I shake my head. "I believe you are the hand of God. You must be the hand of God. Otherwise, it makes no sense. That's what I believe"

"Then you are truly a fool," he says. "As I said, I am living hell on Earth. I don't want this; I never wanted it, and I would pass this along to whoever wished to have it, if I could simply die." Death strikes a match and leans the cigarette into the flame. He puffs smoke out for a few seconds and then takes the cigarette out of his mouth. "I am tired. Isn't that silly? I am invulnerable, and yet I am so fucking weary of this, the walking, the killing, all of it. I just want to lay down and go to sleep. It has been forever since I have simply slept. Can you imagine what that's like?" He puts the cigarette between his lips and puffs like a locomotive chugging up a steep hill, the smoke trailing up toward the ceiling. He chuckles. "The hand of God? That's funny."

"I meant that—"

"I know what you meant," Death interrupts. "But I think it's more likely I am an abomination. One in a trillion. Either way, I want it to end. I am ready for it to end. To be over."

I consider this for a moment. "Even if it meant your death?"

Death flicks his ashes to the floor. "Especially if it means my death." He shakes his head and reaches for the bourbon. He holds his cigarette in one hand and the bourbon bottle in the other. He tilts the bottle and takes a drink. When he is done, a reasonable amount of satisfaction shows on his face. "It's not like I could give this up and have a life. I would always be known as the man who had been Death. I guess, I could be one of the talking heads on television, right? I could write books about what it was like to be a Death, and it would sell millions of copies around the world. Maybe I could be on Celebrity Jeopardy. I mean, do you really think I could be normal? Would my family accept me for what I was? Maybe a state government would arrest me for one or more of my murders, or maybe one of my victim's family would seek revenge. There's always those worries." He yawns, sets the bottle down, and leans back in the chair with his cigarette. "No, I'm tired, and I am ready for it to end. All of it. If I thought it would kill me, I'd find a way to the roof of the hotel and jump. I'd give up cigarettes and bourbon and jerking off if I could die." Death laughs at his joke. It is not a pleasant sound.

I have so much to ask Death about, but I know the interview is ending, and there is only one pressing issue remaining. It is something I have worried about from the moment his entourage contacted me weeks ago. Now that we are almost done, I have little fear in asking it. I lean toward him. "You're known to always be in motion. You're either killing, or you're moving to your next kill, but you never stop."

"That's right." He crushes the cigarette out in the ashtray and lights another.

"So, how is it you've been able to sit with me for this long?"

Death smiles. "What exactly are you getting at?"

He's toying with me, and I bite back my anger. "In seven years, you haven't sat down for two minutes, let alone two hours. You've said tonight it's not something you have control over. Why now?"

Death stares at me, and finally he says, "You figure it out."

I have an answer ready. "I'm your next victim."

He coughs. "You really thought that, and you still came? You are a tough son of a bitch."

I am relieved. "Then I don't know."

Death takes another one of those impossibly long drags on his cigarette and blows the smoke toward the ceiling. He stretches toward me to whisper, "I am your first victim."

I'm confused. I can't get my mind wrapped around it. "What do you mean?"

"You're my substitute, my proxy" he says. "I wish I could tell you how or why, but weeks ago a name came to my mind, and I began moving this way, putting all of this in motion. It became clear I had to meet with you, and I had my fans set it up. I didn't know why. Between kills, I had my fans read me everything you'd written. I got to know you through your writing. I didn't choose you. Until just a little while ago I didn't even know this was ending for me, only that I was supposed to tell you my story. Now, I understand. You will work fine as my stand-in."

I shake my head. "I have a wife and kids—"

"Yes, that's a harsh reality," he says, "but I don't make the rules."

"There are rules?"

Death shrugs.

"Why me?"

"Why not you? Why was it me? I don't have the answers."

I am getting angry now. Frantic. "I can't! I won't!"

Death removes his sunglasses, and those eyes are more than just tired. He is sad and upset. He sits up straight. "I don't believe you have a choice. I wish I could tell you otherwise."

"And my family?"

"Like mine." He lifts his shoulder. "The government or maybe your fans will keep them out of harm's way. When you are finished, maybe you can return to them. Maybe you will ask your replacement to kill you, as I am asking you. There's so much I don't know and can't tell you. I have told you everything I know."

"My kids will be years older. Will my wife wait for me? Will she want me after I have been Death?" I'm not yelling, but I can hear my voice echo within the room.

Death clenches his teeth. "Listen, I sacrificed my life for seven years. Maybe twelve if you consider the years I fought it at the orchard, although those weren't bad years."

I throw my pad at the wall. I turn to face Death. "It's not fair."

"When is life fair? Was it fair to me? No, of course not. That's why it's called a sacrifice. If sacrifice was fair, then it wouldn't be a sacrifice, would it? Sacrifice is never easy."

I slam my hand onto the coffee table, but it's a weaker sound compared to Death's pounding earlier. "Sacrifice requires a choice. If I have no choice, then it's hardly a sacrifice."

Death shrugs. "Yeah, maybe, but you are now what I was." He puts his knife on the table. It's not the original knife, I know, and it is impressively long. I don't want to touch it, but I find it irresistible.

I wrap my fingers around the hilt and whisper, "I don't want it."

Death shrugs again. "You have no choice."

I feel myself changing. He is my first victim, and not because of his murderous ways, but because of his need for respite. "Please," I say, "take this from me."

Death swallows his last drink of bourbon, and holds his arms out. "No. Won't you take this from me?"

I shake my head, but I find myself lifting the knife, and taking my first life, if there was life remaining. Death collapses in the chair. The weariness in eyes fades. Before I can remove the knife from his chest, Death's body disintegrates into dust, so there is nothing remaining but his cloak. I sit while I wait to find out what happens next. A thought occurs to me. I remove the scabbard and sunglasses from the cloak. I lift his cloak and shake it like a rug, and what remains of Death falls to the floor. I put the cloak on, then the scabbard, knife, and sunglasses. I see in my mind a woman who lights fires. This is my next kill, and she is in Los Angeles. I will walk the desert tonight. I pull the hood up to hide my face. I then reach into my pocket to feel for my cell phone. When I am out of the city, I will call my wife and tell her to go to the government and ask for protection. Death's new identity will be known, but maybe I can delay it. I expect government officials will meet me in Los Angeles to discuss how the change happened and why. I wonder if I will be able to talk to my kids, and whether I can keep my phone charged. I am walking down the stairs of the hotel and with each step I can tell it becomes less important. The need for the kill becomes more important. I have no other purpose. I wonder if I will feel the need to call my wife by the time I reach the desert. I pull out the cell phone to call her. It's not important, but there is enough of me still here that I am able punch her name on the speed dial.

She answers.

"I'm sorry for this. I am now Death."
I drop the phone and move to my kill.

A PERFECT LIFE

◆ ◆ ◆

"Has Joanne lost her pregnancy weight?" Charlie asks. I am a little distracted, wiping rain from my face and neck. It's pouring down outside, wind, thunder, lightning, the whole works, what I imagine a hurricane would be like just outside the eye. The umbrella wasn't much use in my mad dash to the front door of the restaurant. It bent back on itself in the wind and now lay broken beneath my chair. I wipe my hands on a napkin, and then I use it to mop my wet hair. I glance at Charlie. He's dry. He apparently arrived before the storm began blowing its fury. From the line of bottles, I can see he's on his fourth Stella Artois and is ready to order his fifth.

"That's one hell of a question." It's been three years since I last saw him, and he hasn't met my little girl, Erin. She is two and a half years old and is the sweetest little child I know. "I've barely sat down, and you're asking whether my wife is skinny again. I knew you had the hots for Jo. I'll tell you, she looks as good today as she did the day I met her."

Charlie smiles. He has those boyish good looks that women cream in their pants for. His smile will do it every time. "I just wanted to know if she's gotten fat like my divorce clients," he says. "Well, most of my divorce clients."

"She breastfed Erin," I say. "It's the equivalent of running three miles every day, or so she claimed. Whatever it was, the weight evaporated over three months. Like magic."

"Magic?"

"Her words, not mine."

Charlie laughs. "Since it's been alleged I have the hots for your wife, and I do, by the way, I guess I should inquire further into the breast feeding. Did she exhibit her breasts in public places? Did that make you nervous?"

I am saved from this line of questioning when the waitress appears at our table and asks what I want to drink. I order a sweetened iced tea, and Charlie asks for another Stella. The restaurant is basically empty, as if a sane person would be out in this weather.

"Have you ever noticed it's always raining when you come to town?" I ask. He shrugs. He's not interested in talking about the weather, so I ask, "How's the law practice?"

"It's wearing thin," he says. His practice is in Savannah, but he claims to be semi-retired. It doesn't have anything to do with his law practice. Since he received a huge inheritance when his dad died at age forty-nine, he dabbles in the law, but nothing more. "Hell, I don't practice law anymore," he explains. "My secretary does. She runs the office, keeps the clients happy. She holds their hand, tells them everything's going to be alright, and sends them a bill for doing it. All I do is show up in court, and sign documents every once and in a while. Oh, and I meet with my young, pretty divorce clients."

"Isn't there a lawyer ethics rule about that?" I ask.

"What? Meeting with divorce clients?"

"You know what I mean, Charlie," I say. "You told me the last time you were here—and let me get your wording exactly right—let's see—'There's nothing like divorce pussy.' That's what you said. Word for word."

Charlie leans forward and whispers, "I never sleep with clients, if that's what you're getting at. I would never be so fucking stupid. When the divorce is final, she is no longer a client. Please remember that. I don't like your insinuation."

"I didn't mean to impugn your ethics."

"Well, you did impugn my ethics." It is stated with mock

indignation.

"Sorry about that." The sarcasm rolls off my tongue.

"Well, you should be," he says. "Of course, when it comes to sex, I have absolutely no ethics. But you know that already, don't you?"

The waitress arrives with the drinks, and I order a bacon cheeseburger and onion rings. Charlie orders a salad with low-calorie ranch dressing. I raise my eyebrows, and he explains the doctor has demanded he reduce his cholesterol intake.

"High blood pressure," he says. "I inherited that from my dad, along with his money. As if I need another thing to worry about in life."

"Jo's got me walking an hour four times a week now, with sit-ups and pushups on the other three days. She says I eat too many potato chips, french fries, and hamburgers. She only asks me to balance with exercise."

"I don't get that luxury. I get to exercise and eat rabbit food," he says, and then adds as an afterthought, "Whatever you're doing is working. You look great. You haven't changed, not since college."

A few minutes pass in comfortable silence, and I think about the beautiful girl Charlie dated during his sophomore and junior years. I can't remember her name—Teri? Tracy? I don't know. He discovered her in bed with one of his fraternity brothers, and it killed him. Charlie went insane, like she was all that mattered in the world. He beat the shit out of the little fucker he'd previously called a brother, putting him in the hospital with a broken jaw, concussion, and a groin strain, which made Charlie most proud. I bailed Charlie out of jail the next afternoon and took him out. I got him laid by one of my sister's friends, hoping he'd just get over it. He never did, and that's what I am thinking this night. Charlie still hasn't recovered from being jilted, and he is lonely and angry. He gets laid—probably all the time—but it only seems to make him lonelier and angrier. Would it be different if Tonya—yeah, that was her name—if she hadn't fucked him over in college? Would he be married now, kids, playhouse in the backyard, and a normal professional life?

Charlie catches my eye, and it seems as though he wants to ask what I am thinking about, but he's afraid I'll answer the question. Instead, he asks, "How's school?"

I make a non-committal face. "It's okay, I guess." I teach American history at UK. It's lost its appeal for me, regrettably, but I don't want to explain this to him. If I told him my life's work has come undone, he would surely ask why, and as strange as it sounds, I couldn't answer him. The question has plagued me. The answer is on the edge of my mind, but it's as if I can't see the light for the darkness.

"Get any co-ed pussy?" He asks this every time he comes to town even though he knows I am happily married. He also knows if I were screwing a student, I wouldn't tell him or anybody.

"Only my wife." I offer a weak smile.

"That's pretty boring. She's not a co-ed these days."

I shrug. "I'm not the most exciting guy, nor do I want to be. I had my excitement during college." He knows I'm referring to the accident and eyes me for a second. He decides to ignore it. I'm not sure why I mentioned it. Why would I annoy him like that when I know it will only make him sulky?

A longer bout of silence comes between us. I study his face. The years are catching up to him. His eyes have the beginning of lines, resembling a road map, and his hair has strands of gray in it. He looks tired, as though there aren't enough hours in the day.

I wonder if I am showing my age, and I can't remember looking in a mirror recently. What do I look like now? I try to imagine it, and all I see is a pale reflection with few details.

"You look troubled," Charlie says.

"Uh-huh," I say ambiguously.

Worry settles over Charlie's face. "What's going on? Can you talk about it?"

"In a bit," I say. He nods.

He can't stand not knowing. "Is it work? Joanne?"

"It's everything, and it's nothing," I say. "I can't talk about it, yet."

This time he nods emphatically. "Oh yeah. Of course." He takes a drink from his beer. "So, tell me about Erin. What's she like?"

"She likes music," I answer. "She likes the kid music, but she's interested in what I listen to. She likes U2 and R.E.M. *End of the World as We Know It.* The Rolling Stones. Elvis Presley. Oh, and the Beatles. She has good taste."

Charlie is smiling. He's happy for me. "That's great."

"She has the most beautiful laugh and smile," I say. "She's all that matters in the world to me. And Joanne. We have a nice little family unit. The three of us. It's the best time of my life, really." I rub my forehead and scratch my head. I want to tell him he needs a family, but instead I say, "I wish you could spend time with them. You would really like Erin. She's the best kid. It's corny for me to say it, but my life didn't really begin until I met Joanne. It's all been like a fairy tale for me."

Charlie sees an opening. "What's wrong then?"

I shake my head. Before I repeat that I don't want to talk about it, our food arrives. The waitress smiles at me as she puts the plates on the table. Charlie is not interested in his salad. I look to the television above the restaurant bar and begin eating my burger. The Reds are getting beat by Atlanta, nine to two. "Cincy can't catch a break. I'm telling you, man, they are worse now than when we were in college. Do you remember the Reds game when I spilled beer on the guy in front of us?"

"And his little boy," he corrects and barks a harsh laugh. "That guy wanted to kick your drunk ass. He would have thrown you onto the infield if I hadn't been there." Charlie has always been intimidating, not that he was all that big, but he had the attitude. The guy in front of us looked like an accountant. He and his son left and didn't return. I felt bad for them.

"It wasn't because I was drunk that I fell, you know," I say. "The prick next to you tripped me. I couldn't get by."

"That didn't matter. The kid's father didn't know it. He was huffing and puffing, red-faced, ready to turn into the Hulk."

"And you were my savior," I say. I take another bite from my burger, and Charlie begins showing interest in his salad. The silence spreads around us again, and I can hear the announcers talk about the Reds' dismal chances of making a run for the playoffs. They are thirteen and a half games down now. It's unlikely they'll play postseason unless miracles happen. St. Louis always seems to lead the division. I notice Charlie's interest is now invested in the waitress across the room. If he keeps it up, he'll get laid when her shift is over. She's a redhead with screw-me-please eyes and a body curving in all the right places.

I bite into a french fry and think I wouldn't want Charlie's draw—the burden of being beautiful—which only seems to reap loneliness for him. He can satisfy the mechanical urges, but not the emotional ones. I can go through life practically unnoticed, and that's really a good thing for me. A thought that has been a mantra lately runs through my mind: *I don't want to change. I don't want to change. I don't want to change.* I wonder if I'm lying to myself. Shouldn't the mantra be I can't change? Isn't that part of the problem? That I can't seem to get outside of my skin. I don't have control.

I finish chewing the french fry and take a drink of my tea. "My life seems too good to be true," I finally say. "Everything falls into place like clockwork. Like puzzle pieces. It's really a wonder. I am truly blessed."

"You're happy." Charlie says it in a way I can't tell if it is a statement or a question.

I push my plate away. "I'm the happiest person in the world, Charlie. Every part of my life is exquisite. It's perfect. It's what I dreamed it would be when we were in college, and even better. But..." My voice trails off. It's difficult for me to continue.

"But what?"

I take a deep breath. "It's too perfect." Even as I say it, I realize it's nonsensical. How can I complain about a life that's too perfect?

Charlie echoes my thought: "Too perfect? What the fuck does that mean?"

I think about it, before shaking my head. I can't explain it to him like this, so I decide to take another tack. I rub my chin. "Charlie, do you ever think about that night?"

"What night?"

"You know, the night of the accident."

"Never." It's a lie. He knows it. Even worse, he knows I know it. But he won't give it up.

"I do," I say. "It never leaves my mind." He stares at me blankly. It's going to make him angry. I consider letting it go, but I can't. I have a point to make, and I can't make the point without that night. "It haunts me," I say. "I have nightmares often. It's fierce."

"I'm sure it is," Charlie whispers.

"All I know changed that day."

"Get on with it. What's your point?" He's pissed off, and ready to leave, even though it's still pouring down outside.

"I'm not bringing this up to irritate you." He doesn't respond. I feel compelled to hurry on with an explanation, but I force myself to think it through first. I close my eyes, remembering that night—not just the road rushing toward us—but earlier in the evening. I remember I had decided to curb the late nights drinking. I had resolved to stop two other times that summer, and yet the habitual drunkenness persisted. We were in the middle of summer after graduation, but the fact Charlie and I had graduated didn't mean much to either of us. I was returning to school in the fall to get my master's in history, and he was going to law school. So, my summer was wasted getting an education in pre-alcoholism with a minor in chasing skirts. I met Jo during this wildness—she was one of the skirts, I guess, but she was different, and I knew it. She was the one. She was in the process of saving me from the madness, even though she didn't know it. I was headed toward the deep end, and she was my only tie to sanity. That summer she began her nursing career, working nights at UK's hospital. We spent afternoons taking long walks across campus, talking about how to make the world a better place. She didn't know the trouble I was in, and if she did, she would have been long gone. Charlie knew of course, but he was in no position to tell me I was going too far. I never caught the other skirts, but not for a lack of trying—it was only because the other skirts were unattainable to me—thank God. I could never have forgiven myself if I had lost Joanne, even though it was only a budding relationship.

I found perfection in my daily drunken stupor. I had moved on from beer—a college drink—to martinis and Manhattans, which seemed to be more sophisticated and refined. It provided a more sustainable high and didn't require the frequency of urination that accompanied beer. I was full of shit, and I didn't realize it. I didn't see my immaturity. I thought I was being cool, one of the in-crowd. But I would never be part of them. I would never be refined or sophisticated, and a drink wouldn't make me refined or sophisticated. I was only a fool, an absolute ass, and I have been apologizing for it ever since. The difference between Charlie and me was Charlie's goddamned smile gave him a free pass into the in-crowd. He was cool. He let me tag along, and I walked the line right behind him, wherever he led me. I had always been comfortable in my skin—I liked me—but that summer I wanted to be someone else, anyone else—except when I was with Joanne.

The constancy of drunkenness had become the norm for Charlie. He would deny it, but I am confident his jilting a year and a half earlier had altered his mental makeup. He was a match on fire, burning himself up, and either not cognizant of it or just not caring. He survived everything he put himself through, all the women, the drunkenness, the fights, the malnutrition, the injuries, as though he were immortal. He was never arrested, although he drove home drunk most nights and started fights at the barest of words. It wasn't that he was testing fate. It just wasn't important to him. Until that summer, I had always been his stop. I was the one looking out for him. How many times did I say, *stop Charlie, you're going too far?* I was the only one who could reel him back in. Then, when the summer began, he drew me further into his murky world, and I lamented over it. Woe is me, I thought, I've got to get a grip on this. I could feel my spiral into the depths and had to grab a handhold while I still could. That night, I held the final straw: I had spent the afternoon with Joanne in my apartment making first love, wild wonderful, passionate, fumbling love, and I decided I wanted to do nothing to risk this relationship. When Charlie came over, I told him I didn't want to go out. I even explained the extent of my desire for recovery and the reasons for it. He didn't laugh. He didn't tell me I was being a fool for love. He slapped me on my back and told me that was great, just great. He said we needed to celebrate. One last hurrah! One more bout of insobriety! I nodded. *Yeah. Sure. Whatever you say.*

So, after steaks and beer at Shooter's, we went to 803's, our usual hangout. I started off slow, but my glass was always filled with beer, and unordered shots were put in front of me. I drank. And I drank. And I drank. I kept telling myself this is it. This is my last hurrah. No more after this one. I welcomed the spinning that came toward the end of the night. It would not have been a last hurrah without it. What a way to end my sixty-day drunken stupor. A big one to go out on.

I didn't object when Charlie wanted to take a drive out of the city. Sure. Why not? What the hell. But first, he wanted to finish the last two inches of beer in the pitcher. He wouldn't waste it, so he downed it, and we left. He started his Mazda RX7 with a roar, and guided it into the country, where the roads dangerously followed the contours of the land. The roads were especially curvy that night, but it may have been a product of my drunkenness. We had the roads to ourselves, and Charlie gunned it. We floated around the bends, seventy-five, eighty miles an hour, and the road rushed toward us, black pavement, no lines. Rush's *Moving Pictures* resonated in the air.

There was one straight stretch that lasted a half-mile or more, and at the end of it, there was only the slightest of curves, maybe fifteen degrees, which was followed by another straight stretch of a quarter mile. We'd driven this road before and attained the fastest of speeds. The curve had always gripped the tires and pulled us in and then out. But this night, Charlie managed a speed even greater than before. I started to fear the curve, as slight as it was, and a sudden, clear, precise thought pierced my drunken mind: He can't make it at this speed. Seat. Belt. On. Now.

I've never asked whether it was God. It didn't seem important to me then, and still doesn't seem especially relevant. It was one clear thought on a drunken night, and I reacted to it. I reached for my seat belt, pulled it down and across me, and snapped it into place.

I felt the car enter the curve, but it didn't come out. The RX7 ripped through fence posts and three strands of barbed wire and landed in a cornfield. My body crashed forward with such horrific force when the seat belt caught, my glasses were ripped off my face. I pitched back into the seat hard enough to crack a rib. But I was alive and nearly unbroken. I could have been dead. When going through the fence, the sound had been like a hammer hitting a nail followed by the roar of wind. Then deafening silence. All I heard was Charlie wailing, and in that noise, he kept asking are you okay? Are you okay, man? The words all blended together in the wail, and it took minutes to understand it was me he was worried about. I didn't answer. For a long time, I just sat there, not thinking about anything. Finally, I told him I was fine, just fine. I felt for him in the darkness and found him. He was in his seat belt, too. He was okay.

"Do you want to know what I think happened that night?" I ask Charlie now. He shrugs. It's the last thing in the world he wants to hear. He would rather talk about the Reds and their abysmal season. "I think I died that night. I haven't let go—no, no. You haven't let go, and I am haunting you because that's what ghosts do." I hear a note of uncertainty in my voice, but as the words settle in my mind, I become convinced. "I didn't put on my seat belt. I was too drunk. I didn't react. Jesus Christ. I died that night. I know I did."

Charlie is non-responsive; his face is impassive. He doesn't ask what the fuck I'm talking about. He doesn't tell me I'm crazy.

"I should have known," I say. "My life is perfect. My wife, my little girl, it's all so wonderful. Nothing bad ever happens. I teach the same students every year, and they look a lot like the people we had classes with. My colleagues are the same ones who taught me when I was taking classes. No wonder I've been bored with it. I don't have any new friends, no one new in my life. There are parts of my life that don't happen, as if they are assumed—or unimagined—and that's always been okay to me, because there is nothing bad in my life. It's as if you are imagining what my life would be like if I had survived that night. You let me live a perfect life. The most perfect life."

I stop talking. I want him to deny it. I want to go home to Joanne and Erin and let life go on, same as it ever was. I can see in his eyes that this is the first step in a long road of recovery for him. Charlie wants the haunting to end. I see he is miserable.

"You've led me to believe all my life is real," I say. "You've been playacting all of these years. What for? To allay your guilt?"

Charlie shrugs. "It does," he says.

"And Joanne?" I ask. "She must have a life somewhere else. She must have gotten over me. What happened to her when I died?"

"She's works in the maternity ward at Central Baptist," Charlie says. "I see her every couple of years, and we talk about you. You're wrong. She's never gotten over you. She's married to an accountant and she has a daughter—"

"Named Erin?"

Charlie nods.

This hurts, as though Joanne has cheated on me.

"She was going to marry you, you know, and she's still mad at me for taking you from her. A wasted life, she calls it. For years, she wouldn't talk to me, and then only begrudgingly. She's mostly forgiven me."

"Did you forgive yourself?"

Charlie sighs and shuts his eyes for a second. This is answer enough.

"What happened that night?" I ask.

He doesn't want to talk about it, but he does. "You were broken. They tried to fix you, but all the king's horses, you know. You went through the windshield and landed in the field. I couldn't find you until some farmer stopped and shined a spotlight. You made no noise."

All the air is out of my lungs. I'm not sure what to say. "Were you hurt?"

He nods. "Bruised. Sore is all. I'm so sorry. I shouldn't have been driving that night—"

I wave this off. "What's it matter to me?" I close my eyes and wonder when it will all end, and whether it will be painful to me. It's got to end now that I know my life is not real. I open my eyes and see not all is lost yet. There is some part of Charlie doesn't want to give me up.

"Why haven't you moved on?" I ask.

He laughs nervously. "You don't get it, do you?" He leans across the table, as though proximity will help him make his point. "I don't have a choice to move on. You haunt me, not the other way around. You said you believe I'm imagining your life, but that's not it at all. You're imagining my life. When you haunt me, I forget you died, and I remember only this life you've dreamed up for the both of us. I do my little part in the playacting. When you're around, I don't remember my other life, my real life—the life where you are dead. When you go off again, wherever the hell it is you go, I wake up and wonder if I'm fucking crazy. I have tried psychiatrists, and a whole host of tiny colored pills to numb me. After all, it's got to be in my mind, right? The doctors all agree I'm burdened with the guilt of your death, so it must be depression, but it's not like that. When I wake up, after one of your visits, it's like a fugue I've been through, not a dream. The funny thing is, until tonight—until you realized you died in the accident—I thought you were a figment of my imagination, but you're as real as I am. I hope you will let go. I miss you, oh God, I miss you, but I've got a life to live. *Please.* Can you do that for me?"

These words run through me like a cold wind. "Why didn't you tell me this before?"

"I don't remember anything when I see you. Until tonight, when you told me you thought you died, my real life had left from my mind."

"Do you practice law in Savannah?"

He shakes his head. "I work for legal aid here," he says. "My life isn't what you imagined. I'm married with two kids, Marianne and Grace, and I don't sleep around. Not since then. I do criminal law because I saw it up close after the accident. It's a wonder the bar association let me take the exam. I went to jail and worked my way through the maze to get where I am now. My life's been hell. It's nothing like your haunting."

"And I've been interfering?"

He nods. "Not often. Once, maybe twice a year, and only for a few hours. They say it's like I'm in an opened-eyed sleep. They can't wake me from it. When I do wake, I remember everything."

I wonder if I will feel death coming on. I feel nothing really, only an increasing knowledge of loneliness, and this is causing a heavy heart. "I didn't know," I say. "I never meant—"

"You only want to live," Charlie says. "I understand that and forgive you. I love you, and I wish you hadn't died. But I'm tired. I want it to end."

Charlie straightens his spine, like he's about to push his chair back. I understand he's leaving. This terrifies me. "Charlie, I don't know what I'm supposed to do now."

"Well, I've got to leave. My wife and kids are waiting for

me."

"Don't go yet," I plead.

"It's getting late."

"I don't know what will happen now."

"You'll either move on, or you'll continue to haunt me."

"I'm scared."

"Don't be," Charlie says. "Just let go. Be at peace."

I consider this, but it doesn't make me any less scared. Still, I nod. "Yeah, okay. If I can."

He stands and reaches for his wallet.

"No, no, it's on me," I say. He nods, smiles, uncomfortable at first, but then it settles into a loving smile, and he reaches across the table to touch me on the shoulder. It is only for a second, but it's long enough to know he doesn't hate me.

"Goodbye," he says. He turns and leaves.

Now, alone, I wonder if it is of any use for me to go home. Will my wife and child be waiting for me, or will this made-up world collapse around me? The thought of it scares me. The more terrifying thought is what if Joanne and Erin are there? Can I continue this fantasy? Will I forget it's a fiction?

I sit in the restaurant and reach for Charlie's last half-empty bottle of beer to comfort me in my loneliness.

THE DAY AFTER
THE FUNERAL

◆ ◆ ◆

T he day after the funeral Rhoda woke and all was different. It wasn't just that Roy, her husband of forty-five years, wasn't in bed, although that was part of it, of course. It was also that she felt free. She was no longer bound by any ties to anyone or anything.

She rolled over and stared at the parallel lines of sunlight shining through the slats of the blinds and wondered if Roy was in a better place. Did he feel free as well? Their marriage hadn't been horrible, and in some respects, it had been great, or at least she thought so at the time. As with all marriages, there'd been rough patches. The worst was when Roy bought the Mustang, drove it home as proud as a banty rooster, and Rhoda told him he had to return it. That it was a toy they couldn't afford. It was one of the rare times she put her foot down, but she was adamant. The used car dealer, a friend, begrudgingly accepted the Mustang back, ripped up the loan documents, and returned Roy's beat-up Oldsmobile. Roy didn't speak to Rhoda for two weeks. In the morning, he'd sit at the table, eat his breakfast and go to work. For supper, he'd take his plate in the den and watch television while eating. Rhoda bided her time. One night, she sat at the dinner table and ate her grilled cheese. When Roy came into the kitchen, saw her eating, and realized there was no plate for him, he finally broke his silence. "Where's my grilled cheese?" He wasn't angry, just curious.

Rhoda looked up at Roy and smiled. "I decided if you weren't talking to me, then I didn't have to fix your meals anymore. You're a grown up. You can fix your own supper."

Roy blinked at her twice, shrugged, and picked up the keys to his Oldsmobile. He left without a word. She figured he was back to not talking to her, but an hour later, he returned and muted Alex Trebek. He plopped down on the couch next to her. She wouldn't look at him, and he waited.

She finally gave in and glanced his way. "What?" she asked. She was irritable not just because of Roy's silence, but because she'd been doing well on the Jeopardy questions. The category was American Rivers, which turned out wasn't water ways, but Americans with the name of Rivers or River, like River Phoenix or Joan Rivers

He took a breath, and another, before sharing what was on his mind. "I'm sorry I've been an ass. I've been selfish and foolish. I want to make it up to you. Can we go back to being us?"

This is what Rhoda wanted to hear. She cried with relief that the fight was over, and they could go back to being normal. She hugged him, and they ended in a breathless physical entanglement in the bedroom.

As Rhoda lay in bed staring at the shadows the blinds made on the hardwood, she thought of her biggest regret from the marriage. She should have given in to Roy and adopted a child. Early on, they tried desperately to have children. When none arrived, Rhoda's gynecologist said her body had defects. God had left her mercilessly broken. That's the way the gynecologist had put it. She cried for weeks. Roy tried to make things better by telling her they could always adopt. She wanted to acquiesce, if only to get rid of the ache in her heart. She couldn't bring herself to believe she could ever love a child who didn't come from her body. God broke her there, too. Now, with the comforter pulled up to her neck, she thought she could have loved any child. She'd been young and foolish, and it made her feel lonely. Still, this regret didn't cause her to feel any less free. There were no boundaries.

Her life had always been monotony. Tedium. Same shit, different day. For thirty-five years she worked at the same desk, although she worked for different attorneys, and had different cases. At some point, it all began to run together. As the law firm changed, she stayed the same, always the same dependable Rhoda who seldom missed work. Whether she was searching a title at the courthouse, preparing wills, or filing messy divorce papers, it was all busy work. She liked all four of the attorneys she worked for during her thirty-five years, but she loved none of them. When she was passed on to the next, she was glad for that small bit of change, not that it lasted. By the time she retired, two of the four attorneys had died, another had simply vanished after a bar association inquiry, and the fourth offered to pay her more money to stay. She couldn't bring herself to do it. She needed to break the monotony. She stayed on an extra month to train her replacement, as if thirty-five years could be trained.

For forty-two years of their marriage, Roy worked as a maintenance man at the municipal water and sewer company, even though he could have retired after twenty-seven years. Rhoda thought he liked being at work more than home. He told her about his day when they ate supper, all the gossip. She listened with mock enthusiasm. She never told him about her work. Even if it all hadn't been confidential, he wouldn't have been interested. By the time Rhoda arrived home in the evening, he'd showered and was watching the news, which lately had been Fox News, or the Doom and Gloom Network as Rhoda called it. First thing, Rhoda brought him his first beer of the night, and even opened it for him. He drank it in his recliner chair. He'd joked early in their marriage that one thing he expected was for his wife to bring him an evening beer. Rhoda retorted that one thing she expected her husband to do was to bring her to orgasm occasionally. She continued bringing him the beer, but the orgasms had become less often.

No more beer now. No more orgasms. She was free.

Rhoda hadn't slept this late in forty-five years of marriage and felt a bit guilty for it. She no longer had to get up to fix Roy scrambled eggs, bacon, and toast. There would be no more bagged lunches with cold cut sandwiches, chips, and a banana or an apple. She was done with it all.

The weekends were no less predictable. Rhoda worked Saturday mornings, to make sure her attorney was prepared for the next week. She went to church on Sunday mornings. The only change in church was a different minister every two or three of years, the one flaw of being Methodist in a small town. She visited her parents every Sunday afternoon until they both died, and then her sister, Hazel, after that. Roy seldom joined her, only when he wasn't fishing, hunting, golfing, bowling, or doing work around the house. Saturday afternoons she went to the grocery and did what little shopping there was. These were the things expected of her.

It wasn't a loveless marriage, by any means, but there was no passion. She lost the ability to daydream once she became fixed in her routine. She realized early on there would be no relief from the absolute dullness of life, and she endured it. On those occasions, when she wondered if life could be different or if she had a craving for it to be different, she pushed it to the back of her mind. She knew letting her thoughts wander like that would only breed unhappiness. She wasn't unhappy. Just unsatisfied. She accepted it. There was nothing she could do to change it, even if she wanted to. She loved Roy. He was good to her. He bought her thoughtful presents on her birthday, Valentine's Day, and Christmas. He never beat her, and rarely raised his voice to her. He was polite, in his own selfish way. To her knowledge, he never cheated on her, and she would have been surprised if he had. He wasn't the type who wanted something else. He *was* satisfied with what he had.

The morning was growing older, and she finally decided it was time she got up. She stood and stretched, put on her robe. She wasn't cold, but wanted to be discreet, not that anyone would see her through the windows, or would want to see her. She'd never cheated on Roy either, not that she hadn't considered it or had the opportunity. Their neighbor from two doors down, Jasper Hancock, told her at a neighborhood cookout that he wanted to come by when Roy was working. He was divorced and worked out, but she played dumb and told him she didn't play cards anymore and moved away from him. He'd been drinking, so she forgave him, but didn't forget. And Toby Williams, her second attorney, who was twenty years her senior, liked to play touchy-feely and more than once grabbed her rear end. Had Rhoda complained she would have been fired, so she kept quiet and pretended it didn't happen. She blocked his advances as best she could and always kept a smile on her face. She had to be dependable Rhoda, of course.

She never told Roy about these sexual advances, but even today as she bypassed the bathroom and went straight for the kitchen, she wondered what would he have done? Would he have knocked Jasper to the ground at the cookout? Would he have insisted she quit her job? Rhoda didn't think so. This was a man who couldn't even clean up after himself. She came into the kitchen and saw Roy had cereal for breakfast this morning, and he'd left his bowl with the dregs of milk on the countertop. He couldn't bring himself to dump the dregs and put the bowl in the dishwasher. Was it laziness or did he just not care? Rhoda didn't give the mess another thought. Her worry was whether he had fixed himself a bagged lunch for work. He couldn't make it through the day without eating, and he hated fast food.

Rhoda went into the den and counted twelve beer bottles, three of them on their side. By his tenth, he'd probably been so drunk he couldn't focus on setting the bottles gently on the coffee table. He always drank when he was depressed. When his brother was shot at his work, American Technicon, ten years earlier, Roy replaced the beer for bourbon and stayed drunk for a week. He only returned to work when he ran out of vacation days. Rhoda wanted to pick up the beer bottles, but she let them be. She had to let them be.

Seeing the flowers in the foyer brought her first tear. Had Roy brought them home, or had the funeral home delivered them? Why had Roy left them in the foyer? Would he remember to water them? They'd just rot or dry out.

Rhoda's hope was he might find a good woman to clean up after him and fix his breakfast. Someone who would make him a bagged lunch and bring him his first beer each evening. She wiped away the tears with the edges of her robe, and yet they still came. Roy needed a wife. He'd be lost without a good wife.

So, this is what it was going to be like, Rhoda thought. She'd wander all day watching the condition of the house deteriorate. She'd always wondered. It wasn't much different than retirement had been, except she couldn't clean up after Roy or fix his meals. It wasn't the heaven she'd hoped for.

IN HIS FINAL BREATH

◆ ◆ ◆

Chuck Anderson was watching the Reds get their asses handed to them by the Braves when he abruptly felt like a thousand pounds weighed down his chest. His diaphragm wouldn't lift to allow air to flow in. The thought he might be dying didn't enter his mind until he heard the desperation in his voice as he called for his wife, Mildred. It was a whimper.

"Mildred?" He doubted she heard, especially if she was still at the sink cleaning up from supper.

When he looked over his shoulder, he saw her standing in the kitchen doorway, a curious look on her face. "Come here," he wheezed.

She hesitated, as if he were the big, bad wolf.

What big teeth you have, Chuck!

Better to eat you with, Mildred.

"Call 911. Having a heart attack."

She didn't look worried. She looked angry. "Don't waste your final breaths, Chuck," she said.

"*Please,*" he gasped.

It wasn't the first time Chuck had seen murder in Mildred's hazel eyes, but tonight she looked at him like she was watching a snuff film. He tried to reach for his phone on the coffee table, but she put the palm of her left hand on his chest and held him there. He struggled but was too weak to fight her.

"What'd you do?" he asked.

She smiled, satisfied he was figuring it out on his own, as if it were important to her he knew.

He should have been dead years before now, but always came out unscathed, except for scratches and bruises. How many times had he gone to bars and not remembered how he'd gotten home? How many fisticuffs had he been in and lost? How many car wrecks had he walked away from?

He claimed the luck of the gods gilded his soul.

He said it last November when Rufus Rickman shot up American Technicon's product line. Chuck drank too much during the Bengals' fiasco the night before and lay passed out on the couch. He woke enough to tell Mildred to call in for him—*call it a stomach bug*, he'd said. As Chuck slept it off, Rufus carried a handgun into the factory at the start of the shift and shot and killed three people at Chuck's workstation. Then he stuck the pistol into his own mouth and put an end to what Chuck called a miserable fucking life. *Good Riddance*, he'd thought at the time. He'd known Rufus was gunning for him because he'd consoled Angie Rickman during the breakup of her and Rufus's marriage. It was dumb luck he hadn't been at the factory that morning. He marveled at the fact he had avoided the violence. He felt like Superman.

The fact Mildred was unhappy in their marriage hadn't concerned Chuck. If she didn't want to be part of it, she should have divorced him, but she couldn't survive without him. She'd never worked. She'd never contributed to the family unit in a significant way. She drove the brats to school and picked them up. She cooked frozen dinners during the week and a big meal on Sunday. What was she supposed to do if he died? Her family had disowned her when she married Chuck. Her friends were non-existent, except for the mommy-friends who spent all day discussing how to lose weight. She hated them. She had no one —no one but him and the kids. Chuck had isolated her.

"Oh, for God's sake, Chuck," Mildred hissed, standing over him. "Stop wasting your final breaths. Let go. Go toward the light. You're almost there. You see it now, don't you?"

Chuck saw, but he fought it. He struggled to breathe. Most of all, he refused to believe his mousy fucking wife would have the guts to talk to him like that. He wanted to strangle the life out of her, but he was helpless. He could only stare into her eyes with all the hate he could muster, still not equivalent to the hate Mildred had for him. She would lose everything if he died. The trailer. The cars. Maybe the kids if anyone suspected she'd poisoned him. Why would she do this? How could she benefit with him being dead?

She must have seen the question in his eyes. "Rufus had a life insurance policy, you big galoot," she whispered, almost lovingly. "Through work. I heard your girlfriend, Angie, talking about it at the funeral. Imagine, fifty thousand bucks. Every employee has it, even you."

Chuck didn't respond. He couldn't have, not now, but he registered what she said. He shut his eyes to block her out.

"That you weren't at work when Rufus shot the place up was a missed opportunity," she continued, "but it got me thinking. You're worth more to me dead than alive, but how to do it? I read about some former child-actor who'd OD'd on beta blockers, and you already had a prescription, for your nerves. You got it after Rufus's rampage, but never took the pills when you found out they wouldn't make you high. Did you know twenty crushed beta blockers will dissolve in a beer? You didn't taste it, did you?"

Chuck couldn't focus on the words well enough to make out exactly what she was saying.

"Tonight, Junior's at a Boy Scout camp, and I sent Sallie over to Judy's for a sleepover. I made you your favorite: Meatloaf, green beans, mashed potatoes, and gravy, just the way your momma made it. I wasn't going to do it. I'd talked myself out of it, until you walked through the door, smelling of Angie Rickman's pussy. What do you do? Walk into her house after your shift, wham bam, thank you, ma'am, and leave without washing her skanky juices off you? Just so you can get home in time for supper? I thought, either you're stupid, Mildred, or you're okay with him fucking that twat? So, I put the powdered beta-blockers in your beer, and you didn't notice a thing, did you? The Old Milwaukee tasted fine tonight." She paused long enough to lean down and put her face right next to his. "What I really want to know is this: What do you think of Angie's pussy now? Satisfied? Got what you needed?"

She asked too many questions he couldn't answer, even if he had the breath to do so. If she spoke any more, he didn't hear her. The pain in his chest took all his attention. Maybe Mildred would have said it was selfish of him to focus only on his pain now. It didn't matter.

He was dying, and in his final breath, Chuck saw the void that was Hell. He fought for another breath, but it wasn't there. With each heartbeat, the trailer paled, and the nothingness surged.

When there were no more heartbeats, his soul was free of his body, and Chuck felt the emptiness of the void as it consumed him. He was almost no more, or just a part of the constant churning abyss, when a different force snatched him out of damnation.

He was given another chance, an undeserved one, perhaps.

He woke, but remembered nothing. He screamed like a banshee, until he was placed in his mother's arms to suck.

CONTEMPLATION
& CURIOSITY

◆ ◆ ◆

There is a box on my desk. It is wooden, the size of a shoebox, and burned into the wood is one word. Pandora. I don't know if I should open it.

It's Christmas Day, and no one else is here. I'm not supposed to be here at the office, not on a holiday, but I wanted an hour alone. I needed to be away from my family and my wife's family. My daughter's new boyfriend, too. I do not like him. He has a nose ring and a small star tattoo below his left eye. He says he celebrates Christmas as a pagan holiday. He's the guitarist in a Nirvana tribute band, which is better than saying unemployed.

My excuse to get away was I'd gotten an e-mail from a client and had to have the file in front of me while I talk him off the ledge. I'm an accountant, and there are always end of year tax emergencies. It wasn't odd any time in the year for me to drop everything to come to the office. More often than not, there is a client who has a question. My office went paperless two years ago, and it's never necessary for me to leave home. My entire office is at my fingertips from my home computer. If I didn't have to meet with clients, I would never leave the house, but my wife and daughter don't know that. I'm not planning on telling them.

When I go to the office on unplanned visits, it's usually to contemplate. I'm a contemplator. I think. When I'm irritated about something, I need to be alone. I can't be in a house full of people. Or in a house with one person, especially if that one person is part of what's bugging me. During business hours, I shut my office door, and put my phone on *do not disturb*. My staff knows to not bother me unless the office is on fire or there is a policeman with a subpoena, not that I expect either, since my office is now paperless. There's nothing to burn, and there's nothing for policemen to obtain with a search warrant. All my data is stored offshore and cannot be retrieved with a warrant. My clients don't always report their cash income, and it's understood I will protect their interest.

I have a bottle of Woodford Reserve in my locked desk drawer to help me contemplate. I am not an alcoholic. Except for a glass of wine or two on the weekends, I don't drink at home, and that's because I never contemplate at home. I have to sit at my office desk to let the free flow of thoughts happen. The bourbon opens the pipeline of the thinking process. I need one shot, sometimes two, to get the thoughts moving, and then I can solve any problem. When I contemplate, I'm on the level of Einstein. This is true. The world lights up for me, and I see everything.

When I took the IQ test as a kid, I remember thinking it was too easy, but it was only easy to me. Maybe that's when I realized I was different. I could have done whatever I wanted in life. But I liked numbers. I liked that numbers can lie when you want them to lie, and those numbers can tell you whatever truth you need.

My daughter didn't get my brains. Not that my wife isn't smart, but she doesn't have the mental faculties I do. Anne's a high school English teacher, and I love her more than I love life itself, but sometimes I have to slow down to her speed just to have a conversation with her. It's like slow motion, and even then, I repeat what I've already explained to her a thousand times so she can understand it. Anne's close to retirement. In Kentucky, teachers retire after 27 years, with full benefits, beginning immediately, and then she can work at a private school and have double income. You've got to love those numbers. Anne has talked about taking it easy, but I told her if we want to live comfortably when we retire, we've got to earn every penny we can now while we're in our fifties.

I almost have her convinced, although she doesn't know I will never retire. I can't imagine what retirement would be like. What would I do with all the free time? What would I contemplate?

Tonight, I planned to contemplate my daughter, Julie. I love her, too, and I want the best for her. But she's settling in life. She could have been a doctor, but she became a nurse, and not even a nurse that makes decent money. She works the night shift at the nursing home. She sits at a desk all evening while the aids go around and change diapers. She responds to emergencies, but otherwise she makes notes in the computer. Any monkey could do her job.

She doesn't contemplate. She reacts, and that's no way to live, is it? Like her mother, Julie is emotional, and emotions get in the way of contemplation. It's not that I don't have emotions, but I'm able to set them aside. I wish Julie could do that as well, but now she told us she's marrying Ralphie, her unemployed, Kurt Cobain impersonating boyfriend. She has a ring and everything. Who gives their girlfriend an engagement ring for Christmas? The wedding date is my birthday in June, and so my birthday will now always be celebrated as the day Julie got married. My God. Of all days to get married. When Julie and Ralphie told us earlier tonight, I had to escape the house. I had to contemplate.

I sit here with a box on my desk. I contemplate the box, and not my daughter's engagement as I had planned. My initial thought was the box was a gift from a client, but I was the last to leave the office yesterday at five. The rest of the staff left at noon, only because I didn't want to be considered a Scrooge. My wife asked *why* I had to be open on Christmas Eve at all. I told her there was work to be done before the end of the year. Oh, the end of the year! What a wonderful excuse for everything in December!

I consider calling my office manager to see if she knows anything about the box on my desk, but she is clueless. Anyway, I have a better way of finding out. I turn on my computer, something else I wasn't planning on. Unbeknownst to my staff, I have motion detector cameras in every room of my office. I know everything that happens here. The good, the bad, the ugly. There's enough ugly to make a grown man blush (not that I ever blush) including weekly evening trysts between my office manager and the chiropractor next door. I do not watch the encounters, and I don't give a damn about their fucking, but I know which couch to never sit on.

The video will show me leaving, almost twenty-three hours ago, and the next video will be the person who broke in and put the box on my desk. I'm careful typing in the password, since any mistake will delete all video. When the program comes up, there are three rows and three columns of camera angles, all nine cameras at once, and I see myself at my desk, and the wooden box there. I click the timeline to five o'clock, when I left, and I see myself talking on the phone to a client on the one camera angle, but no one else is in the office. I was talking to Arnie McElroy about the tax implication of gifting to his idiot children. His word for them, not mine. It was a short conversation, and I watch myself hang up the phone, shut down my computer, put my coat on, and leave. There's nothing until I opened the front doors a half-hour ago, which means there was no movement. The cameras only come on if there is motion. How can it be? I click the camera above my desk and see the box was not on my desk when I left, but it was when I came in thirty minutes ago.

I switch the video to still images taken every hour. I scrutinize the images from the camera above my desk. Nothing changed until the midnight shot. There in the darkness is the box. I go back to the eleven o'clock still picture, and there's nothing on my desk. Only darkness.

I contemplate this.

I consider one of my clients broke into my office, without triggering the motion detectors, and left the box. I doubt this. Not that one of my clients wouldn't break into my office or leave me a *gift*, but that it could be done without being recorded. I have clients with the ability to hack my computer and the various passwords and delete the video. I narrow the list to three clients—two are out of town for the holidays, and the other wouldn't do so. Any of them could have hired someone to leave the box and delete the video, but at great expense. *Why?* There is always a *why* for everything anyone does, and none of the three have a *why*. If the wooden box is a gift, then *why* erase the video?

I have enemies who would leave something other than a gift. Maybe a bomb, or poisonous spiders, which is part of the reason I have the video cameras. I doubt those enemies have the wherewithal or the finances to perform this feat. And *why* leave the box? *What's* in the box? There are easier ways to kill or hurt me.

Now, the question: Why write *Pandora* on the box? I know the Greek mythology. Zeus gave Pandora a box and ordered her to not open it, but her curiosity got the better of her. I know the implications of this being Pandora's Box. If I open it, disease, sickness, jealousy, and all bad things will storm out. Those things already exist. What could be worse than cancer, AIDS, COVID, drug addiction, racism, hunger, climate change, selfishness, and all the other issues we suffer with? If I opened the box, would I really make the world much worse than it already is?

I cannot bring myself to lift the lid. There is no lock, which Pandora had to deal with, according to the myth. Pandora was told not to open the box, but I have not been given such an order, and yet, my curiosity is not any less.

I struggle with all of these thoughts. My impulse is to rip the lid off and meet my fate, whatever it is, but I don't. I have a better idea. I reach into my garbage and find the wrapping paper from a gift of a block of cheese from my staff, which my wife adored. I hate cheese, and my staff knows this. I rip off the bow from the wrapping paper and check to see if there's enough adhesive, and once confirmed, I put the bow on top of the box. I look at it, contemplate its appearance, and feel it's Christmassy enough with the bow.

I lift the box and discover it is heavy, as if it holds lead, but I'm able to carry it to my least favorite employee's desk. Laura Cordell has worked for me as an accountant for two and a half years, and she has no desire to do anything but be my employee. She's only passed one part of the CPA exam in two years, so all she'll ever be is a glorified bookkeeper. If she passed all four parts of the exam, I expect she would want to buy into the practice, but I wouldn't sell. I wonder if she would go off on her own, which is what every other accountant I've hired has done once all parts of the exam have been passed. I don't think I'll have to worry about this with Laura.

Her desk is always in a state of disarray, and there are days I want to fire her just for this abomination. Tonight, there are papers strewn about the desk, as if a tornado had hit, and I try not to be irked. But I can't leave it this way. I sit the wooden box in her chair, before stacking the papers up in a tidy mess, trying to put them in some semblance of order. I move the box to the center of her desk and slide her chair back into place. All looks normal, except for the tidiness.

I return to my office, and sit at my desk, and the questions remain: *Who* put the box on my desk and *why?* There is a possibility I have repressed thus far, and I shudder to think I'm releasing it to the forefront of my mind. It's not something that can be contemplated because it's beyond my capacity to understand. No one can understand God. Or gods, if there are more than one. There is no way to contemplate the unknowable, the unseeable, and I have always thought it would take being a god to comprehend God or gods. As it is, it's like a spider trying to understand a child.

I go to church most Sunday mornings, only because it

helps my business, and not because I believe in the supernatural hoodoo that is taught. Faith is belief in the unknowable, and for me to believe, I have to see. The seer is a believer. If it weren't for the video, or lack of video, the unknowable would never have entered my mind, but I have considered the other possibilities, and all seem just as unlikely.

So, what is on the video? Nothing. Could it have been some godly intervention in my life? And if so, why *me?* There's nothing special about me to bring a gift *or* a curse down upon my house. Although I admittedly participate in my clients' income shell games, my crimes are harmless in the grand scheme of things. I treat people the way they treat me, and usually that's with respect and kindness. I'm not a bad person. I try to help when I can, whether that's giving the random homeless person a twenty-dollar bill or paying for my longtime assistant's dental surgery. Still, I don't go out of my way to assist anyone. I'm not a bleeding heart.

My curiosity to know what's in the box is doused by my fear of the inexplicable.

My head hurts. I decide no contemplation is going to resolve it. There are two choices. I go into Laura's office and rip off the lid, or I go home and wait for her to do it in the morning from the comfort of my study—a safe distance away.

Despite the cells of my being aching to know, I resist. I send an e-mail to all my staff, notifying them, I'm taking the morning off. I turn off all the lights and shut and lock the doors to my office.

As I drive home, I prepare myself mentally for my family and the Kurt Cobain impersonating future son-in-law. It's a thirty-minute drive, mostly on the interstate, but not near enough time for me to be ready to celebrate Christmas. When I reach our neighborhood, I drive around and look at Christmas lights. My wife pays a man to put up our lights, and it's as nice as anybody else's, but I find the costs of such endeavors are never worth the effort. It's not just a waste of expense on purchasing the lights, wreaths, and trees, but the electric to run the lights, and the time putting them up and marveling over them. Even as I think this, I admit seeing all the lights does get me into the mood to socialize.

I park in the garage. When I step into the kitchen, Anne is standing by the counter with a glass of wine. She says she didn't think I'd ever get home. She kisses me on the cheek and tells me the natives are restless and hungry. She says she's kept the food warm for the last half hour.

If I had I come straight home to the party, the food would not have been delayed, but I would have been mood inappropriate. Now, I am mood appropriate. I thank my wife for holding the natives back, and then go to the closet in the foyer to hang up my coat.

Ralphie sees me and wants to make small talk. I listen and respond as best as I can, and wonder if my daughter will have to support him. This thought makes me sad. We walk into the den, and my wife's parents, brother, and sister and their children are in the room talking politics. I know better than to get involved in a political conversation with family. I am anti-political, almost an anarchist. Rather than any good in politics, all I can see is the bad. How can government solve any problem, especially here where it's based on conformity? Or worse, on money. One person should be the decider. A person who has no benefit to the decisions he or she makes. Our plutocracy disguised as a democracy has not worked since *politician* became a career choice. These beliefs are best kept to myself, of course.

I stay long enough so Ralphie becomes embroiled in the conversation, and I take three steps back before turning. I move quietly into my study, hoping for a moment of solitude before the meal starts. But Julie is there, and she pounces on me for abandoning her and her mother with *the family* for hours. I shrug, not wanting to respond. She asks why I don't like Ralphie, and I know I can't tell the truth, so I tell her I never liked Nirvana. I never saw what the big deal was screaming into a microphone about young do-nothing angst. *It's not poetry if it's complaining.* She rolls her eyes and leaves the room. I call out to her, but I'm secretly glad she's given me a moment alone.

I think about the box. I stand in front of the bookshelf as though I'm searching for something to read, all the while wondering what's in the box. For a second, I convince myself I'll drive back downtown once supper is cleaned up and the last guest has left. I'll lift the damned lid off, but I can't think of any rational reason to do so. If it's a gift and Laura keeps it, then it will probably be something I wouldn't have wanted. If she realizes it was meant for me and puts it on my desk, then it's something she wouldn't want but I would. If it's not a gift, then I don't want to be within 20 miles of the place. My curiosity is eased by my brief moment of contemplation.

Anne calls me for supper, and I take a few short breaths before going into the kitchen to grab a plate. The food is laid out along the kitchen counter. I fill my plate with turkey, ham, dressing, and everything else, except for the green bean casserole. Whoever thought green bean casserole might be appetizing has no pallet at all. I grab an iced tea and take the chair at the head of the table, with Anne on my left and Julie on my right. There are fifteen of us but only ten chairs at the dining room table. Ralphie gets placed at the kid's table in the kitchen because there are no seats left. I think it's appropriate. I tell my daughter we can squeeze Ralphie in, but she shrugs. I take that as potential disinterest.

The table talk ranges from sports to stories from childhood Christmases. I listen and laugh at the appropriate places, but don't participate in any of the stories. Even when asked, I deflect the question to someone else. I am not much interested in small talk. There is a moment when I feel a compulsion to tell there is a wooden box with the word *Pandora* burned on it sitting on my desk. I want to scream that I resisted opening it. Of course, my wife's family would look at me like I had gone mad. So, I sit quietly. I eat and smile. I refuse dessert, and just want them all to finish eating and go home.

I listen to my wife's brother, Oliver, tell about the new boat he's purchasing in the spring. He's a lawyer and when not talking politics, he spends his time, bragging about whatever purchase he has made in the last month. It is monotonous, but I think when he buys the boat, maybe he and I can take a trip to South Carolina alone and I can push him off the side of the boat into the deeps of the Atlantic. It is difficult for me to not smile at this thought.

When the dessert is finished, I stand at the sink and wash the dishes. We used the good china, and my wife won't let me stick it into the dishwasher. So, I wash, and Ralphie dries. It makes me dislike him a bit less, but not enough to be happy he's fucking my daughter, which I know he is. The washing goes slowly, and people start leaving before I'm done with the dishes. Each time I wave a soapy hand goodbye, tell them Merry Christmas, and thank them for coming. I am the perfect host. My wife walks them to the door, where she listens to another protracted story about someone she and her sibling knew in high school having a child or about their mother's best friend falling and breaking a hip. I'd rather wash dishes with Ralphie than pay attention to the drivel.

I have a small amount of washing left when the final guest leaves, and I tell Ralphie I'll finish. He refuses. He says Julie will wait. While he thinks this will put him in my good graces, it only annoys me, because he's purposefully kissing my ass. All I can think of is the possibility my daughter will have children with this fool, if I don't break them up, which I'm capable of doing. It must be done with subtlety. I endure another fifteen minutes of him prattling on about getting a gig on Kurt Cobain's birthday in February at one of the better clubs in the area. He's convinced it will get him a recording deal, and I resist asking whether his band has original songs, yet. Even Julie has complained about his inability to write a lyric or original music. She says it always sounds like some other song. Like a bad Nirvana song, probably, not that there are any good ones.

Once all the dishes are clean, Ralphie and Julie make a big

deal about leaving, and I shake Ralphie's hand and kiss Julie. When they've gone, Anne helps me wipe down the table and counter tops. We don't talk. I can tell she's exhausted, and I tell her I'll finish up so she can go shower. Yes, I'm sure, I tell her. I just want to be alone. Finally, alone. The box is still on my mind, and I can't wrap my mind around it. Not here. Not while doing housework. To contemplate, I must be at my office, but I can't go there now.

I finish cleaning up, perhaps not as good of a job as I normally do, but well enough for Anne, who's not particular about cleanliness. I decide to go to my computer and see video of my office. I want to see the wooden box. I don't believe I imagined it, but I do think there is a possibility that I did.

When the computer boots up, I click on the remote desktop connection, and it's the same as if I am sitting at my desk at work. All programs and data on the office server are available. I click the left mouse button on the video camera icon, type the password. The nine camera views come up and I look at the camera pointing at Laura's desk.

The box isn't there.

Where is the box?

I feel relief. I had imagined it after all. It was all in my head. I grunt, and I think I must have been working too hard in the last couple of weeks.

When I look at the camera positioned over my desk, the wooden box is there, exactly where I had found it this afternoon. There's no bow on the box. I look back at Laura's desk and see the bow in the space I had cleared. I want to know who is fucking with me. If someone went to the office after I left, four hours ago, then I am being fucked with. I will find out who it is and beat them to a bloody goddamned pulp. Why are they fucking with me? My rage goes on for so long I lose time, then it subsides so I can think again. I need to contemplate.

I consider reporting a break in, but that would be a mistake. What would I report as missing? I don't need the police sticking their noses in my business. I rub my forehead and decide to check the video made since I left. If it's the same person, I don't expect the video will show anything. I left click on the timeline to go back to when I left earlier, and I see myself leave, and then nothing, as expected. I go to the still pictures, and it's there on Laura's desk twenty minutes after I left at five, but at six, the box is back on my desk.

I stare at the box and click the mouse and zoom in on it. I know it's a curse. My curse and it's calling to me. I can't ignore it. I hope it goes away. It won't. I know if I call my assistant in the morning and tell her to go open the box in my office, it will disappear. It's there for me. It is *my* fate, and it involves the gods, the inexplicable. If I never returned to my office, the box would still be my curse.

No contemplation is needed to know what I must do.

When I tell Anne I have to go back to the office, I don't even lie. I tell her there is unfinished business that must be dealt with before morning. She's in bed, reading a cooking magazine, probably looking for a recipe she can use to recycle leftover turkey. Her look lets me know while she's not going to question what I'm doing, she's not happy about it. Still, she reminds me to take my phone. I go to the bed and kiss her cheek and tell her I love her. I realize I do, and that I haven't paid enough attention to her in the last two decades. All work, and no play. We've had vacations, even Europe twice and Thailand once, and the beach at least once a year, but I've always worked. The phone is my friend, and once computers and the internet took over my life, it meant I could leave the physical office, but always be at the office. The vacations were lonely for Anne. That makes me sad.

She tells me not to be gone too long, and I tell her that I won't. In the car, I turn on satellite radio and sing to Creedence Clearwater Revival *Who'll Stop the Rain*. I drive 90 mph on the interstate, knowing no state trooper will pull me over. This is my fate, and I'm rushing toward it, nothing to stop me. The seventies rock continues and my drive is cut down to 25 minutes. I'm mindless. There's nothing to think about. I sing Wings *Band on the Run*, ELO *Evil Woman*, Foreigner *Head Games*, and Boston *Hitch a Ride*. When I pull into the strip mall and park in front of my office, Zeppelin *Going to California* is playing. As I shut off the engine the line about the wrath of the gods echoes in my mind. My mouth goes dry, and I feel like I'm being laughed at. I feel like a pawn. I feel like a goddamned monkey.

I hear the click of my shoes echo in the night air. I push against the office's glass door, expecting it to be unlocked. It's not. I put the key in the lock and turn it. I go in and turn the lobby lights on. All looks undisturbed. I go into my office. The light comes on, and my final hope that it's my imagination is snuffed. The wooden box is where I had found it.

I walk around my desk and sit at my chair. To open or not to open. That is the question. And as with *Hamlet*, the question may actually be *to be or not to be*. The only way to know is to lift the lid and let what's going to happen, happen.

For the first time, in maybe decades, I feel discombobulated. No amount of contemplation will answer this question. I either do it, or I go crazy. It's really no choice, is it? How can I contemplate this? I find out what's in the box, or I'm haunted by not knowing what's in it. If I did set it aside, hide it in my safe, I may last a day, two at the most, before the curiosity undid me and I opened it anyway.

I lift my fingers to the lid, hesitating a second. I feel beneath the lip of the lid, gently raising it out of position. It's no wood I've ever seen, and the stale air seeping out smells dank, of wet earth. It makes me think the box has been buried for a millennium.

I pull the lid all the way off and set it aside. I stand and lean over the box to see what's inside, half afraid something's going to leap out. Nothing does. There is a single yellowed page in the box. I reach for it, careful, not wanting to be bitten or burned. I lift the page from the box and realize it is a thick, dry paper, preserved, but fragile. I think maybe it's thousands of years old. I set it on my desk, and peer at the written words. At first, the letters are archaic and unreadable, then the letters change, still oddly formed.

After a moment, I make out the words: *Because the end had to begin somewhere.*

It's an answer to my question *why me?* But I don't know what it means. What end are the words talking about? I still don't know *why* me? Why not someone else? Anyone else? What ending is the message speaking of? The end of the world? Who wrote this?

A small whirlwind of dirty brown dust rises out of the box, and it's like watching a cartoon character spinning around in a cyclone shape. It hovers, as though it is sentient and deciding what to do next. I'm as still as I possibly can be. Two seconds. Three. Four. Five seconds pass. The dust from the whirlwind hits my nose, and I feel the tickle of a sneeze coming on. I clamp my mouth down and stop breathing, hoping to deter the sneeze, and yet, I can't. My sneeze is explosive, maybe because I fought it, hoping it would go away. My whole-body sneezes, and my head jerks down. I lose sight of the whirlwind for a second. When I look up, it's slowly moving toward me. I move my chair back to escape it, but it follows. Before I can get up, the whirlwind has covered my face. I can't see, but I feel the dust in my nose and mouth. There's no escaping it. There's nothing to do but give in.

Finally, I can see. The whirlwind is gone. All is fine, I tell myself. It was just my imagination after all. The box and yellowed page are still there.

I sit and contemplate. I realize I should throw the box out. I stuff the page into the box and then lift it. It is light, like balsa wood, not lead as I thought earlier. I go to the rear of the office, open the back door, and without letting the door shut, I first toss the box then the lid into the dumpster. I go back to my office, as if nothing has happened. It could all be my imagination.

I'm hungry. So fucking hungry. Would any restaurants be

open this late on Christmas? I could stop and get some chips at the gas station. I need to fill up anyway. But I'm not hungry for chips. I think maybe I can eat turkey at home, and as hungry as I am, there won't be any turkey left for Anne to recycle. As I walk out of the office door into the parking lot, I realize my hunger won't wait for me to get home. I see lights a quarter mile away in the distance, and realize I'd forgotten about the diner, open twenty-four hours, even on Christmas. I'm not myself right now. I'm too hungry to contemplate. I decide to walk to the restaurant when I should know it would be quicker to drive. It's not that far, and if I'm going to eat that much cholesterol, I need the exercise. I should find this funny, but don't.

After a few minutes of walking, I smell the food. The glorious, wonderful food. I run like I'd never been able to run before and reach the diner in less than a minute. I see the food inside and open the door.

Before the waitress can tell me to sit anywhere, I reach for her, pull her to me, stronger than I've ever been, and I begin eating.

SIRENS

◆ ◆ ◆

For the first time in six weeks, Ulysses Albright walked about his house with a certain purpose. He made the bed, cleaned dishes, wiped the counter tops, all so when Penelope returned home from work at the hospital, she would find order, but not Ulysses.

By that time, he'd be five hundred miles away.

As he walked into the garage, he thought he would feel better about leaving, but he didn't. His heart felt like it was about to implode from the heaviness. He thought about Penny coming home and not finding him. She may wonder where he was, but it would be dark before she began to worry. He didn't leave a note, and the only clothes he took were the ones on his body. She would call, but he left his phone in the sock drawer, turned off. When she got good and worried, after the police told her she needed to wait twenty-four hours before reporting a missing person, she'd call the credit card company to see if he'd left a credit trail, but his credit cards were with his phone. She'd find those eventually, a few days or weeks, maybe. How long would it take for her to discover he'd taken half of their savings? It wasn't a great deal of money in the grand scheme of things, but it would last him six months if he lived meagerly. Maybe he could work for cash, but doing what? He was a professor and had no real skills. By morning, Penny would be frantic, thinking he had hurt himself or someone had hurt him. He knew this and felt bad about it, but it didn't stop him from pulling the new Toyota Camry out of the garage and driving out of their subdivision. It wasn't that he didn't love her. He was leaving because he did love her.

He stopped at a Starbucks, and the drive-thru was backed up almost to the parking lot entrance. He went inside, expecting to see someone he knew, but it wasn't his usual Starbucks. He ordered black coffee, paid, and waited at a table, feeling awkward without his phone. He thought he should stop and get a prepaid cell phone, but not yet. He wanted to take his coffee and move down the highway. Later, when he stopped for the night, he'd go to a Wal-Mart for a phone and some clothes. He knew he was traveling north with no idea of where he'd land. Tonight, he'd stop in Georgia maybe, and then Ohio or Illinois the next day. After that, he didn't know where.

When his name was called, he picked up his coffee, left a tip for the barista, and walked out without a word. He moved the Camry through the streets of Miami and merged onto I-95, keeping his speed at seventy.

He wanted his mind to be clear as he drove. Alone in the car, music and talk radio didn't keep his mind from drifting back home. He wondered how Penny was dealing with her first day back at work. The lab would occupy her mind, although he imagined the day was difficult. How long would it take for the looks of sympathy from her co-workers to fade? His leaving wouldn't help matters at first but staying would have made it worse. He was an open wound that would never heal, except maybe in death. He'd considered killing himself, but he couldn't bring himself to swallow a bullet. Or pills. He believed he could save her by leaving. He was beyond saving.

The University had turned a cold shoulder to him. Two weeks ago, Ron Maxwell, the chairman of the department, said his fall semester class load was covered, adding they could talk in November about the spring semester. When Ulysses asked if he was being fired, Ron said they were giving him time to properly grieve and *get his shit together*. Ulysses had nothing to say to this. He let thirty seconds pass before he stood, held his arms out with unasked questions, and left. He wanted to storm out of the office and slam the door, but he had too much self-control to let it get out of hand. It helped him keep a good face on for when Penny got home later. There'd been no reason for her to know he'd been placed on leave for the semester. Now, as Ulysses passed by the exit for Boca Raton, he knew there was truth in Ron's statement. His shit was fucked up. His soul was damaged. No priest could absolve the sin. No therapist could ease the guilt. For six weeks he had held it all in, all the while wanting to implode. He wanted to get as far from Miami as he could. Maybe Penny could heal without him there.

Ulysses approached an underpass, and he touched the accelerator. His speed edged up to eighty-five. All he needed to do was turn the wheel a fraction and *bam!* He wouldn't survive the crash, would he? He didn't think so. He let the Camry drift to the right. The tires hit the rumble strip at the edge of the shoulder. He jerked the wheel back to the left into his lane of travel and let off the accelerator. He was afraid the airbags would cushion the crash. He'd be saved, and all the world would know he'd tried to kill himself. He could say he hadn't slept well and that's why he'd bought the coffee, but the coffee hadn't worked. He'd drifted off to sleep. Still, they'd know he wanted to end the pain, wouldn't they? His pain. Penny's pain. All the world's pain. If he didn't exist, the world didn't exist either, right? But if he survived the crash, the pain would be unimaginable, and he couldn't bear it anymore.

Ulysses reached for the radio knob and turned the channel. He kept turning until he found NPR and listened to new measures outlined by the President for stabilizing Iraq, which Ulysses thought was foolishness. Ulysses lectured to the radio about the changes, as though he were in class.

NPR moved on to a story about the economy. Ulysses hit the *seek* button and kept hitting it until he found a station playing Dylan's *A Hard Rain's A-Gonna Fall*. He listened to this for a few minutes, sang along even, but before the song ended, his thoughts were back to concern for Penny. How long would it be before her worry turned to anger? He thought it would be an immediate reaction, but hadn't she thought of leaving in the last six weeks? He was sure she had. Who would blame her? At the funeral, she wouldn't hold his hand, and she had been hot and cold since. One night, she'd sleep against him, holding him or letting him hold her. Other nights, if he tried to get close to her, she'd move away and even once had slapped his hand from her hip. He understood, and he stopped trying. He simply let her come to him if she needed solace. He wouldn't force it on her. How could he?

He was lost in his thoughts, and almost missed the turn off onto the Florida Turnpike toward Orlando. A few songs had played but he didn't hear them. Now, as he merged onto the turnpike, Sting droned on about *Roxanne* not having to put on the red light. Ulysses hit the seek button until he'd determined every station was either in commercial or playing country. He didn't want to wait for *Roxanne* to be over, so he tapped the CD button. Had he even played a disc in this car? He couldn't remember. The screen showed a disc was about to play. Penny had driven the Camry home from the dealership after picking it out, and maybe she pulled a disc from her car and put it in.

When James Taylor began singing *You've Got a Friend*, Ulysses felt like he was being punched in the stomach.

Six weeks ago, Ulysses spent the day deep in research and was unsettled by his lack of success. He hoped to relate the fall of Troy to the Union taking Atlanta, only to see if he could. He found no correlations, and this agitated him. It had been a year since he'd written an original paper that wasn't a critique. He needed something different. Relating a Civil War loss to a mythical loss would get attention. The ambition would set him apart from his colleagues, and it could make his career, if it had worked. It hadn't, and now as he drove home, his professional disillusion crushed him. It'll pass, he told himself. Give it a few days, and another idea will take ahold.

He put in James Taylor's *Greatest Hits* and drove the long

way home. James Taylor had always soothed him, and by the time he pulled into the garage, he had put aside his unhappiness. He sat in the car a few moments, breathing in and breathing out, almost meditatively. He wondered now why he delayed going into the house. He still didn't know, but he'd lost three minutes sitting there, singing along to *Sweet Baby James* barely above a whisper.

In the house he found Helen on the floor of the den reading *Where the Wild Things Are*. Seeing him, she squealed *daddy!* He picked her up and held her. She wrapped her arms around his neck. Ulysses felt a love from her like nothing he knew or would ever know. He wondered if she would love him unconditionally like this as she got older, or would she even like him. Why did that worry him? He said she was the best little girl, squeezed her one last time, and put her down. She returned to her book, and he moved toward the smell of Penny's spaghetti. When Helen was born, Penny's fixation had become food, and she bought every cookbook she could find. She wanted her family to eat real food, not the microwavable processed food she brought home before. He couldn't remember what that even tasted like. Penny liked compliments about her food, more so than her looks, and she blushed when Ulysses went back for seconds.

He crossed the threshold into the kitchen. She stood at the stove, not turning around as he moved close to her. She knew he was there. She let him lean down and kiss the back of her neck. She shivered when he did, her pleasure sensor.

As she cooked, they talked, probably something to do with her work. It was all high drama, who was leaving who, who had slept with whose boss, on and on, and Ulysses listened, but not closely. It was meaningless prattle he cared little about. He nodded, smiled, and laughed at appropriate times, as he always did, only to be polite. He knew better than to tell her about the state of affairs at the University. He never talked about the office only because he knew she wouldn't care. Why bore her any more than necessary? Penny wouldn't care that Henry

Oakes had published an article about infection during modern warfare, or that Maggie Atkinson had been given tenure, and not just because she was sleeping with the chairman. She'd earned it.

They drank a bottle of Pinot Grigio while Penny cooked, and Penny asked him to open a second bottle as she set the table. He didn't really want another glass, but wasn't going to let her drink by herself. He filled their glasses as she dished out the spaghetti, then he went in search of their daughter. Helen was on the potty, and he stood outside the closed door waiting for her to finish. After a minute of her hand washing, he knocked on the door and told her to hurry up. When she opened the door, his daughter told him to not rush her. "You owe me a minute of my life," he told her. She rolled her eyes and walked past him into the kitchen. He followed her and helped her into her booster seat. Even before he could push her chair in, she had grabbed a handful of spaghetti, stuffing it into her mouth. He'd tried to explain table manners to her and that she ought to use a fork, but she was set in her ways.

As they ate, Ulysses talked mostly to Helen, trying to get her to tell him what she'd done in daycare, but all she would say was *I don't remember, daddy*, which was a four-year old's way of saying, *I really don't want to talk about it*. She did answer Ulysses' most important question, the one he asked every night: *What'd you read to your friends?* She proudly told him *The Cat in the Hat*. She loved Dr. Seuss. Helen was the only child in her preschool who could read, and Ulysses didn't know how she had learned. He didn't teach her, and Penny claimed she didn't. While the daycare would love to take credit, they spent most of their time teaching the alphabet and the sounds of the letters, but nothing more advanced. It seemed to Ulysses that reading was something Helen just knew how to do.

While Penny gave Helen her bath, he cleaned the kitchen and watched a rerun of *Seinfeld*. The cleanup took longer because of the amount of food on the floor around Helen's seat. He'd simply accepted the fact that half of her food would make it to the floor.

Once the kitchen was clean, he found Helen in her bed reading Roald Dahl's *Matilda*. She put a bookmark in the crease. He wondered when Penny had bought her a chapter book. "What do you want me to read you, daddy?" she asked as part of her nightly ritual. Ulysses wondered how much of *Matilda* she retained, but put aside that thought and told her he'd like for her to read *Alexander and the Horrible, No Good, Very Bad Day*. It was one of her favorites. She went to her bookshelf, fingered the edges of the books until she found it, and settled back into bed. She read the first page silently, memorized it, and turned the book around so Ulysses could see it. She repeated the text in character, as if she were Alexander. Six months earlier Ulysses read to her like this, and he missed seeing her face as she took in the details of each picture. Hearing her read was the best part of his day. He never expected that being read to by a four-year old would give him such joy and amazement.

When Helen finished the last page and said *the end*, Ulysses told her she'd done well, and kissed her forehead. Penny timed it so she walked in as he was saying his good night, and he stood back, waited for her to finish. All of this was the ritual, and it always felt right. When they turned off the light and walked out in the hallway, they waited for Helen to yell *goodnight mommy, goodnight daddy*. Ulysses asked her once why she called out to them after they had tucked her in, and she said *to see if you are still there*. Ulysses thought it was a small bit of fear of the dark but wondered if it could just be loneliness. Once they gave a responsive *good night*, Helen would drift off to sleep.

Penny smiled at him in the hallway and put her hand on his chest. A gentle touch. He wondered what the look and physical contact was about, and when he didn't react, she sighed. He realized what she wanted, and he bit his lip and smiled. She took his hand, and they walked into the bedroom. They undressed, and she slid on top of him. It was the last time they had sex, and it was good. Passionate. They fell asleep in each other's arms, naked, not bothering to clean up from the sex.

He didn't know if he failed to set his alarm, or if he just turned it off when it rang the next morning. In either case, he woke late on a morning he didn't have the luxury of taking his time. He rushed around in the bathroom so he could make an eight o'clock meeting. He showered but didn't shave, and he dressed in record time. Penny was cleaning the syrup from Helen's face when he walked into the kitchen. He considered asking Penny to take her to school so he could take an extra five minutes to eat breakfast, but it was in the opposite direction from the hospital. He poured a cup of coffee in a travel mug, and grabbed two bananas. "Ready to go pumpkin?" he asked Helen.

She held up her Mermaid lunch box as an answer, and he held up his coffee and smiled. Another ritual. Penny kissed them at the door, then Helen turned and ran back to her room. She returned holding *Matilda* and smiled at Ulysses. She had to have something to read in the car. At the moment, his Lexus had ten or twelve books in the backseat because Helen rarely brought them back inside. He didn't mind, and occasionally asked if Helen wanted a bookshelf for the backseat. He buckled her into the car seat and rushed back into the house for a folder he needed for his meeting. Penny gave him another kiss at the garage door and told him to *have a good day*. He told her *he loved her*. More ritual.

When he settled into his seat and turned the ignition, the last note of *Sweet Baby James* played and *Country Road* began. He didn't sing along this day. He wanted to focus on driving. Once he had backed out of the driveway, he looked at the stereo's clock. If he hurried and Helen didn't protest being left at preschool, he could make the meeting.

He started to reach for his coffee but held back. He should save it for the meeting. He'd need the coffee. The University had put a hiring freeze on most departments two years before when state funding had declined, however his chairman had tackled the administrative quagmire to get authorization to replace one of several professors who had retired. Ulysses was in charge of the interview committee, and today's meeting was a review of the twenty-five resumes and writing samples that had been filtered by the chairman's office. Ulysses had glanced at most of the paperwork, and there were only three that had his attention. The others seemed bland from their resumes, although all of them were more than qualified. Ulysses hoped to find someone who would challenge his ever-increasing complacency. Why hadn't he written an article for so long? It seemed all too easy, especially teaching the same curriculum every year. The chairman prodded him, but didn't require the additional work outside of teaching. He thought maybe the chairman had been too relaxed with the department staff, and even Ulysses found himself stuck in that trap. He desperately needed a colleague to argue with about some of his ideas, someone who would stir his atrophied brain. This was an opportunity.

Traffic was heavy, and Ulysses thought there may be an accident ahead, and he decided to take a shortcut. He did a U-turn and then made the first right so he could travel to a parallel street. He had lived in an apartment a short distance from here, and he knew all the back roads. After a half-mile he turned right onto a four-lane road in a business district, and traffic was lighter. If he could make it through three stoplights, he could turn right at the fourth, and this would lead him to the backside of the pre-school.

"Hang on, sport," he said. He turned to the backseat, smiled at his daughter, and added, "We're Helen Wheels, aren't we?"

"No, daddy," Helen said. "We're hell on wheels."

Ulysses laughed and looked back to the road. This was the first time she'd corrected him. Had Penny explained the right phrasing? He'd have to ask her. Surely, Helen hadn't learned it at preschool.

James Taylor sang about being down and out and needing a helping hand. Ulysses hummed along as he passed through the first two lights. The third light turned yellow, but he could make it if he sped up a small bit. Hell on wheels indeed, he thought and laughed. His speed increased to fifty-five. When it was almost too late, he realized he'd misjudged the distance. He could slam on his brakes and come to a skidding stop in the middle of the intersection, or he could maintain his speed even though the light would turn red just before he passed beneath it. He chose the path offering the least amount of risk. He would pass through the light before vehicles from left and right entered the crossing.

What Ulysses didn't know was a Chevy pickup moved toward the intersection and wasn't going to stop or even slow down. Mack Bricker had seen Ulysses' light turn yellow and knew his light would turn green the moment he reached it. He could go through the light without ever touching his brake. It was Mr. Bricker's lucky day. Approaching a light about to change was like winning the lottery. Lady Fortune had visited him. Later, Mr. Bricker told police he was late for work. He even admitted to accelerating as he advanced toward the red light because he *knew* it was about to turn. He knew. And the light *was* green when he went through it. *He* had the *fucking* right of way.

Ulysses knew one truth: Two physical objects cannot occupy the same space at any one moment. Had either of them varied their speed, ever so slightly, the vehicles would not have converged upon the same space.

The collision was loud. It's what Ulysses thought a bomb would sound like. The force of the blow caused the Lexus to spin. Ulysses' body went to his left, his jaw struck the window, and the airbag inflated into his chin with a stiff uppercut. The vehicle made a full turn and another half turn before coming to a forceful stop. Ulysses was slammed to his right until his seat belt caught him, pinning his arm against his chest.

All that noise from the collision, and then blessed silence.

The absence of sound was not blessed, as he had first thought. There should have been noise. Something. His mind was clouded, and it took him a second to realize he should be hearing his daughter's screams or something from her. He looked over his right shoulder and saw Helen's slumped body and so much blood. *"Helen!"* he screamed. *"Helen! Oh God, Helen!"* But he already knew. He jumped out of the car and ran around to the passenger's side crumpled door. He ripped it open and reached to the car seat, unclipped the straps, and pulled out her lifeless body. He sat in the middle of the street holding her, rocking back and forth, unable to cry.

A wire in the stereo must have reconnected because James Taylor began telling Ulysses that he had a friend. He heard sirens in the distance calling to him.

His tears dried up. He didn't notice he'd driven into Georgia. He hadn't seen the *Welcome We're glad Georgia's on your mind* sign. He didn't feel welcome, but he wouldn't feel *welcome* anywhere. What he did feel was numb to the world. For the moment he decided he was far enough away from Penny he could stop for the day. Still, he wanted more distance. He thought she could find him if she tried, but he didn't think she would. Not yet, anyway. If he stopped, what would he do for the rest of the afternoon? Stare at the four corners of a hotel room until the sun dropped below the horizon? Could he even sleep after that? He'd rather drive mindlessly and when he reached Chattanooga, he'd rent a room to sleep. Maybe putting that much distance between him and Penny would allow him to finally rest. He didn't think so, but he'd try. If he didn't sleep, he'd worry about it tomorrow. For now, he'd just drive with the radio off.

For a bit, the changed scenery kept his mind occupied, fewer pines and more hardwood, and a few small hills. No matter how hard he tried to block his mind, Helen and Penny seeped into his thoughts. It was no use to fight against the onslaught. He didn't cry this time.

Since the accident, Ulysses felt like he'd been cast out into the middle of the ocean to drift, and where he went emotionally any particular day depended upon Penny's gravitational pull. He wanted to be there for her, but she made it fucking impossible at times. Could Ulysses blame her? How could she even consider staying with him? They were both miserable, whether together or apart. Ulysses felt the chill between them. She would never forgive him, no matter how often she denied it. If he stayed, she'd become the moon plunging into the earth, destroying everything around them. She could get on with life now, but he was stuck in that one moment as he sped toward the traffic light. There was no reason for her to be stuck there with him.

The EMT with the bright green eyes sat next to him on the pavement and told him she needed to take his daughter. Ulysses only clasped Helen tighter. The EMT brushed Helen's hair. "Mr. Albright, I'll take good care of your daughter. I promise. I'll make sure she gets cleaned up good, okay? She needs that. You want her to get cleaned up, right?"

What got his attention was her delicate tone. *This is what we're going to do, and you agree we need to do this, right?* She didn't command him, like the police officer and other EMT had. "Let him have a moment with her," the green-eyed EMT had told them. "He needs this." They agreed, but only because it was obvious Helen was beyond saving.

Now, he lifted his daughter from his lap and put her gently into the arms of the EMT. "She doesn't like cold water, okay?"

He still wondered why he told her this. Helen was dead. It didn't matter whether they cleaned her up with cold water. The EMT nodded and whispered, "I'll make sure she keeps warm."

Holding Helen's body, the EMT reached down and touched Ulysses' shoulder. She held his eyes with hers, which were almost emerald green. He felt the need to speak again. "I'm not going to be okay," he said. "Nothing in the world can ever be worse than this moment."

She nodded. "I know. I won't tell you any different," she said. "I won't lie to you, but you've got to carry on. Can you do

183

that?"

He didn't answer. He couldn't tell her *no*, but he also wouldn't say *yes* because he didn't believe it. At that moment, he wasn't sure he'd make it through the end of the day. The hurt was great. He wanted to find a hole to crawl into and cover up.

The EMT left with Helen, and Ulysses watched her strap the little body on the gurney and then lift it up into the back of the ambulance. She climbed in, and he figured the ambulance would drive off, but she rummaged around until she found what she was looking for. She jumped out and walked back to him.

"Hold your hands out," she said.

"What?" he asked.

"The blood," she said. "We need to get your hands and arms clean."

That's when he noticed the stickiness. He held his arms out, and she poured the water over his arms.

"Rub your hands together," she told him. When he did, she poured some more water over them. He held his clean hands up. "Good," she said. "Now dry off and change into these." She handed him a towel and some scrubs. He took off his bloody shirt and put it in the trash bag she held out. He put on the scrubs shirt.

As soon as she went back toward the ambulance, the police officer came and held his hand out to help Ulysses up. Ulysses looked away from the officer and hugged his chest. "Sir, you need to get up," the officer said.

Ulysses tried to say he wasn't ready, but instead he put his arms behind him and lifted himself off the pavement.

The officer pulled back his offered hand. "Are you okay?"

Ulysses didn't answer, feeling unsteady on his feet. He didn't know if it was physical trauma or emotional.

"Look, I got to ask," the officer said. "Can you tell me what happened?"

Ulysses looked at his Lexus, the passenger back door

bashed in, and then at the front of the pickup with its hood crumpled. He didn't want to talk about it. "I've got to call my wife," Ulysses said. He started to turn away, but added, "My light was yellow. That guy came from nowhere."

He moved to the shoulder, his back to the police officer, and he called Penny's cell phone. When she didn't answer, he called her office. The receptionist put him on hold. He turned and saw the officer speaking with Mr. Bricker in what seemed to be a heated exchange. Mr. Bricker's hand gestures were theatrical as he pointed from one side of the intersection to the other, his face the same red as his truck. Ulysses heard the phone pick up. He turned away.

"What's wrong?" Penny asked.

Ulysses hadn't planned on what to say. He was silent as he tried to put the words together to tell her.

"Ulysses, are you there?"

He detected the irritation in her voice. "There's been an accident," he said.

"Are you okay?" Now there was concern.

"It's not me," he said, although he was banged up and beginning to feel the ache in his neck and shoulders. "The pickup hit Helen's door. She... She... She didn't—"

"*Oh God!*"

"I'm sorry," he whispered, and collapsed to the pavement again. His wails began. He finally cried.

The green-eyed EMT rushed to him and sat down. She pried the phone from his hands and began talking to Penny. Ulysses sat with his legs beneath him, bent over, head to knees and his arms over his head. He couldn't hear what was being said, only that the EMT comforted Penny as she had him. Finally, she put her hand on his back. "Ulysses?"

He sat up. "What?"

"Come on," she said. "I'll take you and your daughter to your wife. It's not the closest hospital, but you need to be together."

Ulysses nodded. She helped him stand and led him to the

185

ambulance, not letting him ride in the back with Helen. "That's not for you, now," she said. He sat up front in the passenger seat, next to the other EMT. The green-eyed EMT sat in the back with Helen.

Ulysses didn't remember the drive. He had his eyes shut and ignored the questions by both EMTs. He kept seeing Helen's damaged body. Grief shut the rest of the world out. There was a certain amount of unreality to it all, and he kept wishing he'd wake up from the nightmare.

He startled to awareness with a hand on his shoulder. The ambulance had stopped moving. The driving EMT said, "We're here."

He opened his eyes and saw they were at the entrance of the hospital's emergency room.

"Is that your wife?"

He looked around and didn't see her at first. Then he saw her sitting by herself, her eyes shut as well. He had to go to her. He gripped the door handle and then nearly fell out of the ambulance. He left the door open as he stumbled away from the ambulance and through the hospital doors. He sat next to Penny, placing his hand on her shoulder.

She opened her eyes and looked at him. She'd changed. It wasn't just the grief for the loss of their daughter. There was blame there. He saw it. She realized she should be hugging her husband, so she wrapped her arms around him. "I'm sorry," he whispered in her ear.

"I'm sorry, too."

After a few minutes, they were led away by a grief counselor, and after what seemed like hours of conversation, they were taken home. But it wasn't home without Helen there. Their little girl. Who would read to Ulysses in the evening now?

He considered turning the steering wheel into the path of the Atlanta rush hour traffic around him but resisted for fear of harming others. In Chattanooga, he stopped and had a burger and fries. He ate a few fries but was able to get half the burger down. He paid and tipped the waitress the full cost of the meal. He went into a Walmart and bought a prepaid cell phone, some clothes, and a six pack of beer. All he needed. He found a motel, paid cash, and watched television long enough to drink a couple beers. Finally, he slept the sleep of the dead. When he woke, sunlight streamed through the window. His first thought was maybe he'd be okay. Maybe the distance from Penny was his cure, or at least a temporary fix. Maybe he'd outrun his troubles. He showered, put on his new clothes, and packed the rest in the plastic bags with the beer. He had bacon and eggs at the restaurant from the night before. He held the phone, staring at it. He wanted to call Penny, but he didn't want to call. He was able to get most of the food down. He did feel better. Last night's sleep was the real thing, and for the first time in six weeks, he had a glimmer of hope. Was it illusory? Would it all catch up to him as he drove in the quiet of the car?

Back on the road, he traveled north on I-75. Hills and trees, mostly hardwoods. He listened to NPR. Another school shooting. Bombings in Israel. Unrest in Syria. The economy rebounded. He didn't care. When NPR went off, he scanned the channels to find only country and talk radio. He turned the noise off and rolled down his windows.

Penny would be frantic by now and wouldn't go to work. He tried to guess which of his family members she would call, and he hoped they calmed her. *Ulysses wouldn't hurt himself. He probably just needed to get away. He'll be back.* That would be the line from his siblings, except for his little sister, Annette, who would stir the drama. She may even bring up the word suicide. He hoped her husband, Arnie, was close by to take the phone from her and tell Penny to give it a little bit of time. Had Penny called the police last night, or did she wait until this morning? At first, the detectives would tell her there was nothing that could be done, and she'd accept this. As the day wore on and her hysteria rose, Penny would call in favors. She would find someone who knew a political person in the mayor's office or in police administration. At first, it would be a quiet investigation. By tomorrow or the next day, the police would report it to the media. His face would be a fourth page article in the Herald and maybe he'd make the local television news as being missing. Once that happened, it would be difficult to return to the University, which liked its professors to be low key. It wasn't as if Ulysses was going back to Miami, but still, he'd like his academic name to be untarnished.

He wondered if he should call Penny and tell her he needed time to think and ask her to not look for him. He decided to send a text when he stopped for lunch, just to reassure her, and maybe she'd calm down and go about her day as normal. But it would infuriate her. She'd think he was escaping and would be bitter because she couldn't. She would never understand he had no escape. His pain went with him, no matter where he was.

He kept with late morning traffic as he traveled through Knoxville and followed the signs for Lexington. North of Knoxville, he started the ascent over Jellico Mountain. He was reminded of reading *The Hobbit* and wondered if there was a dragon protecting its treasures in a nearby cave. The Rockies were bigger than the Appalachians, but there was something majestic about being here. Helen will never experience these mountains, he thought. She'll never stop on the side of the interstate and look out over the hills and get that feeling of awe a child gets when seeing something so powerful for the first time. Ulysses thought about all the other things she wouldn't do, and with each thought it was like another nail in his heart. Her first day of school will be missed. She'll never have a best friend or worst enemy. There won't be any crushes or first loves, and she'll never be broken hearted. She can't graduate high school or go to her first day of college. She'll never hold a job, get married, or have children. She'll never cause the death of her only child. Helen will miss it all.

Ulysses didn't cry as he crossed the mountains, but as he descended the mountains into Jellico, the overpowering sense of loss made his chest ache and his head hurt. What in life could be worse than this, he wondered. What else could make a person give up everything? He wanted it to end. He was ready to give in, and yet he held back. What if there was a *hell*? Could it be any worse than living like this? Maybe. Maybe it could. If he knew there was *nothing* at his death and this life was it, he'd accept it and give up. Give in. But not knowing was just enough to keep him moving forward.

He passed through Jellico and saw the *Welcome to Kentucky Unbridled Spirit* sign. He considered stopping at the Kentucky welcome rest stop to stretch his legs, but he still wanted to put miles between him and Miami. He wanted to eat up the road.

As he passed the rest stop, he saw her. A thin, stringy-haired teenager wearing shorts and a yellow tank top with her thumb up and a smile that made him think of Helen. This was someone's little girl on the road. She may have been sixteen, but couldn't have been older than seventeen. Here she was, thumbing a ride. If it had been Helen, he'd have wanted someone to help her, give her a ride and talk to her. Find out where she's going, but more important, where she has been. He'd want someone to find her help.

He hit his break before he could talk himself out of it. He'd never picked up a hitchhiker and knew there was risk, but what the fuck did he have to lose? If she pulled a gun out and shot him in the belly, so what? He wanted to die anyway. What better way to die than wanting to do some good in the world for a person that needed it?

Once he stopped, Ulysses watched this rail of a girl in the passenger side door mirror as she ran toward the Camry. Her clothes were too loose, as if she'd been on the road for a long time. He hoped she wasn't selling herself for money or drugs. She had one bag flung over her left shoulder, and it looked heavy. He was tempted to get out and help her put it in the backseat, but decided it might be seen as an aggressive behavior. She was a butterfly, and he wanted her to land. He wanted to hear her life story. He suspected hers was worse than his.

When she reached the passenger door, she opened it. "Oh man, thanks. It's so hot. How far are you going?"

He shrugged. He almost asked *how far she wanted to go*, but decided it might be misinterpreted. "North of Cincinnati today," he said.

Her blue eyes lit up. "Can you take me that far?"

"Yeah, I can do that," he said.

"You're the greatest," she said as she got in. She tossed her bag in the back and put on her seatbelt.

Ulysses turned away and looked in the mirror at the traffic. He waited for a spot to open before moving back onto the interstate. Once he got up to speed, he asked, "What's your name?"

"Thelma is what my parents named me," she said, "but my friends just call me Thel, as in Thel from Hell."

He smiled. "I'm Ulysses."

"I appreciate the ride." He glanced at her and realized how pale her skin was. She didn't have the road weary tan most hitchhikers have or the suspicious exhaustion. Her eyes lit up her face and showed no fear, even though she'd just gotten into a car with a stranger.

"Where are you going?" he asked.

She processed the question a little too long, and Ulysses knew whatever city she named would be a lie. "Cleveland," she said.

Ulysses didn't care that it was a lie. He considered maybe she was going to see a boyfriend, or some guy she met on the internet, but he didn't think so. Thel seemed to be directed by no one but herself. She had self-confidence that young women don't have, and that was a good thing.

The thought that she was someone's daughter eased into his mind again, and he needed to know more about her. "You look like you're sixteen. Should you be hitchhiking across Kentucky and Ohio by yourself? Where's your family?"

"I'm eighteen," she said. "Do you want to see my license?"

He did, but he shook his head. He wondered if she had made a calculated risk he would refuse. He hoped she was telling the truth, but he doubted it. He'd intended on asking her questions, but figured whatever she told him would be a story. Why ask for lies?

After ten minutes of silence, she asked, "What are you running from?"

He glanced at her. The brightness in her eyes from before was gone, replaced with dark clouds. There was turbulence churning there, and he wondered where the fuck that came from.

"What makes you think I'm running from something?"

He changed lanes and passed a semi doing fifty-five. He saw the interstate was cut into a hill, and on both sides were the sides of cliffs made up of limestone. He had passed other cuts in the hills, but this one was fifty feet tall, and he wondered about the engineering. When he moved back into the right lane, she said, "You had a daughter."

That she knew of Helen didn't bother him. It was that she spoke of her in the past tense. *You had a daughter but no more* was what she meant.

He ignored that she used the past tense. "What makes you think I have a daughter?"

He glanced at her, and she seemed to peer through him. "You wouldn't have picked me up from the side of the road if you didn't want to protect me, like you would want to protect her, right? You couldn't pass by and think of me being left on the road."

He wasn't going to deny it. "Yeah, I have a daughter," he said.

A few minutes passed. "But you don't anymore. What happened to her?" Thel asked.

He was silent, but couldn't stand the question being unanswered. "She died," he finally whispered. He turned to her, and Thel's eyes were now the dark blue-green of the Atlantic Ocean, and she seemed to be pulling him into them. Such beautiful eyes. He heard the thumping of his tires striking the rumble strip, and he pulled away from her gaze back to the road to correct his course. "How'd you know?" he asked.

"Your face is sad," she said. "You look like you've buried her a thousand times over, and you've been crying. Didn't you know?"

He reached to his face and wiped the wet from his cheeks. He hadn't known. How could a person cry and not know it?

He thought about Penny and wondered what she would think about him having a pretty teenager in the car. He felt the sudden urge to stop the car and send her a text to let her know he was alive. He even let his foot off the accelerator. He looked to Thel to explain and got lost in those stormy eyes again. He took a deep breath and jerked his head back to the road, pressing on the gas to bring them up to speed. Her eyes welcomed him. They wanted him to fall into them.

"What are you thinking?" she asked.

"I wanted to send my wife a text," he said.

"I can do that for you," she said and reached for the phone in the console before Ulysses could stop her. She punched buttons on the cheap phone, so it lit up. "You don't have your wife's number or anyone's programmed into your phone?"

"It's a new phone," he said.

"Yeah," she said as if she didn't believe that was the only explanation, but it seemed she knew the full story. "What's her name?"

"Penelope," he said.

"Really? It's lovely. I bet she's just as lovely as her name."

"She is," he said.

Thel's fingers moved over the phone as she typed in the name. "Now, what's her number?" Ulysses reluctantly told her the number, and she punched it in. "What do you want to tell her?"

Ulysses thought about it. He knew it needed to be an abbreviated version of the text he intended to send. He didn't want to give Thel too much information about himself, but he wanted Penny to understand. "Just write: Don't worry. I'm alright. And sign it Ulysses. She won't recognize the number."

In the corner of his eye, he saw Thel still watching him. He wanted to turn to her but was afraid of getting lost in her eyes. "That's not what you want to say," she said.

Anger rose up in his chest. "What do you know about it?"

"You want to tell her you love her, don't you?"

"Maybe," he said.

"And you want to tell her you're not coming home."

Ulysses turned to Thel and wondered what she was. "You can't know that," he said. She paid him no attention as her fingers flitted about the face of the phone. "What are you typing?"

She ignored him, and he turned back to the road. When she looked up, a chime played on the phone, which must have meant that the message had been sent. "It'll make her feel better," she said.

He gripped the wheel. "Tell me what you wrote."

He knew she was smiling. "The truth," she said.

"How do you know what's truth or not?"

This young girl sigh almost rose to a moan. "I was born with a gift of knowing what people want, and I try to give it to them. For Penny, you above all else want her—"

"I never told you that's what I called her."

"But I know," Thel said. "You want Penny to forgive you for the death of your little girl. You want her to understand why you do what you do, and to forgive you for that. But most of all, you want her to carry on."

"You can't know all of that," he said.

"But I do," she said. "And I know other things."

Ulysses was hesitant to ask, but how could he not? "What else do you know about me?"

"You were a good father," she said. "You carry your daughter with you still, her life and her death, and she speaks to me through you. She begs me to give you what you most desire, because there is no honor in you giving it to yourself." She sang the words, and it drew him in.

"What does she say I want?" he asked.

"Sweet, sweet death," she intoned.

193

With each word her voice rose in pitch, and it pulled him in. He couldn't concentrate on anything but her words. He could barely get his question out. "You will give me this?"

"No pain. No loss. No grief. No guilt."

Ulysses turned, taken in by her godly voice, so beautiful, and he saw those dark violent eyes and was consumed by them. She could give him death. Sweet death. She could take him to the other side where Helen waited for him. Or was it Hell beckoning with its fiery persuasion? Did it matter?

"Come to me," Thel called out. "Be with me." She sang in a thousand voices, each drawing him in.

She held her arms out for an embrace. He let go of the wheel, and reached toward her. He enfolded his arms about her. He found she no longer had the body of a lithe teenager, but that of a woman. Her chest heaved against his, and her mouth sought his. The eyes hadn't changed, except now he saw they were old. Ancient. She wanted to consume him. As he gave in, he heard the tires cross the rumble strip, but it was distant in his ears.

She still hummed his death song. Her tongue vibrated against his as she pulled him into her.

In the small part of his mind not taken in by her, he felt the Camry shudder. He guessed it had moved off the shoulder onto the grass, vaguely noting his foot had pressed the accelerator to the floor. Horns of nearby cars trumpeted Thel's song.

Her eyes still held his as she sang about his death.

Just before the Camry struck the limestone, time seemed to stop. He came back to himself and realized what he was holding wasn't human, but something monstrous. She fed off him, and in exchange, she gave him the death he desired.

The crash was loud, like a thousand thunders at once. Ulysses felt his body thrown this way and that. He was shattered but didn't die just yet. He heard voices, none of them Thel's. She was gone. He lay, unmoving, listening to the sounds of waves breaking on the rocks. Such a peaceful sound. He opened his eyes long enough to see he was mistaken. The sound was rocks from above falling onto what was left of the Camry. He took one last breath. All faded to white. He died hearing sirens wailing in the distance.

BORN FALSE WITNESS

◆ ◆ ◆

"Hey, brother, I'll be right back. I need a smoke."

Ed Casteel glances at his sister, Janine, and nods. "Okay, Sis. Take whatever time you need. She's resting now."

"Yeah. Ma's a fighter." Janine slides through the hospital room door, already pulling the pack of Virginia Slims out of her back pocket.

When the door shuts, Ed is thankful for the moment alone with their mother. It might be all he'll get. He's got to tell her the truth—everything he's kept from her—so she'll know.

He glances at the little monitor reporting her vitals. She's holding her own for now. She's always been as strong as steel. Her eyes are closed, and her breathing labored. The nurse told Ed earlier she could pass any moment or hang on for days, depending on her will to live. The light from the screen casts Ma's lined face in a pale blue light, reminding Ed of the hazy, summer skies of his childhood. Not an unhappy time, but not a time he likes to remember. At about eleven or twelve, he got lost, and never found his way back. He discovered blue skies weren't meant for him, not even a little bit. It made for a jarring realization.

Ma groans, and for a moment Ed thinks she's trying to tell him she's sorry about how it all turned out. It's alright, Ed, you're okay, she says in his mind. Be who you are, not who the rest of the world wants you to be. Be true. Just be yourself. He

196

wants with all his damaged soul to hear her say this, but he recognizes it's not her. It can't be. If she knew him, truly knew him, he'd have been cast out. He still loves her, even if she wouldn't bend. Not when he was a child. Not now. He hated his father, but it was Ed's love for his mother that made him leave. He couldn't stand the thought of her even suspecting his darkness. He seldom came back, but when he did, she doted on him like a child returned from a forgotten war.

His brothers and sister stayed close, remaining under Ma's watchful eye, constrained to the ideal she created. She only wanted them to be happy. That's what she said. But her idea of happiness was being confined within her small world, and not being creative with life: Do what you're supposed to do and don't question it. If her children were close, she could maintain control of them and make sure they did not stray.

Is that why she fights death? he wonders. So, she can keep them in the fold? Make them be true to her? Once she dies, what will happen?

He slides his fingers into her hand, and it reminds him of holding a claw. He shivers. He holds on, hoping, if nothing else, she can feel his touch and know she's loved. By one of her children, at least. His presence here means something, doesn't it?

He's not getting younger and knows he must speak his piece. He clears his throat. Takes a breath. "I'm not good, Ma. It wasn't anything you or Pa did. You gave me a good life, but there's something in me. It's spoiled. Rotten. I'm everything you feared any of us might be. Worse even."

It's all said in whispers, but it fills the room, even the dark corners. Ed glances at the door, waiting for someone to walk in. No one does. After a minute, he breathes easier, but feels like what he said has soaked into the walls and can be heard if someone listens close enough. He resists the impulse to leave the hospital. Not yet, he thinks, I can't leave yet.

Twenty minute later, Janine returns. She brings Ed a coffee and tells him the cafeteria makes a good brew. The bitterness of it soothes his thoughts, and he thanks her. They sit in silence. The only sound is their mother's labored breathing, until Janine says, "Ma never worried about you. You were a thousand miles away, but she always knew you were fine."

Ed has nothing to say to this.

"If I had a bad day at work," his sister continues, "she would want to pray about it. I didn't tell her anything. None of us did, but she still worried about each of us." Janine pauses. "Except you."

Janine's voice is soothing and non-confrontational. Ed knows she's leading up to a question, and he waits for it.

"What did she know about you that the rest of us didn't?"

Ed shrugs, comfortably. He's dealt with inquiring minds his whole life, and he's learned confidence is usually accepted as truth. "That I could take care of myself, that's all."

Janine nods, and Ed knows he's struck a nerve. "And the rest of us couldn't, that's what you're saying, right?"

It's not what he's saying, but he doesn't mind that Janine thinks so.

She twirls her wedding ring around, and Ed wonders if it's his stare or if there is something else making her nervous. "You haven't been back home for six or seven years, and probably not been here for more than a month's time since you left when you were—what? Twenty-two?"

"Twenty-one," Ed says.

"Gone all that time, and in one sentence, you've defined us. It wasn't even a sentence about us, but about you. Well done, brother."

He finds no animus in Janine's tone, but he detects curiosity, and that must be prevented. Always, the best defense is offense, but he knows he can't make it about her. "Why isn't Jimmy here?" he asks.

Jimmy is the oldest, and Ed the baby. Bookends, so to speak. In their childhood, Jimmy thought it was his place to be in control. Janine, Tommy, and Robbie fell in line, but Ed learned to not be seen.

"He was here this afternoon," Janine says. She assumes Ed's question is marked with speculation. "If you're thinking he's not here because you are, that's not it. He and Wanda are having a rough patch."

Ed glances at their mother, and then back to Janine. "Keep your voice down, Sis. Ma might rise from her death bed."

"If I thought it would pull her out of this, I'd tell Ma Jimmy's planning to file for divorce as soon as she's gone. Hell, he's had a girlfriend for six months." Janine huffs. "He thinks it's a secret."

This fact settles between them. Ed has to press his lips tight to keep from laughing. He's got so many questions he doesn't know where to start, so he asks the most obvious first. "Who is it?"

He hadn't hidden his humor well enough because Janine says, "It's okay if you think it's funny. I do. She's some skank from Richmond he met at work, so I am told."

This leads to the second question. "Who told you?"

She smiles, but shakes her head. "No one you know."

Janine has always had her secrets, and Ed likes this about her, but at this moment, it irritates him. He's not asking for a name, but he wants to know if she has a reliable source of information. "Is it true?" he asks.

"Yeah."

He thinks she's being coy with him, but only because there's something else she wants to tell him. He can see it in her eyes. But she's waiting for him to ask the right question. She wants him to know.

"How long's Ma been sick?" he asks.

"Six months."

In Ed's monthly phone calls, there hadn't been a word of his mother's illness, and he hadn't detected failed health. She sounded no different at eighty-one than she had at fifty-six when he left. Had Janine not left a voicemail, he wouldn't have known she was in the hospital.

"I talked to her three weeks ago," he says. "Ma was fine, or she said she was." Even as he said it, Ed realizes his mother had lied, although she would have called it born false witness.

"She didn't want you to know."

"But everyone else knew?"

Janine nods.

"Why didn't she want me to know?"

Janine leans her head back and shuts her eyes. "Ma never said. She looked forward to your phone calls and told us everything you said. It'll sound strange, but we lived vicariously through all you've done."

He'd only told Ma lies, so he knows they hadn't lived vicariously through what he'd done, only through the fiction he provided. He'd escaped his family, giving Ma a post office box address and a cell phone number, but not telling her he'd legally changed his name when he left. He told her fairy tales, and never regretted it. He'd saved her from the truth.

"You've been paying Ma's bills?"

Janine's eyes light up, and Ed knows he gotten closer to what she wants him to know. He waits for the story, but all Janine says is, "Yeah, about six months ago, when she found out about the cancer. She went to a lawyer. Had papers drawn up."

Ed knows the answer, but he asks anyway. "What papers?'

"Power of attorney. Will. She wouldn't sign a living will until the lawyer told her it'd make it so God could take her when He chose, not when the doctors chose." She glances at Ma, as if their mother is going to rise and walk out of the hospital just to prove the world wrong. "She's breathing on her own, but barely, and she hasn't had anything to eat or drink for forty-eight hours. The hand of God is coming soon, I guess. Maybe tonight."

Ed thinks so, too. That she'll die soon, not that God will take her. He doesn't believe in God, not the one Ma believes in. "Has Ma ever been to a lawyer before? Maybe when they bought the house sixty years ago." He knows if he keeps asking questions, he'll touch on what Janine wants to tell him, and she'll blather what's on her mind.

"When Pa died," she says, "I took her to the lawyer in Richmond, and he went through the assets. Ma and Pa owned everything together, so she didn't have to go to court. She was nervous, like it was a first date. I kept telling her the lawyer was just a man. He puts his pants on just like the rest of us. She said, 'No. Lawyers are smart. They're rich.' This lawyer set her mind at ease and treated her respectful. He listened to her stories."

Ed laughs. "Oh, Lord, sis. You let her tell stories?"

He sees Janine flinch at the Lord's name being taken in vain, but she's heard worse on television hourly. "Like I could stop her, brother. The lawyer didn't mind; he listened. He didn't charge much either. When she passes, he said he would help me with the estate."

The light strikes Janine's face in a way Ed knows they'd arrived where she's been leading them. "You're taking care of the estate?" he asks, and then says. "Just the house and twenty acres, right?"

Janine's eyes are round like pale, gray moons. She leans back in her chair, her eyes go unfocused for a few heartbeats, and then she sits up, her expression just shy of unwanted ecstasy. "You remember when we were kids, and Pa was never home. He worked two or three jobs, weekends, and Ma worked at the dry cleaners when we were in school? Did you ever ask yourself how they could work so much and never have anything? How many peanut butter sandwiches did we take to school? Do you remember Christmas was always clothes, no toys, just things we needed, but nothing we wanted."

Ed is confused. "Yeah, I remember. So, what?"

"They worked, and they saved."

"What? How much?"

"Three point five million dollars," Janine says, her smile stretching across her face. "It's been invested well all that time. Our lifetimes. The will divvies it up between the five of us. The lawyer said no taxes."

Ed remembers having a hole in his sneakers all of eighth grade, but he never asked for new shoes. Jimmy had worn the shoes new and then Tommy had his turn, then Robbie, and finally Ed. Wouldn't common decency have led parents to get new shoes for the youngest?

"They had money the entire time?" Ed asks.

"Yeah, lots of it. They saved every dime."

"Jesus."

"They behaved as if we were dirt poor, and now, we're not going to be rich, but we won't be hurting, will we?"

Ed shakes his head, speechless. He doesn't care about the money. He has money. But how would his childhood have been different? He thinks on this for a few minutes and decides nothing would have changed. He would still have been discontented, but more comfortable. When he looks up, he sees Janine is excited, and it all makes sense now. "Let me guess. Jimmy's spending his money to get a divorce?"

Janine nods. "His lawyer says his wife will get nothing."

"What's Tommy and Robbie spending theirs on?"

"Tommy signed a contract yesterday for an in-ground pool, and Robbie put a trip to Hawaii on his credit card."

Ed leans toward her. "And you?"

"I'm going to file for divorce, too," she says. "Then I'm going to lift this here—" She points to her chin. "—and tuck this." She points to her stomach. She grins. "And maybe a boob job."

"You got a boyfriend?"

She shakes her head. "Not looking like this. I've not been my best. I can quit my job, start exercising, and maybe find myself some happiness. That's what the others are doing."

None of this shocks Ed, and he knows it has less to do with money than it does their mother dying.

"What are you going to do with your share?"

He blinks a few times, to make it seem he's considering the question, but he already knows. "I don't want any part of it."

Janine's gray eyes narrow at this answer. "Why? You can use that money, can't you?"

He shrugs.

Janine grunts and holds her arms across her chest. "I don't

understand you, brother. It wasn't that bad of a childhood, was it?"

"Have you put it so far out of your mind?" Ed watches Janine bite her lip, and he waits for her to answer. When she doesn't, he smiles. "It's all I can do to eat beans and cornbread now. My God, didn't we have it almost every other fucking day?"

How does Ed know this will be a catalyst to her anger? Her cheeks bloom in red, and she looks at him as if it's blasphemy. In a quiet voice, she says, "I like beans and cornbread."

"Me, too. Just not every other day," he says. He wants to turn the conversation, so he asks, "A divorce? Really? Is Buddy that bad?"

Janine looks sad and shakes her head. "Nah, he's just not that good. He doesn't beat me. He has a good job. He's a little overweight, but not that fat. I just don't love him."

Ed sighs and says the only truth he knows. "Love isn't all it's cracked up to be, sis. Sometimes, if something works, you go with it, because you don't know what's around the corner."

Ma chooses that moment to groan, as if she's expressing her disappointment or maybe echoing agreement. Her eyes are closed. Ed has turned to Ma, expecting her to have more to say, because she always spoke her mind, but she settles deeper in the bed.

To Janine it must have appeared Ed cowered away from Ma because she asks, "Are you afraid of her? Even now?"

He lies. "I am; always have been."

"Yeah, me, too. All of us were, even Pa."

Ed smiles. "We were all God fearing and Ma fearing."

There is silence as his joke settles in Janine's mind. She starts laughing, as if it's the funniest thing she's ever heard.

Ed looks at the door, worried a nurse will pass by. "Sister, someone's going to hear you."

This only makes Janine laugh louder, so he lets her be.

When the laugher fades, Janine cocks her head to the side and says, "Hey, brother, when Ma dies, you can finally come out. You know that, right? Only Jimmy will be judgmental about it."

Ed doesn't understand what she means for a second, and when it strikes him that Janine thinks he's gay, he says, "I'm not gay, sis." He laughs, but he keeps it controlled.

"You've never married, and you live out west. You're thin. Good looking. We all thought…" She doesn't finish.

He shakes his head. "That's not why I left."

"Why did you leave then? And don't say to get away from Ma and Pa. You could have gone to Lexington if it were them. What's so terrible about you that you had to live across the country?"

He wants to tell her, so she can be a stand-in for Ma. He wants to be honest for once in his life. He knows he can't. He should have agreed he was gay. This would have been a good lie, and it would have ensured his siblings would never try to find him.

He decides to tell the truth, or at least, a truth. "I'm an atheist," he says, "and I needed to get away from the godliness here. It was stifling and has been since we were kids. Having to go to church on Sundays was like driving a stake through my heart. I was different."

The silence stretches uncomfortably long, not uncomfortable for Ed though. When Janine's ready to talk, she bites her bottom lip. "I understand. It's okay. I still love you, brother, and would rather have you close by."

This may be true, but Ed doubts her love. She doesn't know anything about him to love. He's known for all his memory love fostered by family is watered-down. You take care of your own as an act of responsibility, not of love, and it's the easiest love to walk away from.

He unexpectedly feels close to his sister, and this makes him uneasy, so he chooses to put the distance back between them.

"You know what's funny. Ma's dying and leaving us her fortune, and you all are changing, becoming what you always wanted to be and what our parents didn't want us to be. I'm holding true to what I always have been. You and the others let Ma and Pa think you were good, and maybe you were, but you sacrificed yourselves for them."

He especially likes that he's damned his siblings as being untrue to their nature, but it falls flat with Janine. She sees it as mean. "You should get off your high horse, Ed, and stop acting like you're superior. It's not fair. Ma was a good parent. The best, and she loved us."

Ed starts to speak, but holds it in. What good will it do to argue? Ma was a terrible parent. She let her five kids go to school with holes in their shoes and holes in their stomachs. But that wasn't his point, and Janine is too dense to get the point. She could have said that, unlike him, at least they stuck around to help take care of their parents as they died. He wouldn't have disagreed.

He's done making small talk, and he takes their mother's hand again and leans in close. He listens for her breath sounds and faintly hears the gasping of Ma's lungs.

Janine can't stand Ed's silence. She shifts in her chair, and finally stands up. "I'm going for another smoke."

Ed nods and says he'll come find her if anything happens. When the door shuts, he almost laughs. She's pissed because she thinks he's being judgmental, and that's a joke. He'd never pass judgment. Not on anyone, except maybe himself. He knows his own damnation. He feels like he's alone in a burning house, throwing gasoline on the fire.

He can't help himself. He likes the burn.

He stares into Ma's face, and he's mesmerized by the lines etched into her skin, as if they're a road map of her life. What had she been born into that made her so hard? Had she gone without in her childhood? Had her father emotionally abused her? Was she different like him?

He always felt connected to Ma and wanted to tell her about what he had become, not because she would absolve him or give him her blessing, but because someone needed to know.

Yet, he could never bring himself to ever say the words. Until now.

"I'm not good," he begins, his voice only a whisper. "Seventy-one is my number, Ma. I remember every face."

She groans, and her hand tightens on his. It's a reflex, he thinks, but he's not sure. The grasp is firm.

"I want to quit, Ma," he continues. "Every time, I tell myself it's my last, but it's like I got a disease that must be fed. I'm not right, and I know I can't be right, okay? I got to be myself. This is who I am. You never saw me, truly, but you never saw Jimmy, either. Not Janine, or Tommy. Not Robbie. They've not even been honest with themselves. I always knew what I was. I was true to myself, at least. But Ma, you didn't make me like this. I was always like this. I would have been, no matter what you did for me. It's them you made, and if you're damned, that's what it should be for. Not for me."

He pauses. Breathes in. Breathes out. He feels lighter, as if he's unloaded a thousand pounds from his shoulders, but there's more.

"I'm invisible when I want to be. Not truly invisible, but people don't notice me. I don't know if it's because I blend in, or that they don't want to see me. I don't choose my numbers randomly. I study them, follow them, become them, a part of the backdrop of their lives. I am organized. Always prepared." He pauses, then adds, "I'm sorry I lied to you, but I had to. You wouldn't have let me live as I have if I told you."

He stands, takes a few steps toward the door, but stops. He walks back to Ma, leans over her, listens to a few breaths, and whispers, "I promise to stop killing, Ma. I'll try." He rises and looks down at her, wondering if there is anything else he needs to say or do, but all he does is whisper his final goodbye and leaves.

He doesn't see Janine in his walk through the parking garage to his car, and he is thankful for this. He'd made a promise to Ma, and he doesn't want Janine to be one of his number.

A ROBOT DOESN'T CRY

◆ ◆ ◆

My wife is a robot.

She changed. She no longer laughs at my jokes. She doesn't smile. She won't reach to me in the middle of the night or lay close on a cold night. When I come into a room, she leaves. She goes to work early and stays late. And the touch of her skin is three to four degrees cooler than it should be. She has a pulse—I've felt for it in the middle of the night, on her wrist, her neck, her temple—but a pulse doesn't make her human.

At first, I thought Maggie had a boyfriend, so I followed her. I read her emails, texts, social media messaging, all of it. There is no boyfriend. When she leaves early, she goes straight to work, and she's at work until late. She eats lunch at her desk and doesn't talk to her co-workers.

At home, I asked if she felt okay, and she said she was fine. I told her she should make a doctor's appointment. That she wasn't herself. She smiled at that, but she went to the doctor anyway. Nothing was wrong. I wondered if he was part of it. Was the doctor fucking her?

For weeks, I racked my brain. Why is my wife different? Had I done something to deserve the stares that freeze me in my tracks?

We still fuck. Usually, on Sunday morning. And it's not that she lays there. She's not impassive. She works it like she's fighting for her life. But it's all an exercise. An act. Before, her hips never moved. Her tongue didn't explore. And her orgasms, when she had them, were soft, quiet whimpers, not the monolithic, aggressive struggles she has now. It's as if she wants to pull me into her and consume me.

Two weeks ago, she said she had a business trip out of state at the end of the week, and I offered to tag along. Her lips stretched across her face, and that's when I first imagined the mechanisms necessary to extend the lips. I could see it all. The cogs and wheels shifting and turning beneath the skin, reacting to what I'd said, all so she could smile. Once I saw it, I couldn't unsee it. No, she told me. It's only one night away.

Until she left for the trip, I didn't want to believe. But I watched her, and what I had always thought was indecisiveness, was the lag of the computer chip in her brain calculating what would most be like Maggie. *How* would Maggie respond to this or that? *What* would she say or do? The *fucking* could be programmed, to the final heave and moan, but how can day to day life choices be anticipated? It's not as simple as making a decision. It's making a decision that will mimic Maggie. No algorithm can predict every act.

She left for her trip, and I couldn't sleep. I thought about all the changes in her, and I finally understood. That she was a robot explained it all. The cold, detached way about her. Her savage lovemaking. The expressionless, pale intonation of her usual voice.

They'd made her a robot, but why? Nothing could be gained from me. My time of knowing had passed. What I knew was likely public. Anyway, those synapses no longer fire. All that's there now is a bright flash and the noise of thunder. And pain.

As far as I knew, nothing could be gained from Maggie, either. She's not part of the machine. A paper pusher is all. Her office handles nothing unknown.

I was missing something, but I didn't know what.

When she returned, she told me she loved me. She missed me. She put her lips to mine, and we made love on the couch.

She held me and told me she'd try to do better. She said she hadn't been herself. She told me she was sorry. She traced my scars with her fingertips and tried to not cry. But she did. A robot doesn't cry. It can't, can it? Had I been wrong?

A week passed, and life was like before. We watched television together and drank wine while we cooked. We made love. She laughed. She smiled. I had my wife back.

And yet, I didn't.

This morning, after she left for work, I cleaned the bedroom. Made the bed. Put water glasses in the dishwasher. Carried her suitcase to the closet and lifted it up to the shelf, but I had a thought. I set it back down, and opened zippers. What was I searching for? Dirty clothes? Maybe. What I found was a business card. Rosalyn Edmonson, PhD., Life Planner. On the back was a time and date. There had been no business trip. She'd been to this life planner. Was this code for reprogrammer?

Now, I knew. The robot had noticed me noticing her. She extrapolated that I knew she wasn't my wife. Data collected. Then analyzed. A new program written by the doctor. I think they failed to take into account the effect war had on me. It's said that war makes a man, but it doesn't. War undoes a man. I'm undone. And how's a good wife supposed to respond to this? She leaves her broken husband. That's how. Only a robot would stay. They made her into a robot so she would stay.

And now, as she sleeps next to me, I wonder if robots bleed.

THE FADING OF LIGHT
IN HER EYES

◆ ◆ ◆

"John? John? What would you sacrifice?"

John Edward Simpson startled awake and sat up in bed. The voice echoed in the walls of the house—or was it in his head? A dream, maybe? He waited for more to be said, but there was nothing. No breathing sounds to indicate someone else was in the room. No smells of another person. He sighed and laid his head down and listened. Nothing but a cold November wind.

The next time John heard the voice was in late January, and he was awake this time. Or at least he thought he was. "John? John. What would you give up to see the world?" He lay still, but all he heard after that was the wind. Had it been the wind? The voice had sounded next to his ear, right above him. But no one was there now. The alarm would have sounded if someone had come into the house. He knew that.

It was morning before he drifted off, not because he feared someone was in his home, but because of the question. He hadn't answered it. Not yet. But he thought about it. He was preoccupied with it. What *would* he give up?

The question remained in his mind during the remaining cold days of January, but by early February, it faded, as daydreams that have run their course will, like the smoke from a burnt-out candle.

Unlike January, when John had regular visitors at the farmhouse, weeks passed in February when no one came. He felt isolated. Then Gus Dent brought the month's groceries a week late, blaming his delay on the snow. John waved the delay away. "Can't change weather, can we?" he said.

As Gus labeled the packages and put them away, he talked about college basketball and John listened. John was starved for conversation, and he hung on every word. He even gave his own insights, based on talk radio and the Kentucky games he'd listened to.

John agreed to email March's grocery list before the end of the month, noting that it would be filled with usual misspellings. Gus laughed. "I figure it out, don't I? I knew peanut mother was peanut butter, didn't I? What if I had brought you the mother of all peanuts?" The hilarity between them was real, almost tangible.

When Gus left, the house felt quieter than usual. That was when John remembered the voice, and he had the irrational thought that the question had been asked by Gus. He was one of the few people who had the code to the security system. But why would Gus do it?

The first Saturday of March, when the icy weather cleared, Angie Erickson resumed cleaning John's house. The Kentucky winter had loosened its grip, and Angie opened all the windows to air out the house. Angie called him *darlin'* and *hon*, and always touched him on the shoulders or neck when she passed by. Was it a sign of affection, or did she do that to all the men she cleaned for? He liked her voice; it was almost silky. It was a skinny voice. Not a smoker, and not overly educated. She may have had some college, but would she clean houses if she had a degree? He often wondered if she was beautiful, but did that really matter to him?

Before she left, Angie kissed John on the temple, as she did every time, and asked if he needed anything. He considered the question, and he thought of all the things he wanted from her, but did he need any of them? He didn't like his thoughts and wondered if he blushed.

What would he give? What would he give up?

The spring rains blew in, and John could hear the creek at the bottom of the hill rushing by. He could smell the damp and hoped the sump pump worked to keep the crawl space dry. His brother, Mike, called, and he listened to his only sibling make pediatrics in Green Bay sound challenging. Everything was *fucking* in Wisconsin. Fucking cold. Fucking snow. Fucking wet. Fucking house. Fucking wife. Fucking life. Just before he hung up, Mike asked if all was well with living on the farm. The obligatory *fuck-my-life-but-yours-is-worse*. John answered he was fine; an acknowledgement he didn't need his brother's interference. He didn't want it either.

At the end of April, John heard the voice again. "Johnny? Hey John. Tell me what you'd do to be able to look into her eyes?"

John sat up in bed and shouted, "*Who's there?*" When no one answered, he said, "I *know* you're there." He waited a long time, but he was the only one in the room breathing. Still, he asked, "What do you want?"

But John knew. The voice wanted him to answer the fucking question, and the owner of the voice was waiting.

John got up and went to the kitchen. He found a Coke in the refrigerator, opened it, and drank. It was a different question this time. What would he do to look into her eyes? Whose eyes? There was no woman in his life. Only the cleaning lady. Angie Erickson. But there had been other women. Women he'd been close to. That he'd loved. That he'd screwed.

He thought of Rose Inman, the feel of her body against his and how her tongue explored. Her tongue had no fear. Had it been two years? Or three? When was the last time he thought of her?

Before that was Alice Freeman. She'd been soft and gentle. She'd been kind. And yet, she'd stolen from him. She'd wiped out half his savings and disappeared. When she called from Phoenix a few months later, she admitted to taking the money, but wouldn't say why she left, just that she had to get away. He figured she meant *get away from him*, but he wasn't sure. He wasn't that bad of a guy, was he?

He sat the Coke on the counter and wondered if he was losing his fucking mind. Why did he get so worked up over someone who wasn't there? If no one was there, why was his subconscious asking these questions? What was so important about these fucking questions?

When Angie cleaned the next Tuesday morning, she mentioned he was being quiet. He held up his book and said the feel of the story had taken him so deep, the world disappeared for him. Everything else was backdrop.

He intuited Angie wanted his attention, so he put the book down and listened to her hum as she cleaned. Her infectious merriment distracted him from his thoughts. When she moved back into the room, he asked her why she was in such a good mood.

"No reason," she said. He could sense the smile in her voice.

"Yeah, there is. I can hear it."

She stood quietly, weighing her response, it seemed. "I just like being here," she said.

He waited for her to continue, and when she didn't, he said, "I like you being here, too. It's nice."

He didn't know what she was thinking, but he could almost feel the heaviness of her thoughts. Then she said it: "Do you ever feel alone?"

It felt like a thousand pounds had landed on him. The unfairness of the question made his chest hurt. His answer was obvious, and he considered not answering. Finally, he said, "Yeah. I get lonely."

He thought she might suggest he get a cat or a dog to help with that. But she moved to him, leaned down, and kissed his cheek. "I can come over later, fix us some supper. We can sit on the back porch and listen to the crickets. We can be lonely together. How about that?"

John wondered why she was lonely, but he said, "Yeah, I'd

like that."

After she left, his daydreams swallowed him whole, and he fell asleep on the couch. It was as if he were wrapped in a cocoon, preparing himself for a rebirth, and he wasn't ready to emerge.

The voice woke him: "John, what will you give up to see Angie? What will you sacrifice?" There was a sense of mad urgency in the voice, a desperate need to have an answer.

John satisfied that need. He sat up, took a rush of breath into his lungs. *"Everything!"* he shouted.

He wanted to take his answer back. He should have said his left nut or pinkie toe, something ridiculous that would not bind him. He didn't want to have something taken from him he was unwilling to give.

Nothing happened. It had been a dream. Just a dream. There was no one in the room.

Yet, John felt an uneasiness in the pit of his stomach for the rest of the afternoon. He blamed it on nervousness. It was his first date in years. Or was it a date? What else would it be called? He paced a well-worn path throughout the house as he dwelled on the frustration of the not-knowing.

When Angie arrived, she led him into the kitchen, and he leaned against the counter while she cooked. She did have a degree in biology from Vanderbilt University, but she'd never used it. She had a failed marriage. Aging parents. A brother with a heroin addiction. "But I manage," she said.

"You're a saint," John said.

"Not even close."

They ate pan-fried trout at the table, and then took their wine out on the deck. Angie talked, and John listened. At some point, she grasped at his hand as if she needed saving, and maybe she did. She said there were days she felt stuck in a well, unable to see the light of the sun, and didn't think she'd ever be able to climb out. She said those days were insufferable. Those were the days she asked the big question: Haven't I suffered enough? He said he knew those days well, and that those days seemed to come in seasons.

They talked of happier times. She told him about being wooed by a singer in a band and the near fairy tale that led to her only marriage. She stopped at what caused its demise. He told her about his favorite poets, and recited parts of T.S. Eliot's *The Waste Land*.

After several hours, Angie complained about mosquitos draining her of blood, and John thought it was her prompt to go home. When they went in, she filled their glasses and led him to the couch. He wasn't sure if he was pulling her out of the well or climbing in with her. He wondered if she thought of him as her liberator. He didn't want to be a rescuer. It was too great of a burden. She was so close to him, how could he not lift her up?

There was a moment where they'd both grown quiet, and she leaned into him, bringing an unexpected physicality to the night. John didn't shy away from it. He pulled her to him, and she took him into her, clothing tossed aside to the floor.

John was attuned to the feel of her body as she moved against him. His fingertips ran a path along each of her ribs and circled her vertebrae as if her body were a map. He could smell the jasmine in her hair and the sweetness of her breath, and he tasted the grape of the wine. The rush of breath into her lungs sounded like the song of the crickets. This was everything to him.

In the midst of this magic, he heard the voice whisper in his ear, "Now John, you get, and you give."

He could see the halo of light around Angie as she moved above him, but he focused on the blue of a summer sky in the iris of her eyes which was circled by the yellow of the sun. He smiled at seeing her, and wondered at what price. Any blind person would give almost anything to have sight, if only long enough to see the light in a lover's eyes.

He sat up with her long, lean body wrapped about his, and they moved together. With each movement, John felt a loosening. It was as if he took a step back within his mind. He felt unbound, as if he were losing control. He now had sight, but with the sight came discord.

His body continued, but it wasn't him anymore. He was in the back seat, along for the ride, while the owner of the voice controlled his body. John was in the well now, able to see all that happened through the lens of the eye, but he had lost everything else.

Everything, he had said. *He'd given everything.* He had struck a bargain.

John had been blind since his early, and it was never enough to say he lived in darkness. What's darkness to a person who's not known light for decades? How is sunlight different from the dead of night? And yet, now he was enveloped in a worse darkness. He'd given up everything.

He'd lost the smell of jasmine.

He could only imagine his taste of fear.

He couldn't feel the touch of her neck.

He didn't hear her screams.

But he could see the fading of light in her eyes.

THE SOUNDS OF WAR

◆ ◆ ◆

I love my wife, Jeanie, and would walk to the ends of the earth for her, but she's a run-on sentence. She babbles in a stream of consciousness, and I'm drowning in it, but no one seems to notice. No one thinks to throw me a lifeline or even acknowledge my struggles.

The constancy reminds me of the sounds of war. Not that we fight or even raise our voices, but when it starts, I want to escape. I will do anything to get the noise out of my head.

When she drones on, I think about 1971, when a Viet Cong landmine obliterated Sammy Cook's left leg from the knee down. Much of his leg ended up on me. Our unit had been walking across a rice paddy twenty klicks from Huế. There weren't supposed to be landmines. The next thing I knew, I woke up looking at the bluest of all skies and I couldn't hear a fucking thing. It was the only peace I'd had in all the months I'd been there, until Jackie Dawson leaned over me and looked into my face to see if I was alive or not. When he grinned at me, his teeth were brighter than the sun. Jackie turned and yelled something to someone behind him, probably that I was still alive. He helped me sit up, so I could see the chaos.

The medic, Arnie whatever-his-name-was, had tied off Sammy's leg to stop the bleeding. He was yelling something at me, his mouth moving with his skinny little mustache going up and down, but I heard nothing. Only silence. In a war, si-lence is a blessed thing. Arnie walked over to me, put his hands under my arms and dragged me over to Sammy. He put my hands on the tourniquet and motioned for me to hold it. I had to look away from the mangled leg, but I held tight in the bustle of activity around me.

It seemed like an eternity before I felt someone pull my hands away. I looked into Arnie's dour face, and he nodded at me and pointed to the transport. I thought maybe he was the angel showing me the bus out of Hell. Even as I saw Sammy being lifted onto a stretcher and carried to the transport, I didn't move. Arnie handed me a sheet of paper. *Can you walk?* I nodded. I got to my feet and limped toward the vehicle.

I don't remember getting on the transport, or the drive to the field hospital. When I woke, it was like I was hearing time slipping away—a sucking sound, and I wondered if this was what it felt like to get old. I lay in bed, staring at the ceiling, watching the day turn into night and the night turn into day, the nurse feeding me broth, and people talking about me. *Shell-shocked. Unfit for war. Damaged.* I acknowledged none of it.

Sammy held a note in front of my face, and when my eyes focused, I read:

You need some pussy

There was no punctuation, but from the look on his face, I knew it was a question. He wrote:

That will help

I turned to my best friend and smiled.

You still can't hear

I could, but I shook my head. He scribbled:

You can talk

I shrugged. I hadn't tried and didn't want to try. I pointed to

Sammy's missing leg, and he wrote he'd get a prosthesis when he got back stateside.

As long as you can't hear you got your ticket too
You know that don't you
Don't fuck it up

In the middle of the night, a nurse I hadn't seen before stopped by my bed and asked how I was feeling. I smiled. She rattled on about the weather, local insects, and hating war. She told me I wasn't much of a talker, but wondered if I was a kisser. She leaned over me, put her lips to mine—her breath smelling of menthol cigarettes—and she kissed me. It was nothing spectacular, but I liked it. She told me to scoot over and then motioned with her hands. When I still didn't respond, she put her hands on my side and pushed. She climbed in next to me and pulled the cover over us.

My world became hot as we kissed, and in a way, I still don't understand, she adjusted me, then herself, and took me inside of her without ever shedding her nurse's uniform or removing my hospital gown or underwear. It didn't take me long to explode like that goddamned landmine, and she rolled off me but lay close, her head on my shoulder. She was on the chubby side, but I was in love. I wrote her a note that I was a virgin and she shut her eyes. It was too dim to see much, but I bet her cheeks were rosy from embarrassment. I guess you don't expect virgins in war. She wrote on a card that her name was Carol and she was from Ann Arbor, and she promised to come back in a few days. But she never did.

Sammy was shipped out the next day, and a week later, I got my discharge papers and left the war a different person. I was soft clay when I went to Vietnam, and the war shaped me, made me something I wasn't and wouldn't have otherwise been. I was brittle and broken, and I didn't want to be fixed.

I spent the rest of 1971 and the first eight months of 1972 living in my parents' basement. My mother described the recovery of my hearing as nothing less than a miracle. *Praise be to God, praise be to God*, she kept saying, and I wanted to tell her it wasn't God. How could a god allow war?

I started at the University of Kentucky in the fall and met Jeanie Lipetsk on my first day. I was sitting in freshman English, half asleep, when she walked in and sat next to me. She had a *you-have-no-chance-to-get-into-my-pants* curl to her lips and an *it'll-be-worth-it* curve to her body. She ignored me, but I didn't give up. After a half-semester of asking, she finally half-heartedly agreed to go out with me.

The night we went out, I told her about the noises I heard in the war. The rat-tat-tat of gunfire in the middle of the night. The whirring of the cicadas in the jungle. The insistent buzz of helicopters. All the hopeless screams. I'd been back in the states almost a year, but when I closed my eyes, I still heard those sounds. They were deafening.

She brushed a strand of dark hair from her eyes and said, "You'd give up what you've seen for innocence."

As if life experience is something you can trade for. I bit my tongue, knowing you can't explain war. Not to someone who's never been. And not to anyone who has been. War is inexplicable.

Later, in bed, she caught me smiling and asked what it was about. I couldn't tell her I'd realized war had gotten me laid twice, so I said I'd been thinking about how beautiful she was.

Jeanie wouldn't marry me until after we graduated and had jobs. She became a dental hygienist, and I was a shop teacher. I taught my students how to make everything but love and war.

It was a good life, though quiet. We chatted in the evenings, a little *how was your day*, and a few *love me do's*, but nothing excessive. No children, only each other, and happy. Maybe life was a bit monotonous, but I liked the monotony. It was the opposite of war.

I had a habit of comparing each day to a day I spent in the war. There were mind-numbingly rough days, but not once did

I hear a noise and think: Someone just died. Never did I worry that I could die.

We slept late most Saturday mornings, and then she went to the grocery store while I worked around the house. We went to movies in the afternoon or watched a game. On Saturday nights, we were partners in a bridge club. In between games, the women chatted in the kitchen, and the men drank a beer on the deck.

Sunday mornings, Jeanie and I went to church, and then had lunch with my parents or her parents and spent the day with them. When our parents passed, we had Sunday meals with our siblings.

Through all of it, war had a constant presence. Maybe it was a stapler, but I heard a sniper. In every clap of thunder, there was a camp being shelled. I thought incoherent whispers of casual conversations were the enemy.

I learned to steel myself against the sounds of war and to never flinch in the face of potential battle. I wore a mask to hide my fear.

There was nothing to fear, of course, but the war had changed me, unhinged me, and broken me. No one knew.

I retired a year before Jeanie, and the quiet was bliss. It was what I had worked for. It was my reward. I took in the silence of the day as if it were the only sustenance I needed to be alive.

I think I was healing. And then, Jeanie worked her last day.

You would think after being together forty years, married thirty-six of those, I would have known my wife. There's great comfort in being able to finish each other's sentences and not having to speak every thought.

The day after retiring, she woke me to say she had forgotten to put the garbage out the night before, the trashcan was almost full and was going to smell, and could I borrow the Donaldsons' truck and take the trash to the dump this morning?

When she was finished, I smiled and told her it would be

okay. I rolled over to go back to sleep because that's what I had done for the last year.

She didn't. She sat on the bed and outlined our day and all that we needed to accomplish. When I realized she wasn't going to leave me alone, I got up. I followed her along that day, busily helping her feel she was making good use of her time. I thought she'd realize the pace of retirement was slow, and silence was bliss.

Two weeks in, I figured out that for the last thirty-five years, she'd spent her day with her fingers in patients' mouths, asking them *yes* and *no* questions, telling them all that was on her mind. She carried on a one-sided conversation as she brushed and flossed. By the end of the day, her words were used up. In the evening, she had nothing left. I'd always thought she was at peace, but it was only that she'd used up her word count for the day, and maybe for the week. Or perhaps weekends were simply the days she rested.

She needs socialization, and I need solitude. I need the void. She needs to fill the void with words.

I'm her victim, immobilized by my own retirement. It's not like I can leave when a half-hour passes, like one of her patients. I must suffer through it. She's not the enemy, but her need to make words is.

That I stopped listening matters little to Jeanie.

I went to the VA Hospital last week. I told Jeanie it was for hearing aids, but it's the dreams I've been having. I'm in the middle of a battle with no weapon, and I see Sammy Cook die a thousand deaths. I do nothing. The fact I know Sammy made it back stateside doesn't make a difference.

The doctor told me I have PTSD, but he doubts the war is the cause of it. Not if I haven't had battle-related dreams for forty years. He kept asking what has changed, and I would only say, "Nothing. All is the same as it ever was." He said he could give me an antidepressant or something to help me sleep, but did I really want to feel like a goddamned zombie?

When I got home, I told Jeanie I was losing my hearing. "It's the old war wound," I said. I told her the doc thought it would help to have silence.

There is truth in this lie, and that gives me some comfort. But Jeanie's struggle to be non-communicative is unsettling. She began by speaking in whispers, letting the sentences die a tragic death of murmurings. Then she compensated with loud, one-word sentences. *EAT? SLEEP? WALK? TV?* This went on for about three days before she got tired of seeing me flinch at her every word, and she relapsed into non-stop discussion of the meaningless. After a half-day of this, I covered my ears with muffs and her monologue ceased, but the words built up in her head so each day became a field of landmines unleashed with one simple misstep.

My dreams are worse than ever.

Her need to talk equals my need for silence. She and I are at war, and our marriage is the casualty.

This morning I got up before she did and left a note. *Will be back before lunch.* I drove around the nineteen-mile loop of New Circle Road three times before stopping at Walgreens. On the way out, I deposited the box and instructions for the ear wax drops into the trash and ripped off the bottle's label so all Jeanie would see was a clear liquid.

I told her my doctor at the VA had spoken to a specialist at New York University who had suggested experimental drops for my ears. I said my doc was cautiously optimistic, but he also prescribed at least four hours of complete silence per day.

Jeanie was hesitant at first, but by mid-afternoon she began speaking in complete sentences. She edited all she said, and she mandated every other hour as silence.

I am hopeful, but doubt a truce constructed from lies will last. Perhaps it will be a path toward ending the war. If nothing else, Jeanie made love to me today. By my count, war has gotten me laid three times.

GROUP THERAPY

◆ ◆ ◆

Elliot Mann needs to sneeze, but he's holding it in so he can hear what Janice Dixson says. "Oscar gave me the clap the first time we slept together. I started itching a few days later, and it burned when I peed. I didn't know what it was. I thought maybe a UTI or we'd had too much sex, but my gyno told me it was gonorrhea, and said I needed to tell my partner. Oscar was the only man I'd been with for a year. Still, he blamed me."

Dr. Rick's grief therapy meets on Thursday nights in a run-down shopping center on the east side of Lexington. Tonight's group is small, only eight patients, and so far, there haven't been any tears, but Elliot knows there will be. He sits outside the group circle, almost in the corner, as he always does. At his first session, six months ago, Dr. Rick told him he should move his chair into the circle so he could join the group. Elliot shrugged. Dr. Rick let it go. Elliot likes being on the outside looking in.

Tommy Roark, pronounced Ro-Ark, sits with his back to Elliot, but Elliot sees him lean his brutish body forward as he says, "Why'd you marry him if he gave you an STD? That's fucked up." Tommy's a lawyer, but Elliot thinks he looks like a thug—greasy hair, thick shoulders, no neck—the kind of guy you imagine breaking legs for a living.

Janice shuts her eyes and slumps in her chair. "I got the clap *on* our wedding night," she says. There are a few groans in the

224

group, and she squeezes her eyes tight until it stops. When she opens her eyes, Dr. Rick encourages her with a nod, and she sighs. "It was prudish. I know, I know. I made Oscar wait to get into my pants, and so yeah, maybe Oscar was right. It was my fault. He had to satisfy himself somewhere, right?"

Elliot's need to sneeze has passed, but he burps a laugh and covers his mouth. Janice doesn't notice. "I'm so worried about Oscar. He's been gone for seven months. *Seven months.* Not a word. He wouldn't just leave me. I mean, he loves me. Or loved me. I know he's dead. Every time the phone rings, I think it's the police calling to tell me they found his body. I'm so freaking worried. It makes me ill."

Elliot gets a whiff of dirt—that wet, musty smell that bursts forth with the breaking of good soil. He can almost see the earthworms wriggling on the end of the shovel. It's not an unpleasant odor, but it's one that Elliot doesn't smell often.

"I'm so heartbroken," Janice says.

And a murderer, Elliot thinks. He doesn't know how she killed him or why, but he knows her husband's not breathing in the sweetness of the flowers growing above his decaying flesh. Elliot wonders if a boyfriend or a brother dug the hole while Janice idly sat by worrying over her story. She doesn't weigh more than a buck and a quarter soaking wet. She couldn't have dug the hole by herself, or lifted her husband into the grave. But she smelled the pungency of the dirt. That much, Elliot knows.

Janice bows her head, dabs at her eyes with a tissue, and then groans so that it's clear she's done for the night. Dr. Rick looks around the room, stops at Elliot and starts to speak. Elliot moves his head left and then right, one time. Dr. Rick moves on.

Elliot has never shared in group therapy, and maybe that's why he feels as bad today as he did the day of the fire—what he's deemed the worst fucking day of his life. He'd rather cut his wrists in Dr. Rick's office and bleed all over the other patients' sadness than share his story with them. But he fears if he did open his veins, he'd become a story for the others to tell, and he refuses to give them fodder for their self-inflicted drama.

For a long time, Elliot couldn't figure out why he came to therapy. He dreaded it for days leading up to the session. He couldn't sleep. He didn't eat. His stomach hurt. But he arrived early and paid attention to every word spoken with great anticipation and anxiety. Therapy was always a letdown. He felt miserable for all of them. Then one night, in an unexpected moment of clarity, he understood why he came. He thought —*he hoped*—eventually one of them would tell a story sadder than his own and he'd be able to move on with his life. He realized only someone else's story would move him to release his own. Let him forgive himself. But so far, Elliot had suffered through only mundane and ordinary tales of woe, albeit with near-hysteric effect from each delivery so he always felt beaten up afterward.

Dr. Rick finds another volunteer. After clearing her throat, Agnes Gillespie smiles like a wilted flower. She gathers herself and says, "Grief's a funny thing. I can go all day and not think one time about Ruby, and then I'll be getting in the tub, and I'll think about how she used to sing taking a bath when she was a little girl. That awful Hannah Montana stuff. And Barney. Ugh. Then I'll wonder what the fuck I could've done different to keep her from trying heroin that first time. It only takes the once to get addicted, you know. It permanently changes the chemistry of your brain. For Ruby, I think heroin made it so she wanted to die. I think she thought there was nothing she could do that was ever good enough for anyone, me included. Why live when you have no expectations of greatness, right? All this will go through my mind as I'm sitting on the edge of the tub, and I'll bathe myself in tears. Once they start coming, they won't stop. The tears will never stop."

Elliot breathes in the soap; not what Agnes uses, but the baby soap she used to wash Ruby when she was little. There were no tears when Ruby bathed, only laughter.

"I blame myself," Agnes adds.

Tommy Roark nods an affirmation to the admission of guilt, and Elliot wants to smack the back of his head, but resists, waiting for Dr. Rick or someone to defend Agnes. Surely someone will, but the confession is met with silence.

Except, within Elliot's gut, words rise up. He clenches his mouth tight to keep them unspoken, but temporarily loses the battle. "You can't—" he starts, but cuts himself off when he sees every eye in the group is on him. He waves his hands in a *never mind* gesture.

"What were you going to say, Elliot?" Dr. Rick asks.

"Yeah, say it," Tommy Roark says. He's turned in his chair to face Elliot, who now searches each face until he gets to Agnes. Her eyes plead with him to save her. She's wanting to be liberated. She wants redemption.

Elliot's nose tickles with the scent of the candles Agnes lights every night, and he can almost see the light of the flame in her eyes.

"It's not your fault," he says. "You can't blame yourself. Listen. Life's a crapshoot. A guy gets cancer, and he wants to know why so he can blame someone. Or blame God. He asks if God chose him, like, 'He's a sinner. He gets cancer. Incurable.' Boom! But it's not like that. There are no causes. There's no God issuing judgment. It's just dumb fucking luck. Someone has to get cancer, right? It's the roll of the dice or turn of the wheel. You become the unlucky bastard with the gene making you more susceptible. Tough shit. Life's a bitch. It's a cruel world. Sorry, Charlie. See you later, alligator. You're dead. All for chance."

The words rush out, and Elliot hears himself talking. He doesn't like the sound of his own voice, so he stops.

Tommy Roark turns his chair halfway so he doesn't have to crane his neck all the way around. "What the fuck does that have to do with Agnes' dead daughter? Your boyfriend die of cancer or something?"

Elliot ignores him and looks at Agnes. He speaks directly to her. "It could have been a million things that made her vulnerable that day, but none of them was you. Maybe she was just wired that way, willing to take extra risks for a chance of euphoria. Maybe she thought it would give her a religious experience. Something made it okay to her."

Tommy Roark grunts. "And maybe you're full of shit, Mr. *I-Won't-Talk-Unless-It's-To-Take-Away-Someone's-Need-For-Guilt.*"

Elliot looks to Dr. Rick, but Dr. Rick shrugs. It's not his fight.

"You got a story, don't you?" the lawyer asks. "You listen to us, on the edge of your seat. You take in our pain and grief, but you don't open your mouth. Why not?"

Elliot smells grass, as if Tommy's face is right in the green of a freshly mowed lawn. It's fleeting. When it passes, Elliot stands. "I shouldn't be here."

He moves through the group toward the door, stopping only when Dr. Rick says, "Wait, Elliot. Group therapy will help if you talk. You *should* be here, but you've got to tell us what happened."

Elliot turns, and looks around the room. He doesn't want to speak, but he wonders if it's true. Will speaking the words help, or is it just some psychoanalytical bullshit dreamed up by Dr. Rick? "My wife and kid died in a fire, and I didn't save them," he says.

He takes a measure of what he said and decides that saying it did not help. He knows he should leave, but his feet are planted.

"Could you have saved them?" Dr. Rick asks.

Elliot considers how to answer the question, and finally says, "Could I have taken action that would've prevented their deaths? Yeah, I think so."

Tommy Roark puts his right leg over his left, as if he's getting comfortable for the ensuing conversation. "Like Agnes could've done something to save Ruby's life? And I could've kept Amy from going to the grocery? Or Jackie-O could've feigned a stomach virus to keep John F. from the Dallas motorcade? Dude, get over yourself. Your story is no different from any of ours."

Elliot runs his hands through his hair and rubs his forehead. "You don't understand. I smelled smoke for a week. I smelled it. I didn't know where it came from. I could have gotten them out of the house."

"You mean, a fire burned in your house for seven days?" Agnes asks. "How can that be?"

Elliot doesn't understand what she means at first, and when he does, he shakes his head. "No, no, no. The fire hadn't started. I smelled it. I smelled the fire before it happened. Before the place burned to the fucking ground."

"But what do you mean you smelled the fire?" Agnes asks. Now, she's trying to save him.

Elliot wants to leave with the question unanswered and his story unspoken, but much to his surprise, he feels a need to explain. He didn't think he ever would. "I was on a business trip to Milwaukee. It was one of those trips you can't avoid because the industry is changing and you've got to figure it out so you don't get left behind in the dust. The moment I got on the plane, I smelled smoke. The flight attendant assured me nothing was burning. She said smoke alarms in planes are hypersensitive and would detect smoke. So, we took off and landed, and nothing happened. I smelled smoke the entire time we were in the air, like a forest was burning. When I got off the plane, the smell faded, but it was still there, like a memory of it. I considered that maybe I had a brain tumor. I smelled it the entire week, just faint enough that I didn't go around checking the hotel for fires, but I never stopped asking waiters if there was a kitchen fire."

Elliot moves back through the group and sits in his chair. "I hated being away from home. I missed my wife, Ella, and my son, Lil' Scottie. I called them, but the distance was there. I should have been home.

"It was a late flight out. If all went right, I would've been home by four in the morning, in time for me to hold Ella for a few hours before she woke up. I could see Scottie off to school.

It didn't happen like that. When the plane took off, I smelled smoke, burning, and I could barely take in a full breath. I told the flight attendant, and she went to the pilots. One of them came out of the cockpit and walked up and down the aisle, sniffing the air. He came to assure me everything was fine. He asked if I'd had anything to drink, and I told him I hadn't, but I still smelled smoke. He could see it was the truth. He could tell I was worried, but he didn't land the plane. He thought it was a panic attack."

Elliot takes a few breaths before he continues. "You see, I smelled smoke when I thought about leaving home and when I thought about coming home, and I should have known. I should have called Ella. I should have told her to get out of the house. I didn't know what was going to cause the fire— it was electrical, a time bomb waiting to happen—but if I had thought long and hard about it, I would've known she and Scottie were not safe. I didn't kill my family, but I'm guilty."

There is silence in the room, not a breath is heard, and then Tommy Roark cocks his head to the side. "You smelled your house burning from an airplane two states away? And you blame yourself? That's the craziest thing I've ever heard. You're a fucking lunatic."

The smell of grass is stronger now.

Elliot ignores this. "Since then, I smell things."

"What do you mean?" Dr. Rick asks.

Elliot breathes deep and captures a new car smell. "Since we've been here, you've been looking at your watch, and I didn't know why until just now. I smelled the interior of a brand-new car. The BMW in the lot? You can't wait to get in it and put the pedal to the metal?"

"Yeah," Dr. Rick admits.

Tommy Roark grunts. "You saw him pull up and get out."

"Maybe," Elliot says. "But how about this? Last week, when you told us about Amy's violent death in the Kroger's parking lot, I got a whiff of a cheap perfume and the smell of condoms. A girlfriend, right? While your wife was being murdered, you were cheating on her. The police called while you smoked cigarettes in bed with your girlfriend. You showed up to identify her body smelling of sex, right?"

Tommy Roark's silence is answer enough.

Elliot glances at Janice. "I smelled dirt earlier tonight. Why is that? Do you know?" Of course, he knows why, and Janice pleads with her eyes for him to say no more.

None of the others make eye contact, except for Agnes, who asks, "Is this a gift or a curse?"

Elliot stands. "I don't know. I wish I did. What I do know is that Dr. Rick was right. Talking has helped get the poison out of my brain. I'm not cured, but I'm done with group therapy. Thank you."

He moves through the group again, and this time he doesn't stop. In the lobby, he hears movement behind him, and he knows who it is. He makes it through the door of the office to the courtyard outside before a hand grabs his shoulder and twists him around. "You son of a bitch. How'd you know?"

Elliot brushes Tommy Roark's hands off him. "Does it matter? You can't be helped in there if you don't tell the truth. Your grief has stuck around because it's tied to your guilt. So fucking obvious."

Tommy Roark's fist moves in slow motion, and Elliot leans back just enough to only feel the rush of air as it misses his chin. He catches himself at the edge of losing his balance, just in time to see Tommy Roark's body pitch forward with momentum. Elliot reaches over and grabs the lawyer's thick shoulder and eases his unbalanced body to the ground below, resting his angry, contorted face inches from the fresh cut lawn.

Squatting on the ground next to Tommy Roark, Elliot says, "No one blames you. Amy wasn't murdered because of what you did."

Tommy Roark rolls over and looks up at Elliot, and there is no longer anger in his eyes—only sadness. "And you shouldn't blame yourself, dumbass. There was nothing you could've done to stop the fire. How could you have known? You need to get over yourself if you think you got superhuman powers."

Elliot nods and stands, then reaches a hand down to help Tommy Roark up.

THE KING OF TASTE

◆ ◆ ◆

Rooney Rodriguez had been a prep cook in the kitchen at Bebe's for three months before he heard the rumor that Chef Bilbao's taste buds had been chemically removed by a competing chef who wanted to settle a score for the theft of a roux.

"Acid-washed tongue," Marla whispered.

They were smoking on the restaurant's loading dock during a work break when she interrupted his harmless flirtation to share the rumor. Rooney cocked his head to the side and shut his eyes, unnerved at the thought of Chef Bilbao's professional castration. He repeated *acid-washed tongue* as if saying it could give it more meaning. "It'd be like breaking the fingers of a pianist. Harsh. Why the fuck would anyone do that?"

Marla leaned toward him like she had all the secrets in the world, but she hesitated, as if she wondered whether she could trust him. This made Rooney more curious about what she was going to say. To pry this from her, he looked into her dirt-brown eyes and gave a half-smile. She smiled back. "To get revenge, of course."

He puffed on the filtered Pall Mall, but could still smell Marla's flowery perfume—something vague, like Red. Her answer disappointed him. He hadn't meant to ask about the perpetrator's motive, which he thought was obvious. It was the human condition he'd been thinking about. It'd been a rhetorical question, anyway. Still, Rooney wanted to get in Marla's pants—he ached to screw her—so he acknowledged her statement with a nod.

She asked if he believed the rumor. He didn't, but he didn't say so. He lifted his thick shoulders and tossed his cigarette into the September rain. From what Rooney had seen so far at Bebe's, Chef Bilbao was an artist in the kitchen, with no signs of any handicap.

Before he returned to the line, he asked Marla who'd told her about the rumor, and she deflected the question. "It wasn't anyone here," she said, but of course it was. He could tell she was lying by the way she sucked in her fat bottom lip.

Rooney put no credence in the rumor, and he thought less of Marla for repeating it. He wouldn't tell Chef Bilbao, but someone would. Rooney began thinking of Marla as *dead-waitress-walking* and wondered if he could get into her pants before she was fired.

He couldn't. The next Tuesday, she didn't show up for work, and he figured she'd been shit-canned. No one lamented her loss except for Rooney, but that was the restaurant world. Here today, gone tomorrow. It was like she didn't exist anymore.

Six months passed, and the rumor faded from Rooney's mind, but then it was uttered by another prep cook. This time, it wasn't an acid wash by a competitor, but tongue cancer from a vengeful god. "It's why he speaks with a lisp," Hodges whispered. They'd finished their shift and sat in Rooney's car in the parking lot smoking a blunt at one in the morning. Hodges had asked Rooney to wait with him for Marco, a dishwasher who owed Hodges a hundred bucks as part of a deal for quality weed. Hodges had admitted Rooney's presence was meant to intimidate Marco. "Size does matter," he'd said, and laughed at his own joke. Rooney was six-four, two-forty, mostly muscle, but he wasn't a muscle freak like most of the guys at the gym. He worked out because it calmed him. He said it was meditative, like cooking.

"Bilbao doesn't have a lisp," he told Hodges. He took a long hit, held his breath until his lungs burned, and then blew it out. "He's Spanish. It's an accent. What the fuck's wrong with you, man?"

Hodges squinted at him. "No, no," he said. "I mean, yeah, he's Spanish, but he used to talk plainer, and now, because of the cancer, he can't express himself for shit. Haven't you noticed, man?"

Rooney shrugged. "What do I know? I mean, he tells me to add salt, I add salt. He tells me to julienne carrots, I julienne carrots. It's plain enough."

Hodges shook his head. "I mean, yeah, it's plain, but when he opened Bebe's, his voice was all over the place. Now, it's a whimper here, a whimper there, like he's half of himself. The cancer's got him."

Rooney shook his head, a bit stoned, but not wanting to give up the argument just yet. "If Bilbao's taste buds are shot, how can he give us all such precise directions about seasoning?"

As if he had all the patience in the world, Hodges put his hand on Rooney's shoulder. "Chef is just that good, and he can still smell like a motherfucker. Haven't you ever seen him put his snout into the food? It's like he's a goddamned bloodhound."

Rooney started to argue no chef could use his sense of smell to determine seasoning—especially salt—but Hodges opened his car door, jumped out, and began running. To intimidate Marco, all Rooney had to do was open his car door and stand there. By the time Hodges made it back to the car, the conversation had moved on to Hodges calling Marco *a fuckin' pussy.*

Rooney woke up in the middle of the night thinking about Chef Bilbao's tongue.

On Rooney's next shift, Chef Bilbao made him throw out a bolognese because he'd used unripe tomatoes. The chef had been working at the station next to Rooney's, stirring a bé-chamel, when he leaned over and dipped his left forefinger into the bolognese, lifted the finger to his nose, sniffed at it, then put it to his tongue and shut his eyes. There was calm in his face, and Rooney imagined those taste buds soaking in the sauce, measuring the acid against the earthiness, and the freshness against the depth. When the chef opened his eyes, Rooney's heart sank.

The chef loomed over him, even though Rooney was nine inches taller and a hundred pounds heavier. He arched his eye-brows and, in a thick accent, said, "You used unripe tomatoes? Really? One day, maybe two days, those tomatoes would have been ripe, but not today. Just throw it out. Throw it all out."

Rooney did as he was told, and when he returned to his sta-tion, Chef Bilbao put his hand on his shoulder. "Wasting food. I won't tolerate it in my kitchen. There's no worse crime."

"Sorry, chef," Rooney said. "I'll pay for it."

Bilbao grunted, almost a laugh. "He says he'll pay for it. No, no, my dear boy. You'll make it again, but this time, you will taste the tomatoes to make sure of—what?"

"That they're ripe, chef."

"That's goddamn right. Now get to work."

Even after being humiliated, all Rooney could think was, Chef Bilbao's tongue was fine.

As if it were a train station, cooks and serving staff came and went, and no lasting friendships were made—not even with the waitresses Rooney screwed. But Rooney gained some-thing shy of respect from Chef Bilbao. To say they were friends would be an overstatement, but Bilbao grew to depend on Rooney. At the end of Rooney's second year, a sous chef quit to open her own restaurant, and Chef Bilbao asked Rooney if he was up to the task. "You've been here almost two years, right? You're here every day, like clockwork. You have an in-nate sense of flavor, sometimes better than mine, I think. You have no formal education, yet you have a palate of the gods. Your only fault is not keeping your cock in your pants. As long as it doesn't interfere with my restaurant, what do I care? *Entiende?*"

"Sí, el jefe," Rooney said. "I live for this place."

"Bueno," Chef Bilbao clapped him on the back.

As staff moved on, Rooney moved up, and at the end of his fourth year, Chef Bilbao made him head chef. Chef Bilbao made his presence felt on the menu, but he let Rooney run the kitchen.

The rumor about Chef Bilbao's damaged taste buds had surfaced on occasion, but each time, Rooney stamped it down as if it were a blasphemous affront to him personally rather than Chef Bilbao. He told each propagator it wasn't true. *Can't be true. Haven't you seen the chef in the kitchen?* Rooney asked where they'd heard the rumor, but the response was always vague, as if they didn't know or couldn't remember. Or could it be that they were scared to say who had told them? The rumor consistently held that the chef's sense of taste had been destroyed, but varied on the how. Acid wash. Birth defect. Cancer. Syphilis. Burns. Infection. Medically.

Rooney decided the rumor could only be coming from one person. Chef Bilbao himself. He'd been the only person besides Rooney who had been at Bebe's throughout all the iterations of the rumor. He didn't understand why the chef would fabricate it.

After ten years, Rooney had become restless. He wouldn't admit to being a master, but he knew he was no longer a student. He was ready to fly away, be free, maybe to the Spanish mountains Chef Bilbao reminisced about so often. Maybe he could start fresh in a small restaurant.

He went back and forth for months before deciding to tell the chef. A shift had finished, and the staff had left, except for the cleanup crew. Rooney considered every platitude he could think of about a boy becoming a man, but what he finally said was, "Bebe's has been a home for me and you've been a father, but it's time for me to leave."

They sat at the bar having a drink, and Chef Bilbao put his

palms to his forehead. "Oh, no, no, no."

"Yes," Rooney said.

The chef stuck his forefinger into his glass and lifted a drop of bourbon to his tongue, and then he drank deeply from the glass. "Of course, of course. I know I've got to let you go, but know you have a home here, and can return once you've found what you are looking for."

Rooney appreciated the sentiment, and he promised Chef Bilbao he'd not forget that. They discussed Rooney's plans and drank. The cleaning crew left and they were still at the bar, drinking, talking big, telling outlandish stories, laughing, being brazen, because what did it matter now?

In the swirl of Rooney's drunkenness, the rumor came to mind, bright like the color of honey gold, and Rooney had to ask. "Why'd you keep telling the staff you lost your sense of taste?"

Chef Bilbao made no noise or movement for what seemed like a full sixty seconds as he stared into the amber of his drink, and then his laughter erupted. It was a deep, guttural laugh that Rooney recognized as an admission.

Rooney didn't think the laughter would ever stop, it was so raucous and profound, but it eventually died down like a car running out of gas, with coughs and gasps. Still, the chef smiled, almost as if he had pride in the rumor.

Rooney shook his head, wondering how to get at the mystery, and he decided to push ever so gently. "I mean, you keep a rumor going, and I tap it down. What was in it for you?"

"But it's not a rumor," Chef Bilbao said.

Rooney leaned forward and squinted. "What do you mean?"

The chef took a drink of bourbon and wiped the traces of liquor from his upper lip. "I told the truth, but the truth's been a little muddled. I have a sense of taste, but not in my tongue, or my mouth, like you."

Rooney tried to sober up and get his head clear, but he could think of nothing to say. He waited, like an audience for the first note of an opera, and Chef Bilbao seemed to gather himself to tell his story.

"In 2005, I was abducted," he began. "Bebe's had been open for about two years, and I was making a name for myself, becoming a rock star, or so I thought. Everyone had to get into Bebe's to taste my food—movie stars, athletes, the *Food and Wine* circle. Our reservations were months out. I thought I was a god. And like you, I couldn't keep my cock tamed. Every pretty waitress was a conquest, and I was a conquistador, right?"

Chef Bilbao poured more bourbon into the glass and offered Rooney another draw on the bottle, but Rooney shook his head. Chef stuck his finger in the glass, and then sucked on his finger, and smiled. "I chose the wrong waitress to screw. We don't always know who the conquest is, right? She may seem like a normal human being on the outside, but inside, she could be anything. We don't know her psychology, what makes her tick, what her motivations are, but it doesn't matter. We're young and full of piss, willing to mesh with whatever piques our interest. There's always risk, and we fly in the face of it."

These truths made Rooney discomforted. He wanted Chef Bilbao to get on with the story, but when the chef reached for his drink, Rooney leaned back and shut his eyes. The room spun in this darkness, and he got caught up in the motion, and maybe he even lost consciousness. When the chef spoke again, he woke.

"This waitress was lithe, athletic, blonde. So buxom. Curves in all the right places. I chased her for months before she slowed down enough to let me get within reach. She took me home, and I thought I was in love. Don't we always think that? Just a little lie we tell ourselves. But she had the better lie. She was the bait, drawing me in, like a fish to the worm, and when I was hooked, she and her kind snatched me."

Rooney leveled his gaze at the chef and asked, "Her kind? What were they? Italians?"

Chef Bilbao shook his head emphatically. "No, no, no. She

was a monster from another world, living in a waitress' skin. I don't know *what* she was, only that I was taken, strapped in, and studied, always with a bright light in my face. I never saw what they looked like. My mouth was clamped open. You see, it was my tongue they wanted. They harvested my taste buds, one by one; a tedious, meticulous process. I'd become a donor for a transplant team. A fucking science project. For whatever reason, they wanted to taste food as I did. They called me the king of taste. They promised to return my taste buds."

Rooney leaned forward. "But they didn't?"

Chef Bilbao laughed, more bitter than any coffee. "Oh, they gave me my taste buds back, but not like you think."

Rooney blinked twice. "How then?"

The chef's left hand rose, and he held up his forefinger. Rooney didn't understand what it meant, until the chef put his finger to the bottom of his glass and said, "This is how I taste, now."

"Huh?"

"My taste buds are lodged in the tip of my finger."

"That can't be."

Chef Bilbao held his hands out. "You may not believe me, but when you leave here, you'll remember where my hands were when I tasted food on the line. How often did I wash my hands? I see it in your eyes. You're starting to understand, but may not able to admit it."

"But your finger? How is it possible?"

"Like I know," he answered. "They put me under, and I woke up in my bedroom with the waitress sitting next to me. She told me to be careful about what I touched, and she left. Nothing else. But I soon found it was true, simply from the saltiness of my skin when I rubbed my forehead."

Rooney stood up from the bar stool, stumbled, but held himself up by the back of the chair. His face felt thick, and his mouth didn't want to work. "This is all weird, but I'm drunk. Maybe it'll make sense in the morning." He started to walk away, but stopped. "You still haven't said why you started the rumor. Why tell anyone?"

Chef Bilbao yawned. "I couldn't keep the staff from seeing me touching the food, so I hid within the rumor. It's the safest place if your secret has to be out in the open. And you, my friend, you took the air out of each rumor, and doubt reigned."

"You used me?"

"Of course."

"Aliens? Really?"

The chef shrugged. "How would I know?"

"I'd better leave. If I don't, what'll you tell me next? That you shit gold and breathe fire? Jesus *fucking* Christ." Rooney turned away again and stumbled toward the restaurant's entrance, wanting to say goodbye, but unable to form the words with his mouth.

Chef Bilbao raised his voice. "Don't tell anyone, or ..." He paused as he considered his word choice, and then finished, "... or the Italians will get you."

As the doors closed behind him, all Rooney heard was gales of laughter.

THE CHILL OF THE
WATER BELOW

◆ ◆ ◆

You have a feeling of flight, soaring high, warm air on your face, the moon shining in your eyes. Time seems to have stopped, nothing moves, the air is still, there is peace, and you have a sense of wonder. It's a beautiful moment to be caught up in. It's endless. And yet, fleeting.

As if a switch is flipped or a dial turned, you find the brief moment of flight was illusion. You were never flying. You were falling. You feel the pull of gravity, and the water comes rushing towards you like a locomotive. Nothing slows your descent. Still, you have time to process your thoughts at a speed faster than ever before, like Einstein on one of his best days.

You understand it all now.

Between the top of the bridge and the chill of the water below, you realize you don't want death, or maybe it's that you don't want the pain that comes just before death. You want to reverse what you've done, go back, have a redo, hit reset.

You want redemption.

As you fall towards the cold river, you think about threads unraveling. A perfect life came undone, untied, frayed. You can identify the exact moment when it all came apart at the seams, when entropy was no longer just an idea but a way of life. You think of that moment as your life's schism.

And jumping—a terrible decision, you realize—was your

way of fixing the schism. You understand now that it will only make the schism worse; not for you, but for others.

You don't know what's below the surface of the water. Pain, you imagine, but only for a moment, right? Or does the pain follow you into your inevitable death? Your initial sense of wonder is replaced with fear.

You want to take it back, not just this decision, but the one from before that created the divide. You want to make it so you don't have to regret, but when did the regret begin? Was it when your lips and hers first brushed against one another, or were you too caught up in the moment for compunction? Maybe it was when you felt her wetness swallow you. Or perhaps the next morning, when you woke with her arm draped over you.

Your initial thought that morning was to blame the alcohol. You still had the taste of bourbon on your tongue. You'd only had a few drinks, enough to flirt, but not enough to become uninhibited.

Then you'd thought: She's a succubus. A siren. She used her song to pull you into shore so she could bash your brains against the rocks, but she fucked you, she didn't kill you. She was beautiful, sure, but you knew what you were doing. You just didn't give a shit, right? Why didn't you give a shit?

Ainsley had pissed you off, something about you forgetting to pay the electric bill and getting charged a twenty-dollar late penalty. You'd left the house, wanting to get back at her. All you heard was the shrill of her voice in an argument that was no longer about a bill. You were going to get drunk, call for an Uber, and fall asleep noisily next to Ainsley with your clothes on. That'd show her, wouldn't it?

But the succubus—*do you even remember her name?*—she sat next to you and from the first glance, you wanted to fuck her, not because she was a siren, but because she looked like your wife at nineteen. That's why you started flirting, acting interested that she was from Harlan.

You told the succubus you were an attorney like it meant

you had a huge cock, and she responded like that's what it meant. The drinks were flowing; for you, bourbon and cokes, and for her, gin and tonics. She drank three to your one and only became more herself, but not more interesting.

You didn't take your wedding ring off, so maybe she was a succubus. You liked the attention she paid you. You liked the feel of her fingertips gliding along the back of your hand, the way the little hairs on your arm rose up to attention, an autonomic reaction to stimuli. When she did that, still at the bar, you wondered why Ainsley didn't touch you like that. You decided she was too fucking worried about the cancerous little details of life that sucked the marrow out of your marriage and made you painfully numb to it all. You wanted to feel a little bit, to have joy about something, and if it wouldn't come from your marriage, where would it come from?

When the succubus said it was too loud in the bar, you suggested getting coffee at the Starbucks a block away. She smiled as if you'd made the funniest joke ever. She leaned forward, put her lips on your ear, and whispered, *I'd rather you do something to make me scream.* The vibration of her words ran through your body like a ghost on hallowed ground.

She hooked her fingers into yours and led you out into the warm night, and you let it happen.

The water is closer now, and you wonder if there is any way to unhinge yourself from the grasp of gravity. You feel like you're being embraced from all sides, wrapped in a blanket of air. You worry about how deep you will slide beneath the water's surface, how cold it will be. Will you rise and float downstream like a cork, or be a buried secret in the river's mud? Will you feel the decay of your flesh, the rotting of your soul?

Your only worry is whether it will hurt.

The succubus consumed you, ate you up, spit you out, drove you, moved you, filleted you, and flayed you. Your body was her instrument, and she played you like a symphony. It was glorious. It was torture. When you died, she brought you back to life, until you had no more lives, and you were rubbed raw.

As the succubus fell asleep, she spooned against you, breathing onto your neck and pushing the wetness of her sex against you, as if she were trying to get inside of you, rather than you inside of her.

You drifted off and thought of Ainsley and felt the crushing of her heart. It hadn't been good before, but now it was broken. The sanctity of your marriage was desecrated. Still, you fell asleep.

You dreamed the night through, just colors and sounds, all made of unstated guilt. When you woke, you lay on your back, and the arm of the succubus stretched across your chest. You felt sick.

What had you done?

If your marriage hadn't been over before, it was now, unless you could clean yourself up and forget it ever happened. You tried. You put the succubus out of your mind, but thoughts of her surfaced at odd times. The guilt enveloped you like gravity and pulled you down.

You may have quietly rolled from beneath the arm of the succubus without waking her, but she still had a hold on you. You may have washed away her smell and stickiness, but you couldn't get her off of you.

You made it home to a teary-eyed Ainsley, looking unkempt and worn through. You told her you'd drunk too much and spent the night at the Hyatt. She believed you.

But lies have mass, and they weigh you down. These lies made it hard for you to breathe, as if they were stuck in your windpipe, like a bitter pill swallowed wrong you couldn't cough up. But you realized you would have to cough it up.

This is it, you think as the river reaches up to you. You want peaceful thoughts, to die with acceptance of a chosen fate, but all that comes to you is a concoction of fear and shame.

In the light of the moon, you see your reflection in the river. You don't like what you see. You're haggard, beaten up, bruised, worn through—all self-inflicted wounds.

Ainsley knows nothing, only the lies. She doesn't know that for weeks you've been eaten up from the inside by a parasite of guilt that's wrapped its tentacles through your heart and mind. You've carried on a show, acting like all was fine, even better than before, only letting the darkness come when Ainsley had fallen asleep. How many tears can a grown man cry?

And your pain brought you to the bridge.

You couldn't live with your burden any longer.

You couldn't live with yourself anymore.

You would rather die than tell Ainsley the truth.

You are a coward.

As the cold water embraces your ankles, you wonder what you did to deserve this life, to be imperiled by your own selfishness, to fail to see the wonders of the world. It's all about you. Forever you.

Your body breaks as gravity slams you into the water. You shatter within your bag of skin. Your mind lights up with a register of pain so immense, the only reason you remain conscious is that I want you conscious. I want you to feel this agony, so you'll have something to compare to the hurt you'll cause Ainsley when you tell her of your succubus.

The cold water eats you, takes you into its depths, holds you down, hugs you, suffocates you with as much love as you've shown your wife. You breathe in the river, and even in your wrecked state, you thrash about, fighting for a life you wanted to throw away.

You feel the thickness of the silt drawn into the caverns of your lungs, and your chest expands, wanting to explode. Still, you fight. Why didn't you fight like this before? Why did you so easily succumb to a life of misgivings?

The river tries to spit you out, but your foot is hung on bottom refuse, maybe a rope or chain. Your neck extends upward, you look up to the surface and see me staring down, laughing.

I want you to feel every last second of your madness, or

perhaps mine, before I rip you out of Death's clutch. I want you to catch a glimpse of the nothingness you desire before I shine light in your eyes and pump life into your lungs.

I want you to know me for what I am, and the power I have over the tiny lives of men. I remember all my children, and watch over them the best I can, as only a father can do.

Your eyes swell, and you can't shut out the river. You believe you're going to die looking at the muck of the depths. The river's current is strong, and it tugs at you. It wants to take your story downstream, but your foot is still caught. You no longer kick to get it free. Your surrender is delightful. A delicacy.

The residue of the river pelts your skin, but you no longer care. You don't know why you jumped. You no longer remember your wife. You only know you want the pain to end. You want the darkness. You want the nothing.

What you want matters not.

It's what I want that matters, and what I want for you isn't this pain. If I lifted you to the river's edge and breathed life into you, but left you shattered, you'd garner compassion. The reason you fell would matter less than the physical pain you suffered as a broken man. That's too easy for the likes of you.

I will lift you up to the bridge, mend you, fix you, make you as you were before you jumped, burdened only with your lie. Should you reach for Death again, you will fail. I will follow you, protect you, make you safe. I will do this again and again until you confess the blackness of your heart. Your path will always lead to telling your wife that you lied.

Only moments are left now. Death is here, but I wave him aside, and I reach for you and save you from yourself.

Time comes unhinged, six minutes tick back, and you stand at the edge of the bridge, remembering being ruined by the waters below, the pain, the drowning, and then being saved. You look down at the blackness of the river and still feel the impulse, but you remember.

You step back, hesitant, confused. You still want it. But not

247

the pain.

You have a moment of clarity and you think about me. You know I am a vengeful god, a just god, but you don't know why I care. You can't explain my interests in the likes of you.

I am also a lustful god. I have had many brides. Your wife's mother knew me as Lucky, and maybe I was for her.

THE HOLDEN DEVICE

◆ ◆ ◆

I. *"We could see the pyramids being built."*

I watched him watching her.

I didn't want to be there, but he had asked me. You don't turn away a dead man's request. Johann Hart and I had been best friends for life, and now he was dead. She was dead, too.

Johann sat at his desk, his back to me, looking at his computer screen, and what he saw on the screen was his beautiful wife, Denise, being unfaithful. The camera angle was from above the bed. Denise was on her back, staring into the camera, although presumably she didn't know the camera was there. All I could see of the man who moved atop her was the back of his head and his hairy shoulders. The rest of him, and of her, was covered up. I was told at the funeral he was a neighbor. Denise looked like a woman who was being fucked by her neighbor, not so much enjoying it, as needing it. Whoever he was, he violated a commandment and was now dead.

I watched Johann on the same computer he'd watched Denise and the neighbor three days earlier. He twisted in the chair so he faced the camera, but he kept his head down. His face was pasty white. He was sickened, but he gathered himself, business-like, because he knew what he had to do. He made an unthinkable decision, but he didn't act rashly. He was too rational. He squinted at his watch and reached into a drawer. He lifted a notebook out and started writing. He filled two pages with his precise handwriting, but I couldn't see the words he wrote. I didn't need to see them. I had read the words only hours before. He referred to a data file on his computer twice as he wrote and scribbled certain dates and locations. When he finished writing, he took his lab key off the key ring. He stuck both the key and the two pages into an envelope, wrote out my address, and sealed the envelope with a five-inch strip of Scotch tape. He cautiously looked about the room, especially at the ceiling, as though he expected to see something. He didn't see it, and that was okay with him because he smiled, shrugged his shoulders, and left his laboratory.

He went home and killed his wife, her lover, and then himself. But first, he mailed the envelope. I followed him through all of it, except I couldn't watch once he walked into the bedroom. I didn't want to see it. I turned away from the computer. He shot them both, then went to his car and shot himself.

I looked up at Detective White, and he stared over my shoulder at the computer screen. He couldn't turn away. It was like fucking reality television to him. Once it's on, he couldn't bring himself to turn it off.

Johann Hart was always secretive about his projects as he worked on them. He would call me when it was done, whatever *it* was at that time, and ask if I could come over and let him show it to me. He was a physicist at the University of Kentucky. I was a history professor there. What Johann designed, I didn't get at all. It's not just that I didn't understand the workings of what he created. I didn't understand the application of it. I realize it makes me sound daft, and I'm not. It's just that his work was so beyond me, I felt stupid when he explained it. It would be like me trying to explain the significance of the Gettysburg Address to a two-year-old. I wouldn't waste my breath. Johann knew this, but it never diminished his enthusiasm or the twinkle in his eye when he told me about it.

In the letter, Johann described his creation. He joked it was his first creation that had a practical application. He called it *the Holden Device*. He said he named it after me because it would change my life

Johann called me Jack when we talked about our childhood, Holden when we drank a few beers, and Professor Holden or Dr. Holden when we discussed our respective careers. He was more interested in my field than I was in his. He was an avid reader and seemed to know something about everything. I would talk to him rather than my colleagues about my ongoing research. He knew more than them, anyway. He read the first drafts of my papers and offered critical analysis, but he was always fair. When he disagreed with my theories, he didn't lash out and belittle me. He posed certain solutions, and on the occasion when he deflated my theory to nothingness, I rethought it, and either reconstructed and resurrected it or threw it out and began anew.

He was a genius. I knew it. Denise knew it, too. That's why she married him and not me. When I introduced Denise and Johann seven years before, I thought she was going to be the future *Missus* Jack Holden. I was in love, or thought I was. But I was Denise's thesis advisor, and it would have been entirely inappropriate for me to act on it, if indeed it was love. I never imagined bringing her to lunch that day in September would lead to a marriage nine months later—well, a marriage not my own, the hell with university rules. As it turned out, I was best man at the wedding, and accepted it gracefully. Johann never knew of my infatuation with Denise. Neither did she, I guess.

She was good for him. Denise drew Johann out of his laboratory, and this was something I couldn't do. He was a workaholic, long days and nights, weekends, and holidays. After Johann married, he arrived to work late, left early, was home on weekends and holidays, and he took an occasional vacation. He finally got it into his thick skull that physics was not the be-all and end-all of life. He was happy with something besides his career. I was happy to see it, even if I didn't get the girl. She was happy, too.

But her happiness ended, and Johann lost her.

When Johann told me three months before that he had made a revolutionary, un-*fucking*-believable discovery, he didn't tell me what it was. I didn't ask. I assumed it was beyond me anyway. I wouldn't have understood it. I was focused on my own research and spent most of the conversation explaining what I thought was a revolutionary, un-*fucking*-believable theory. It wasn't that revolutionary or un-*fucking*-believable. Had I not been so self-involved, perhaps I could have drawn him out a bit more. I think he would have been reserved about it though. The Holden Device wasn't ripe for picking, yet.

This is what I think happened: He made the discovery and told Denise to be patient, then spent seventeen hours a day, seven days a week at the laboratory for months on end. He had returned to his old habits. Denise was lonely and acted on it. Can you blame her? I saw him several times a week on campus, and went to their house at least once a month. I saw nothing out of the ordinary. They appeared as happy as they'd ever been. Johann may have been preoccupied, but that was an accepted norm. He often stared at the wall unfocused. Had Denise told me how unhappy she was—that she needed to be held by her husband—maybe I could have talked some sense into Johann, or at least prepared him for the breakup, which was inevitable, given his detachment.

The proper reaction to learning your wife is fucking the neighbor is to ask for a divorce and maybe punch a hole in a wall, not to kill her, him, and yourself. I have always wondered whether he suspected Denise of screwing around, maybe a stain on the bed, or a different smell in the house. That could have been why he was watching her with the Holden Device. But I don't know this. I would love to believe Johann was merely testing the device, to discover its parameters, when he happened upon Denise and the neighbor. Once he saw them, he flew into a rage and killed them. Still, there was no immediate detectable rage. It took him ten minutes to write the letter explaining the device, and on the way home, he stopped to mail the envelop. Under the normal circumstance, a husband who discovers a cheating wife would be so besieged with fury he could have no other thoughts. But Johann was a masterful chess player. He could see six or seven moves ahead. This is a possible explanation why he paused in the midst of his mental break to write a letter. It was more important to pass on the technology of the Holden Device than to surrender to the anger boiling in the blood of his veins. The anger must have called him, like a thousand voices. Yet, he kept it at bay, for a little while. That's all he needed. Had he given in, I would never have learned of the device, and even worse, the University would have gained control of it. Johann could not stand this. If the University had it, the government would have it, and that had to be averted.

I hoped Detective White would see it this way.

Detective White was at the scene on the day of the murders. When I heard there had been violence at the home of a University physics professor on Cooper Drive, I ran out of my office to my bike and pedaled across campus as hard as I'd ever pedaled. Students stared at me as I rushed by. I rode down Cooper Drive, passing the football stadium, where I could see the flashing lights of police vehicles and ambulances ahead. The road was blocked three houses down from Johann's. I stopped and let the bike drop to the sidewalk. I bent over and tried to catch my breath. When a uniformed officer advised me to stand back, I told him between breaths that Johann was my best friend. I needed to know if it was him who had been hurt. The officer wouldn't answer my questions. I made a scene, and it was necessary for Detective White to intervene. The detective listened when I told him who I was and how I knew Johann. He took me aside and told me the details of Johann's actions. At his request, I went to Johann's car and identified him and then into the house and identified Denise. I told the detective I didn't know the other man.

He ushered me away from the crime scene, and as an after-thought, he handed me his card and told me to call if I needed to talk. At first, I thought it was an offer of friendship, after all I had lost my best friend, but this was ridiculous. He was a policeman investigating a crime and apparently wanted details, or maybe an explanation. I mindlessly put his card into my shirt pocket—that's what you do when someone hands you his card—and usually the card goes from the pocket into the trashcan. This time it sat on my dresser until my third day of grieving. When I got home from the funeral, Johann's note had posthumously been delivered to my mailbox. After my first reading, it seemed necessary I speak with the detective. To be perfectly honest, contact with the dead had unsettled me, and my thoughts were somewhat muddied.

On the phone, I didn't tell the detective what the note said. I only told him it might be a suicide note, and he might find it of interest. I asked him to meet me at the laboratory in thirty minutes. When Detective White read the note at the lab, he told me to turn on the computer to see what Johann wanted us to see.

"Do you believe him?" Detective White asked.

He still watched the computer screen with interest. The police would arrive at Johann's house shortly to discover the double-murder and suicide, if they weren't there already. I couldn't watch, so I was still turned away from the computer. I didn't know if I believed the note, so I asked, "Do you?"

The detective looked at me, pondering the question long enough to blink three times. "No," he said and turned back to the computer. "Your friend is making fools of us. Or he's trying to do so. That's what I think. He must have an elaborate video recording system."

"Maybe," I said, "but how'd he get it to this computer? It's an island. There are no phone lines. There's no modem. No wireless connection. As far as I can tell, it's not connected to the internet."

"Why wouldn't it be?"

"Johann was afraid of a hacker getting his research."

"Yeah, right," Detective White said. He still didn't believe it. Detective White was over six feet and thin, too thin to be a cop, but I figured he could prove his physicality if necessary.

I considered his original question, but only for a second. "I believe what Johann's letter says. He's never lied to me before. There's no reason for him to do so now."

"But—"

"And Johann expected some disbelief, didn't he?"

"You mean you want to check out the grassy knoll?"

"Don't you?"

The detective sucked in a lungful of stale air. When he exhaled, he flung his arms out. "That doesn't concern me."

"It should," I said. "You're a police officer, aren't you? A crime was committed. You should investigate. You could put the conspiracy theories to rest. Was there a magic bullet? Were there other shooters? Come on. Aren't you the least bit interested?"

Detective White folded his arms across his chest. He didn't answer my question, but he didn't leave. So, I turned back to the computer and hit the X in the right corner of the opened window. Before the window closed, I could see Denise's dead, naked body. It broke my heart.

All that remained on the computer screen was the desktop and a dozen or so icons. I double clicked on the icon labeled *Holden*. A new window opened with a plain blue background. Large, white letters simply asked for the date and time. I looked at Johann's note and typed 11/22/1963, hit the tab, and typed *13:25*. Johann's note explained all times were military and based on Eastern Standard Time. The time should be adjusted up or down as necessary for the time zone—something to be fixed later if Johann had the chance. The beta version needed only be rudimentary. The next window asked for longitude and latitude. I typed in the coordinates provided by Johann. The number included six digits after the decimal, and I assumed there was a reason it needed to be exact. When I clicked on the *next* button, there was whirring and buzzing from across the laboratory sounding like a furnace igniting. Earlier, I discovered the sound came from a metal box about the size of a large microwave, sealed on all sides except for the power cord plugged into an outlet and a cable trailing across the lab to the back of the computer. The first time the noise lasted ten seconds, but now, it went on for several minutes. I thought something had gone wrong and was about to click *cancel*, when the whirring and buzzing stopped. The screen went blank, and a new window opened.

I was looking down at building tops, trees, and a curved city road from a hundred feet up. A crowd lined both sides of the road. I clicked on the right mouse button and scrolled down to move the visual on the screen down to ten feet. Even though it wasn't physically a camera, it felt like a camera. Earlier, I had maneuvered it through the roof of Johann's laboratory and other levels above, as directed by his note. It seemed to have no substance and couldn't be blocked by any physical object. I held the left mouse button down and scrolled so the angle was thirty degrees. I slowly rotated the camera three hundred and sixty degrees by holding the left mouse button and pushing the mouse forward.

Spectators were lined up along Elm Street in front of the Texas School Book Depository. I'd seen pictures of the Book Depository, of course. If Johann's note was correct, President Kennedy's motorcade would turn onto Elm and drive by in five minutes.

I'm watching history, I thought. It's for real. I am convinced. Johann has made me a gift. He named the device after me, and he had known I would be spellbound. His note said it would let me *get to the truths of history so there will be no discrepancy about what happened.* If he was right, the gift was not the device itself, but the truth it would bring. The one truth for today was whether there was a second shooter on November 23, 1963. Later, I could return to this moment and study the killer—and I wanted to do this—but for now, I had only the one task.

After getting a bearing, I moved the camera to the field on the left of the Book Depository. This is what the conspiracy theorists have labeled the grassy knoll. There were several people in the grass, squinting in the bright day as they waited for Kennedy's motorcade. None of them were the shooter. It would be nothing so obvious. But shots had been heard from this area, and the President's head had rocked backward as though a shot had come from the grassy knoll. Yet, there was nothing suspicious here. There was a wooden fence separating the grassy knoll from a parking lot, and I remembered some theorists suspected the shooter was hidden behind the fence. I moved the camera across the knoll to the fence and then to the other side where I found a little bald man with coke-bottle glasses peering over the top. A rifle leaned against the fence near the man's left foot. A cigarette was gripped between his lips.

This has to be him, I thought.

I had enough proof. I could turn the computer off now and know there was a second shooter. But I had to watch it. I wanted to see this little man lift the rifle and put a bullet into the President's brain. I wasn't morbid. I had heard all the theories and had never put much credence in them. Now, I knew.

I positioned the camera behind the shooter, looking over his right shoulder so I could see the motorcade as it approached. The shooter was calm, patient. He was cold. It wasn't the first time he had done this. Murder was his business. It all happened quickly. When the President's Lincoln Continental appeared, the man lifted the rifle, aimed, and shot twice. All hell broke loose. The motorcade rushed off. The people on the sidewalk and grass scattered.

The little man with the coke-bottle glasses briefly watched all of this, calm, almost curious. When his interest had been satisfied, he bent down, broke down his rifle, put it in a case, and walked away.

That was all I needed to see for now. I closed the window and turned to Detective White. He was ashen white. He rubbed his chin. "I'm still not fully convinced," he said. "It's impressive if he's duping us. It's the greatest con I know. It's incredible."

"What can I show you to make you believe?" I asked. It was suddenly important Detective White believe.

"I want to see me."

I was confused. "You want what?"

"I want you to go back to the day your friend watched his wife on the computer screen and find me. I wasn't far."

"You want me to find you?"

"Yeah, he can't fake me. He didn't know who I was."

I finally understood, and turned back to the computer and typed in the date, time, latitude and longitude. When the window opened, the camera looked down onto the roof of the chem-physics building, and I knew I could go inside and see Johann watching his wife and her lover, but it wasn't necessary, thank God. I turned to Detective White.

"I was on Preston Avenue, at Smithfield's Grocery, getting a sandwich for lunch. I had finished eating when I got the call."

"I go there, too," I said. I maneuvered the mouse so it appeared we were flying over the treetops. It took me two minutes to get to the parking lot of Smithfield's. Using the mouse to move the camera was a bit problematic, but I was getting used to it.

"Go inside to the deli. There was a long line," the detective said.

I entered the grocery and went to the back of the store. "There you are," I said and pointed to his lean form. I positioned the camera so it was behind the counter, looking at the line of customers.

"Jesus-*fucking*-Christ," Detective White whispered. I turned to see that he looked sick to his stomach. He pulled up a chair, sat down, and watched himself as he moved forward in the deli line. When he made it to the front, he said, "Shut it off. I can't watch anymore."

I did so. "Anything else you want to see?"

"*No*," he said, perhaps too strong. In a softer tone, he added, "I'm convinced. It's unbelievable. The repercussions are big."

I nodded. I knew. Johann had known, too. He told me in the note to destroy it and how to do it, but he added, *do as you will.*

The last thing on my mind was destroying the device. I was too busy wondering what the limitations were: Could I watch Columbus land at the Americas? Or the pilgrims share a meal with Native Americans? Could it travel to the other side of Earth to see the Colosseum in Rome being built? Or China's Great Wall? Could I see the dawn of the Ice Age? Could I watch dinosaurs graze and their extinction? *All the wonders of the world.* I was calculating where the machine fit on the scale of the world's most-important inventions when the detective whispered, "You know we have to destroy it."

I looked at him like he'd lost his mind. "Destroy it? What the fuck are you saying?"

"There's too much power," he whispered. "It's bad for us to know everything." He held his hand in the air to emphasize his next words. "Certain things should be left alone."

"You don't believe that," I said. I felt as if he had taken on Johann's role in one of our epic arguments, and it felt comfortable.

"I do believe it. There would be no such thing as privacy. I could watch my neighbor's wife taking a shower. Or watch her screwing her husband. Or you jerking off last night. It's a voyeur's wet dream. It's messed up. I could watch my girlfriend lose her virginity."

"But it could do great things, too."

"Perhaps. But in the wrong hands..."

"It won't get in the wrong hands," I reassured.

The detective leaned toward me. "Don't lead me into temptation. You're like Frodo offering Gandalf the ring. I've got to resist it because I'm afraid what I might do with it."

"I know what *I'll* do with it," I said.

"What's that?"

"History. I'm a history professor. Johann made this for me. He named it for me. I'll confirm historical facts. It'll make my work simple. I'll see every bit of history happen."

"If that's all it could do," the detective whispered.

"No, it can do so much more."

"And that's the problem."

I shook my head. "No. That's what makes it great. Think how it can change your life."

He looked confused. He hadn't thought about it.

"There'll never be another unsolved murder," I said. "Every crime would have the face of a criminal to go with it. They'd all go to jail. You'd be the *crime whisperer*. That should mean something to you, right?"

He took a long time before answering. "Yeah, it does. That would be great, but we have to look at the bigger picture. Think of this. There would be no national security. If this device got into the hands of our enemies, they would know everything."

I laughed. "Yeah, and it would make the government honest. There would be no more deceit."

"*Jesus Christ!* Listen to yourself. Just think. Extremist would see our weaknesses—"

"And we'd see the extremist before they got here. But I'm saying no one would know but us."

Detective White held up his hands. "Okay. Forget that. Think of this. Even if you kept it and passed it on to your kids, you couldn't jerk off anymore without wondering whether your kids or grandkids were watching over your shoulder. They could watch themselves being conceived. Now, you don't want that, do you? It creeps me out."

"I don't have kids, and don't plan to have any," I said. "Once I'm too old to use it, I'll destroy it. I'll just use it for history. You and I could see the Declaration of Independence being written and signed. We could watch the bombing of Pearl Harbor. The rush of troops onto the shores of Normandy. All the presidents' men. All the presidents' women. Marilyn Monroe screwing Kennedy. Nixon ordering the break-in. We could study every monarch in history. We could see the pyramids being built. There would be no mystery anymore."

"Mystery isn't such a bad thing," the detective said. He gazed at his feet, gathering his thoughts. "And you could watch Jesus die on the cross with his crown of thorns."

"If you want," I said. I didn't see where this was going.

"And what if he didn't rise from the dead? What if Mary conceived Jesus not through Immaculate Conception? What if she wasn't a virgin?"

"What do you mean?"

"What if there was no flood? What if Noah didn't gather the animals, two by two, or build an ark?"

"What if he did?"

"What if God didn't create the world in seven days?"

"*What's your point?*" My voice echoed in the lab.

"My point is that some things are supposed to be a mystery. If this machine gets out and breaks it all down, smashes it to smithereens, so nothing remains of the religions, there will be disorder. Panic in the streets. There'll be a loss of cohesion in society—what holds us all together."

"You think religion holds us together?"

The detective shrugged. "It doesn't matter what *I* think."

"What do you mean?"

"The world has a lot invested in its religion, and it won't give it up without a bloody battle. Even if one of the religions is right, which I doubt, the other religions will hold on with all their might."

"Who the fuck are you?"

He looked confused but answered the question. "Alfred White."

I smiled. "No, I mean, you're a cop. You're not supposed to be the philosophical type. You've gone from referencing *Lord of the Rings* to talking about jerking off to being a Biblical scholar."

"I'm just different," he said. "I don't do things the way most cops do. I read a lot about everything."

"You mean you use your brain."

He was hesitant, but did give one nod of his head. "Listen. If you continue with this, it'll cause trouble for lots of people. It's destroyed the lives of three people. How many more lives will it destroy?"

"You've made your point," I said.

"No, this is my point. Even your friend's note said it would do harm. He told you it should be destroyed, but he gave it to you. It's your decision, and I will respect whatever you decide."

"Will you?"

"I have to."

"Won't it be in your report?"

"This is no longer police business."

"Are you sure?" I asked.

He nodded. "This is magic. It doesn't have anything to do with me."

At that moment, I wished I hadn't asked Detective White to meet me at the laboratory. Johann had warned me in the note not to call the police, but how could I not have contacted them? Johann was *dead*. I had just come from his funeral and was dealing with my grief. The detective needed to know about the note. It had been a hasty decision. Now, I needed time to think—not about what I was going to do with the device—I had already decided to keep it (how could I not?)—but about how I could get the device out of the laboratory. Would the detective even let me take it? Would he tell anyone else? "I can't destroy the device," I said. When Detective White looked up, I shrugged. "I just can't do it. Not yet. I see so much good it will do the world. It would be insane to let it go."

"How much good it'll do you, you mean."

"That too," I admitted. "But it's my decision. You said it."

He nodded. He wasn't going to fight me about it.

"You and I are the only ones who know about it," I said.

"What about the University?"

"Johann's note says the University didn't know. He developed projects for the University on a continuing basis, but he was always honest with them that he had other projects which

262

didn't concern them."

"And this was one of them?"

"I'm sure. If the University knew, Johann would have told me to destroy it without telling me what the fuck it was."

"Because if the University learns about it—"

"The University would lay a claim," I finished. "It was developed on their property with their equipment. For *this* invention, the University would put up a fight, and they'd win. It's not going to happen, because they won't learn about it."

"Okay. Fine. What are you going to do with it?"

"Explore the past," I said. "I'm an historian. Johann created this so I could watch history happen, the good, the bad, and the ugly, and I'm going to write about it. I'll give my *theories*— and maybe my theories will be wacky as hell—but I will corroborate the theories as much as I can. *I'll* know it's the truth. All future evidence from whatever source will corroborate the theories, too, and what doesn't will be false. Research is what I do. Right now, I'm confined to the evidence I can find through writings of the time, which is a desperate limitation. Now, there'll be no limitations. I'll be subtle and try not to blow the world's collective mind with what I learn."

"You don't want to be a fruitcake."

I smiled. "I will be, though. I don't care. So will you."

"I don't understand," Detective White said.

"When you solve crimes, it'll be like you're a mind reader. You'll know the truth of what happened before you investigate."

He shook his head. "No. I won't—I can't use it."

"You can make good use of the device."

"No fucking way. I value my privacy and wouldn't want to invade someone else's. It would make me feel dirty."

"If you know when the crime was committed, and where it happened, are you really invading someone's privacy to witness it? Doesn't a criminal give up his privacy when he commits a crime?"

He thought about this and shrugged.

"What's the problem?"

"I would need a search warrant to use it," he said. "Most evidence is discovered inside a person's home."

I nodded. "But if the crime happened anywhere else, would it be okay to watch it? If a mugging happened on a street corner, could you watch it happen? And then follow him home?"

"Sure, that'd be fine, but it doesn't help me much. Even if I know who committed the crime, unless I can produce evidence for probable cause, the judge won't give me a warrant to go into the home."

I nodded. "You're right. The device can't be used as evidence."

Detective White smiled. "The judge would think I was whacked in the head if I tried."

"What if the mugger threw the purse into a particular dumpster, it might give you a fingerprint, right?"

Detective White nodded. "For the fingerprint to be useful, the mugger would need to be in the system."

"But it would give you a beginning place."

"Yeah."

"You wouldn't have qualms about using the device for this?"

"Listen. I don't want to use it."

"Don't be absurd," I said. "How many murders go unsolved in a year in this city? In the country? You could find out who killed that little girl, what's her name? In Colorado."

"Jon Benet Ramsey."

"Yeah," I said. "Once you knew, you could find the evidence. The problem with unsolved murders is you don't have suspects. If you had a suspect, you could find the evidence. What about all of the children who go missing? We could follow them and see where they go. We'd know whether they were alive or not, or where they were. It's not just your career we'd be helping. It's all these people."

"It's not that I'm not considering it," Detective White said. "I see all of the advantages, and I agree with you, but the risk is *huge*. It'd be the end of the world if it got out. I think the world would go insane."

"There is no risk so long as it's just you and me. Think of all the people you can help. You can be a goddamned superhero if you want."

"I don't want to be a superhero. I don't want to be a voyeur."

I took a deep breath. I was exasperated. "You won't be. You're not like that at all. You seem like a good man. You see the evil that could be done, and you can keep it from happening."

I could see he was breaking or maybe he was tired of arguing. His face slackened and he took a deep breath. "Okay. Maybe. We'll be the other's checks and balances."

"That's fair. And no one will know, right?"

"That's right. Now how do we get it out of here?"

I shrugged as if it was unimportant. "We carry it out," I said.

"No one will question it?"

"You're a cop," I said. "You tell me." He gave me an odd look, so I continued. "I mean, I can pull my SUV into the loading zone, and in five minutes, load it up. I'm a professor at the University, and you can flash a badge. Once we're gone, no one will know we were here."

"That easy?"

"Yes, detective."

He held his hands up. "Let's get something straight, okay?"

"What's that?"

"My name is Alfred. I don't like being called Detective White by my friends, and if you call me detective one more time, I'm likely to start calling you *professor*. Got it?"

How could I not nod my head *yes* to this? But I asked, "Not Al? Or Fred? It has to be Alfred?"

He tried his best to not to smile, but he did. "I like detective better than Al or Fred in case you're inclined to not call me Alfred at any point in the future."

"So, we're going to be friends?"

"I hope so," he said.

"Okay then," I said. I'd lost a friend, and now I'd gained one. It was important to me. Johann wasn't replaceable, but I needed a friend.

The difficulty was the weight of the Holden Device. It was two cubic feet, but weighed five or six hundred pounds. Later that night, Alfred looked at me with one eye open larger than the other. "What's in here?"

"The walls of it must be lined with lead," I suggested.

"You're saying there's radiation?"

"Who knows," I said. "Here. Wheel the cart beneath when I lift it up."

He nodded and stood behind the handcart. I put my hands on the far edge of the device and pulled it toward me. At first there was no movement, and then it lifted off the ground and Alfred slid the cart beneath.

I took hold of the cart and wheeled it through the office building. Alfred followed with the monitor and cables. He rushed ahead and pushed through the door and held it open for me. I wheeled the cart into the night and down the handicap ramp, and across the parking lot to my Chevy Traverse.

"How are we going to lift it?" he asked.

I already knew we had to take it apart, but I didn't want to involve Alfred. "I got this," I said. "Go back inside and straighten up Johann's lab so it looks like we weren't there."

"You sure?"

"Yeah."

As he walked back into the building, I retrieved a flashlight from the glovebox. I had seen the release earlier on the back edge, and now shined the light on it. When I pressed the release, the top lifted off, as if it moved with hydraulics. I put my hands on the underside and struggled to lift the top into the back of the Traverse. How would I ever get it into my house? I told myself to keep moving forward. There was a release for each side, and I carefully placed each on top of the other. When I had put the last side in the back, I shined the light on what remained. It looked like the inside of a clock, with cogs, wheels, chains, and pendulums. In the center was a glass case with purple and red smoke twisting and turning about, as if the smoke were alive. I wondered if Johann had trapped something supernatural inside the glass, and whether I should let it out. The thought doing so scared me.

I cautiously lifted the bottom into the back. Even in the darkness of the Traverse, I could see the purple and red smoke searching the four corners of the glass case for a way out. It had to be alive. I didn't want Alfred to see the smoke and have morality issues, so I pulled the rear door of the Traverse down and went back to the lab.

We agreed he would meet me at my house at midnight, and test the device. He wasn't overly happy about the delay, but I told him I needed to clean a space in my house.

I labored to carry the device in from the garage, but once I did, the pieces snapped together with precision. I had the device ready to test well before midnight.

As I waited, I marveled at the history in the making. Like I was about to step foot on Mars. The world would be changed forever, and I was the gatekeeper of the device. What came from it would be determined by me. Alfred, too. I may never sleep again.

Alfred arrived fifteen minutes early, and handed me a coffee. He followed me into my home office, and I sat at the desk. I turned in my chair and arched my eyebrows at him. He stood in the corner of the room. It was then I realized how thin he was, maybe hundred and sixty pounds with his over six-foot-frame. "So, what do you want to see?"

The look on his face was thoughtful, but indecisive. He had more than one thought and was trying to decide between them. His face relaxed. "Last night," he said, "there was a murder of a gas station clerk at the intersection of East 3rd and Race Street. We have a video and made an arrest, but we don't have the murder weapon. I want to find it."

I inspected Alfred's face, and found a hardness in his eyes I hadn't seen earlier in the day. This was the policeman. He was a force to be reckoned with when he had this face on. "What's so important about this one?"

He shrugged. "It's not important to anyone but the clerk's parents. She was nineteen. She had a lot of life to live, and it was taken from her for a couple hundred bucks in the till. Just doesn't seem right."

I realized Alfred was sanctimonious. A do-gooder. This concerned me. Would he judge me for the use of the device or let me be? As soon as these worries surfaced, I smothered them. It was too late to worry about it. Maybe he was the right person to battle me about use of the device.

The screen asked for coordinates. I turned on my laptop and googled latitude and longitude, and when I found an appropriate website, I typed "Race Street, Lexington, KY." A box with the coordinates opened up. I turned back to the device's monitor and typed the coordinates.

I looked over my shoulder. "What time did it happen?"

Alfred cleared his throat. "According to the video, the gunman shot her at 7:34 p.m.," he said.

I punched in 19:25 to allow an additional nine minutes. The device whirred and buzzed for less than a second. When the machine stopped, the camera was positioned over a baseball diamond. The bases were loaded, and a big kid was up to bat. I was too stunned to do anything but watch as the pitcher moved into his windup. He threw a hard strike across the inside corner of the plate. The batter arched his head up and looked directly into the camera. Even a hundred feet in the air, I could read his lips. *Fuuuuuucccck.* He turned and threw the bat to the ground then stomped toward the dugout. His teammates on the bases walked toward the dugout with their heads down. The teams lined up to shake hands. I realized it had been the last pitch. "Had he hit that," I said, "the game could have been different, right?"

When Alfred didn't answer, I turned and saw he had moved

up behind me and was now peering into the computer screen. "You punched in the right numbers, didn't you?"

I nodded. "I checked twice."

"There's not a baseball field on 3rd Street," he said. "But that's Castlewood Park. The gas station is close."

I took the camera angle down to street level, and Alfred directed me until we reached the gas station with less than three minutes to spare. I stopped outside the doors. "Go in. Go in," Alfred said.

I did. I had no desire to see the murder of this clerk, but I didn't want to let Alfred touch the device. It wasn't mistrust exactly, but I was protective already. I positioned the angle so we were able to see both the clerk and the door. I turned away from the screen. I knew if I looked at the clerk, I'd see death surrounding her. I couldn't take that. Instead I cocked my head behind me. "You had another choice of a place to visit. What was it?"

"Not a place. A person. My father," he said.

"Really? We can still do that."

"He died when I was thirteen. Heart attack. I still miss him."

"I'm sorry."

When I looked back to the screen, the clerk was ringing up the sale of an elderly gentleman. Gas. Cigarettes. A lottery ticket. As the old man was leaving, a man in his thirties wearing jeans and a t-shirt walked in.

"That's him," Alfred said.

I followed the man through the store. He was the only person there except for the clerk, who was busy checking Twitter or TikTok on her phone. The man was short, maybe not even five and a half feet, but he was stocky. His eyes were vacant, as if he were one of the soulless. He stopped at the chips aisle and grabbed a bag of Fritos, and then a Mountain Dew from a cooler.

When he moved back toward the front of the store, I saw the pistol sticking out of his jeans. I figured he'd simply shoot

269

the clerk, but he passed by her toward the door. He put his hands on the glass and pushed. I thought he would just leave. I hoped he would. Maybe this isn't the murderer after all.

But the clerk spoke up. "Hey, you've got to pay for that."

The man stopped, his eyes grew dark. With one foot across the threshold, he turned to her. "Why would I pay?"

"If I let you leave," she said, "my boss will know, and I'll get fired. I can't lose another job. My folks will kill me."

The man grunted. "I can help you with that," he said.

She looked surprised, then fearful as the man removed his pistol from the waist band of his jeans and lifted it toward her. I didn't want to see it, so I turned away. Still, I heard the shot and her body hitting the floor. I heard the cash register opening. I turned to watch him pull the small amount out of the till. Then he left the store.

"Follow him!" Alfred shouted.

I flinched at the voice but put my hand on the mouse and moved the camera outside. At first I didn't see him and turned to the right just as his tennis shoe was moving out of view around the corner. I moved the camera forward and then around the corner. The man walked at a steady pace. He had just killed a woman, but had no urgency. He passed out of the parking lot onto the sidewalk along Race Street. I could hear him whistling, like nothing had happened.

He turned the corner at East 4th Street, and then onto Hawkins Avenue, still not hurrying. This was an older neighborhood in Lexington. The white clapboard houses were close together, and many of them had chain-link fences around the front yards and large barking dogs sitting on porches. The killer didn't notice any of this.

"Was he stoned?" I asked.

"Blood tests aren't back yet."

If he was stoned, he had enough mental capacity to pause at an abandoned house. Alfred leaned in close and watched as the man opened the front door and moved about the discarded junk as though he owned the house. He went down the stairs into the basement, lifted a towel covering an old television and wrapped the gun in it. He walked to the back corner of the basement where it was dark, and deposited the gun on top of a concrete block between two floor joists.

"There it is," Alfred said. "That's fucking great. You did it."

Alfred left.

Alfred had a backup unit meet him and the elderly owner at the Hawkins Avenue residence. The owner waited in the yard while Alfred and the patrolmen went into the abandoned house. He told me later about the patrolmen's elaborate stories of how they had followed him in, and he had gone to the gun without looking for it. Alfred's colleagues questioned how he knew where it was, but he only said, "It's not magic, if that's what you're thinking."

This behavior would earn him the nickname of *Sherlock*, which he did not particularly like. He felt it was mostly used in a derogatory way by his colleagues, but in my mind, it seemed to fit. Alfred grew tired of hearing *let Sherlock figure it out*. He knew challenging the name would bring attention to it. So, he let it be.

The only peculiarity from that night was why the device hadn't started above the intersection of 3rd Street and Race Street, but above the baseball game at Castlewood Park. I had entered coordinates correctly. It was obvious moving the device had caused the coordinates to be inexact, and while this was problematic, I could work around it. A few months later, with Johann's copious notes about the device, most of which I didn't understand, I discovered that for reasons Johann hadn't figured out, the device occasionally needed to be calibrated to space and time. Moving the device from Johann's lab caused an additional fluctuation. Johann suspected the instability had to do with a shift of the polar axis, but hadn't had time to gather the data. Not that it mattered. So long as I followed the calibration procedures in Johann's document files, the longitude and latitude remained precise.

II. *"They called me God."*

Throughout academia, life flows like a big, lazy river, a constant push downstream, never ending. I always seemed to stay within the wide channel, never against the current. I knew where I'd be in one year, or five years, or even ten. Life was predictable. The students changed, but the course work was the same, and the research was an investment of months and sometimes years or decades. Nothing happened quickly. I found myself carried forward by the momentum of all that had already happened. There were signposts, but there were not many destinations in academia, except for tenure and retirement. While there was comfort in the consistency, there was also boredom.

With the device I had something that was against the grain of the usual course. It was a diversion, for better or worse. I was no longer bound by the current. I wasn't even in the river now.

I'd lost a friend, and I missed him, but he would still speak to me through the device. Johann had given me the gift of the gods. In many respects, I'd become omniscient. There was no past that was a barrier to me and no secret to be held from me. It's true, I couldn't see what the future held, but no future is set. So, even if I could see a future, it would only be one of many. Had I known what the future contained, especially if it involved me, it was likely to be changed by my knowledge of that future. Seeing what has happened and what is set in stone holds power. Seeing what can change doesn't.

All of this rolled through my mind that night after Alfred left my house, and it kept me from sleeping. I was wound up. I mentally made a list of all the moments in history I wanted to see, not for the sake of my career, but to see history being made. I'd be the only person alive to witness the shot heard around the world at the Battle of Lexington. I could see Muhammad Ali defeat Joe Frazier in the *Thriller in Manila*. I'd hear Mozart compose *Eine Kleine Nacht-Musik* and watch da Vinci paint the *Mona Lisa*. My list was endless. I rearranged the list in my mind over the next few months, but I never wrote it down.

After the first few months, Alfred feared his presence at my house was drawing attention, but he only imagined it. What attracted more attention was my late hours and haggard appearance. I had tenure, so my job was safe. I showed up for class, taught as I always did, but I stopped appearing for faculty functions. I blamed it on *research*.

Placing fault on research was laughable. I realized in order to study history with the device, I needed a team of researchers tracking events, otherwise I might never make a momentous discovery. I had only *me*. I spent the first few days following Benjamin Franklin, and I learned the man liked to hear himself talk. Otherwise, I found nothing useful for my academics. It was interesting, but after the novelty wore off, it was rather boring and tedious. It was the unedited version of a person's life with all the waiting for something to happen, but nothing ever did. How would I ever find something worthwhile that was previously unknown? I chose significant historical events that had a set date and time. I watched John Wilkes Booth shoot Lincoln during *Our American Cousin* at Ford's Theater, and I saw Lincoln give *the Gettysburg Address*. I cried for both. I saw the beginning of the Normandy Invasion, but shut the device off because I couldn't bring myself to watch all the death within the heroics. I watched the cowardly suicides of Hitler and Eva Braun with a detachment I didn't like. I knew I should feel something as the monster swallowed a bullet, but I felt nothing. *Good fucking riddance* is what I thought. I saw the making of *Monty Python's Holy Grail*, and laughed more at that than the movie. Then for the hell of it, I went to the set of *Debbie Does Dallas*, and saw that no love was involved, only sex, and I couldn't decide if it was a factory or a sporting event.

That the device had limited use for my research caused me to be disheartened. I could care less about trivial facts of history, like what F.D.R. ate for breakfast while President. No one cared. There *were* important unknown moments within the triviality of these lives, but how could I find them? I could mine one life and unearth the gems of that life, but it would take years. I couldn't have much impact on the world that way.

I spent much time watching my childhood. I was less interested in me than I was Johann. My parents moved into the house next to Johann when I was four. Johann and I discovered each other within a few days. He was different than other four-year-olds. He was brilliant. He understood all that happened around us, but was smart enough to not let the adults know he knew. It frustrated him I didn't understand the complex ideas about the world he had already grasped. But as only Johann could do, he forgave me for it, and was my best friend throughout it all.

I watched a seventeen-year-old-me lose his virginity in his bedroom to Emily Sue Dean. What I had always thought of as a beautiful act of love-making was awkward. I was all elbows and knees and she was filled with worry and uncertainty. Getting undressed lasted longer than the sex, and the jubilant seventeen-year-old me failed to notice her sadness. I watched him walk Emily home, and rather than returning with that immature-me to hear him describe it all to a curious Johann, I remained with Emily. She wailed in grief on her bed for the loss of her virginity, then wrote about it in her diary. She wanted it back, although she did write she loved me and it had been her decision to be done with it. She wrote that it felt like a friend had died. She described it as grief.

I remembered that Emily and I screwed like fiends throughout our senior year and the summer before she went to the west coast to study film making. I always thought the first time was the best, but it was just clumsy sex. Still, it had a certain meaning, and maybe that's what has colored my memory. The act of screwing is little without meaning to back it up.

I watched me being conceived late one night after my parents had too much wine, and I watched me being born. I randomly followed my parents throughout their lives, and I learned how much they cared for one another. I watched them die in a car accident while I was in college.

I did nothing useful for myself with the device. It was my entertainment, my reality television. Alfred's use of the device progressed slowly at his request. Be patient, he told me.

I spent much of my time searching for ways to help Alfred, so I could at least feel useful. He didn't know the extent I was doing this. If I found something I thought he could use, I'd tell him I saw it in the paper or on the television news, but not that I had already watched it happen. Sometimes, he was interested and told me to pursue it, and other times he said it was procedurally not a crime he could reach. I think he meant that the crime was too far out of his jurisdiction to assist the detectives on the case. On those occasions, I sent anonymous tips to investigators. I didn't tell Alfred this either. He would worry my anonymity would be compromised, but I took precautions.

One morning, fifteen months after Johann died, I sat at the kitchen table with my cup of coffee scanning the newspaper for unsolved crimes. The front page of the paper had stories about bombings in Syria, a reversal in a senatorial poll, and an indictment of a local minister for child pornography. It wasn't until I flipped to the City/State section of the paper that something caught my attention. It wasn't a crime story. A husband and wife lost a lottery ticket worth $320 million. I read the article three times before it occurred to me *why* it drew my interest. Jerry and Smyrna Gibson from Cressy, Kentucky about ninety minutes away, had thrown a party the night following the lottery drawing. They had shown the ticket to their friends and family, and lost track of it. Jerry said Smyrna had it last, and Smyrna said Jerry had it, but when they woke the next morning, the ticket was gone. They searched the house from attic to basement a dozen times, but hadn't found it. A color copy had been made of the lottery ticket for framing, and was presented, but the lottery office said winnings could only be redeemed with the actual ticket. Now, time was running out. Presentation of the ticket had to be made within six months of the drawing. Only a month remained. The Gibsons were desperate and filed suit to force the lottery company to accept the copy. The lawsuit was the focus of the newspaper article.

My coffee got cold that morning as I thought about it. I called Alfred and told him about the lost ticket. "Well, what do you want me to do about it? There's no crime."

"No, of course not," I said. "But *I* can find the ticket."

There was a pause on the phone. He wasn't disinterested, but he was unwilling to commit a favorable comment. "Okay," he finally said. "Find it. Just keep us out of trouble, and leave my name out of it."

There were hundreds of details to be worked out, but my first concern was finding the ticket, and this turned out to be simple.

With the device I went to the Gibson's home on the day of the party and watched them go about their celebrations, which had apparently started early in the day. I followed the ticket from person to person and room to room. People came and went, and the ticket was always with Jerry or Smyrna. Alcohol of all kinds flowed at the gathering, but the Gibsons maintained sobriety throughout. The fact they hadn't slept since the drawing the night before was their only weakness. Smyrna got sleepy at about midnight and went into the bedroom to lie down. A short time later, the guests started leaving the party, and Jerry finally shut the door after the last person left, and... *he didn't have the lottery ticket.*

I went back to the point where Smyrna went to lie down, and I watched Jerry slip the ticket into Smyrna's shirt pocket, but she didn't seem to notice. *I* hadn't noticed. I followed Smyrna into the bedroom, and without turning on the light, she took the lottery ticket out of her shirt pocket, presumably

276

not knowing it was the lottery ticket, and put it on the dresser. The lottery ticket stayed put until Jerry came into the bedroom an hour and a half later, holding a Stephen King novel. He picked up the lottery ticket and slid it between pages as a bookmark. It was dark. He hadn't known the lottery ticket marked his page. *Misery* sat on their dresser for several days while the Gibsons searched the house. Neither of them opened the book. A few days later, Smyrna put the book on the shelf, and it had been there since. As of the day before, I could see the smallest edge of the lottery ticket peering out between the pages of the book.

When I showed it to Alfred later that evening, he said, "That's brilliant. What are you going to do now that you know where the ticket is? Be a Good Samaritan and let them know, right?"

I shook my head. I had thought about this, too, and I had an outline of a plan. I explained it to Alfred, and he reluctantly agreed I should proceed, but again, admonished me to be careful. I hired an attorney to prepare documents for Finders Keepers, Inc. and an agreement in which the Gibsons agreed to pay ten percent of the lottery earnings in exchange for disclosing the location of the winning lottery ticket. It was a simple agreement with the exception of the penalties for revealing any information regarding the corporation or any person connected to the corporation. The confidentiality clause was necessarily three of the agreement's four pages. When the attorney asked how I knew where the lottery ticket was, I said, "I could tell you, but I'd have to kill you." He laughed uncomfortably when I didn't smile.

Before making initial contact with the Gibsons, I implemented the necessary legalities. With less than a week before the lottery ticket expired, I knocked on the Gibson's door. Smyrna answered in a bath robe.

"What are you peddlin'?" she asked.

"Mrs. Gibson, my name is Jack Holden. I'm president of a company called Finders Keepers. We find things, and I understand you have lost something of value." I brought my hand up to shake hers, but I let it fall when her hand remained motionless at her side.

Her smile was lopsided. She didn't quite understand.

"Ma'am, I don't want to waste your time. This won't take long, but I want to discuss it with you and your husband together. I would rather your attorney be present, too. Is your husband here?"

"He's working in Richmond," she said.

"Can you call him and tell him to meet you at your attorney's office?"

She nodded. An hour later, I made my pitch to the Gibsons and their Richmond attorney, and the attorney's main question was *how exactly are you going to find it?* I pointed out the paragraph in the agreement stating the Gibsons and their representative were not allowed to ask that question. The attorney reread the paragraph and grunted. "You expect my clients to believe—"

"They don't have to believe anything," I said. "Just tell them it is an enforceable contract. I only get paid if they get paid. I mean, what else are they doing today?"

"And you get thirty-two million dollars?"

I smiled. "No, I want ten percent of the cash value; it'll be somewhere around seventeen or eighteen million. This is not a scam. If I don't find the lottery ticket, I leave with nothing. Zero." I turned to the Gibsons. "If you sign the agreement, then we will go to your home and find the ticket right now. No delays. If I am correct, you have until next Wednesday to present the ticket to the lottery office, right?"

Jerry turned to his attorney. "It's enforceable?" His attorney started to hem and haw, but finally nodded. Jerry looked to Smyrna with raised eyebrows. "What have we got to lose?"

"Nothing, I suppose."

They signed, and the four of us went back to the Gibsons' house in Cressy. I asked Jerry what book he was reading when he bought the lottery ticket.

"Oh dear God," he said. "I don't remember. Do you, hon?" He turned to Smyrna.

"That Stephen King book, I guess," she said.

Jerry nodded. "That's right. I didn't finish it."

"When did you put it down?" I asked.

"I don't know," he said. "I think we were looking for the damned ticket."

"Did you ever look inside *Misery*?"

"How'd you know it was *Misery* I was reading?" Jerry asked.

"Never mind that. Did you look in the book?"

Jerry and Smyrna looked at one another and shook their heads. I went to the bookshelf, slid my hands to the third book from the left on the top and pulled it down. I held the hardback of *Misery* in my hands and let it fall open to the marked page. I showed it to Smyrna. She reached to the book and lifted out the lottery ticket from the crease.

"Shit," Jerry said. "Oh, Jesus Christ."

"Thank God," Smyrna said. She had fallen to her knees.

"Unbelievable," their attorney whispered.

"You shouldn't waste time. Go to the lottery offices today," I said. "I'll send wiring instructions to your attorney for my fee." I left.

The Gibsons paid the finder's fee without questioning the enforceability of the contract. At a news conference the Gibsons credited God with recovery of the lottery ticket. They called *me* God.

Once the money was secure in the company's bank account, Alfred and I breathed a sigh of relief and celebrated with Chinese takeout and a chilled Pinot Grigio. I talked about the money in terms of *freedom*. Alfred saw it more as a *burden*, but all of it was a burden for Alfred. He didn't want any of the benefits of the Holden Device. In spite of celebrating with the payday, he refused to take any part of the money. When I asked if he had a moral opposition to accepting it, he shrugged and said he didn't want to have to report it as income on his taxes. He added he had to avoid any appearance of impropriety, and an influx of cash from an unknown source could be questioned. I didn't believe him, even though it was a plausible answer. It seemed too perfect, too detached, and the vibe I felt from him was that this was personal, as though he felt the device had bad mojo and anything from it was tainted. I wondered if that bled over to me. I wanted to ask why anyone would look at his bank accounts, but I let it go.

It wasn't my intent to continue with Finders Keepers, but on a whim, I put an ad on *Craigslist*. The ad asked: *Have you lost something? Send an e-mail to finderskeepers@xyz.com with your story, and Finders Keepers may be able to help find whatever you've lost (for a fee).* Requests trickled in for a few months, mostly to locate jewelry or money, then it became overwhelming. I pulled the ad, but still requests came, I assume from word of mouth. I became selective about who I helped and *why*. It wasn't always for the money. There were also bizarre requests. One person asked me to find the Duncan Butterfly yo-yo he lost when he was eight years old. I wrote back telling him to buy a new one. I couldn't have found it anyway, since he couldn't pinpoint the month or year he lost it. Another person begged me to find the 1965 Mustang he sold in the eighties. I suggested he contact the DMV. There were numerous requests to find people, which I always declined. I figured if a person was lost, there was a good reason he or she didn't want to be found. I located all kinds of things. Big things. Small things. Important things. Unimportant things. Sometimes I charged a fee, but more often than not, I waived the fee, thinking of it as a good deed.

I quit my job at the end of the next spring semester, but I didn't stop being a historian. I wrote journal articles based on theories that could only be proven with the device, focusing on big issues I could prove without a great deal of time investment. My peers at the University thought I was a loon, but I didn't care. I was free to think what I wanted, and say it, too, without many repercussions. I was also free to *do* whatever I wanted. Alfred requested if I wrote any controversial articles to use a pseudonym so I could avoid unnecessary attention. Since notoriety wasn't my goal, I agreed. I took on an alter-ego and wrote what Johann would have called my wild-assed theories. These articles did cause a stir, especially the one called *The Homosexual Presidents*. It was labeled as conjecture, of course, and yet others added to my proof, and a movement was started.

I purchased a large farm, ten minutes from town, and constructed a relatively modest looking house to live. From the outside, the house looked like a typical farmhouse, but it was a fortress. Anyone could walk across the farm, hunters did all the time, but not without me knowing. To break into the house, a thief would need heavy explosives, and that may not have done it. It's never been tested. Within the house, a second fortress—a fortress within a fortress—was built with the same material used for bank vaults to hold the device. I called it the vault. The room was impenetrable. This was Alfred's idea. It was his fear our secret would be discovered, and extra security was the only way to protect it from the rest of the world. He had shady friends design and install the security system, but none knew *why* it was needed. I told Alfred I was surprised he rubbed elbows with that type. He shrugged and said sometimes the good guys wear the darkest of clothes. He trusted them, and that's what mattered.

Alfred continued to resist my assistance on his cases. I'd presented him with hundreds of possibilities, but he used only a dozen. He didn't want to be noticed. We argued about it, and neither of us would back down. I pointed out all the good people he could help but wasn't, and he said he could only help those within his path. To stray outside his path would lead him to trouble. When I said he helped the guilty, his hackles rose. He said it was none of my goddamned business. He always rebuffed my suggestions as unreasonable searches under the Fourth Amendment.

"Your precious Constitution," I said one night. "You know,

only a minority wanted the Fourth Amendment, and that minority forced it on the majority, like bad fucking medicine." He started to speak, and I held up my hands. "This is not something you want to argue with me about, Alfred. Trust me on this. I've watched it all, and I know what was said in the backrooms. I know what no one else in the world knows. Here's the thing: That all of this has held together for so long is remarkable when you realize how fragile it was. So, don't tell me about the importance of the Constitution. What I'm talking about is removing reasonable doubt from *your* mind so you can find evidence to remove doubt from a jury's mind. As a person who knows the founding fathers intimately, I'm telling you this is something they would support."

Alfred leaned against a post on the porch and sighed. "You're drunk Jack," he said.

I smiled and held up my glass of bourbon. I wanted to say *hell, yes, I am and I'm right whether I'm drunk or not*. But I kept silent.

"You're right," he said. "The Constitution is just words on a piece of paper, and mostly worthless, except for the fact it's been interpreted for two hundred years. It's the interpretation of those words that gives them real meaning. That more than two hundred years have passed and this fragile society hasn't imploded means something, doesn't it? I mean, maybe it wasn't as fragile as you think it was. You know, if I start deciding how the words apply to the device, I'm making the words weaker."

"*No one else will know*," I yelled.

"*I'll know*," he yelled back.

That's how the argument always played out, with a few varying themes, but the end result was he walked away...unless I could guarantee no rights had been violated in my review of the crime. Even though Alfred had an aversion to the device, he still wanted to spend time with me, and talk about it.

When I moved to the farm house, Alfred and I spent more evenings together than apart. As I cooked, we talked and drank wine or beer. I told him much of what I was doing on the device, and he told me about his cases, mostly in generalities. I looked forward to seeing him, as he was often my only contact with the outside world. I was his only contact with what he labeled the normal world, although I smiled when he called me normal.

I realized Alfred had indeed replaced Johann in my life. They were different, of course, but like Johann, Alfred carried his own in most of our conversations. Like Johann, he often took the other side of an argument just to test my theories on the topic. He enjoyed our verbal sparring, and while he may not have been as brilliant as Johann, he kept me maneuvering to stay caught up with him. What he did most like Johann was to take a great interest in what I was doing. He questioned me for hours about historical issues, and he let me show him the more interesting parts of what I discovered on the device. He loved all history involving twentieth century wars, which were my least favorite topics. Sometimes I pulled up bits from World War II or the Vietnam War for him to see. I wanted to keep his interest in the device, and continued to hope he would begin using it for his work.

Occasionally, I wondered if we were friends only because I had the device. Did he just want to keep an eye on me to make sure I wasn't acting outside the norm with it? He never confronted me, so if that was his purpose, he set it aside so we could remain friends.

But even now, I question this.

III. *"That was the moment he needed the device."*

Alfred's surrender to the Holden Device came once he'd been softened by marriage and then hardened by divorce. The night he told me he and Julie were getting married, I considered using the device to get to know her, and this thought made me feel unclean. I hadn't met Julie and felt a little left out. I only knew the small bit that Alfred had told me. Even though he and I were best friends, he kept me at arm's length from the other people in his life. It was as though we were superheroes and had to keep our identities secret. He was at the house four or five times a week until he met Julie. Then it was once or twice a month. He was always interested in what I'd been doing on the device, and I asked him about Julie. I told him everything, and he told me very little. On occasion, he called to ask me to use the device to find evidence, but all he would let me tell him was where the evidence could be found. That I had additional information didn't matter. The crimes were always insignificant, but I obliged.

I was surprised to receive an invitation to the wedding. When a wedding list is created, isn't there a conversation about who each guest is and why they are included on the list? I wondered what exactly he'd told Julie about me, but I was scared to ask.

I put on a suit I hadn't worn in a decade and sat in the back. I'd been to large church weddings, but nothing like this. It was something out of a movie. As they said their vows, my only thought was how uncomfortable Alfred must be.

On the way out of the church, I watched with interest as Alfred and Julie greeted wedding guests. She could have been an actress or model. When I made it to the front of the line, I congratulated Alfred and shook his hand. I was happy for him. He turned to Julie. "Hey, Jules. This is my friend I was telling you about, Dr. Jack Holden."

Julie took my hand in both of hers and smiled. Her hands were warm. "Nice to meet you, Jack," she said. "You're the history professor. I hope you can have dinner with us, so I can get to know you."

I didn't think it was something Alfred wanted, but I said, "I would love that. You're a beautiful bride."

She thanked me, and I moved on, leaving the church. I considered going to the reception, but I knew I would sit in the corner by myself, nursing a bourbon and coke, wondering why I had never met the love of my life. I knew the answer, of course. I spent all of my time in my house on the device. I only left the farm to go to the grocery or liquor store. How would I ever meet a woman? Was I even interested in falling in love? I had normal sexual desires, but having someone in my life would complicate matters. How could I have a girlfriend or a wife without her knowing about the Holden Device? Could I trust anyone else with knowledge of the device? As I got into my car, I felt like my chest had been pried open and my heart removed.

That night I went to a bar and met a woman. We fucked at her place, and I never felt more alone.

After the wedding I didn't see Alfred for six months. I continued my quest for something useful on the device, but much of my viewing was for entertainment. I watched the NCAA tournament run of the 1996 UK Championship team. I was in the huddle at timeouts and in the locker room at halftime. I spent a month following Charles Manson around before the murders began. He was more conman than madman. He was a humbug. I floated down the Mississippi with Mark Twain. I was in the NASA control room when Neil Armstrong put his boots on the surface of the moon. I investigated several ghost sightings, one of which I could not disprove. There was a news report about a Sasquatch sighting I determined was fake, and it led me to other sightings. The extent people will go to keep this legend alive is troubling.

In the late fall Alfred reappeared. I was alerted by a message on my phone when the front gate opened. I looked at the security camera and saw it was him and turned off the device. To kill my boredom, I had been watching a day in my life as a seven-year-old. It was something to entertain me. My life had become monotonous, but I didn't want Alfred to know that.

I waited for him at the door, and as he walked up the porch steps, I understood he was sad. "What's wrong, my friend?" I asked.

"Her," he said.

"Who?"

"My wife. She's wrong."

"Come in. I'll get some bourbon and you can tell me about it."

We sat at the kitchen table, the bottle of Woodford Reserve between us. He sipped at his drink, and I waited. "I think she's fucking someone else," he finally whispered.

"What makes you think so?"

"I found some text messages from him, her lover, on her phone. If they're not fucking, then I don't know what she's doing."

I took a drink and considered how to respond. I wondered why he had come to me, but I already knew, didn't I? I proceeded carefully in the conversation.

"Have you asked her?"

"No," he said. "I found out a couple weeks ago, and you're the only person I've told. What am I supposed to ask her?"

I smiled. "You ask her if everything's okay."

"She'll say *yes*."

I leaned across the table. "When she does, tell her you love her and forget about it."

"I can't. I...I don't want to be a cuckold." It was unlike Alfred to be this emotional. His thoughts were always rational, and never scattered. He was never scared of the unknown. I thought of him as fearless, but only because he would never show his fear.

Yet, today, he was scared. He was terrified. I waited. I knew what he was going to ask.

"Can we find out?"

I shrugged. "What are you going to do if she is? Will you kill her like Johann did Denise?"

He looked offended. "No. Of course not. I just don't want to sleep in the same bed as her if she's fucking someone else."

I believed him. Even if I didn't, could I deny him?

As it turned out, Julie had a lover, but it wasn't exactly what Alfred thought it was. He told me the date of the text messages and where she worked. I followed her during the last thirty minutes of her shift at the hospital with Alfred sitting next to me. Nothing happened out of the ordinary. All was professional. When she clocked out, she drove to a house Alfred didn't know. She knocked on the door, and a woman answered. When the door shut, there was an immediate peck on the cheek, but nothing lurid. The evening wore on, and I noted how they smiled at one another. I knew they were lovers, but I said nothing to Alfred. After a meal, Julie led the other woman to the bedroom. Alfred and I watched a sexual encounter that was both beautiful and mysterious.

All Alfred would say is, "Oh my God."

I asked if he knew the woman, and he shook his head.

Later, we sat at the table drinking coffee. "The text messages were from Shawn," he said. "I figured it was another man. I had no idea."

"You didn't know she was a bisexual?"

He shrugged. "I knew, but not that it was ongoing."

"What are you going to do?"

"I don't know. I'll confront her at some point, I guess, because it's still her being unfaithful. I'll talk to her, and find out if we can make it work."

Alfred never confronted her. He let it go, accepted it, but the marriage declined anyway. Julie complained Alfred was never home, and when he was home, their time together was interrupted by police business. He blamed it on himself, too. "I couldn't give her what she wanted," he said. "I'm not the kind of guy that can give up everything at a whim, and that's my fault, I know." But it wasn't his fault. I knew more than he did. Julie's affair continued, and Shawn subtly picked at Julie. *Come on, babe. You know you're happier when you're with me, don't you? He's a great guy. I know that, but he doesn't make you feel special, like I do, right? I make you feel special, don't I?* I never watched Alfred during this decline. I spent twelve months in the house with Shawn and Julie. They'd become part of my life, people I visited daily, only a few hours delayed. They weren't bad people. What Shawn did was out of love, and I couldn't fault that, even if it broke up a marriage.

I had reduced myself to reality television, and the difficult part came when I realized I had to let them go. When Julie left Alfred, I was no longer tangentially part of Julie and Shawn's life. There was no reason for me to watch their drama any longer. For a long time, I felt empty and listless, as though my friends had abandoned me.

I had Alfred, or what was left of him after the divorce. He claimed he'd never trust anyone again. He went through the motions of his job, just showing up, but not really working. Whatever criminals he put in jail was from the absurdity of their crime, not because of Alfred's investigations. Those criminals simply fell into his lap. Away from work, he had little motivation to do anything useful. Alfred had no joy.

But he had me. After six months of listening to his heartbreak, I showed him something to help him rise above it and move on. On a Friday night, I already had the device running. Once I heard the front door shut out the cold of the winter, I yelled, "Come in here, Alfred."

I had a coffee cup ready to hand him as he walked into the vault. "What's this?" he asked.

"Have a seat in my chair," I said.

"What for?"

"Just do it."

He took the cup and sat down, but he didn't look at the screen. If he had, he would have seen his childhood home. Early on, he'd told me where he'd lived as a kid, and now seven years later, I'd pulled it out of my memory and chose his fifth birthday. I'd seen much of it. "Have a look?" I said.

"What for?"

"Just look, goddamnit," I said, but not harshly.

When he turned, he saw it. "That's..." His voice trailed off.

"Go inside," I said. He did and was lost in wonder. I clapped him on the back as he fumbled the camera about the house. He found his younger self sleeping in a day bed. He had a Mickey Mouse poster on the wall, and checkers set up to beat his next victim, although I think his parents let him win. He moved to his parents' bedroom and saw his father spooned with his mother. He was awake, but still wanted her warmth. His father was happy.

"I'm going to see a movie," I said. "I'll see you when I get back."

Alfred glanced up, but just for a second. "You don't have to go," he whispered.

"I don't," I agreed. "But I've seen this already. Happy watching. This was a good day in your life."

I left.

When I got back, Alfred hadn't moved, but I could see he was different. "You okay?" I asked.

"I'm great," he said. "They loved each other so much." He pointed to his parents who were making him lunch, laughing at something. "It's so fucking beautiful, you know?"

"It is."

"This is a gift," he said. "Thank you."

"I brought a pizza home," I said. "I'll bring it in here and we can eat and watch your birthday party. You had pizza that day. Do you remember?"

He shook his head. "It was a surprise birthday party," he said. "At the skating rink. I didn't know. All they fed me was cantaloupe for lunch, and that's why they're laughing. I kept asking if I could have peanut butter crackers, and they wouldn't answer me. It never dawned on me why."

I smiled. That night we ate pizza and watched the younger Alfred as he tried to skate. It was but one block to breaking down the wall he had constructed. Still, it was a start. He kept asking for more over the next few months. He would tell me what he wanted to see from his childhood. I would set it up and leave him alone. It made him want to live again, but not love. That was more than I could do.

Alfred renewed his pursuit of those who commit crime. Had he followed my lead and used the device, I could have made him a superhero. Instead, he followed his instinct as a tenacious investigator—a junk yard dog that wouldn't let go of anything.

Late at night, sitting across from me with a beer, he told me more than he should, as if I was his confessor. I never passed judgment. I merely listened, and the next day, with his approval, I watched the more interesting parts of what he told me had happened in his day. In the interview room, he looked each suspect in the eyes and talked to them, treated them with respect, like any human being deserves. It was less like an interrogation and more of a chat. He'd draw them out, build trust, then he'd ask about the crime. They'd tell him everything. Even the hardest of criminals eventually talked, only because Alfred never gave up. He was ruthless, searching for something to get into their minds, and when he found it, he didn't let it go. One tack was to make the suspect feel guilty, not because of his or her crime, but because the *one* person who mattered to them most would be disappointed. In ten minutes of conversation, Alfred knew who that person was and why there was a bond. When there was no remorse, Alfred used fear, but not by screaming or making threats. He used a calm, guttural voice from deep in his diaphragm. What he said mattered less than how he said it. You only wanted to make the voice go away so you could get on with your life without the unqualified oppression the voice caused. The suspect's eyes bugged out like Alfred was inside him. All he ever did was talk. Alfred could see the fear, and he chased it relentlessly. He was unforgiving.

I often wondered if the obstinacy that made Alfred a great policeman is what caused the failure of his marriage. Did he ever give in to Julie when they argued? Did he apologize afterward and tell her he loved her, or did he walk away uncompromisingly mad and expect it to be a new day when the sun rose the next morning? Stubbornness was an essential part of who Alfred was as a person, and it must have been noticed by Julie prior to the wedding. Wasn't it part of what she was attracted to? Would she have even noticed him if he was acquiescent?

The marriage and divorce changed him, made him colder, but there was warmth buried within for the right person to find. That person would have to burrow beneath the surface and be patient. Alfred's dry sense of humor had become sporadic, and I had no gauge on what he thought was funny. I was hesitant to make jokes. Who wants to make jokes without an audience? Despite this, Alfred and I grew closer. I think he had better friends, but I was the only one he could talk to about everything. He kept few secrets from me.

And when he was in trouble, he came to me. That was the moment he needed the device.

I had become obsessed with Richard Nixon. It was less a political obsession than a personal one. I was fascinated by what drove him as a man to be an unlikely candidate, let alone elected as president. He was so much more than the failed president we all know from the television news and documentaries. There was a depth of thought in him that conservative presidents since have regrettably lacked. These presidents may have had more charisma than Nixon, but none have thought for themselves like he did. In the end, he didn't stay true to himself and got caught up in the need to be reelected, which caused his inevitable downfall. I saw him as his family saw him. He resisted the forces that pushed and pulled him toward this end, but in due course, he met his fate, albeit in disgrace. I read his biographies and his writings, and I made elaborate notes. I called all the people who had surrounded him during his presidency and arranged for interviews. I realized my outlining wasn't for an article, but a biography. There were elements I could bring that no one else had. I knew who hadn't been interviewed and what those individuals knew. I could bring it out of them. It was like mining for gold I had placed in the ground myself.

On a Friday in late September, I'd had an impossible day looking for a discussion between Nixon and Gerald Ford referenced in his most recent biography. Either the discussion hadn't happened, or it had happened at an unlikely moment. Following a president is tedious. Ninety-nine-point-nine percent of the time, nothing happens. Then, in twenty seconds, a world-changing event transpires. If you're not paying attention, you miss it. On this particular evening, I fell asleep at eight o'clock, thinking it was strange the sun still sent its rays through my bedroom window as I drifted off with a book against my chest.

I dreamed I was being chased by men in dark suits who wanted the Holden Device for themselves. The sirens resounded.

I sat straight up in bed, still fearful of the men in dark suits, but relief flooded over me as the dream state subsided. I realized it was the alarm system blaring. This wasn't an uncommon occurrence. It was usually a deer or coyote that had wandered onto the farm and was spotted with the motion sensors. As typical, I wrapped myself in a cover and went to the vault to confirm nothing was amiss. I saw Alfred's car barreling down the long drive. I suspected this would be a long night, so after I shut off the alarm, I went back to my room and pulled on a pair of jeans. I had just poured water into the coffee maker when Alfred walked into the kitchen, blinking at me.

"What are you doing awake, Jack?"

"You forgot the secondary code," I said. The gate at the road had a main security code to open the gate, but also a secondary code turning off the alarm.

"Sorry," he said. He looked haggard and worried. His eyes kept darting away from mine.

"It's okay," I said. "What the fuck is wrong?"

"Everything."

I inspected his face to see if he meant to be melodramatic. All I saw was his worry. "Okay. Let's talk, but I need to piss

292

first."

When I came back into the kitchen, he had sat at the table, staring into the darkness of the coffee cup cradled in his hands as if there might be answers in the brew. I poured myself a cup and sat across from him. I took a sip. "Talk to me, man."

He leaned back in his chair, winced a bit as he tried to summon the words he needed. "You've heard about the Hannah McBride case, haven't you?" he finally asked.

For the last week, Hannah McBride's picture had been above the fold in the Lexington newspaper and on the local news of all four TV stations. The day before, it had even been picked up by the national media. Hannah was a pretty sixteen-year-old who had gone missing. She looked like every pubescent boy's wet dream. A girl-next-door type. According to the newspaper, Kyle Gruber, her longtime boyfriend, had taken her to dinner and a movie, then drove her home. He claimed he kissed her on the front porch, an innocent peck on the cheek, and watched her go inside. When the door shut behind her, he left. Hannah's parents were awake, watching television. They said the door never opened, and Hannah never came home. The local media focused on this discrepancy and questioned why police were looking for some unknown suspect and not the boyfriend or the parents. The coverage suggested the investigation had been botched and Hannah would never be found.

I arched my eyebrows at Alfred. "You've got that case?"

"Yeah," he said. He bit his lower lip and shut his eyes. "I've got the team investigating the boyfriend, Kyle, and there's another team looking into the parents' story. I wanted to break this one. I decided since Kyle was the last one who saw Hannah, he had to have information about where she was, right? So, I've been at him, like I do, you know? You've seen me when I push them. Three meetings in the interview room, and I've been at his home, trying to break him. He's been resistant."

"Is he telling the truth?"

Alfred always had an instinct for what was going on in

a suspect's mind, but he sighed and elaborately shrugged his bony shoulders. "I think so. But he knows...something. He's lying about something. I had to break him. If Hannah's alive, we need to find her. If she's dead, we need to find out what happened to her. Her parents are putting stress on my bosses."

I was confused. "Was she found? Is that what's wrong?"

"No. I pushed Kyle. I pushed him too much. He tried to hang himself in the basement of his parents' house. He left a note, saying he felt responsible even though he hadn't done anything. He mentioned me."

I didn't want to ask, but I had to. "Is he okay?"

"The rope broke. His parents found him passed out from hitting his head on the concrete floor. He's in the hospital and will be fine, but his parents are in my shit. The only way I can save myself—*my career*—is to find Hannah. If I don't, I'll be the scapegoat."

I considered all of this. He'd come for my help. "You want me to find her with the device?"

He nodded. "I was going to let you sleep and do it myself, but since you're up, I would appreciate the help."

"Of course."

"You can find her, can't you?" Alfred asked. The furrow across his forehead was deeper than usual.

"Of course, I can. I will."

He stood, but I sat still. He looked down at me. "Is there something else?"

I had one more question for Alfred, and he wasn't going to like it. "Are you sure you can do this without violating your principles?"

He nodded.

I stood from the table. "I want to do some good with the device and I think we can. The two of us."

"But—"

"No," I interrupted. "I don't fucking care about their precious rights. We've had this argument, and as long as you hold onto those ideals, you'll never move forward. Give them up.

Let's help people."

He looked at his feet, then raised his head. "Okay. Fine. The Constitution is dead to me."

It was said with sarcasm, but I took it as truth. "Good."

I tossed out Alfred's coffee and poured us both a fresh cup. Alfred followed me to the vault, and I booted up the device. In the last year, the monitor started dying, and I replaced it with the largest screen I could find. It was especially nice when I watched old sporting events, almost as if I was there in the stadium or arena.

"Where do we start?"

"Kyle said he picked her up at six on Saturday night."

I turned to him. "He dropped her off at eleven?"

Alfred nodded.

"So, you want to spend five hours with them on their date?"

"Something happened on the date," he said. "I have to find out what."

I sighed. "I'll fix more coffee in a bit."

He gave a slight nod.

I converted the McBride home address to latitude and longitude coordinates, and keyed the information into the device. I punched the time in and clicked *start*. The device buzzed for about three seconds, and then the screen showed the roofs of several houses.

"That house," Alfred said and pointed to the house in the center.

I moved down and hovered the camera viewpoint so we stared at the front of a split-level home constructed sometime in the 1970s in what was an upper middle class subdivision then, but was working middle class now. The houses Johann and I grew up in were only a half-mile away. When we were kids, we rode our bikes by this house a thousand times.

I moved toward the door and through it to a foyer. The stairs went up on the right and down on the left. I went up and found a landing, what would probably have been a living

295

room, but had been turned into a library or maybe a reading room. Built-in bookshelves lined the walls. To the right was the kitchen and an open dining room, where Hannah's mom stood, looking out the back door. I thought about moving toward her, but went left into a hallway toward the bedrooms instead. I found Hannah in the back bedroom on her bed reading. I moved closer and turned my head so I could read the binding of the hardback. John Green's *The Fault in our Stars*. Not a book I had heard of, but I didn't read much fiction. I moved above the book and then forward so Hannah's face filled the screen. She was waif-thin, but had the face of a flower with bright aqua-green eyes any teenage boy could lose himself in. In a few years, she'd fill out and be beautiful.

Alfred was impatient. "Find her father. See what he's doing."

The other bedrooms were dark, so I moved back into the library and saw that Hannah's mom was still staring out the backdoor.

I moved down the stairs into a den. Hannah's father lay in a recliner, snoring over the blaring of the local television news. His hands were folded across his thick chest. He had broad shoulders and solid arms, but his stomach bulged like he was pregnant. An empty beer bottle sat on the coffee table making a water stain, and two empty bottles were on the floor.

"He's a carpenter," Alfred said. "Look how big his hands are. Chunky fingers, like sausages."

I started to move out of the room, but Alfred put his hand on my arm. "Wait a second. Do you see anything odd in this room?"

I turned the view about, but saw nothing out of the ordinary.

Alfred sat straight up. "Put the camera angle right above her father's head, looking at the television." When I moved as directed, he pointed. "Now, do you see something?"

I said I didn't.

"You've read the news reports? What Hannah's parents

said?"

"They were watching television. Saturday Night Live, I think."

"That's right. But they also said the door never opened. Look. They can't see the door from this chair. Or the couch."

Alfred was right. None of the seating created an angle with a view of the stairs to the foyer or front door. "So, you think she came home without them knowing then left?"

"I don't know," he said. "I only know her parents saw nothing. Not what they claimed, anyway. If the television was up this loud, I doubt they could hear the door open and shut."

I went back upstairs to Hannah's mom in the kitchen where she still stood at the door, now smoking a cigarette. If she was thirty pounds lighter and twenty years younger, she'd be Hannah's twin, except she no longer had her daughter's innocence. I had a sense of her being used up and discarded.

Alfred walked close to the screen and peered into her face. "Do you see the sadness in her?"

"Maybe sadness, but I think it's regret."

Alfred rubbed his chin as he stared at this woman. "If that's the case, then I guess the question is, what does she regret?"

She sighed and blew a funnel of smoke into the window.

Alfred's squeamishness finally got the best of him. He turned away from the screen. "Leave her in peace. Go outside and wait for Kyle."

I moved the camera to the front yard and positioned it so we could see Kyle as soon as he drove up. Having to wait for Kyle bothered Alfred. "Why wouldn't your friend have added a fast forward to the device? How much time do you waste waiting for something to happen?"

I could have told him most of my time was wasted, but sometimes the in-between moments were important. "Why don't you go home and sleep? I've got this. I'll mark the time anything significant happens, just like always, and you can come and watch later."

He shook his head. "No. I've got to see this to the end. Even if I went home, I wouldn't sleep."

"You'll have to be patient."

"Yeah, okay," he said, but he paced the room.

Ten minutes later, a black Kia SUV parked in front of the McBrides' house, and a tall, lanky kid with thick glasses got out. "That's him. That's Kyle," Alfred mumbled.

Kyle Gruber wasn't who I expected to date the girl next door. He had a crop of zits on his face, and his glasses rested on the end of his nose. He seemed to be unsure of himself as he walked to the front door.

Kyle rang the bell and stood with his hands in his jeans pockets. When Hannah opened the door, she leaned into him and kissed him on the cheek. She beamed at him, and he beamed back. Young, mismatched love.

Hannah turned and yelled she was leaving. She waited for a second, but neither parent responded. Hand in hand, she and Kyle walked to the SUV, and he opened the passenger-side door for her. As he walked around to his side of the car, he seemed to have grown to ten feet tall.

I moved into the backseat, but when Kyle accelerated the camera angle was left in front of the McBride home. I moved the camera forward and followed from about thirty feet back and forty feet up. When the mouse moved off the pad, I lifted it and put to the front edge, again. I'd grown accustomed to the difficulties of keeping up with moving vehicles.

"That's another thing your friend failed to do," Alfred said.

"What's that?"

"I'd like to hear what's being said in the car."

"As would I."

I had tried to perfect movement of the camera so I could stay within the confines of a moving vehicle, but all I ever got were short snippets of conversation. Not enough to make sense. Speed and direction were never consistent enough. Had Johann had time, I figured he would have made it so the camera could be affixed to a particular object, like the dashboard of the car or maybe even a person.

I felt intrusive as we watched them talk and eat at the Pizza Hut, but mostly it was conversation about television shows, their friends, their parents, and school, all normal teenage banter.

It only took thirty minutes of this for me to come to a conclusion. "You know Kyle didn't hurt Hannah, don't you? He worships her."

Alfred nodded. "So it appears."

I followed them to the theater, and when they parked, I moved into the car and watched them make out. It was a little touchy-feely but Kyle's hands never went below her waist and only briefly touched her chest. Hannah did graze Kyle's crotch to make sure he had a boner. "After the movie," she promised.

Alfred looked away while they made out, but this got his attention. "What the fuck is that supposed to mean? Can't we fast forward through the movie to find out?"

"Oh, you want to get to the dirty part of this?" I said. When he started to object, I reminded him to have patience.

The movie was a romantic comedy, but I was more interested in the play between Hannah and Kyle. They held hands and didn't talk, except to say something was funny. When Hannah told Kyle she needed to go to the bathroom, he walked her out and waited. How could Alfred have thought Kyle took part in Hannah's disappearance? I glanced at him and considered admonishing him, but it wasn't necessary. Alfred knew he'd done wrong, and it pained him.

After the movie, Kyle didn't drive her straight home, and Alfred's attention was piqued. It was five in the morning now, and he had become irritable. He sat on the edge of his seat. "Where the fuck is he taking her?"

It wasn't a question I could answer, so I followed silently. Kyle parked the SUV at the rear of the high school. "He didn't say anything about going there before taking her home," Alfred said.

"If you were him, would you?"

"Not at first," he said. "But by now, I would have. Someone

may have seen them. If he lied about this, he could be lying about anything."

"But he's not," I said.

Again, they made out, which Hannah concluded by giving Kyle a dry hand job. It took less than thirty seconds once she had unleashed him from his jeans and underwear. She laughed. "I'm not losing my virginity in a car, but I'm hot for you right now. You should know that."

"Can I touch you?"

Her knees went together. "Not tonight, okay?"

Kyle looked sad, but he smiled. "Yeah, yeah. Of course."

He started the car and drove her home. As he had told the police, he walked her to the door, kissed her goodnight, and she went inside. He turned and skipped down the walkway.

I turned to Alfred. His eyes were shut. When he opened them and saw me staring, he said, "I'm happy for the kid. But I'm fucked if I can't find her alive."

I thought he was fucked, too, but didn't say it. I went into the McBride home, and what I heard got my attention. The roaring voices weren't coming from the television. Hannah's father stood in the center of the den downstairs, arms wrapped around his chest, wailing. There were no intelligible words. Just a sound of pain. Misery. Or maybe even grief. Hannah was at the bottom of the steps, staring at her father. Hannah's mom sat on the edge of the couch, her head down, tears quietly flowing into her hands.

They hadn't seen Hannah, yet. From the bored look on her face, this behavior by her parents wasn't unexpected. This was the norm. "I'm home," she finally said. When neither parent responded, she screamed it. "I'm home! Can you stop with the drama now?"

Her father jumped and turned to her. His wails were silenced. Hannah had scolded him, and he was embarrassed. Her mom peered through her fingers at her daughter.

"What's it about tonight?" Hannah asked.

Her father took a step toward her. "Your mother's in love

with another man," he moaned.

"Oh, Jesus," Hannah said. She looked at her mom, but her mom refused to look back.

"She wants me out of the house," her father continued. His words were slurred, and his cheeks red. He rocked back and forth and shook his fists at his wife. "I ought to beat the life out of you, woman!" he screamed.

At this, I thought Hannah's parents were responsible for her being missing. I glanced at Alfred, but he was too intent on what was happening.

Hannah's father took a step toward his wife, but Hannah moved across the room and stood between them. "You're tired, and you're drunk. Why don't you go upstairs and get some sleep, okay?"

"You're going to protect her?" he asked, his voice soft.

"I don't need protecting," Hannah's mother said. Her words were also slurred, but she wasn't as drunk as her husband. I thought maybe she was pushing him so there'd be violence.

Hannah turned to her father. "It's just there's nothing you can do here, unless you decide you want to hurt her. That's only going to get you in trouble. I need you. Let me talk to her, okay?"

"I'm not done yelling," he said. "The last time she did this, I yelled until she decided to let me stay. I want to stay. Can I keep yelling until she agrees I can stay? I won't lay a hand on her. I promise."

"You're leaving!" Hannah's mom screamed.

Hannah glanced over her shoulder at her mom. "Please, shut up, mom. You're not kicking him out." She turned back to her father and put her hands on his shoulders. "If you start making threats, I'm leaving the house. I can't be here as long as you're acting like this."

Her father looked too drunk to understand her words, and ten seconds of silence passed while he considered his response. Finally he said, "Go then. Go stay with a friend. Get out of here."

"Fine. That's it," Hannah said. She turned, went up the

stairs to the front door which she opened, stepped through, and slammed behind her. She stood on the front porch and pulled out her cell phone, but she didn't use it. She turned it off and walked to the sidewalk.

"Where the fuck is she going?" Alfred asked.

"Why didn't her parents tell you what just happened?" I asked.

"They feel guilty."

"But it would have helped. It wasn't them *or* Kyle."

"In the beginning, maybe they thought she'd come home, so their story didn't matter much. When she didn't return, they couldn't change their stories, or it would bring suspicion on them."

I continued to follow her on the sidewalk. She held the phone in her hand, but it was still turned off. "You have her phone records, right. Does she make a phone call?"

Alfred shook his head. "She hasn't turned it on."

She walked as if she knew where she was going. She turned left and then right and after three-quarters of a mile, she turned right again onto one of Lexington's major thorough-fares. After another quarter mile, she went inside an all-night diner and sat down. She ordered a coffee and a basket of fries. She asked the waitress if she could use the phone, claiming hers had died. The waitress nodded. She reached into a back pocket and handed her cell phone to Hannah, who looked at it as if she didn't know what it was. As she walked away, the waitress said her boss wouldn't let anyone use the restaurant's phone. I deftly moved in so I could see the numbers Hannah punched in and wrote them down.

"Hey," Hannah said. "Can you come pick me up? They're at it again...I'm at the all-night diner...yeah, that one."

She ended the call, and gave the phone back to the when she came with the coffee. Hannah quietly ate her fries as she waited, and we watched the door over her shoulder. I hoped she'd called Kyle so he could take her home, but I knew that didn't happen. She didn't want her parents' actions to bleed over into the good thing she had with him. She thought he'd disappear if he knew, and maybe he would.

The door of the diner opened, and a man in his early forties walked in. He was dressed casually, but there was nothing casual about him. When he sat across from Hannah and started eating her french fries, I turned to Alfred, held out my hands, and asked, "Who's that?"

"I don't know," he said. "I hope it's a family friend."

I hoped so, too, but the familiarity, the way he looked at her, told me this man was something else. Maybe a lover. But I didn't want to believe it. "This is a fucking soap opera," I said.

Alfred didn't answer. He was mesmerized now.

Hannah and the man talked about the nice fall weather and school, surface type stuff, but nothing about why she called *him* of all people. She didn't look at him like a lover, not flirty or interested. She was somewhat indifferent to him, but there was an ease between them that made me uncomfortable. The man, she called him Hank, paid for her coffee and fries, and they went out the door to a Chevrolet pickup, not what I expected. I would have thought he drove a Lexus or maybe something sporty. He looked like he bled money. He was someone who had everything except something to prove. I didn't want her to get in the truck, but she did.

He drove into an older neighborhood lined with tall oaks and sycamores. The houses were set a short distance back from the road. I knew this neighborhood. I always asked why anyone would need such a large house and so much yard. Hank drove the twisting roads until he reached a two-story Tudor, which I guessed had five or six bedrooms. I wondered who else lived in this enormous house, if anyone. The other car in the garage was a Mercedes. When they got out, Hank led Hannah into the house. He went to the fridge and opened a beer. He offered her one, but she declined. She sat on a stool, her elbows on the countertop of the island, and told him about what had happened with her parents. She said they'd been arguing for weeks. "I think they'll get a divorce," she said.

"You wish."

"It's for real this time." She didn't say her mom had a lover, but *another* lover, which alluded to an earlier lover. She also speculated her mom didn't really have a new lover, but just said it for the drama, to stir things. It had. She told Hank her father had slept on the couch for two weeks. "I don't understand *why* she'd tell him if she wasn't wanting a divorce."

Hank was quiet at this, but the edges of his lips turned upward in a faint smile. Hannah didn't notice. "You've got one and a half years, and then you'll be off to college, far, far away. You've got to make it until then."

"It's toxic in the house."

"It always has been toxic. They've just hidden it from you. I think they care for one another, but they're both filled with self-loathing. They need to get over themselves. You can't do that for them."

"But—"

Hank leaned over the counter toward her. "Let's hope they can survive this. They are the best thing for each other."

"I can't go back."

"You have to. You have nowhere else to go."

She looked at him with pleading eyes.

"No, no, no. Don't even think about it. You have to go home and keep them together."

"Can I stay here tonight, at least? Let them worry about me."

Hank shut his eyes. He knew what she asked was trouble, but he wasn't in a position to deny her. He opened his eyes and stretched his lips into something short of a smile. "Yeah, okay."

"I'm wiped out. I think I'll go on to bed."

Hank nodded. "Okay. I'll see you in the morning."

She walked through the house as if she owned it. She found a bedroom and closed the door, but didn't lock it. Her familiarity with the house was a clue, but I didn't know of what. She went into the bathroom where she had her own toothbrush, lotions, makeup remover, and skin cleanser. All the things a girl would need. When she was finished preparing herself for the night, she went back into the bedroom and changed into pajamas. She climbed into the bed, turned off the bedside lamp, and shut her eyes.

I saw Alfred had turned to look at the wall. He must have looked away when she undressed. "She's in bed now," I said. When he turned back to the screen, I asked, "What now?"

Alfred pressed his lips together and looked at his watch. "See what Hank is doing right now. While you're doing that, I'm going to borrow your laptop for some traditional investigation."

I shoved the laptop toward him, and I heard him tapping away while I moved the view of the device through the house. I found Hank in his bedroom watching highlights of the day's college football games on ESPN. He held the neck of a second beer, but wasn't paying much attention to the television.

"Whatever's going on here," I said, "he's not malicious."

Alfred looked up. "I don't think so, either. His name is Henry O'Roark. He's never been arrested. He has a few speeding tickets. He owns a company called O'Roark Strategies, but I don't know what it does. The tax office has his home valued at just over one and a half million dollars, and he doesn't even have a mortgage."

"How do you know all this in just a few minutes?"

He grunted. "It's what I do."

"More than I found in five hours on the device."

He shrugged and stood up.

"Where are you going?"

"You've given me a lead," he said. "Now I just got to follow it up."

"What lead?"

"The restaurant," he said. "The waitress saw her that night. Why hasn't she called the police? With the coverage this story has gotten, she should have called us. Once I get her to tell me Hannah was there, I can ask what she ordered, whether she was with someone, how Hannah paid for it. Then I've got him.

I'll be able to go to his house."

"How are they going to identify Henry O'Roark?" I asked.

"If the cameras in the restaurant are hooked up, I'll have a video of him, which won't be as good as the device, but good enough. And he used a credit card to pay for her food."

I smiled. "You don't really need me, do you?"

"Oh, I do," he said. "You're going to make sure Hank tells the truth, because you have the truth. You are the only person who will know what really happened. I don't want to be wrong with this one. Once *he* falls asleep, skip ahead six hours. Back-track if you have to. See what happens in the morning. I'll call you when I know more."

I shut my eyes for a second. "You think she's alive?"

"It all depends on who he is," Alfred said.

"Let me skip ahead six days and see if she's still at this house."

He shook his head. "No. I need you to sift through what happens between them. I only need you for confirmation of what he tells us, okay? Don't tell me anything else, unless I ask."

I nodded, and he left.

Once Hank fell asleep, I went to the kitchen and made more coffee. I returned to the vault and moved the device ahead to seven the next morning and changed the coordinates to Hank's house. When the camera popped above the house, I could see the sun just rising. I went inside and found Hank reading the newspaper at the kitchen island. Hannah was still asleep. I kept the view on Hank, and I read a Nixon biography.

Two hours later, Hannah appeared in the kitchen, where Hank was still lodged at the stool, clicking at a laptop. I had read his emails as he typed them, but could not follow enough to grasp much useful information. I thought he may be a soft-ware designer, but it seemed less technical, as if he were the marketing person behind the software.

"Good morning," he said.

"Morning." She wore different clothes than the night before.

He scrambled eggs and fried bacon for them both. When he sat down next to her to eat, she said, "Thanks Hank for letting me stay. I'm sure all has calmed down at home."

"You're welcome."

They continued eating, but he had something on his mind. He kept glancing at her. I had a sudden expectation drama was about to occur. I leaned toward the screen and tried to figure out what was on his mind by the look in his face, but it was of no use.

"I've been thinking," he finally started.

"Oh, that's dangerous," Hannah said and laughed.

He ignored her. "Are you tired of this life you're leading?"

My heart sank. His statement was ominous.

She repeated his words from the night before. "Only a year and a half more. That's what you said, right?"

He nodded. "What if you wanted it to end now? You can stay here, with me. All you have to do is say the word. You don't have to decide now. You can think about it."

Hannah squinted at him. "You can make that happen?"

"Of course," he said. "I hate to see them put you through this."

"Yeah," she said. "I don't know. I thought we had it all planned, but I had to wait until I was eighteen. What's changed?"

"It's just you're so unhappy when you don't have to be. I can change that."

She looked at him. Maybe I was wrong, but I saw a certain amount of discomfort in her face at the suggestion. "I'll think about it," she said. She went back to her food.

I followed Hannah about her day, mostly she stayed in the den, reading and watching television. She picked up her phone a few times, and seemed to debate whether to turn it on. Hank left the house for an hour, and returned with groceries. After he put them away, he continued working on his laptop. There was little conversation.

Late in the day, Alfred called and told me I could stop watching. He said Hannah had been found and he would explain later. Before I could ask whether she was alive or dead, he hung up. Still, I continued watching Hannah as she read. This was a normal pattern for me. It was hard to let go once I had become interested in a person's life.

After the sun had gone down, the gate buzzed. A quick glance at the security camera showed the gates opening for Alfred's sedan. I didn't wait for him to get to the house. I left Hannah watching a Seinfeld episode, the one with the soup Nazi. I went into the kitchen. I heated up oil in a pan and started cutting up vegetables for a stir-fry. When Alfred came into the kitchen, he sat at the table and watched me cook. After a few minutes of silence, I asked, "You going to tell me what happened?"

"I'll wait until we're eating," he said.

I nodded. "Okay. But at least tell me she's alive." I wanted her to be alive more than I had wanted anything lately. I was emotionally invested in a good result here.

"She's alive and well," he said. "She's been reunited with Kyle, and all's well with her mom and father. Well, kind of." I turned and looked at him. "It's complicated," he said. "Just cook and then I'll explain."

"Get us some beer," I said.

"God, yes."

I tossed chicken into the hot pan, and took the beer Alfred handed me.

"Did you see anything today of interest?"

I shook my head. "Not much. Hank asked Hannah if she wanted to end her life." Alfred's eyes got big, and I shook my head. "No, not suicide. He wanted her to stay there with him. But I don't know why." I stirred, then salted and peppered the chicken. "You know though, don't you?"

"Yes," he said. "Finish that and I'll explain."

I removed the chicken from the oil, and added broccoli, onions, carrots, mushrooms, fourth of a cup of sherry, and sesame oil to the pan and mixed it all up. I put in the zucchini, ginger, sugar, and cornstarch, and finished by adding the chicken back in.

As I put the meal on the plates, I realized I hadn't cooked rice. "I forgot the goddamned rice," I said.

"If you could get me another Sam Adams, I'll forgive you," Alfred said. "I don't need another starch, anyway."

I set the plate before him and mine across the table. "Too many donuts today?"

"Too little sleep."

I opened both of us another Sam Adams. I handed him his as I sat at the table. "So, talk," I said.

"Before I do, I'm curious what you think happened."

I considered the question as I chewed a broccoli floret. "I think Hank is mostly innocent, and yet he wants to stir matters between Hannah's parents so they get a divorce. But I don't know what he gains from it, if anything. He has to have an interest, doesn't he?"

Alfred nodded. "*That's* the key to all of this." He took a big bite of food, as did I, and I realized I had been a bachelor for too long. I had become too good of a cook. "I went to the all-night restaurant," Alfred continued, "and I got the address of the waitress who had served Hannah. I found her at her apartment. I lied. I said a witness had seen Hannah enter the restaurant. I showed her a picture of Hannah. She said she'd seen her but wanted to know *why* I was asking so early in the morning. She doesn't have a television and doesn't pay attention to the televisions at work. 'None of it affects me,' she said. Right. She said she had never seen Hannah before that night, but had seen Hank. He ate there once or twice a month at odd hours of the day and night."

"Did she know his name?"

Alfred smiled. "She didn't need to," he said. "I called another detective to get the credit card receipt, and in twenty minutes, I had his name. I went to the house, knocked on the door, and Hannah answered. Hank wasn't there."

I stopped eating as I waited. "Well, what did she say?"

Before answering, Alfred looked out the window, gathering his thoughts. When he turned back to me, his eyes were bright with knowledge. "I asked if she knew everyone in town was looking for her. She said she was sorry. She kept meaning to return home, but couldn't find it in her. She said Hank wasn't keeping her against her will, and she could have left at any time. She wouldn't explain more without Hank there."

He delayed by taking a long sip of beer, and I had to know. "Did you ask *why* Hank had to be there to discuss it?"

"Of course," he said. "But she wouldn't talk about it, not a word. When he got there, I told him who I was and I asked what he was to Hannah. He said he was her father." I started to protest, but Alfred held up his hands. "Yeah, yeah, I know. You don't have to say it. Hank proved it. He showed me DNA tests confirming Hannah was his daughter. There will be additional tests, of course."

"He and Hannah's mom?"

"Were lovers seventeen years ago," Alfred said. "He wanted her to leave Hannah's father, but she claimed she couldn't." He paused, considering the situation, then took a bite of food. "The fool never fell out of love with Hannah's mom, but he hasn't spoken to her since. She didn't tell him she was pregnant. He found out only because he saw her with Hannah when she was a few months old. He did some math and determined Hannah had been conceived while they were still together. He waited until Hannah was fourteen to approach her. When he did, he told her he was her father."

"How could he know for sure?"

"He confirmed it with a blood sample, freely given by Hannah. It's not that she hates the man she's known as her father, she just hates the tension between her parents that's always been there. Hank was aware of it. He kept tabs and had pictures of her throughout her childhood. When the moment was ripe, he came to her. He's been talking to her ever since."

I shook my head. "I don't believe it. How did he get Hannah to agree to a DNA test?"

"He showed her pictures of her mom and him together. Hannah said it was the only pictures she'd ever seen of her mom happy. She only wanted her mom to be happy like she was in the pictures. The affair between Hank and her mom went on for six or seven months, then she abruptly ended it. He thinks she did it because she was pregnant."

"What's Hank planning for Hannah now?"

"A paternity claim," Alfred said. "The paperwork was filed today, and Hannah's parents will be served tomorrow by the Sheriff's office. It took four days to get new DNA tests."

I pushed my plate away and leaned back in my chair. "Is he being vindictive or does he have good intentions?"

"It doesn't matter to me," Alfred said. "I told him until the judge ruled otherwise, Hannah was not his daughter. I called the Commonwealth's Attorney, and he came to the house to hear the story. I think it's technically kidnapping because Hank deprived the parents of custody. Hannah insisted it had been her choice all along. The Commonwealth's Attorney told me to not arrest Hank, yet, but he would review it. I think it'll go away. It helps that Hank has more money than God. Did I tell you he's an electrical engineer and he designed a different way to use the lithium-ion battery for computers? He didn't invent the battery, just a different process for it. Not that I understand what that means. But what he said is that he gets rich when people buy computers and battery-powered hedge clippers, and all that shit."

"How'd he meet Hannah's mom?"

Alfred scratched the back of his head. "They knew each other in college, but never dated. Then they saw one another in a coffee shop, and it was love. He said it was the greatest seven months of his life, and he'd dated very few women since."

"That's tragic."

"It is," Alfred said. "Here's the good part of all of this. I took Hannah to see Kyle in the hospital. I left her there to explain, then I brought the McBrides to the police station, and I interviewed them. I explained that Kyle had hung himself because he thought he was responsible for Hannah being missing. I asked them if there was anything about that night they weren't telling me. They looked at one another, then back at me. They innocently said *no, not at all, we've told you everything*. So, I put them in separate interview rooms, and let them be for ten minutes. When I went back to her mom, I lied. I told her that her husband said Hannah had left because she'd been having an affair for months. She said it wasn't true. She'd told him that, but she'd lied. She said Hannah left because he had made physical threats and told Hannah to leave. When I went to her father, I told him what she'd said, and he claimed he hadn't made threats. He said Hannah left because his wife had an affair."

"And you think the device is bad?" I asked. "You tricked them."

"I did nothing illegal," he said. "When I put them back into the same room, they wouldn't look at one another. Tomorrow, when they're served with paternity papers, I think their marriage will be done for. I told them Hannah was alive, and neither asked me where she was. I explained that I didn't think she was safe with the likes of them or the media that swarmed around them. I told them if they'd just told us Hannah had walked out of the house, I wouldn't have been so harsh with Kyle, and he wouldn't have tried to kill himself. I didn't tell them the suicide was their fault. I'm the one who made that miscalculation."

I thought for a second. "What about the media? Have they been told yet?"

"I had my first press conference," Alfred said. "I told them the break in the case happened when a confidential informant advised Hannah had been seen in a restaurant, and this led to the location where she'd been staying. I explained in a few days, more details would be revealed, but for now, Hannah was safe and that's all that mattered. They wanted to know if arrests had been made, and all I would say is the Commonwealth's Attorney was reviewing the case. I was on CNN, Fox News, and all the network channels, I guess. I'm famous."

I could see a glint in his eyes. "You liked it, didn't you?"

He nodded. "I did."

"Good."

There was a few minutes of silence. I was about to get up from the table to clean the dishes when he said, "I was wrong."

I squinted at him, confused. "About what?"

"The Holden Device," he said. "I should have been using it. I should solve every case I can, *not* for the thrill of being on national television, but because I can make things better, right?"

"You can," I said. "You know if you hadn't found Hannah, all would have worked out anyway, don't you?"

"By finding her first, I got to control the story," he said. "I'm confident Hank will stay out of jail. Really, he's innocent. Only guilty of a technicality."

"So, what do you want to do now?" I asked. I knew what I wanted him to say, but it had to be his choice.

He smiled and finished his second beer, setting the bottle on the table. "You're wanting to know if I'm ready to start using the device."

"I am." I went to the refrigerator to get Alfred another beer.

"Let's use it. Solve all the fucking crimes."

I handed him the beer. "I've understood your hesitancy all along, and I've respected it. There's a joke I used to tell my classes. I said I was fine with a monarchy as long as I got to be king, and a tyranny as long as I was the tyrant. I'd pause, scratch my head, and turn to the class and say, I'm fine with a theocracy as long as I get to be God."

Alfred grunted at the joke.

"Yeah, I know," I said, "it's not that funny. But the class always liked it."

"What's your point?"

"Since it's just you and me, I'm fine with criminals losing

their privacy, their constitutional rights. And dead people, too. They don't have rights, do they?"

"Goddamn, that's morbid," he said. "But yes, only the two of us."

"I think we will help lots of people."

"Indeed."

As I cleaned the dishes, I wondered if I had created a monster.

4. *"Let's destroy it."*

Finding Hannah McBride wasn't the career-making move for Alfred I thought it would be. The other detectives resented him, and his superiors wanted the publicity he'd gotten. He took it in stride, but he was given nothing cases —liquor store robberies, bicycle thefts, property destruction, missing persons—none of which would get him in the newspaper or on the news—not that Alfred wanted the media attention. He only made it worse by solving all the nothing cases. I found evidence, and Alfred used it to get a confession. No one ever questioned how he did it.

One night Alfred stormed into the house, frustrated his chief had given him what he called a *shit, unsolvable case.* It was a rape and murder of a freshman student two months earlier at the University. His predecessors had no leads, no suspects. *Not one*, he told me. *Nothing.* "The chief is setting me up to fail, and he knows I know it."

Angela Dubcek had been found dead in a wooded area of campus the morning after she'd broken up with her boyfriend, Tom O'Reilly. They'd been at a party, and she caught him drunk dirty dancing with a senior. According to witnesses, Angela stormed out after making a scene. Thomas was the obvious suspect, but his senior dance partner said they'd screwed in the basement on a couch and fell asleep. Alfred said the prior detectives found nothing to prove the senior was lying. The problem wasn't that no one noticed Angela at the party, it was that everyone noticed her. The breakup had been shrill. How could they not stop and watch her berate her now ex-boy-friend? Everyone saw her leave, but no one at the party saw her afterward. She was discovered in the early morning by two runners. She had been beaten lifeless.

Alfred and I followed Angela as she left the party, and we saw the killer just before he grabbed her and lugged her into a wooded area. I turned away as the killer raped and beat her, but there was brutality in hearing it. When it was done, we followed him to his car and to his house. When we got a good look at his face, I told Alfred the man had been at the party. We went back to the beginning and followed the killer. He leered as Angela fought with her boyfriend. The fight was loud, and all the partygoers watched. But he moved out of the house before it was finished. He waited across the street in the dark. When she left, he followed her like a bad dream. Alfred and I made a list of all the people in the party, by name if we had it, or by description if not. There were forty-seven people there, in-cluding the killer and Angela. Alfred's predecessors on the case had located only twenty-one of them, which Alfred called lazy. He went to each of the twenty-one people and asked for copies of all photos they'd taken that night, hoping to find the killer, but he was in none of them. Alfred figured he actively avoided being photographed. Alfred did get thirteen more names, and he went to those thirteen for their pictures. In the end, he knew the name of every person at the party and had every pic-ture taken that night. The killer appeared in only two of them.

No one at the party knew who he was.

The campus police showed the photo to students and staff, but no one recognized him as a student. Alfred extended the search into the neighborhoods around campus, and finally went door to door on the killer's street. The next door neigh-bor identified him as Alan Millett, and said Alan lived with his mother and worked at Starbuck's. At the Millett house, Alfred found his mother home, but not Alan. She told him her son was at work. She was quite upset. She said her son had done nothing wrong. Alfred asked if he could take a look at Alan's room. The mother refused at first but relented when Alfred asked for a unit to pick her son up and take him to the station. She knew whatever was in the room would inevitably be found. In Alan's bedroom, Alfred put on gloves and looked about the room as if a clue might jump out at him. Finally, he opened the closet door, leaned down, and picked up a shoe box. He asked Mrs. Millett to open the lid, and she said she didn't want to, but he could. When he lifted the lid, he saw jewelry. He pulled out a necklace with a cross. He asked Mrs. Millett if she knew where it had come from. She didn't, and he showed her the engraving on the back. *To Angela with Love.* He asked if she knew who Angela was. She didn't, of course. The other jewelry in the box led to the closing of three other rape cases. Before a warrant could be issued for Alan's DNA, he confessed.

It took one week for Alfred to close this case, although we knew *who* the killer was that first night. Alfred couldn't simply arrest him. He had to build a case, a trail from the crime to the killer, otherwise a defense attorney would pick it apart. While I was an integral part of the process, only Alfred could take the information I provided and painstakingly build the evidence. He played his part meticulously, and much of it I watched later on the Holden Device. He didn't know this, but I was particularly interested in how he did it.

The local media was interested as well, and they took note. He deflected as much of the attention as he could, giving the credit to his predecessors for their work. He said all he did was take an extra step. Everyone knew he'd put it together. They didn't know *how* he did it.

Only a few months later, Alfred quit his job, weary of the hierarchal and administrative issues on the force. He applied for his state private investigator license. He was selective with his cases. His primary goal was to do good acts, as if he wanted to balance his karma between the device and his squeaky clean version of morality. His investigations were primarily charity work, but he charged a fee when a job required it. He gained a reputation of being a genius by laying his hands on evidence without much effort, as if he had a sixth sense where to look. This was me, of course. Alfred was no genius, except for his skills at acting. He knew this.

To the rest of the world, I was his crime-solving sidekick, providing endless support as Alfred went about the country. I was his Dr. Watson. I stood by professorially and whispered in his ear, but otherwise I stayed out of the spotlight. Still, I liked taking a part in it, an actor's part in a play. Alfred would walk into a crime scene and look around the room from all angles. After ten or fifteen minutes of moving from corner to corner, he would state what he thought happened and recite the evidence. Sometimes, he would leave the scene and start walking, like he was a bloodhound following a trail. He always found the evidence that broke the case. He could do this when cases were months or years old. It was theater for me, but it was genius for everyone else. I was the only person who knew what Alfred did was a façade. The credit was all Johann's for creating the device, not mine, not Alfred's. When the clients asked how Alfred did it, I wanted to scream, *it isn't Alfred! It's Johann!* It's always been Johann. Alfred merely presented the pieces of the puzzle and played his part.

He took every precaution to avoid publicity, and for that he deserved credit. Yet, he did become a celebrity. The media gave him movie star status and one book was written about a case he solved. He refused to be interviewed for it. After a decade of avoiding it, he did one interview with Rolling Stone magazine in which he diffused as much of the hype as he could. Then he disappeared. He called it being on sabbatical. That was five years ago. Some people thought he'd died. Others figured he had become a recluse or a hermit. He let his hair grow long and thick, so he looked the part. It was all so he could go about unnoticed, without the entourage. I fed him information as he did his good deeds. Even though he was still working, maybe more now, he avoided the attention, and performed most acts anonymously. No one hired him. He'd become a true super-hero.

Alfred took it all seriously. He brooded about it. There was little enjoyment in the investigations for him. It was a burden to him.

It's still a burden.

Tonight, he came to the house, and said he was done. He sat across from me at the kitchen table, where so many of our conversations have taken place over the last twenty-five years. "I can't do it anymore. I don't want to explain."

I nodded. "You don't have to."

He took a drink of his beer, set it down, and looked at me. "Why doesn't it affect you like it does me?"

This was a question I'd asked myself from the beginning, and I debated whether to tell him the truth or make up a fiction. I chose truth. "I think, maybe it's because I've become immune to it. I've seen it all. Murders. Rapes. Heinous acts of all types. I seldom turn away. It's not that I don't have empathy, but I'm able to separate it, put it aside, like a surgeon does. As she cuts the skin, the surgeon's doing harm to the body, but it's a necessary harm. I don't like watching the crimes, but I know it's necessary."

"It's not now," he said.

"Without you, you mean?"

He nodded.

"What are you suggesting?"

He sighed. "Let's destroy it."

I've known for years it would come to this, but still I feigned shock at the suggestion. "You can't mean that, Alfred,"

He nodded. "I do."

"It's like asking a wizard to give up his magic."

"I only want to be free of it," he said. "I want to live my life and not take on the worries of all those other people."

"Alfred, why do you think I'd agree to it?"

"Because it's the right thing," he said. "We're old men now."

"You're only fifty-eight, and I'm sixty-two. That's not old."

"It's too old to have to worry about the device getting into the wrong hands. I'm worried about our deaths. What happens to the device when we die? It bothers me. You understand the risk if the device is taken. You do. I know you do. It would be awful."

Of course I knew. We'd talked about it the first day, but those risks had little impact on me. "I've got to think about this, you know?" I said. "It's been a good life. We've had twenty-five years making the world a better place. There are crimes that would never have been solved if it hadn't been for us."

"A drop in the bucket."

"Indeed," I said. "Can you give me a week?"

"Of course."

We drank a few more beers and talked about nothing of note, mostly college basketball and the stock market. When he left, I began writing this detailed accounting of how our lives were changed by the death of my friend, Johann Hart.

I'll agree to destroy what Alfred thinks is the Holden Device. It won't be. It can't be. You see, I knew the day would come when Alfred would want to destroy it, and it would be wrong. I must protect the device. Alfred will need something to smash or have melted down. Years ago, I had a new box constructed, with the same amount of lead, and transferred the parts into it, including the glass box with the purple and red smoke twisting about, still wondering whether it was alive. I put computer components in the original box, and knew Alfred wouldn't know the difference. He can destroy the original box and think it's the device, but the Holden Device will be safe.

Maybe I'm damned for doing this, but I can't let it go. I'd rather die. I have plans for its use. I'll be more aggressive.

There are beliefs modern society and religion are based upon, and I'll research those. I'll determine the truth of those beliefs, and I'll share my findings. It's dangerous information, I know, but why shouldn't the world know? I understand I can't make proclamations of all that I discover. The world would want to know how I know. But I can discover proof, and ease it into the world's consciousness. Whatever I do will be subtle, and never associated with the name Jack Holden. The world will never suspect it is me.

Alfred put the thought in my mind. When he told me some things in life are supposed to be a mystery, it created a desire to solve every mystery. That desire has been dormant until the last year, as thoughts of my impending death grew. I have to know the truth so I can go gentle into that good night.

When I die, the Holden Device, and this accounting will be placed into the hands of the person I feel I can trust. I haven't met that person yet, but I hope to soon. If you're reading this, you are that person.

ACKNOWLEDGEMENTS

◆ ◆ ◆

There are many people to thank: My wife, of course, who is First Reader of all the words I write and the most honest critic.

My daughters for taking me away from my writing when I fall too far in.

Michael Fehr for being Second Reader and providing his unique perspective.

Bob Nailor for making my words shine with his immense copyediting skills.

Early on Twitter, I got involved with group of writers who wrote stories with 140 (and later 280) characters stories called Friday Phrases (or #FP). Many of the stories in this collection originated with an #FP (i.e., He realized between the top of the bridge and the chill of the water below that his worries were not that desperate after all. #FP; There is a box on my desk. It is a wooden box with the word Pandora burned into it. I want to open it, and yet I resist. #FP; In his final breath, he saw the void that was hell, just before his soul was snatched & given another chance as a new born babe. #FP; When her car went over the cliff, the lives flashing before Jenny's eyes weren't hers. She wondered how many lives can one person have? #FP). The Friday Phrases group is too numerous to name them all (and I will forget some), but those that affected my writing the most need to be thanked (although, I do not know all of their names): Maria Carvalho, Kristen Falso Capaldi, Reena Dobson, Aseem Saxena, Hope Denney, Alex Alvarado, Beth Deitchman, Jason Zwiker, Joanne Blaikie, Jane Lightbourne, Callie Gay, Willow Dawn Becker, TipTim, J.D. Estrada, The Devil's Advocate, Sid Black, PrairieSky_27, Ayla Ault, Katsyarina, The Mad Monk, Crystal Martin, Karina Lawrence, The Real Marj, Sarah Brentyn, Mr. Micawber, Adele Gray, Clive Moore, Lynne Blaszak, Roger Jackson, and Nillu Nasser.

Finally, five of the stories ("The Fading of Light in her Eyes," "The Sounds of War," "Group Therapy," "The King of Taste," and "Chill of the Water Below,") were part of a collection entitled *Falling into the Five Senses*. The idea was that four writers would produce one short story for each of the five senses. When Reena Dobson asked if I would be part of the *Five Senses* anthology, I was hesitant, mostly because of self-doubt. Could I produce five different stories worthy of this theme in a short amount of time? Once I got over the doubt, the stories exploded onto the page, and I am thankful I allowed myself to be part of this. The other writers were Reena Dobson (who also served as anthologist, copy editor, publisher, etc.), Maria Carvalho (who served as copy editor), and Roger Jackson. If you like my stories in this collection, you should checkout *Falling into the Five Senses*, which can be found on Amazon.

ABOUT THE AUTHOR

◆ ◆ ◆

Cedrix E. Clarke is a non de plume. He lives in Kentucky and has a day job, which pays the bills. He writes at nights after everyone else is asleep and on the weekends. He has published a children's novel called Lucinda's Ghost, which can be found on Amazon. You can find Cedrix online at cedrixclarke.com. His Twitter handle is @cedrixclarke.